Three Tales In Lastima

Fantasy Of Old New Mexico

James Nathan Post

This book is entirely a work of fiction. No character, tribe, clan, church, or other organization described herein represents any such real or actual entity.

www.postpubco.com

CONTENTS

THE DEVIL'S OWN HORSE

Prologue

This is the story of a miracle. I was baptized Cristoforo Mescalero Colon, after my father's Italian ancestry, but I have always been called Cabrito — which means "little goat" — because of my curly hair, maybe. It is also the word used for roast goat, so it might just have been a joke. My mother was Apache, as my middle name indicates. Her people don't like any of the white-eyes, Spaniard, Anglo, or Italian, and Mexicans don't like Apaches, Spaniards don't like Italians, and the gringos don't like Mexicans, Apaches, or Italians either, so I was never very popular around here.

As the result of my anger and my youthful pride, I did some very stupid things, which got my wife killed, and my child, and my mother and father. I was left alive to suffer the shame of it, with an Apache spear through my ankle so I would never forget. Perhaps it was also pride which led me after that to behave as a bitter outcast, instead of becoming a more contrite and penitent man. Perhaps it was another stupid thing to do as well, but I became a recluse, and I lived alone on the little piece of valley land which my father had owned. Like him, I farmed chile there.

Years ago, the river, the Rio Grande, flowed over that place, leaving beds of river sand. Then it moved, and the bosque grew there. The thick patches of salt cedar, reeds, tall grasses, sage, mesquite, and willow lay down fine thick beds of humus. Then the river moved again, and those fields were covered with a layer of adobe clay brought down from the hills by the arroyos. Years of weather eroding, and people plowing that clay to bring up and mix the layers below has produced an exceptional soil. Everyone always agreed it produces the very finest chiles in the entire Rio Grande valley.

The name of Lastima, the little community closest to my farm, means a pity. "*Aie, que lastima, mi Lastima,*" the people like to say. In the year of the miracle, it is still in Mexico, but the border keeps getting closer. Only a few years ago, the border was hundreds of miles north of here, in the headwaters of the Rio Grande, beyond Santa Fe, and Mexico extended up the coast all the way to San Francisco. Now it is only a few miles away, and right across it is the fort of the United States Cavalry. It is quite certain one day soon the gringos will come down here and swallow us up.

I suppose I could have been a commercial grower, and traded in the local market, perhaps even in the big markets a day's ride south at El Paso Del Norte, where the river has cut a gateway through the long chain of mountains it follows in its journey from the north. I might have made good investments, bought more land, and become one of the influential and respected citizens of Lastima. But I did not. I worked only hard enough to produce just enough chile to buy hay and salt for my old horse Huevon, all the beans and tacos I could eat at La Cantina La Fuente, and all the tequila I could drink. I reckoned I was working very lightly and drinking very heavily, and so I was somehow getting over on those more foolish people who worked hard and drank little.

This is the story of a miracle, and how the redemption of an angry, crippled, chile-farming but otherwise useless half-breed town drunk was brought about, in part at least by his meeting the Devil himself, and the Devil's own horse, the greatest horse that ever was, the mighty Cesar.

Chapter One

There is something particularly beautiful that happens all the way up the valley of the Rio Grande, from El Paso to Santa Fe. Miles to the west, the mountains of Mogollon and the Gila stir up tall thunderstorms in the clear skies of late summer afternoons. These great anvil-topped piles of boiling clouds become like free-standing pillars of fire when the setting sun goes behind them, and they turn the most stunning shades of crimson and gold. When the dark hollows beneath the anvils are ringed with such blazing splendor, they look like huge cathedrals, and the distant rumble of their thunder sounds like chanting choir. Sunbeams stabbing through the gaps shine down upon the ground, and as the sun settles, the rays appear like huge glowing lodge ladder poles, like those of the pueblo people, being raised up in radiant glory as though to secure the great kiva of the sun itself for the night. Then as the blazing disc slips below the columns of cloud, just before it sets, when it is its deepest red, it is reflected from the bases of those clouds, and it shines across the valley and strikes the mountains on the east side. For just a few moments, the mountains all turn the most astonishingly bright blood red. For this they have been given such names as the Sandia, and Sangre De Cristo Mountains, Spanish for watermelon, and the blood of Christ. If all who live in Heaven could have the most beautiful sunsets the great Father ever created, surely they would all enjoy these.

Across the valley from Lastima rises a ridge of granite crags that catches that light and shines like a huge jagged-toothed jawbone carved of the reddest Indian pipestone. The gringos call it The Organ, because it looks like the big row of pipes of the organs in the cathedrals of the great cities far away.

Seen in silhouette, a lone rider moved slowly along this spectacular horizon. He slouched in the saddle on his skinny slow-plodding old horse, and if he was impressed by the view, he showed no sign of it. He wore the rough trousers and buttonless tunic of a peon, with an ancient and ragged woven wool vest and a floppy old leather hat. He appeared to be about forty, his thick curly black hair and his sparse and scraggly beard going to gray.

At dusk, the valley still glowed with last warm brown light as the purple curtain of the night rose up over the mountains. He rode into the little town plaza of Lastima, a flagstoned and tree-lined square of low adobe buildings, with a bandstand gazebo in the middle. On one side of the plaza the biggest business was clearly The Romero General Store, and on the other, the Romero Hotel. A block away stood the newest building in town, the stone-faced two-story brick edifice of Romero's First Bank Of Lastima, where the mayor also had his office. Behind the square were a few blocks of simple adobe residences and a few frame houses. Beyond that were the well-tended even if small fields of the valley, and beyond them, the desert.

He did not have to tell his horse where he was going, or when to stop. He rode directly to the end of the plaza, climbed down from the saddle, draped his reins over the halter rail, and limped to the door of La Cantina La Fuente.

The saloon he entered was a long narrow room with a polished hardwood bar along one side and a row of tables on the other. Behind the bar a window opened into a kitchen area. At the far end there was a bigger room with more tables, and a fireplace with a broad hearth. In the winter, that fireplace was the most comfortable and congenial place in town. As the chiles were then ripening in late summer, there were pillows on the hearth, and two little tables close by. As he stepped into the room, he reached over and put his hand onto the smooth dark wood of the bar, like he might pat a horse, to relax and reassure it, and himself.

Through the window from the kitchen, a woman called out to him. "Hola, Cabrito. Do you want some tacos?" She was Corona Baca, the bachelor businesswoman who leased the kitchen and ran the town's bakery out of it, in addition to serving nachos and meals over the bar. To some of the old wives of Lastima, she was an embarrassment, an old maid who sold the culinary service a wife should provide as a prostitute sells other such service. Corona was an imposing figure to look at, as befits such accomplishment, at twenty-six a very large, double-barrel-breasted powerful-looking woman, long black hair tied back from her broad moon face, her body wrapped in a huge apron. He nodded curtly to her, and moved down the bar, limping just a little on his twisted right foot. "Ok," she called after him. "Concha will bring them to you."

Most of the clientele at La Fuente were simply the local Mexican farm laborers, and they looked a lot like Cabrito, if more tidy and alert. The vaqueros, the cattle handlers, wore more denim and leather, some favoring the classical Mexican sombrero and others the flat-brimmed felt Stetsons of the gringos. At one of the tables sat a pair of grubby-looking gringos, the only gringos in the place, each nursing a shot of whiskey. Homer and Wilbur Colby were pretty unusual there, being very much a minority as gringo farm workers. At another table sat three black men in US Cavalry uniforms. They were pretty unusual around there too. They all came from Fort Selmore, which sat on the border a few miles north of town. They were part of an experiment the US Army was conducting with freed slaves. The Indians called them buffalo soldiers, and they seemed to like that. They seemed to get along fine with the Indians, matter of fact, which sometimes distressed their commanding officer, General Cooley, probably because if the Cavalry had to fight a war, it would be the Indians they were supposed to fight.

At the bar sat a pleasant-looking young man wearing the garb of a peon and carrying a guitar. Everybody just knew him as Flaco, though of course everybody also knew he had a good name from a good family, and was well educated and able to translate and write in both Spanish and English. With him was a short, dark, hawk-nosed Apache in the uniform of a Cavalry Corporal, with two gold chevrons on his blue sleeve.

"*Hola, Cabrito, que tal?*" asked Flaco, cheerfully.

"'*Tal*," Cabrito grunted with a curt nod.

Corporal Geronimo Jones didn't say anything to Cabrito. Being Apache wasn't something he sought to share with him, though they had in common that they were in a way, both half breeds. Jones was all Apache, but he had been captured by white settlers as a child, and raised as one of them.

As Cabrito worked his way back toward the corner table he liked best, Concha the waitress called to him. "The usual, Cabrito?" He nodded, waved his hand. Concha was seventeen, the most voluptuous and tempestuously tempting young heifer in town, and she was desired by almost every man she ever met. That made her the perfect barmaid, as men would order drinks all night just to watch her come and go.

In the room at the back of the bar, two older men sat together at a table, with a third younger man. Both of the older men were dressed in expensive suits, and the other wore the vest and rolled-up sleeves of a clerk. The larger of the two, the one in the classical Mexican suit with the silver-tipped boots, was cigar-puffing Arturo Melendrez. He was the mayor of Lastima, and also the owner of La Fuente. The dapper little caballero with the glasses sitting next to him was Alonso Romero, who owned the bank, the hotel, and most everything else in Lastima. The third, the good-looking if a bit bovine and phlegmatic young man enjoying the privilege of their company, was Emilio Sapogrande. He worked for Romero, and had dreams of someday being elected to Melendrez' job.

"*Buenas noches, Cabrito,*" said Romero. "How is your chile crop looking this year?"

Though they treated Cabrito civilly enough, it always seemed to him that he could see a certain distaste, and a certain self-praise in their condescending to be so civil to him. "I don't see you walking on water either," he wanted to say to them, but he maintained a dark and sullen civility too.

"Best I've ever had, Alonso," he said. "Best looking chile I've ever had."

"I can hardly wait to start serving *rellenos* made with

your chiles, Cabrito," Martinez said to him. "They have always been the best in the valley."

"You know that's true," said young Sapogrande, "though I don't know why, since you spend more time in here than you do in your field."

"My chiles don't like too much supervision, so I leave them alone, Emilio," said Cabrito.

"Leaving the weeding and cultivating to God, no doubt," said Romero.

"I leave it to the Devil," said Cabrito. "If anybody understands chile, it is him. A good evening to you, *Señores.*"

Concha brought Cabrito a tray with a plate of tacos, a short glass of tequila, and a large mug of beer, and set it on the corner table at the hearth. He tucked himself into the space close to the wall, tossed back half of the tequila, and sat for a moment as though in prayer, letting the warm agave burn spread out from his middle. He followed it with a pickled jalapeno, and winced against its fiery bite. In a moment, the sweat broke on his forehead, his ears began to ring, and he knew he was ready to relax and enjoy his tacos as they should be enjoyed.

As Concha walked back past the bar, she passed Pancho Huarache, a scruffy-looking young man who had taken to wearing a military shirt with epaulets and a large pistol-belt, letting his hair grow long, and fancying himself a revolutionary. Corona of course always kept Pancho's pistol on a shelf behind her bar. It was always understood that if anybody needed to get shot in La Fuente, it would be Corona who was going to do the shooting. She had never actually shot anyone, but when she did draw down on a pair of rowdies with a shotgun one night, she was definitely taken seriously.

"Concha, I hear you're getting married," Huarache said as she passed him.

"Married? *Hijola*, Huarache, not me. Where did you hear that?"

"I don't know. It didn't sound much like you."

"*De veras,*" she said. "I like my independence too

much."

"That's good to hear," he said. "I agree one hundred percent. Freedom begins at home. You've got to be free to enjoy the important things in life."

"Oh yeah, like what?" she asked.

"Like love without strings," he said.

"*Aie, pendejo!*" she snorted, and moved quickly past him.

Sitting at the bar, Flaco nudged Corporal Jones and nodded at Huarache beside them. "You catching this act, Geronimo?"

"Something I'd expect to hear come out the back end of a bull," Jones said, shaking his head. When Concha came past again with more drinks, he stopped her and spoke to her, close. "Concha, when these people give you a break, come have a glass of wine with me, will you?"

"Sure, Corporal Jones, I'd love to," she said, "but it won't be right away."

As though nothing had happened since the last time he was talking to her, Huarache started in on her. "It's a sad thing how much pain is caused in the name of love," he started running on poetically. "We have so many rules, so many inhibitions that say we can't love each other freely. But if we all demanded the right, exercised the right..."

Jones interrupted him. "Huarache, I hear you don't approve of military service."

"That's right, I don't," Pancho said loftily.

"And why is that?"

"The army is just another tool the rich use to exploit the poor," Huarache explained. "The rich buy an army, call themselves the government, and shoot anybody who won't pay taxes."

"You think soldiers exploit the poor?" Flaco asked. "Most soldiers I know are poor."

"No, soldiers are exploited too," Huarache assured them, "except the officers of course. The government makes us pay taxes to build an army to protect us from enemies. But when the enemies come, we are the ones who have to go get shot to protect them."

"Just looks like a good job to me," said Corporal Jones.

"Sooner or later, they will fall, and the poor will get the money they deserve," said Huarache.

"Let me see if I have this straight, Pancho," said Flaco. "Anybody who is rich now is an unrighteous exploiter, and anybody who is poor now deserves to get rich, is that right?"

"The meek shall inherit the land and the wealth they deserve, yes."

"Then they won't be poor anymore, they will be the rich, right?"

"Exactly."

"Won't that make them into exploiters then?" Flaco asked.

Huarache frowned. "You're twisting around what I said."

From his table across the cozy space of the room, Sapogrande held up his hand. "I think I understand, Pancho. You mean when the poor finally get the money they deserve, then they are righteously rich, is that right?"

"*Seguro,* exactly," Huarache agreed. "People who have seen how the rich are corrupted will not permit that to happen to themselves. They will see to it the wealth gets spread around, and nobody gets puffed up with it."

"Ok," said Flaco, "so it's all right to have wealth, as long as you continue to live like a poor person, right?"

Huarache scowled, and glared from one to the other of them. "You guys think you're real smart, but that kind of thinking leads to the rich getting richer, and the powerful getting more powerful. If there is no way to redistribute the wealth, we all becomes the slaves of the rich."

"Speaking of redistributing the wealth, I'm about as poor as anybody these days," said Flaco. "How about buying me a drink, Brother?"

Huarache looked at him in disbelief, his jaw falling open. "What? Here are the two richest men in town, and you turn to me? I have even less than you. Why don't you get the rich to buy us all a drink. If the rich are taxed, and the money given to the poor, then we would spend it and the rich would get it right back, so why not?"

Sapogrande scoffed and waved a deprecating hand. "You leave out something important, Huarache. Work. If you want things the rich have, why not start a business, and get them honestly? You refuse to work, you make an issue of your poverty, and then you demand to be given what other people have earned, just because you don't have it. You're not poor, Huarache, you are *jodido*. You stay poor to get something for nothing."

"I represent the poor, that's why," Pancho said, standing up taller. "I endure the hardship of poverty, because I'm the only one who will stand up and champion their cause."

"You know, if you were rich, you could give something to the poor yourself," said Sapogrande, "instead of going around crying for somebody else to do it."

"I'll give you a choice," said Mayor Melendrez. "I offer you a job, Huarache, working for the town of Lastima. Mostly labor, very low pay, but a beginning, and a year well spent in community service could win you a friend at the bank. You have a flair for politics, it seems. Perhaps you could run for office someday. What do you say?"

"A job. Is that right? A government job and a mortgage. Well, let me tell you something, Mr. Mayor..." Pancho began, working up a head of steam behind a wagging finger.

"Are you about ready for another drink, Pancho?" Concha interrupted. "It's getting pretty late." A quick look around showed that the evening had wound on in conversation, and there remained only a few customers, and themselves.

"What? Oh, no, no, not now," Huarache backpedaled. "I was just..."

"Let's have another round, Concha," said Emilio. "I'll even buy the revolution a drink."

"Don't try to buy my sympathy, Sapo," Huarache persisted. "Mayor, you want me to sell out to the system, then when I've clawed my way to the top with the other cutthroats, I can give it all to the poor, right? No, we want our rights now, not a generation from now."

"Can you think of a faster way?" Melendrez asked him.

"Absolutely," Huarache said with great confidence. "The working people will inevitably rise up and demand it. They will destroy the oppressor, and his wealth will be shared."

Alonso Romero wiped his glasses with a linen handkerchief. "You amaze me, Huarache," he said. "If people won't give you their money, you will take it from them in the name of the people? I am thinking you should be locked up."

They had another round of tequila shots, and another of beers, and the evening passed. Then from behind the bar, Corona called to them, "You're the last ones left. It's time to close up."

"That time again already, Corona?" asked Sapogrande.

"*Si, Senor*," she said. "You don't have to go home, Good-looking, but you can't stay here."

"All right, I'm ready for a good night's sleep," said Arturo Melendrez, stubbing out the butt of his cigar in an ashtray. "Good night, Pancho, my zealous young friend. I hope I don't have to shoot you someday."

"I hope so too, Mr. Mayor," Huarache replied genially. "Just be sure you don't miss the first time. *Buenas noches, Señores.*" He put on his sombrero, gave them a salute, then turned to leave them, as though expecting trumpets and applause. Then he walked past the bar, looking all around, and into the window to the kitchen. He turned to Flaco, who was sitting at the bar finishing off his beer. "Hey, Flaco, did you see where Concha went?" he asked.

"She left a few minutes ago, Huarache, with Geronimo Jones," Flaco told him.

"She what?" Huarache looked stricken. "Jones?"

"Yep." Flaco nodded and smiled. "You'll be pleased to hear what she said before she left. 'I think Pancho is right about loving each other more freely.' That's what she said. I guess you helped to awaken her consciousness, Huarache. Congratulations."

"*Aie, la puta,*" Huarache groaned, and he stood grumpily waiting for Corona to come to give him back his pistol. When she came out of the kitchen and gave it to him, he departed kicking the furniture.

Cabrito came up to the bar to catch her attention. "There is a tequila moon out tonight, Corona," he said to her. "I'd better have the big one, OK?"

"Sure, Cabrito, I'm keeping count. You just take good care of those chiles."

From a shelf in the back, Corona brought him a large crockery jug, with a handle, and a cork plug in the neck. He took it, carefully worked the cork loose, popped it open, and then held it up in salute. He took a swig. Breath suspended, he stood with eyes bulging. Then with a gasp he sucked in air and held it, his veins looking like roots growing out of his face. He smacked the cork back into the neck of the jug with his palm.

"*Para Diablo!*" he swore.

Chapter Two

Clutching his jug and pulling his old leather hat down over his eyes, Cabrito stepped out into the night. For a moment he stood peering out from under its floppy brim, taking in the space before proceeding. The late summer air was still warm at midnight, and it felt thick and close and reassuring. He made his way slowly but resolutely across the few yards to where Huevon stood waiting for him, and he paused, hanging on the saddle horn. Using a loop of rawhide he had made for the purpose, he hanged the jug on the side. Wincing a little as he raised his good left foot to the stirrup, he swung himself up and settled into the familiar seat. *"Andale pues,"* he sighed, then leaned down and patted the horse's neck. "Take us home, Huevon."

The old horse whinnied softly. *"Si-mon, hombre,"* he said.

There was a lantern still burning in the gazebo which served as a bandstand and ceremonial place in the center of the plaza. Mayor Melendrez had decided it should be kept lighted from dusk to dawn, so people would know the town of Lastima was always vigilant. There were a few doorways near the plaza still lighted by lanterns, but they were not needed for Cabrito to see his way, nor Huevon, for that matter. High in the sky hung a baleful fat half moon, casting eerie shadows from the tattered high clouds shifting slowly before it.

Past the second street there were only the fields of cotton, and chile, and corn, and then only the wagon road south to El Paso, and north to Fort Selmore, and on to Santa Fe. Huevon took the saddle trail which led between them, down through the mesquite dunes to Cabrito's chile field. The dunes looked like big spiny-backed creatures, and the eerie shadows made them appear to almost move. The only sound Cabrito could hear was the steadily plodding ka-lump ta-clop of Huevon's hoofbeats, echoless in the eerie still. He began to hum and then to sing a sad Mexican tune, its words only half remembered, and cast in tatters into the shadows.

Suddenly on the crest of the highest dune above him appeared an apparition that stopped his voice in his throat. Before him rode a man on horseback, a huge and proud Conquistador, dressed in Spanish armor, mounted on the most awesome black stallion he had ever seen, the most awesome he could imagine. The moonlight flashed from his armor in gleaming spikes, and the dust rose up from the pounding hooves of that horse in great swirling clouds as he rode thunderously down toward him.

Huevon shuddered like a scrawny dog. He slid to a stop, planted his back hooves wide, and pissed between them. With a screech like a cornered goat he bleated, *"Cesar!"*

Raising up a gauntleted hand, the dark warrior pointed his finger at Cabrito. With his eyes flashing rainbow sparks in deepest black like Mexican opal, and his face a demonic leer, he called out in a voice that enfolded him and hung close upon him like the coils of a snake. *"A donde vas, Cabrito?"*

Cabrito's scalp bristled, and his hair felt like a live thing crawling on his head. His heart pounded and stuttered, and felt like it was dropping right into his stomach. His eyes were stretched so wide open with horror he felt he couldn't even blink. But Cabrito had been terribly frightened before in his life, and he had seen terrible things before. He had suffered terrible things done to him, and he had done terrible things to others. He was not one to be easily impressed by the terrible, even by one as terrible as the great dark dignitary who confronted him. "Who in hell wants to know?" he demanded.

The Devil laughed, and he settled down to a smaller apparition, and reined up beside Huevon. "That's very funny," he said. "*Buenas noches, Cabrito.* I heard you toast to my name in the cantina, and I have come to have that drink with you."

Cabrito gave him a second look, and noted that he seemed to be very much the grand old Spanish gentleman, a very affable caballero. Though he had been sure for many years that such a meeting would one day take place, he was surprised to find it happening in such a genial fashion. "I see," he said. "*Pues,* I happen to have some very fine tequila with me tonight, and I would be honored to have a drink with you."

He took the jug of blue agave elixir from the loop on the saddle horn, and he pulled out the cork bung. "For the hell of it," he toasted, and took a big swig. Then he handed the jug to the Devil.

"And to hell with it," toasted the Devil, and he took a big swig. The clouds around the moon began to roil and twist, never quite obscuring the moon, and from somewhere far off the rumble of thunder grumbled like the chanting of monks. "Aie, that is good," he said. "Now, lets ride together. There is something I must talk to you about, and I have come to settle an affair with you."

"Is that right? Well, I'd say neither you nor I is drunk enough for that, Mister."

"Ha ha, you are surely right about that. We had better have another drink, then."

"Yes," Cabrito went on, emboldened by the tequila, "and if we are going to come to a final agreement, we should first agree to sing together. Men who cannot sing together cannot deal as men either."

"I agree," said the caballero, "so what shall we sing?"

"Tonight you are dressed as a Spaniard, but Spaniards sing only in church. My father did not live long enough to teach me to sing an Italian song, so we will have to sing a Mexican song."

Cabrito began to sing a passionate Mexican song about how a man must stand up against the sorrows of life, and the Devil joined him. They passed the jug back and forth, and as the Devil became more drunk, his image began to slip, and by the time they reached Cabrito's little farm, he looked like a skinny old white man in an oversize caballero's costume, a sentimental drunken Don Quixote bawling the song in gusty machismo.

They arrived at the little farm riding close, arms

around each others' shoulders, still singing. The moonlit farm consisted of one little adobe house under a large cottonwood tree, and a little separate wood barn with a corral behind it, and the long rows of chile plants, each about a foot high.

"Welcome to my home," said Cabrito genially. "Let's go over by the tree and we can finish this jug of tequila."

"If I drink any more of that, I will never find my way back to my home," the old Spaniard objected. "Ah, to hell with it. Let's do it."

Cabrito led the Devil to the big cottonwood tree that grew over his house. Like a dancer leading his partner across the floor, Cabrito stepped this way, leaned that way, and then with one last flourish of the jug, had him where he wanted him. Next to the tree was a very large steel-jawed trap, made for mountain lions or bears, which Cabrito had placed to catch a marauding coyote which had been robbing him of the chickens he encouraged to hang around in the barn. With a terribly sinister clank and a crunch like a locomotive hitting a buffalo, the jaws of the cruel trap slammed shut on the right foot of the Devil, and he was chained to Cabrito's cottonwood tree.

"Ow!" he yelped. "What? Awww, you got me."

"*Si, Señor.* That I do," said Cabrito exultantly. "Looks like you're going to have a foot like mine, Mister."

"Wait, maybe we can make a deal," the captured demon protested. "Come on, there is a way out of everything. I know about your foot, and how your parents died. I can give you revenge for that, make you the scourge of the Apache. No? Then I can make you the leader of a new tribe of Apache warriors, and you can sweep the land of white men. Come on, talk to me, Cabrito."

Cabrito stood over him, shaking his head. "You lying old scorpion, I see your game. It would take a much higher power than you to raise up as fine a people as the Apache, no matter what they did to me. You will never get my soul bargaining like that."

"Your soul?" the old Spaniard sputtered. "I'm not here

for your worthless soul, Cabrito. I came to bargain for your chile."

For a second time, Cabrito was astonished to have so miscalculated the Devil's intention. "My chile?" he asked. "Well, that's different. You will deal with me for chile while you are sitting in my bear trap? Ha ha!"

Cabrito stopped to think a moment, smiling in anticipation. In all of his darkest moments, when he had felt most disadvantaged, this was the moment he had dreamed of. Then another kind of dark suspicious idea tempted his mind. He had always thought in such a moment he would have a thousand things to ask for, but at that moment there was not a thing that sprang up before him as a prize. He had long ago renounced the things of the world as mostly worthless in the long run, and he couldn't think of anything more to desire than what he had, his farm, his chile, his privacy, and his tequila.

Even so, he did not wish to appear to be a fool, so he spoke up boldly. "Well, all right, for openers, I'll take that horse," he said.

Standing a little way off, with his reins trailing on the ground, Huevon gasped out in horror, "Aie, God help us."

Standing beside him, the great stallion Cesar rose up aghast, eyes goggled. *"Mi Señor!"* he whinnied.

"Not a word, Cesar," his master said curtly. "It's a deal. For my freedom from your diabolical trap, I will give you the horse. Then we can talk about your chile."

"No, I think we should do it the other way," said Cabrito shrewdly. "The horse for chile to grace your table in hell, and then we will talk about letting you go."

"All right," said the Devil. "We have made a deal."

Cabrito had just enough time to jump up and hop around once on his good left foot to congratulate himself, when he was surprised for the third time that fateful night. The sky began to rumble, not like thunder, but more like the great pipes of a huge organ, as if the great Organ Mountains themselves were giving voice just softly, just at the very edge of their power. The moon above them turned bright, and from it like an arm extended a beam of sunlight to stab down on the little farm. The ominous droning of the Organ deepened and grew louder.

Standing suddenly exposed in the light, Cabrito looked around him furtively, expecting something to jump out from any direction and grab him. The beam of light was incredibly hot, and he broke out in a sweat. A deep, calm, and unchallengeable voice filled the night. "So, my little Cabrito, you have the Devil in your trap and you deal with him like a bigshot. You know I don't like you dealing with my enemy. So what are you going to do about me? Get a bigger bear trap?"

To his eternal misfortune, Cabrito was drunk enough, and desperate enough to think that what had worked once that night might work twice. "Oh, yeah?" he said. "What is it to you if I deal with him? Maybe you can't handle him, but I have him in my bear trap. What do I need you for?"

"That's what I was waiting to hear," said the Devil. He leered and cackled, and he began to grow, becoming first robust, and then Olympian, and then monstrous. Above, the storm clouds darkened the sky, and the sunbeam from the moon faded. With a triumphant roar, he pulled the jaws of the trap open like taffy. He stepped out with hoofed black goat feet, and pranced back and forth.

In true fear, Cabrito fell to his knees. "Oh, God! No, don't leave me, I didn't mean it. Please! Help me!" he cried piteously. "Please!"

From the night came the calm reply, "I thought you'd never ask."

"I'll do anything," Cabrito wept. "I'll become your priest. Please, stay with me! Just tell me what to do, and I'll do it."

"You a priest?" said the Divine voice, as though surprised Himself. "Now that would take a miracle. So be it."

"Damn," said the Devil. He returned to the size of a normal man, and stood swatting the dust from his striped riding bloomers.

"One more thing," Cabrito was told. "The horse you dealt for? He is yours. I am interested to see what a chile farming priest is going to do with the Devil's own horse."

From somewhere out of the night, a dark whirling dust devil came down from the mesquite dunes. The Devil stepped into it, and he was whirled away, waving his upraised fist in the universal sign of ill will.

The sunbeam faded once again to a baleful moonlight, and Cabrito found himself standing alone beneath a starry clear sky, with the two horses standing a few yards away, both looking at him in great dismay. He turned his back on them, staggered to the tree where the jug lay, and hoisted it to finish the last drop. Then he fell on his back, out cold.

Chapter Three

Cabrito jumped awake as though he had been kicked, and found himself facing bright sunlight. He sat up on his elbows, then clutched his knees and pulled himself up to sit with his throbbing head between them. After a minute, he rubbed his eyes and ventured a look around. The gate to the corral was open, and Huevon stood inside, still wearing his saddle. He picked up the jug at his side, observed that it was empty, and shook his head sadly. He rose clumsily to his feet and walked over to take off the saddle.

"Sorry about this," he said as he unbuckled the cinch. He pulled the saddle down and stood holding it, looking at the way Huevon was looking the other way. "What, you're not talking to me today?" he asked. "Well, all right for you." He turned around to take the saddle into the barn, stopped short in his tracks, and dropped the saddle at his feet.

There, not fifty feet away, stood that most spectacular black stallion, still wearing a fine Spanish saddle, peacefully munching chile plants bearing little green peppers.

"Santo Chorizo!" he gasped. "I'm still drunk. No. No, it's really you. You are Cesar. Oh, my goodness, just look at you." Cabrito walked out of the corral and stood admiring the mighty steed. "Come over here, now," he said firmly.

Cesar held his head up high and came obediently. Cabrito picked up the reins and led him back and forth, applauding as he presented first one profile against the turquoise horizon and then the other. Then feeling a strength in his feet he had not known for some time, he stepped up into the wide Spanish stirrup and swung himself up, up higher than he had thought a horse could ever be, and into the fine plush leather of the seat.

Feeling something flow through him like a flash flood in an arroyo, he rose up straighter and taller in the saddle than he had thought he ever could, and took a huge breath of air. "Yes, this is more like it," he said.

Every move that Cabrito could imagine, Cesar was ready and able to do at the first hint of command, and he put the horse through all he knew of dressage, and he pranced like a show horse, flashed back and forth like a cutting champion, and spun and turned like a barrel racer.

"Let's go for a little run by the river," he said, and they ran along the sandy edge of the bosque and the mesas, at a speed faster than he had thought anything at all could move, much less a horse. This was no mere horse. If he had been a flying horse, he would have been the swift war eagle of horses, and not the swan-like Pegasus.

"Enough," Cabrito finally had to cry. "Oh, that's enough. I can't ride any faster. Oh, my, oh, my, that is so glorious. On this horse, a man could rule the world!"

On the plaza of Lastima that day, young Emilio Sapogrande walked along the street, dressed in his fancy brocaded Mexican suit, carrying a bouquet of flowers. In front of Romero's General Store, he passed two young girls sitting together, with ribbons in their hair, and smiles on their faces. They giggled and flashed their eyes at him.

"Hola, Emilio," said one. "Are those for me?"

"Maybe next time for you, *chiqui*," he replied with a friendly wink.

"Don't forget, now," she said.

A block away, next to the fine brick building of the Romero Bank, was the fine brick house with the sign, "Casa Romero," beside the door. Sapogrande opened the gate of the lovely white picket fence, and paused a moment to appreciate the smell of the lovely honeysuckle blossoms which clustered on the vines which hung there. Beneath the broad overhanging porch of the home he found the object of his pursuit, the beautiful and perhaps soon to be available fourteen year old daughter of Alonso Romero himself, Dulcina.

"*Senorita Dulcina, buenos dias.*"

"Hello, Sapo," she said sweetly. "Have you come to bring those flowers to my father?"

"*Aie, que chulita,* how cute. No, my beautiful Dulcina, I have brought these for you, of course."

"Why that's very nice of you, but whatever for?" she

asked, more sweetly still.

"Listen to you," he said with avuncular confidence. "You know very well how I feel about you. I have already told your father many times that I desire nothing more in the world than to marry you."

"Why how sweet of you, Sapo," she said, "but you know I am too young to marry. I've not even celebrated my quinceanaria."

"You are fourteen now. In the old culture that has always been enough."

"Yes, perhaps so," she agreed, "but only to a man who has already established himself."

"Hola," came a friendly call. Wearing the pajamas of a peon, the young man known as Flaco came through the gate, and he joined them on the porch with his guitar.

"Hola Flaco, how nice to see you," Dulcina said. "Sing us a song, will you?"

"Sure, Dulci, if it will make you smile like that again. Hola Sapo, nice suit. Here, I'll sing this one for you." He sat on the railing of the porch, put his guitar up on his leg, strummed and plucked an opening lick, and sang, *"Que bendiga mi valle, me corazon, mi pais. Que bendiga mi pueblo, que viviran feliz, que viviran. Que bendiga mi valle, Guadalajara a Santa Fe."*

They heard a commotion a little way off, and when Flaco went to see what it was, he saw a crowd gathering on the corner of the plaza. "Come on," he said to the others, and he hurried out the gate.

From out of the mesquite dunes and into the town square rode a vision that drew everyone into the street with eyes agoggle. It was Cabrito, riding on the mighty stallion Cesar, and he had come to town to establish himself. He wore a black outfit like a monk's robe, a big wide black Franciscan-style hat, and he carried a tall staff as he rode. With a dramatic cloudscape behind him, and a holy glow upon him, he rode before them all, his dark curls clean and shiny, and with new bold flashes of gray at the temples.

On the corner, a group of children clumped tightly

together, as though to protect each other, a little fat boy, a spot-eyed dog, a dark-haired girl, and one skinny little black boy who wore a cavalry hat and clutched a chicken. They looked up at the tall rider wide-eyed, like a nest of owls. With the sun behind his head, he wore a blazing halo.

"Are you the Devil, mister?" asked the little cavalry kid.

Cesar's eyes flashed like fire, and he made a single STOMP in front of the kids, sending them scattering and squealing.

"Behold!" cried Cabrito imperiously. "Behold, for verily I have come before you. Forsooth, I have met the Devil, and I was deceived by him. But I have been delivered from his treacherous clutches, and the Lord God has said unto me that I am now your new priest."

There was a moment of silence, and then some dissatisfied muttering and scoffing, and some laughter. The oldest grandmother in town, who seemed to be Abuelita to everyone, waved her hand in dismissal. "Priest? You couldn't be a choirboy, Cabrito. You've never been inside a church in your life."

"You can't just make yourself a priest, you idiot. You have to be ordained," said Emilio Sapogrande.

"I am ordained, and anointed, you can believe that," said Cabrito. "Verily I say the Lord God Himself talked to me last night, when I had the Devil caught in my bear trap."

That got some genuine laughter.

"You were ordained by God Himself last night in your chile field?" asked Alonso Romero. "Next you're going to tell me that horse can fly."

"Did you and God eat Indian peyote cactus together, Cabrito?" asked Abuelita.

"No, we did not, vieja, but I did drink tequila with the Devil," he told her.

That got some genuinely derisive laughter.

"Now that we can believe," said Sapogrande. "So are you going to quit drinking now that you're a holy man, Padre?"

On that, Cabrito looked surprised. "You know what?

The subject never came up." Then he sat up even yet more confidently. "But drinking tequila is how I caught the Devil in my trap, and that is how I ended up with this horse, the mighty Cesar, the greatest horse in the world."

"Come on, Cabrito," scoffed Pancho Huarache, "half of us have met the Devil too, so cut the crap. Where did you find the horse?"

Cabrito pointed at him with the long yucca staff he carried. "Behold, verily I say this horse is given as a sign unto you, so you will know I am not just dreaming this all up."

"That is a pretty fine horse all right," Abuelita agreed.

A few of the men tried to press forward to touch Cesar, but he reared back up, snorting fiercely at all.

"You don't know. You don't even know," said Cabrito. "Come, Cesar, let's show them who you are."

Cabrito began to ride Cesar back and forth before an old adobe wall, cutting back and forth faster and faster, until the earth began to shake, the glass to rattle, and the bell hanging in the town gazebo began to ring. The wall came tumbling down.

The hapless owner of the wall came running out of his house in terror. When he saw what had happened, he was furious. "*Aie, cabron,* that's my wall," he wailed.

"Now you know how they felt in Jericho," Cabrito told him.

"Great," said the man. "So let's see you put it back up, smart guy."

"Who can raise up what the hand of God has smitten down?" Cabrito intoned.

"You better think of something, you crazy drunk, or that horse is going to be pulling my fertilizer wagon."

"That wall was a hazard to public safety," said Cabrito. "Believe me, there's going to be a lot of changes around here. We are going to start setting things right."

Back away from the others, under the awning of one of the stores, Corporal Geronimo Jones stood with two of the Buffalo Soldiers. "You men thinking what I'm thinking?"

he asked them.

"You mean this horse might give Gunpowder a run for his money?" one Buffalo asked.

"You bet," said Jones. "Looks like the classic dark horse to me, and the General's Gunpowder is giving some long odds these days."

The second Buffalo shook his head. "That big butt quarterhorse damn sure can run, though, can't he."

"Tell me about it," said Jones. "Since he's never been beat, the action is always on place and show, not the big win where the money is. This could be our big break."

Cabrito raised his staff and made his announcement. "I have come to announce my first service will be held in my church tomorrow on Sunday. You want to hear the truth, maybe for the first time in your life, you better be there."

Pancho Huarache, with a genius for timing, broke wind copiously. "The only truth you know comes out of the back end of that horse," he said.

"Tell us the truth, Cabrito," said Homer. "Where did you steal the horse?"

"Just be there," said Cabrito, and he swirled the sleeves of his robe around him like a pair of great wings, and he rode out of town.

Come Sunday morning, Cabrito had set up his little house like a church, with a row of pews made from rough planks. Having not been in a church since his childhood, he was at a loss as to what to put into it, or what to do in it, but he was resolved to be the priest he had promised to be, whether or not he was appreciated by his new flock of errant sheep.

The first to come to his service was Corona Baca. She came in, sat down in the front pew bench, and waited. Several other people came out to the little farm that day, though it was obvious that most of them had actually come to see Cesar, not to listen to Cabrito preach. At some point, he managed to get all of them into the little room, and he began to deliver his message.

"You people have got to get together now, and start

acting like a congregation," he scolded. "You need to straighten out your miserable, worthless, petty, and meaningless degenerate little lives. Repent of your disgusting, shameful, wicked, and sinful filthy stinking stupid behavior, and start cleaning up this pitiful no-account patch of God-forsaken dust-blown desert nowhere you are calling a town. Lucky for you, the Lord has sent you somebody who can set you straight. That's me.

"And another thing," he said, to their astonished faces. "If we are going to have a real church here, one people will point to and say, 'There is a place where God can feel at home,' then we are going to have to buy a few things. It is going to take a lot of money to... to make it bigger, and put in some glass windows, and some Santos to stand along the wall. You may be *jodido* cheap with each other, but you better not be cheap with the Lord. You better dig deep in those dirty pockets of yours and come up with some real silver, if you expect to have a real church in Lastima."

At that point people started shaking their heads and getting up to leave. Cabrito stood watching them, exasperated. "Wait. No, I'm not making this up. I met Him. I met both of them. This is for real, you stupid *pendejos*."

The last to leave was Corona, who reached into her pocket and dropped one silver peso to clink in the collection plate. "*Muchas gracias, Padre*," she said.

Cabrito came out of his church that Sunday feeling frustrated, and more than a little angry that he had been put in that position. When he saw that several of the people were standing by his barn watching Cesar eat the young chile plants, he went over in a great rage. He took hold of Cesar's bridle, and led him into the corral, and made a great show of closing the gate. Cesar trotted back and forth, and then jumped right over the side of the corral. When Cabrito let out a squawk, he jumped right back in. When Cabrito turned away to go back to his church, he jumped right back out, and returned to munch the chile crop. The people howled with laughter.

Cabrito led the horse into the barn, and he put a

heavy bar and a chain across the door. In seconds, the wall beside the door exploded into boards and splinters as it was kicked right off the barn. Cesar stepped out just seconds before the roof collapsed.

"*Aie, La Madre*," said Huevon, "there goes my retirement home."

Still determined, Cabrito took the chain from the door and used it to chain Cesar with a loop around the cottonwood tree beside his house. "Go ahead, try to kick the tree down," he said. "I'm going into town to get some things." He waved his hands at the people. "What are you all standing around here for? Don't you have anything to do? Go make some *tortillas* or *adobes*."

Cabrito saddled up Huevon, and with the others, he rode away toward the town. Cesar began to walk around the tree, faster and faster, using the loop of chain to cut through the bark, and through the wood.

When Cabrito returned home a few hours later, he found Cesar in the field eating chiles, and the cottonwood tree had fallen onto the house.

"That's it. That's all I can take," he raged. "I'm putting you up for sale, you big mule, and I'm taking the first offer I get." He did just that, and advertised in the plaza that he was selling the horse to donate the money to his new church.

The following Sunday he made a few quick platitudes from the pulpit, and then concluded that the business of the church could best be done by taking care of the business of the church, and they should at once adjourn to the auction. As the horse had already earned a spreading reputation, there were quite a number of people, including many of the town people, some of the soldiers, and some strangers.

Cesar stood beside the chile field, cropping chile plants. Cabrito put his saddle on and led him before the crowd. He swung himself (but more cautiously) into the saddle and began to put Cesar through his steps. Flaco had his guitar, and he and a couple of other musicians began to play Mariachi music. All began to applaud and cheer, and the horse started to get into the act. Cesar pranced back and forth, reared up high, and danced.

"I am a priest now, and a farmer," Cabrito pleaded, "and I have no use for such a fine horse. What am I offered?"

A well-dressed wealthy Caballero from Mexico stepped up without waiting for anyone else. "I will make this easy. I have an offer no one here can beat. Ten thousand pesos. Anyone? Any other bids? No? All right then." The Caballero took the reins and stepped close to the horse. "Now let's see what you can do in the hands of a master." He held the reins like a conductor and led the horse in graceful passes back and forth. He raised them and Cesar rose to his back legs and posed rampant. The crowd cheered and applauded.

The Caballero bowed, then mounted to the saddle. He gave a command, but Cesar did not move. He took a statue posture, one foot raised, and just stood there, while the Caballero grew more and more frustrated and angry. "Move, damn you, you black ass," the Caballero bellowed.

Cesar began to stamp his hooves, to drums his hooves in a fast flamenco beat, to step this way, and back, and back, and then when the rider was clutching at the saddle horn in terror, with a shrug he tossed that Caballero into the air, and into the chile patch.

"I withdraw my offer," the Caballero howled. "This horse is a monster."

"This horse is very high spirited, and not everyone can ride such a horse," Cabrito said apologetically. "I'm sorry, Señor. Who else has a bid?"

A grey-bearded old rancher raised his hand. He took off his tattered old straw sombrero, and shook back his long gray hair. Holding the hat before his chest humbly, he kicked the dirt from the heels his worn old leather boots, and he said, "I will bid five thousand pesos."

A little way off, Flaco stood watching beside Huarache and some others. "Look," he said, "it's old Pepe, the man who whispers to horses."

"If that horse takes orders in whispers, I'll eat my

boots," said Huarache.

The whisperer stepped up close to Cesar, and began to pet his nose, and to whisper seductively into his ear. Cesar listened, then nodded. Everyone gasped. The whisperer turned to the crowd, winked and grinned, and started to mount. When he put his left foot up into the stirrup, Cesar stepped quite daintily onto the toe of his right boot.

The whisperer tried to push him off, to whisper him off, then to whisper loudly for help, and finally bawled out in pain and frustration, "Get him off of me!"

Cabrito took the reins, and he led Cesar obediently forward.

One of the Buffalo troops with Cpl. Jones stepped forward. "Never met a horse I couldn't ride. I'll take a shot at it." The woolly-headed warrior got as far as throwing his leg over the saddle, when Cesar bucked him out of the stirrup, side-stepped left out from under him, and he went flying right on over.

"Look," laughed Huarache, "a soldier who falls out of the sky. Wouldn't that be nice to have an army of?"

"How about you, Huarache?" Flaco asked. "He looks like a rebel to me. You two might get along."

"I might try it, just to surprise you," he said.

As the morning went on, one rancher, or gentleman, or soldier after another went flying.

Finally, to everyone's surprise, Pancho Huarache did step up. "I don't have any money to bid, but how about donating that horse to the revolution?" he asked.

"Huarache," said Cabrito, "if you can ride this horse, I will join the revolution."

Huarache got as far as approaching Cesar, when the horse turned to look at him, right in the eye, and he scowled, and snarled menacingly like a genuine man-eating demon. Huarache backed off fast, crying, *"No, no, no. Aie, La Madre!"*

After a while all the prospective buyers shook their heads, scoffed, and departed. Cabrito followed after them, trying to get them to reconsider, and Corona found herself alone, watching Cesar eat chile plants. She walked slowly around the horse, looking him over.

"*Si-mon*, you're one good-looking horse, that's for sure," she said. "That's what everybody says. He's a good-looking horse, the strongest, and the fastest. But I know something they don't, don't I? They think you are so stupid you would take orders from them, so they call you untrainable. But I know the truth, don't I? You are The Devil's Own Horse, and you know exactly what you are doing, and you know exactly what everybody is saying. Yes, you do, you don't fool me a bit. You see, I know you are not a rebel. No. You are loyal to perfection... yes, but only to a master who deserves your loyalty. Uh-huh, you see I do understand, don't I? So you can confide in me, and I will help you with your situation."

Corona pulled up one of the remaining chile plants with a few small green peppers on it, and offered it to Cesar. He took it with pleasure.

"*Pues, andale,* Corona," he said with a whinny. "No promises, but let's see what you can do."

Chapter Four

In the kitchen of La Fuente, early in the morning, Corona was working by herself. Arturo Melendrez came into the bar, poured himself a glass of brandy, and stood watching her, appreciating the way her strong forearms worked the dough, and the way the light came in through a window made of colored broken bottles and made rays in the flour dust hanging in the air.

"What's cooking, *muchacha*," he asked.

"I'm making some *albondigas* for tonight, and some *churros*," she said..

"That's good, that's good," the Mayor said. "Too bad you never got married, Corona. Somebody would have a good wife, that's for sure."

"Well, thank you, Arturo," she said.

"You know, I can't remember you ever having a boy friend, or a late night date even," he said.

"My work and my home have kept me busy. So what?"

"Well, sure, you're a hard worker," he went on, "but you shouldn't be busy all the time. I was just thinking... if you don't have time for dating, but you would still like to have a friend who could treat you like a woman, a friend with understanding and experience..."

"Arturo, you old goat," she said with a laugh. "You must think you have *huevos de oro*, the way you keep advertising them to all the girls."

"I am a very generous man, that's all," he said. "I hate to see someone go hungry, when I have so much of what she needs."

"What, are you asking me to marry you?"

"No, no, of course not, not now," he said, "but my wife is much older than I, and I might be a widower soon..."

Corona picked up her big Chinese cleaver and waved it at him. "*Aie, cabron viejo!* I've got a good recipe for *chorizo de oro*, so you better watch out, or I'll serve it to you."

Melendrez held up his hands and backed away, laughing.

Cabrito was up early also. He went to the shattered remains of his barn, and he dragged out his old iron plow, and he led Cesar up to stand in front of it. "Come on, let's go," he said. "You may be a bigshot in hell, but a horse is a horse, and we have to do something about the mess you made of my chile."

"Cabrito, please, let me do it," Huevon whinnied plaintively. "Don't put the plow on Cesar. You must not."

"When I need advice from a horse's ass, I'll ask for it," Cabrito told him, and he fastened the yoke, and strung the traces on the mighty black stallion, and he drove him out into the chile field and commanded him to pull the plow.

Whatever his curse might have been such that he found himself in service to the Devil, Cesar was at heart a beast of loyalty, and he struggled mightily with the desire to rebel outright and to stomp that clubfooted fool Cabrito right down into the mud of his own chile field. Unable to bring himself to that point, he began to pull the plow, stamping potholes into the furrows with each step, and moving faster and faster. Cabrito struggled to keep up, limping and staggering, and then finally he fell to his face in the dirt. Cesar pulled the plow back and forth across the furrows, and faster and faster until the dirt flew up behind him like a wave of mud.

"Come back here, you demon," Cabrito cried, and then wished he had not as Cesar swung around and headed directly toward him, and directly toward the door to the house. Cabrito leaped aside, and Cesar ran right through it. As the plow struck the big stone lintel of Cabrito's adobe house, it struck out a huge burst of sparks, which immediately set the wood floor and roof of the house on fire. The plow cut a palm's width into the stone and stuck, and the harness broke as Cesar charged through the house and then dived out the window on the other side. He shook off the rest of the traces, and he bucked and kicked all around the burning building and the fallen tree.

"My house! My church!" Cabrito wailed. "Lord, Lord, if you love me, send me rain."

Cesar's head snapped up as he heard Cabrito's prayer. He began to stomp his hooves on the ground, creating the sound of thunder, which rumbled out like ripples in a pool of mud. He leaped up and down in thundering tom-tom rhythm.

"No, Cesar, not a rain dance!" Cabrito cried.

Huevon ran over to hide in the limbs of the fallen tree. The sky clouded up fast, with great cumulus boiling up like forest fires, flashing lightning. A flash of lightning hit the fallen cottonwood tree, setting it on fire and sending Huevon fleeing. A torrent of rain started to fall, and then a flash flood came rushing down the valley and swept toward the house. Just as the roof collapsed from burning, the flood swept through it, and washed away the burning vigas and boards.

Then, just as quickly, the sun broke through, and the sky cleared, and Cabrito sat in the mud beside the ruins of his house, defeated and in despair. Huevon stood likewise in resignation, his head leaning on a branch of the sodden and blackened fallen tree. A little way off, Cesar cropped a few remaining chile plants in the ruined, rutted, and eroded field.

In desperation, Cabrito got on his knees and tried to pray. "All right, Lord, you know I don't know much about praying, but please, you see what's happening to me, and I pray... I pray that you will... well, come on, Lord, you remember, we talked. It's you and me now, right? Look, I'm having a lot of trouble with this horse, and nobody believes me. Do I have to make another deal, is that is? When I need you, you're not going to be here? Come on, I know you can hear me."

He slumped in frustration and disgust against the wall and pulled his big black padre hat from the mud and shoved it onto his head, resolved that he would sit there and wait until... well, until he didn't know what.

It was only a little while later that Corona Baca came down to his ravaged house on her mule-drawn buckboard. She walked over to stand above him, fists on her hips. "Padrecito," she said firmly, "it's time for church. Come on."

"How am I supposed to run a church with this?" he

whined.

"I suggest we start by getting this place cleaned up," she said.

It was clear enough that she was quite serious, so he dragged himself to his feet, and they began to carry out pieces of burned and broken furniture and the collapsed roof, and to pile them up for a bonfire in the back yard. Corona quickly demonstrated she was a powerful worker, and whether using her hands, a shovel, or a broom, the disorder was quickly swept away before her. He struggled along limping, trying to keep up with her. After a while, she stopped and went to her buckboard and brought out a basket, from which she handed him a big burrito.

Feeling quite humbled, and also quite hungry, he took it gratefully. "I am surprised you never have married, Corona," he said around a mouthful of frijoles. "You run the best kitchen in town, you have your own house, and believe me, I have never seen anyone who can work as hard as you."

She shrugged, and bit into her own burrito. "No matter how hard they try to be better, Padrecito, most men are *pendejos y cabrones*. They need a mother to take care of them, they want a servant to order around, and they expect a wife to be both. I don't need a man to support me, and I don't need one to tell me what has to be done. I just haven't met a man I liked enough to put up with yet."

"I don't say this much, but I want you to know I am very grateful for what you have done for me. And thank you for bringing this."

"You're welcome," she said, "but I am here because I believe you, even if everyone else thinks you are crazy. You would not give up the life you have created for yourself if this didn't mean everything to you."

"I didn't ask for it," he grumbled, then had to admit, "well, I did, actually. I didn't mean to, but..."

She nodded. "All my life you have been out here raising chile by yourself, and spending every peso of it on tequila at La Fuente. You could have a good home here, and you could be rich with your chile, and raise a family. But instead you have been what you have been. How come you never married, Cabrito?"

For an instant, he started to give her a glib answer, something like not wanting to share the blanket, or talking too much, like he might say to the hombres at the bar. But there was something about her sincerity that he could not hide from, and he found himself telling her things that he had not spoken of for many years.

"I was married once," he said. "I was young, and full of anger and pride. You see, my father was Italian, not Spanish, and my mother was Apache, not Mexican, so mostly everybody gave me a bad time. When my father took my mother from the tribal lands in Mescalero, the Apache told them never to come back. So they came here and built this house. When I was old enough to think I was a man, I decided to run away from the Mexicans and the gringos, and return to my mother's people."

He told her how as a boy of about seventeen, he had entered the lands of the Apache, demanded to be admitted as a brave, and was confronted by the men of the tribe. They had pushed him around, knocked him down, tied his hands, and led him to the Chief's tent. "Your mother is a whore," the Chief had told him. "If you had been raised among us, you might at least call yourself a half-breed, instead of the white-eye bastard you are."

"They decided to let me stay, and they gave me to an old man to teach me," Cabrito told her. "He treated me all right, fed me well, and beat me if I was not brave and hard-working. I was doing pretty well, until I decided to marry Two Deer. They called a council around the fire, and one of the older boys told the Chief they all believed that the real Apache should have first choice of wives, and not mongrels from the valley. Every one of them agreed, so the Chief didn't have much choice. 'Which of you wants to claim this woman?' he asked. Two Deer was not very pretty, and the truth is she was a bit stupid and not very clean. None of them stepped forward. I was ready to fight any of them. They all looked from one to the other, and then they began to laugh. It turned out nobody wanted her after all, so we got married."

Corona brought a corked bottle of red wine out of her basket, and worked the cork out with her teeth. "Here, a little of this will be good for your stomach," she said, and handed it to him.

"*Dios*," he toasted with the bottle, and took a drink. "We had a baby son, and when I took him to the Chief to be recognized as one of the tribe, the men all came around again and objected. His mother's marriage was illegitimate, they said, and his marriage is illegitimate, and so the whelp is a bastard of a bastard, they said. It should be taken to the rocks and left for the coyotes, they said. It was all I could take. I called them the coyotes and cowards and liars too, and I demanded they apologize or fight me, to the death."

Cabrito shook his head solemnly, and his jaw clenched. "You know what they did? They laughed at me, and they made fun of fighting me. They danced back and forth, and pretended to stick me with their short spears. Then... one got too close to me, and he stumbled a little, and I stabbed him with my knife." He shrugged. "He didn't die right away. It took him a couple of days."

"So you had time to run away," Corona said.

"Yes, to run for our lives. I had nowhere to go, and to my eternal shame, I came back here, where my father and my mother welcomed us and fed us and let us into their home. We promised to stay only long enough to get ready for a move, perhaps north to find a place among the Spaniards and the Dineh, the pueblo people of the Rio Grande valley, and of the cliff cities of the north.

"On the next night, we all lay in the house, sleeping. Suddenly there was a hooting and yelling, a terrible commotion, and some of the Apache I knew were there in the house. I heard the screams of my parents and my wife as they were killed. Then somebody hit me with something, in the head. The last thing I knew I was going to be killed. But I was not. I woke up in the morning to find my family leaning against the wall staring at me with empty eyes, and my foot was pinned to the floor with a spear. I could have stayed right there and died. One little day to sit there and bleed away. That was the choice they gave me, a choice they thought was worse than death. So I made my choice. I had to take them all out and bury them."

Cabrito took a second drink from the wine bottle, and heaved a deep sigh. "It took me a long time, and I had to find a way to take care of my foot, because I couldn't let myself die before getting them buried. When I finished, I planted that cottonwood tree over them. Every day when I get up in the morning, I have gone out to that tree, and said to myself, this is what you have instead of your family. Now look what I have done. God help me, I wish I could find a way to be free of that horse."

Corona leaned close to him, so she could look up under his floppy hat brim. "Do you trust me, Padrecito?"

"That comes much harder than gratitude," Cabrito admitted, "but yes, more than anybody else, Corona, I trust you."

"Good," she said. "Then leave this to me. I think I have an idea."

Chapter Five

Corona was kept busy with her many duties in running the bakery and the kitchen at La Fuente, but as soon as she was able to get a few hours free, she went to Cabrito's farm. She told Cabrito to get on Huevon and ride into the plaza and tell Concha to fix him a big plate of tacos. Then she went out to the chile patch to talk to Cesar.

"What a pleasure to see Your Highness Equuinus again. Shall we dance?" She raised up a hand, and began to step lightly from side to side, surprisingly agile for her size. Delighted in spite of himself, Cesar jumped up eagerly, and began to dance back and forth with her. Laughing and applauding, she led him in a game of pantomime.

"That's it, yes, the war champion, tall, proud. Oh, yes! OK, now, the ears back, the eyes of fire... aie, Cesar, even the Devil himself would tremble."

Cesar lowered his head, snorted viciously, then strutted back and forth.

She went over and pulled up one of the last chile plants and brought it over to him, and stood petting his nose as he munched it. "Aie, Cesar, what a horse you are. Your name should be first among all horses. You know the names of Bucephalus and Marengo, don't you? I see you do. They were the horses of Alexander and Napoleon. They were the horses of Generals. That is what such a horse as you should be. I understand, you see. These stupid men do not. You could never be sold. It is beneath your station to be sold. You must be won, as Cabrito won you, or won in deadly combat."

The horse snickered, and nodded his head in agreement.

"You know what? I have an idea. You could be won as a prize in a race, the greatest prize ever won in a race, and you could be won by a General. With you to serve him, he could become a great General. What do you think?"

Again Cesar nodded in agreement, with an eager whinny.

"All you have to do is lose the race," she said.

Cesar reared up, wild-eyed. "Lose? My ass!" he said.

"Oh, come on now, we all know the truth," she told him. "You could beat that Yankee quarterhorse jumping back and forth over him. What you have to win here is not the race, but your freedom from this *pendejo* priest. I can help you win that. Fixing a race is such a deliciously devilish thing to do, don't you agree?"

Reluctantly, the horse had to agree with that much, anyway.

"I knew you would understand," she said. "You have a very subtle and clever mind, Cesar, yes you do." Then she held up a finger, remembering something she had reminded herself not to forget. "Oh, we have another problem. If you want to keep eating chile, there has to be a lot more of it, and if there is no chile for the Devil's table, I'll bet he has a good recipe for making tacos out of a horse."

"I see your point," said Cesar. "Watch this, my lady." Cesar turned his tail away, and Corona gasped at the sound of his copious urination, like a stream, a waterfall. From behind him spread out a growth of chile plants, sprouting and rising up and blooming and fruiting in the twisted furrows until the whole field was filled with ripening fat green chiles.

Corona stood with her fists on her hips and admired the lush growth. "You know, I like it much better that way, without the rows. Maybe a mule would make rows, or a stupid ox, but never one like you, Cesar. Never you."

It was a little while later that Cabrito came back from town, and Corona took him aside, and sat him down on one of the little bench pews remaining. "Padrecito, I have a plan. You desire to be free of this devil horse, and we need some money to rebuild your house into a church."

"You saw what happened when I tried to sell him," he protested.

"He won't let anyone buy him because that is an insult to him, but it would be all right if someone won him, in a contest or a bet," she explained.

"Bet him?" Cabrito started to agree at once, then

suddenly frowned. "I can't. I am a man of God now, Corona. I can't bet the horse, even intending to lose him."

"You won't be betting the horse," she quickly assured him. "I will be making the bets, and you will only be putting up Cesar to me personally as collateral. If I lose, then the winner gets to foreclose on Cesar."

"All right," Cabrito reluctantly agreed, then shook his head. "I can't ride him either, not in a race like that would be."

"Don't worry about that. I have an understanding with Cesar. It delights him to please me because he knows I understand and admire him. He also knows I have the answer to his problem as well as yours."

"Oh? What is that?" he asked.

"You," she said simply. "If his soul were not already mortgaged, he would give it in an instant to be free of you. He is a great warrior, and to be hitched to the plow of a mud-farming priest is the greatest shame he can imagine. Therefore he will follow my instructions to the letter. Let me handle this, Padre."

It was only a few days later that Corona drove her buckboard along the wagon route north to the adobe-walled compound at the foot of the mountains called Los Robledos, the robbers. Above the big heavy gate was a sign reading, "Fort Selmore, U.S. Cavalry." Looking sharp and on the bounce, a trooper on guard raised a hand to stop her, his curly black hair sticking out from under his gold-braided cavalry hat.

"Hey, Corona, what you got for us today?" he asked.

"Everything you love, Calvin," she promised. "Bolillos, tamales... I even made you some biscochitos."

"I'm looking forward to that. The General is over there working the team on the grinder." He pointed toward the parade field, where the commanding officer of the fort, General Burwell Cooley, was drilling a company of troops in close-order rifle drill, riding his handsome quarterhorse, Gunpowder. Corona drove her buckboard close to watch them work.

Though Cooley was a gringo, as Anglo a white man as could be imagined, all of his troops, except Corporal Jones, were black Buffalo Soldiers. Having no war to fight in those pleasant days, the troops devoted themselves to drill. Though she had never seen any other troops doing such spectacular things with their rifles, she was certain they must be the finest rifle drill team in the world.

The troops marched under the command of Master Sergeant Oscar Bonaventure. Known to all as Top, he was the oldest of them, black as aged leather, bristled with gray muttonchops, and with a row of chevron stripes all the way up his arms. (Jones, Corona recalled, had two stripes, and all the rest had none.) With a small brass marching band thumping out a rousing blare of field music, the troops conducted a spectacular drill routine, twirling and throwing their rifles. Top called them to attention.

"Who are we, men?" he barked.

"We are the Cav, Top Sergeant," they shouted in reply.

"Say it again."

"We are the Cav, Top Sergeant!" they shouted louder.

"Who's better?"

"Nobody!"

"Damn right," the Sergeant agreed. "Dismissed."

The troops departed the field running, hooting and howling. General Cooley rode beside them, hooting with them, waving his hat. He rode around the field at a full gallop, letting Gunpowder show off his astonishing speed. Then he rode over to where Corona sat watching. "*Señorita Baca*, good morning," he said.

"Good morning, General Cooley. I've brought the baking as usual, but there is something else I'd like to talk with you about. It's about a horse."

The General reined up close to her and leaned forward conspiratorially. "Aha. Well, I'm very interested. I've heard some rumors about a horse lately. Meet me in my office."

In a few minutes, the General and Corona sat at a coffee table in his comfortable office. Cpl. Jones brought a tray with teacups, poured tea, and withdrew quietly. "I'll be right inside if you need me, General," he said.

"Jones. Now, Miss Baca, about this horse?"

"He is a wonder to see, I must tell you," she said. "I think he is a champion in the rough."

"What do you mean, in the rough?"

"I believe he has never known the hand of a real horseman," she said, "but if he were trained to your standards, he would be unbeatable."

"Aha." The General gave her a long shrewd look. "I don't think you have come here to sell him to me."

"No. I have an arrangement with the owner. He is a farmer who thinks he is a monk, and has no idea what to do with such a horse. So I have become Cesar's manager, and I have come today to challenge you to a race between him and your horse Gunpowder."

"I see. I thought so. You must think a great deal of this diamond in the rough, an untrained horse ridden by a farmer, to think he might beat the finest and fastest Cavalry mount in the United States Army. What do you propose to bet?"

"I propose a bet of one thousand gold dollars," she said. "But I must tell you that I do not have that money."

The General leaned back in his chair and took a slow sip at his tea. "You want to bet big money, but you don't have any? I don't understand."

"I am prepared to offer as collateral... the horse."

"Aha. So if this undisciplined mustang that wandered in from the desert does not win the race against my champion Gunpowder, then he becomes my property, is that the bet?"

"Yes," said Corona, "and if Gunpowder loses the race, then I win the money."

"There is no untrained horse this side of hell can take Gunpowder," said the General. "Your bet is a very foolish long shot, but I'll take it, and when you lose him, I will make a champion of him." He raised his teacup. "To the horses," he toasted.

Corona clinked her teacup against his. "To the horses."

When Corona approached her buckboard a few minutes later to leave, she was met by Corporal Geronimo Jones. "Hey, Corona, come here," he said. "I heard you talking to the General. Why don't you step into my office?"

In a cramped room off the supply warehouse, Jones had his desk, and walls lined with shelves piled with boxes and bags of supplies. "Welcome to the real nerve center of the fort," he said. "Top takes care of keeping the troops in line, the General keeps himself amused, and I take care of business. Tobacco, jerky, whiskey, opium, gold teeth... all the things that make Army life worthwhile. Tequila?"

"Sure," she said.

Jones poured two shots and hoisted his in toast. "Hao." They shot their shots. "All right. It happens I also handle certain other matters on behalf of the troops. There is a dice game, a loan service... and a book on the General's races..."

"I see," she said, "and you just happen to be the first one to know about the General's next race. How convenient."

"How about that?" he asked, pouring two more. "Corona, I've seen that horse run, and I know every man on this base is going to want to bet on Cesar. Now the General expects us all to bet on him and Gunpowder, and every man will, one buck per buck. But what I propose is that I make a single bet with you on behalf of the all soldiers, with their big money."

"You want to put their collective big bet on Cesar, right?"

"Yep."

"And you heard me tell the General I don't have any money to cover the bet, right?"

"Yep. I also heard you talking to Cesar." To her surprised look, he waved a hand. "I'm an Indian, remember? Shamanists? I've got your game all figured out, sister. Cabrito is trying to get rid of the horse, and vice versa, and you're trying to make some money."

"So?"

"So if Cesar wins, then I get to take the horse on behalf of the troops to cover your bet. You get the General's money. If Cesar loses, the General gets the horse to cover your bet, and you get the soldiers' money. Either way, you win."

"I see we think alike, Geronimo," she said. "We have a bet?"

"We have a bet. Honest Injun."

They toasted again with tequila shots, and Corona sang cheerfully all the way back down the valley past the old volcano El Picacho, and past the high flat lava flows called the black mesa, to the plaza of the little town of Lastima.

As the early morning sun came through the colored glass of the broken bottle window at the end of the bar in La Fuente, Corona was doing her baking as usual, kneading dough with her big strong hands, mixing masa, and kicking up a little cloud as she hummed a song and danced a little step, on her great strong legs.

Stopping in for one of Corona's deep-fried apricot empanadas, Emilio Sapogrande came in dressed in a Mexican caballero's suit with lots of piping, and a big brocaded and embroidered sombrero.

"Hola, Emilio," she greeted him. "My, my, look at you. You know, something I like about you is the way you favor the traditional style of old Mexico. That's classy. The sombrero is so much more manly."

"Thank you very much, Corona," he replied, tipping the big wide hat back and smiling. "I think the clothes of the gringos are boring, like they had no *cojones*, like they had no heart."

"No one could say that of you, Sapo. I am surprised every day that you are not married yet. All the girls wish you would like them."

"Oh, I do, I like them all," he protested, "but..."

"Yes, we all know you are saving yourself for Dulcina Romero," she said, "and we all know that Alonso won't let her until you make something of yourself."

"The way you say that sounds like a pitch," said Emilio

suspiciously.

"*Seguro.* Here, let me get you a *cervesa,* and we can talk." She brought him another empanada and a mug of beer from the tap, and leaned across the bar to talk to him. "The General has challenged Cabrito to a race, Gunpowder against Cesar, but there is a problem. Cabrito can't ride fast enough, and he needs a strong and brave young man to ride Cesar in the race. I want you to be that man."

"A race? The General's horse doesn't have a chance against Cesar," he said.

"Yes, and when you win the race, you will be a hero, and then you will win the election for mayor."

"But Corona," he protested, "everybody knows nobody can ride Cesar but Cabrito."

"I know you don't believe in such things," she told him, "but I have an arrangement with Cesar. He likes me. If I tell him you should ride, he will let you. All you have to do is just stay on and don't try to give him any orders. You understand that? No orders, and you'll be all right. Deal?"

Emilio shook his head in amazement. "It sounds crazy, but crazy enough to work. All right, I'll do it. I'll ride Cesar in the race."

"Good for you," she said, picking up his empanada and biting off half of it. "This is going to be a great moment for you. But that's not all. General Cooley has offered to take side bets on the rider of the winning horse, at even odds. If you were able to make a little bet, you could win some money too."

"I don't have much, I'm afraid. Just my savings of one hundred silver pesos."

"All right, do you want to put your money where your... you know what is?"

"Oh yeah? OK, I'll take the job, and the General's bet. Thanks, Corona, I won't forget this." He picked up the empanada and finished it with gusto.

"It's nothing, really," she said with a wave. "And good luck with Dulcina."

Later that afternoon, Corona unpacked half a dozen

more of the little fruit-stuffed pies from her basket at the broken-down house of Cabrito. The clean-up was coming along well, and the barn had been well enough repaired that Cabrito had taken to sleeping there. He was pleased to get the tasty prizes, and sat down with her to enjoy them.

"I have made a wager with the General," she told him. "If Cesar loses the race, then I lose my wager, and the General gets to foreclose on my collateral, and so he gets Cesar. If the General's horse Gunpowder loses, then the General will pay me one thousand gold dollars."

"But that will only solve one of our problems, and not the worst of them," Cabrito protested.

Corona nodded patiently. "I have also come to an agreement with Corporal Geronimo Jones. Since the soldiers deal through him, he represents as much money as the General, and like everyone on the post except the General, he believes Cesar will win the race. If Cesar wins the race, then the Corporal wins the bet, and he would be able to foreclose and so own Cesar. If Cesar loses the race, then the Corporal will pay me the soldiers' one thousand gold dollars."

"But surely Cesar will win."

"That is what the Corporal thinks too. He thinks he will win the world's fastest horse, and I will win the General's money."

"Wouldn't that be all right?" he asked.

"Think about it," she said.. "Cesar would never agree to become the horse of a Corporal, much less a cocky little feather merchant like Geronimo Jones. He wants to lead great cavalry charges with the General. All he has to do is stumble just enough to let Gunpowder win by a nose, and he shall become the General's prize. Then he can run circles around him if he wants to, and I shall have the soldiers' one thousand gold dollars."

Cabrito shook his head in dismay. "Aie, I am not only taking part in a bet, it is a crooked bet, and I admit I don't believe for a minute that Cesar will ever throw a race, not when it is down to the wire, he couldn't. And even if he would, we don't have a rider."

"But we do," she assured him. "Emilio wants to become mayor of Lastima, but he has no money. He bet his life savings, one hundred silver pesos, against the General's silver in a side bet on the rider of the winning horse, so he could win enough to run for office, and he would be a town hero."

"But you said Cesar is supposed to lose the race. Emilio will lose his bet."

Corona giggled wickedly. "*Si, mi Padrecito*, you are correct."

Chapter Six

On the night before the great race was to take place,
La Fuente was filled with people talking, drinking, and making
bets among themselves. Among them were Arturo Melendrez
and Alonso Romero, Corporal Jones and a few of his troops,
and others of the town. The kitchen and the bar were both
kept busy enough that Arturo hired Concha's little sister
Chulita to help Corona. Four of the local ranchers had put
together a pretty good Mariachi band, and they were kicking
up the rafters.

As it was in the region of the tejanos to the east,
more and more of the foreigners coming to settle in Mexico
were gringos, pale white men with their sharp little chins and
noses, but they were still looked on as outsiders by the
Mexicans. As a result of that, perhaps, men like Homer and
Wilbur Colby sometimes made a point of being hard on the
Indian, so as not to be seen as the one on the bottom of the
heap. That happened most easily when there was a lot of
tequila flowing, and the tequila was flowing that night.

Wilbur made the mistake of trying to start some
trouble with Geronimo Jones. "What the hell is an Indian
doing in a US Cavalry uniform?" he asked, loudly. "It's a
Goddang shame. You are a Goddang redskin aren't you?"

Jones gave him a long cool look. "My parents were
Apache, yeah. They were killed by a band of ravaging
settlers who burned their teepee and kidnapped me. I got
raised by those white-eyes like I was their own son."

"Well, that still don't make you a white man," Wilbur
said with a sneer, "and redskins aren't supposed to drink in
white men's saloons."

"You call me a redskin again, Wilbur, and I'm going to
show you an old Indian wrestling trick," said Jones calmly.
"I'm going to put your right elbow in your left ear, and your
left elbow in your right ear."

"Like hell you are," said Wilbur, and he took a swing at
Jones. There were some fast blurred moves, and then Jones
coolly returned to his drink.

On all sides there were astonished faces. "I didn't believe that was possible, first time I heard it," said Huarache.

Wilbur gasped twice, and then whined piteously, "I cain't get 'em out."

On the wall above the fireplace, a rough map was tacked up. Emilio stood up on the hearth, and called for everyone's attention. "All right everybody, here is the map. We go from the start at Fort Selmore, down the river to Brazito Ranch, up onto the Black Mesa, and then down to the finish in the square right here in Lastima."

Alonso Romero rose up from his seat at the table next to him. "Our mayor Arturo Melendrez will hold all of the stakes in the official bets on this race, and the prizes will be distributed right here in La Fuente after the race."

Everyone applauded, and Alonso paused and looked as there was a commotion at the end of the bar. Gradually a hush fell on the room and the people parted as Cabrito came into La Fuente, and he walked slowly up the length of the bar, and he stood looking across the room at them all gathered there. "*Vino, y tortilla, por favor*," he said.

"Sure, Cabrito," said Concha. She poured a glass of wine from a jug, picked up a fresh hot tortilla from the kitchen window, and put them in front of him.

Cabrito tore the tortilla in half and dunked it into the bowl of chile sauce Corona kept full on the bar. "The pleasure and pain of the chile is the perfect expression of the joy and suffering of human life," he said. "It is the perfect complement to the bread and wine." With everyone watching in silence, he ate the tortilla and chile, then raised the wine glass with tears running down his face. He downed the wine, then looked around the room with wild eyes. "I talked with God last night," he said. "God has promised to give his church a sign, and he has challenged me to an act of faith. Tomorrow I shall ride in the race."

There was a great collective gasp, and then immediately an uproar, which Sapogrande was able finally to silence. "What do you mean?" he demanded. "I am riding

Cesar. That is what everybody has already bet on. You can't change that now."

"Never mind, Emilio," said Cabrito. "I am not going to ride Cesar. God has told me to ride my own horse, Huevon."

There was another gasp, and then another uproar, but this time one of hilarity. Finally Mayor Melendrez stood up and raised up his hand. "*Pues*, Cabrito, since you have such a fine horse to ride, what are you going to bet on him?" he asked.

"Nothing," said Cabrito. "I am a man of God."

"Nothing?" asked Romero. "Then what do you expect to win?"

"God didn't tell me what to expect," Cabrito said. "He just told me to run."

When the laughter died down, Emilio said, "Well, all right. I don't have any objections. Does anybody have any objections? No? OK, Cabrito, your challenge is accepted. Welcome to the race."

The party at La Fuente lasted well into the evening. Those who had to ride north to the starting point at the fort went to bed early, and rose early to make the trip.

When the sun was high in the sky, the soldiers' brass band began to toot and thump, and all of those who were to be at the starting point were in a state of great excitement. Corporal Jones found the General sitting out under a big umbrella, and he saluted sharply. With him he brought a leather-vested Indian, a very bull-chested and savage looking man.

"I brought in a communications consultant to send a message to Lastima when the race has begun," he said. "General, this is Skytalker. He's a Navajo. His cousins are at Brazito, and in Lastima, and they can send signals only they can interpret. It is kind of like a secret code that nobody else could break."

"Aha," said the General. "You know, that could have very useful military applications, Corporal Jones."

"Yes, Sir, General, except for just one problem, Sir," said Jones.

"What's that, Corporal?"

"Meaning no disrespect, Sir, but we're the Cavalry, and they're the Indians."

"I see your point."

As the Buffalo Brass Band played, the Buffalo Soldiers came out marching with their rifles. Some on horseback performed mounted drill, and did stunts of trick riding, rope handling, bullwhip handling, and sabre work, and they finished off their show by lining up all four of their artillery cannons.

At the starting line, the three horses stood side by side, as all watched excited, ready for the start of the race. Wearing his sharpest uniform, Top Sergeant Bonaventure stood looking at his watch. "Two minutes, General," he said.

"Two minutes, Corporal," said the General.

"Two minutes, Skytalker," said Jones.

Skytalker raised the blanket from his firepit, and sent a billow of smoke into the sky. He held up a long yucca-stalk staff, and he called out in a mighty voice, "Hey, yah!" The staff began to glow with a shimmering light like the sailors call St.Elmo's fire. He made a vertical stroke and the smoke was parted into two rising columns. He made a horizontal stroke cutting off the smoke at the bottom, so that two short parallel smoke columns rose up together. Then with a flourish like a bullfighter, he put the blanket back over the bed of coals.

"Rabbit ears?" the General asked Corporal Jones. "What's that supposed to mean?"

"I think you've got it, Sir," said Jones. "The rabbit has great symbolic significance to the Indian. But shouldn't there be two rabbits?"

General Cooley mounted to his saddle, to the cheers of the troops and the blaring cavalry charge chorus of the company bugle corps. Gunpowder pranced back and forth tossing his head and mane-trimmed neck.

Cesar stood looking bored and above it all. Sapogrande patted his neck for reassurance, and gingerly climbed into the saddle. He leaned close to the horse's ear and spoke to him earnestly. "All right, now, Cesar, all right, no orders. I'm just a passenger, I won't forget. You're the champion. You're the boss."

Limping on his twisted foot, Cabrito clumsily climbed up to sit on Huevon, who was looking stubborn and sullen as he endured the hoots and laughter of the troops and the others gathered at the starting end of the race at the fort.

With one minute to go, Huevon stepped close to Cesar, and spoke to him earnestly. "Mighty Cesar, you have no idea what an honor it is to stand beside you today. I mean it. This is the greatest moment of my life. I am so moved I must ask you a little favor."

Cesar turned to look at him, surprised. "Oh yeah? What's that, *Viejo?*" he asked.

"When we begin, would you hold back your great power for a few minutes, and just let me run alongside you, so I can admire you for just a little way, before you run off like lightning to embarrass that foolish quarterhorse. I would be most grateful."

The great stallion snickered, then whinnied in laughter. "You're a pretty bold old plug, Huevon, but you got respect. I like that. Sure, stick by me and I'll show you a couple of tricks I know."

"Riders take your places," said Top. "Ready..." He pointed his arm at the cannoniers, who set off their four cannons together. The Skytalker let up a big billow of smoke, inhaled it all, then with a stacatto hoot like a bellowing buffalo, blew out a huge smoke-ring zero, which rose quickly into the sky.

Gunpowder leaped out ahead of Cesar and Huevon, to the cheers of the troops. Huevon ran alongside Cesar, struggling mightily, gasping to utter words of flattery. "What a wonder it is to watch you run. You make it look so easy, and it is all I can do."

"I could do this on two feet," said the great Cesar. "Come, get closer to me. You feel that power? Now draw from it. Yes, that's right, breathe, breathe."

"I feel it!" cried Huevon. "Aie, I feel like I am flying.

I feel young again! Whee-hee-hee-hee!"

Huevon was swept along with Cesar, and his hooves almost never touched the ground. For a little while they ran along behind Gunpowder, and then began to quickly gain on him.

In the plaza of Lastima, Mayor Arturo Melendrez was holding control of the crowd of townspeople and visitors surrounding the band gazebo. Up on top of that stood a second Skytalker, an even more savage looking man with great hulking shoulders. He pointed to the north, and they could see a great round circle of smoke rising up into the sky.

"A chicken egg?" Melendrez asked him. "What is that supposed to mean?"

"Chicken has great symbolic significance to the Indian," said the Skytalker. "It means race has begun."

"The race has begun! No more bets," Melendrez announced to the crowd.

Corona Baca walked among them, selling sweet rolls from a big basket she carried. At one point she brought out beer from a barrel she kept cool with wet burlap wrappings. Instead of using the bar's mugs, she sold the beer in bottles, and at a premium for the convenience of buying them on the open plaza.

"I make them out of the empty wine and whisky bottles from the bar," she explained to Alonso. "I use a hot wire to crack the tops off, and a grinder from your hardware store to smooth them down. With a cork in the top, I can carry a dozen and a half cold beers, ready to serve, in a shipping box with a strap on it."

"And you collect the bottles back up?" he asked her.

"Sure, if I can," she said, "but it doesn't matter. They are already something that was thrown away and reused."

"Cold beer in throwaway bottles?" Alonso mused. "It seems just improbable enough to be very popular. Corona, there is something I like very much about the way you think. I'll take one."

Flaco and the Mariachis played a rousing tune.

Miles north, General Burwell Cooley, United States Cavalry, rode like a madman along the river, yelling wildly, and laughing gleefully. "Charge! Cavalry! Ho-oh!"

A little way behind, Cesar and Huevon followed. Cesar was amusing himself, leaping and prancing, showing off. "The canter. The trot. And hang on now, the gallop! Hyaah!"

"Aie, Cesar, no horse has your style," Huevon cheered. "No horse has your power. No one has ever seen such a horse."

All along the way, the local farm workers waved and cheered as the horses charged by, and as they splashed mightily across the Rio Grande river, kicking up great rooster tails of water, spinning rainbows.

Cabrito and Emilio were both doing the same thing. They were holding on the best they could, and struggling to resist the urge to squeeze their eyes tight shut. Ahead of them they saw the fences of the Brazito Ranch, with crowds of people sitting on them, already pointing and waving, and yelling them on.

"Now watch this," said Cesar.

He quickly ran up close behind Gunpowder, but he didn't pass him.

"I'm catching you, Powderpuff," he whinnied to the quarterhorse. "I'm going to pass you. You better go faster. Faster!"

Gen. Cooley angrily waved his sabre, and he urged Gunpowder to run faster, to come up with whatever it was going to take. Gunpowder did, but Cesar just stayed with him, half a length behind, taunting him. Cesar pressed Gunpowder harder and harder, not passing him, but driving him faster. The General yelled and cursed, and he began slapping his horse on the flanks with the flat of his sword.

Just as they came into the ranch, where the people were cheering them on, Gunpowder began to gasp and wheeze, and then suddenly he stuck his neck straight out, croaked a desperate whinny, and fell straight onto his chin into a cloud of dust, sending the General flying and then tumbling down the road, right in front of the gathered watchers.

Cooley picked himself up and waved his broken sword after the departing Cesar, yelling, "You black demon! You're dog meat, do you hear me? I'll conquer half of Mexico if I have to, but I'll get you."

With great whinnying laughter, Cesar and Huevon climbed with mighty flying jumps up onto the rim of the valley, the flat steep-sided lava flows called the black mesas.

"Did you see the look on his face?" cheered Huevon. "In all time there has never been a horse like you, Cesar. Never one like you. How ironic that you are ordered to lose the race, and must lose to a broken down old plug like myself."

Suddenly remembering, Cesar planted his feet and skidded to a stop, and Heuvon skidded up beside him. "What? Oh, no!" the stallion wailed.

"What great depth of character you must have, to endure the ridicule they will heap on you. I could never do it," Huevon said with feeling.

"You could never do it? I could never do it. It is too much," Cesar protested.

"What's happening? Why did they stop?" asked Sapogrande.

"Shut up," said Cabrito.

"It's not right," said Huevon passionately. "You should never be so humiliated just for a fat girl and a fool. You should dance into Lastima in victory. You should finish this race in a blaze of speed like a falling star. The ground should smoke beneath your hoofs as you fly from the mesa to the plaza like Pegasus on the wings of a hawk!"

"Yes!" cried the mighty stallion. "I'll show them. I don't care what happens to any of them. I'll show them all!"

With Huevon starting beside him, Cesar began to run again, exploding into action on legs like pistons of fire, springing up into the air, and then churning up the sand and the black cinders with slashing hooves, driving himself forward, faster and faster, straight toward the steep edge of the black lava flow.

"Show them, Mighty Cesar," cried Huevon from behind, "Show them your great power! Fly! Fly!"

"No! Woah! Stop, you devil, stop!" screamed Emilio.

"No orders from you, fat boy!" yelled the horse, and with a mighty shrug, Cesar sent Sapogrande flying into the air, and into a big clump of prickly pear cactus. Then with his hooves ringing like anvil strokes on the black lava, Cesar leaped out over the edge of the mesa, as though to fly to the village spread out below. He arched out into the sky like an eagle, front hoofs cleaving the air and mane streaming like smoke behind him.

Though he was the Devil's own horse, he was still a horse, and he began to plummet straight down, his legs folding back along his body. He fell like a black comet, screaming in horror the last few feet, then he struck the ground and rammed headfirst into it half his length. His tail stood straight up like a spearshaft and he broke wind like a clap of thunder, and then collapsed into a dusty heap.

"It is over," said Huevon. The horse shrank back to his own old tired self, and then he gamely began to plod along the path toward the village.

The people lined the streets in utter silence as Cabrito rode Huevon into the square, just clop-ta-clopping slowly along. Cabrito sat smiling sheepishly in awe and humility, tears on his cheeks, unable to move or say a word. Behind him a few yards, General Burwell Cooley walked holding the reins of Gunpowder. Both looked tired and thoroughly beaten, but they made the walk with dignity. A few yards behind them, Emilio Sapogrande limped along also, still pulling pieces of cactus from his pants. As Huevon crossed the finish line, everyone broke into cheers, throwing their hats and confetti and flowers. Flaco and the Mariachi band struck up a lively Mexican beat.

Chapter Seven

In the history of the town, there had never been such a moment as prize night in La Fuente that night. Everyone was there, including the General and many of his Buffalo Soldiers. The atmosphere was festive, with lots of food and drinks.

"All right, now, this is what we have all been waiting for," said Arturo Melendrez, when he had everyone's attention. "The official bets. General Cooley, in accordance with your agreement with Corona Baca, you are the owner of the remains of the Devil's horse, for he has lost the race. In accordance with the same agreement, you owe Señorita Baca one thousand gold dollars, for Gunpowder has also lost the race."

Melendrez handed Corona a leather bag, from which she poured into her hand a pile of shining gold coins. Everyone cheered, and even the General grudgingly applauded. Then Melendrez continued. "Now, Corporal Jones, in accordance with your agreement, you owe Señorita Baca one thousand gold dollars also, as Cesar has lost the race."

Melendrez handed Corona a second leather bag, and she held both of them high in her hands as the people all cheered again.

"Aie, Corona, let's get married," called Homer.

"Not to you, droopy drawers," she told him.

"There is one more important bet," said Arturo. "You, Sapogrande, and the General have each bet one hundred silver pesos on the rider of the winning horse. The silver all belongs to the priest."

Cabrito rose with tears in his eyes to accept his winnings.

"Cabrito, I declare that we have seen a miracle," Melendrez declared. "You have raced against a horse that no other horse could beat, and you have ridden a horse that could beat no other horse, and you have won the race. You have placed no bet, and yet you have won the prize. Praise the Lord, we have a Padre, a real Padre."

"Speak to us, Padre," they began to yell. "Tell us the word of the Lord. We believe you now."

"Please, I am just a man like you," Cabrito protested. "All I know is the Lord is real, and so is the Devil, and if either of them talks to me again, you will be the first to hear about it. I have an announcement to make. I am not going to replant my chile field. I am just going to let it grow wild there, and build a ministry, whatever that means. I confess I don't know yet. But I will give my seed stock to anyone who comes to the church and asks for it, and maybe someday the whole valley will grow that chile. God bless you all."

The people cheered and applauded, and cried, "Amen!"

"Oh, Arturo," Cabrito added, "since I am a wealthy man now, I would like to buy the house a round."

"Done," said Melendrez, "and I will buy them another."

As Flaco and the Mariachi played, and people talked and drank, Corona Baca took Emilio Sapogrande aside, and she spoke to him very confidentially. He looked astonished, and then pensive, and then he spread his arms in agreement. She gave him a great big hug.

Then Sapogrande took Arturo Melendrez aside, and talked to him confidentially. Arturo looked surprised, then he looked up at Corona, who nodded her agreement.

Arturo Melendrez then took Alonso Romero aside, and he talked to him confidentially. Alonso looked surprised, and then he began to laugh heartily, and he shook Arturo's hand.

Emilio Sapogrande took the floor and raised his arms for attention. "I have an announcement to make," he announced. "I am announcing that I will be running for the office of mayor of this beautiful town of Lastima this year. Wait, wait, that is not all. I am also announcing the engagement of myself and Señorita Corona Baca, who has pledged her winnings today as a dowry. I will be placing that money into an account at the bank of my esteemed friend, a man like a second father to me, Alonso Romero. Before the sun sets on us again, we will be married by our own Padre Cabrito."

The crowd applauded and cheered.

Arturo raised his arms. "I have an announcement to make too. I am going to let the town borrow Sapo's money from Alonso's bank, and award a contract to build a town cathedral — well, a small church, anyway - right here on the plaza. We're going to need to buy adobes, vigas, glass, and we'll hire everybody to paint or lay tile, or carve woodwork, or something. When we get done, everybody will have money to pay taxes and tithes. We can be a real town."

Everybody cheered again.

"You're going to run against that, Sapo?" asked Flaco.

"Wait, I have another announcement," said Martinez. "I will not be running for re-election this year. Instead, I am endorsing the candidacy of my courageous deputy, hard-riding man's man, businessman, and soon to be a family man, Emilio Sapogrande. This will be my last act in office, and I will leave all the work to Emilio. I am going to take my retirement pension and invest it in producing a crop of Cabrito's chile."

"Wait," somebody said. "Arturo, if you are not running, why don't we just have the election now, and elect Sapo by acclamation? Does anybody else want to run?"

There was a moment of silence, and everybody looked round at everybody else. Then Huarache stood up. "Stop, I don't like this," he protested. "There is something very undemocratic about a unanimous vote. I'm going to run for mayor too, as the candidate of the People's Revolutionary Party."

"Huarache, you are out of your mind?" asked Martinez. "Let's take a vote. Is there anybody here who would vote for this little *gallo jodido*?"

There was a moment of embarrassed silence, and then Concha held up her hand. "I'll vote for him," she said. "He may be a *gallo jodido*, but he's got some *huevos*, and he believes in something. He'll be important too someday, you wait and see."

"All right, for Huarache, one vote," said Melendrez. "I move we proclaim Sapogrande the next mayor of Lastima, upon completion of my term."

Everybody cheered, and even Huarache nodded begrudgingly and applauded.

When he could catch Concha's attention, Huarache said, "I don't believe you voted for me. All our lives you've treated me like a clown."

"All our lives you've acted like a clown, Pancho," she said simply, "running around trying to stir up trouble. But I know you've always tried to do your crazy things for good reasons. You've got a good heart, and that matters to me." She patted him on the shoulder. "You'd make a very good mayor, but let me go now. I've got a lot of tequila to move."

"I have an announcement to make too," said General Cooley. "It seems every man in the fort re-enlisted, no doubt for the re-up bonus, and unless your revolution gets big enough to give us a job to do, we've got lots of free time up at Fort Selmore. We're going to turn our drill team into a wild-west show. We're going to call it Wild Burwell Cooley's Buffalo Soldiers Show. Here, meet the villain of the show, the turncoat Indian rebel, Big Chief Geronimo Jones."

Jones took a big feather headpiece from beneath his table and put it on. He sneered dramatically at the soldiers, who glared at him menacingly. "Arf!" they barked.

In the middle of these festivities, a messenger entered, a gringo in the leather outfit of a cross country scout. He looked around, located the General, and reported directly to him. "Are you General Burwell Cooley? Sir, I have been sent to tell you that it has been done. The Gadsden Purchase, Sir, it has been signed up in Mesilla. This town is now part of the United States of America."

In the silence, you could have heard an anvil drop.

The General stood up imperiously. "Aha," he said. "Well, well, well, what a glorious day for the Red, White, and Blue. That means you are all now under my jurisdiction. Aha. You there, young Mayor Sapogrande, I guess it's up to you now. We'll have to get you started on a proper census, property inspections, background investigations, we'll get a tax base going, and get some security around here. We've got Mexican terrorists to protect ourselves from, right across the border. Where is everybody going?"

Many of those present made a hasty departure in pandemonium. Making a show of boldness before the watching General, Huarache approached Concha. "I'm going south, Concha, back into Mexico. I'm going to change my name from Huarache to Zapata, and try to make something of myself. Will you come with me?"

"Are you crazy?"

"Yes!"

"Me too. Si, Pancho, I will go with you," she said.

"*Aie, aie-aie, pues andale!* I knew you'd come," he crowed. "I knew you loved me. It will be wonderful. We can live on the road at first. You can do the cooking, and I'll teach you how to fight."

She put her hands on her hips. "Cooking? Fight? Pancho, you *baboso*, what kind of girl do you think I am? If you're going to be a revolutionary, you can start by recruiting some troops to carry my suitcases, and to set up a decent officer's club where I can eat. Isn't that how it's done, General?"

The General bowed graciously. "That is exactly how it is done, my dear, in a civilized army."

"Oh, is that right, mister gringo? You know, if you wore that suit in Guadalajara, you would be a hotel doorman," said Huarache. "Before I am done, my darling, you will be *La Doña Concha*, the grandest lady in all of Mexico." He cried out loudly, "*Viva Mexico!*"

A very few echoed his cry.

"Go ahead, leave," the General called after them. "Someday you'll be wading the river trying to come back."

"Oh, I'll be back, all right," said Huarache. "You'll not get rid of me just by moving your borders around." There were some furtive and embarrassed glances toward the General as Huarache and Concha departed.

"All right troops, let's get to the fort," said the General. "We've got lots of work to do. Corporal Jones... that is, Private Jones, round them up."

There was an audible collective gasp in the room. The

Buffalo Soldiers all turned to look at Geronimo. "Private Jones?" asked one of them.

Jones looked from one to the other of them like a cornered coyote. "Huarache!" he yelled, and turned to flee the bar. He ran directly into the great wide gold-braided chest of Master Sergeant Oscar Bonaventure.

"Where you think you're going, boy?" growled the grizzle-bearded Top.

Jones stopped short, "Ulp. Takin' care of business, Top. Yassuh."

"That's good," said the Top Sergeant, "as you do have some markers to work off, don't you? Let's go, Cavalry. Mount up!"

With Jones at the front, the Buffalo Soldiers all jumped to their feet and departed, hooting and stamping. Everyone shook everyone else's hand, patted their shoulders, congratulated each other, or consoled each other. Cabrito was one of the last to leave, and Corona finally put the last of the cats to bed, and turned off the last of the lanterns, and that was the end of the greatest night in our town's history.

On the plaza the next morning, people stood around watching, some dressed in their Sunday clothes. A small detail of soldiers conducted a ceremony to raise the United States flag on the town's flagpole. The bugler played, "Call To Colors," and Homer and Wilbur stood saluting, to the sidelong glances of some of their neighbors.

Off to one side, Arturo and Alonso stood together. "Maybe I will get used to it, Alonso, if I live to be a hundred years old... or maybe two hundred," said Arturo.

"No, no, don't you worry, Arturo," his old friend reassured him. "Bankers and bartenders will do just fine in America's New Mexico. We'll do just fine."

Emilio Sapogrande and Corona, who was by then *La Señora Sapogrande*, came walking together, taking everyone's greetings and bows. He wore his best Mexican caballero suit with silver-tipped boots and embroidered sombrero. On his arm (and being treated like a queen) was

Corona, wearing a beautiful old Spanish style dress with lots and lots of lace, and her hair piled up in a great black swirl with a tall mantilla. She looked absolutely beautiful, grand, and imperious, like a walking cathedral.

An old villager raised his hat to her. "*Doña Corona. Buenos días.* You know we are going to miss you in the kitchen."

"Don't you worry, *Viejo*," she said. "I just took the day off, that's all. I couldn't let my handsome husband get all the attention."

Sapogrande blushed and gushed, and kissed her hand, clearly then completely her unabashedly infatuated worshipper. "*La Corona de mi vida,*" he sighed.

On the lovely covered porch of the *Casa Romero*, Dulcina and Flaco sat on a bench. "Flaco, I love the way you play," she said. "I wish you could play for me all the time."

"I don't think your father would like that," Flaco said with a laugh. "He wants much more for you than someone like me."

"I know you can already read in both English and Spanish," she said. "You know they have a school up north, near Santa Fe. If you went there to be educated, now that we are Americans, I would be just old enough to marry when you came back."

"Oh, I see. Well, maybe I'll do that," he said. "You don't think I will be too old for you then, do you? No? Well, perhaps that is what will be." Then Flaco played his guitar, and they sang a beautiful Mexican ballad together.

Epilogue

I would like to say that I never saw that Devil again, but that night when the whirlwind took him away was not the last time. As I was riding home on old Huevon that very night, I rounded one of the mesquite dunes, and there he was waiting for me, sitting upon Cesar. I was startled, but he waved a reassuring hand, and Cesar stood with his head down, looking very sullen.

"*Hola, Cabrito. Con su permiso,*" he said to me.

"Well, well, you again," I said. "I'm sorry, but I don't have any tequila with me today. And look at you, Cesar. You look much better than you did last time I saw you."

"Screw you, chile picker," Cesar growled, "and the horse you rode in on."

"Awwwwww. Be nice," said Huevon.

"That was such a pleasure to watch, Cabrito," the Devil said genially. "What a pack of fools. I can't wait to see you try to make something more out of them with your silly little church."

"We'll do the best we can, with a little help from our friends," I assured him, casting an eye heavenward.

"You're going to wish you had stuck to raising chile," he told me.

"You're going to wish I had stuck to raising hell," I told him. "*Vaya con Dios, Señor Diablo.*"

"And to hell with you, Padre Cabrito," he said. "To hell with you." He reared Cesar up to paw the air, then turned, and galloped away into the night.

So I rode upon my own horse to the place I could at last really call my own home. The building was still in ruins, but it was cleaned up and ready for restoration. I took off the saddle and sent Huevon out to pasture on the greens sprouting up all along the arroyo. Then I walked into my chile field. It was rough and the furrows were ragged, but it was lush and green. The chiles were tall and the great long pods were ripe, and every one had turned bright red.

THE END

LA MANTILLA

Chapter One

There were people in the little town of Lastima who thought Flaco was just lazy, and that he was wasting his talents because he did not have a regular job. Everyone knew that he had been sent to a school in Santa Fe when he was a child, and that he could read and write in both English and Spanish. But instead of using such an advantage to become an influential figure, he had returned to Lastima, his little home town just across the border in Mexico, and he had sold his fine suit and put on in its place a heavy old *zerape* which had belonged to his father. He had sold his school books and bought a guitar, and had begun to spend his days sitting in the plaza playing softly to himself, or talking with the other people who lived in the tiny cluster of adobe buildings. It was a scandal at first, but after a few years everyone got used to the idea, and by the time he was about thirty, Flaco's past was just another chapter of the town's legends, and he was well-liked in spite of his failure to meet his neighbors' expectations. He earned what money he needed to care for himself responsibly by writing letters for people, and translating things.

On a cold, clear day about two weeks before Christmas, Flaco sat on the steps of the town bandstand. Slender and long-haired, the man was wrapped in his old *zerape*, and though the cold made it difficult for him to keep his guitar in tune, and his fingers were too stiff to play quickly, he carried the instrument anyway and strummed softly on it as he watched the other citizens of the town move about on their daily errands.

The plaza was dominated by three structures. One, in

the center, was the bandstand on which Flaco sat. The second was the church, a simple adobe mission-style chapel with a bell, and heavy carved wooden doors. Though many of the little villages of the Rio Grande valley had been built around the old Spanish missions of previous centuries, the church was one of the newest buildings in Lastima. Building it had been the first thing done by Mayor Emilio Sapogrande when he was elected the first time. There were several long low buildings on the plaza which served as storefronts for the businesses of Lastima, including the fine stuccoed and painted Romero Hotel, with its vigas and covered walkway paved in terrazzo brought up from Guadalajara. It was the saloon, La Fuente, which stood opposite the church, which was probably the second most frequented place in town... after the church. About halfway between the two buildings, in front of the bandstand, was the town flagpole.

Flaco watched as a solitary bird flew high over the town, steadily beating its wings toward some destination far to the south, and as he watched it, his attention was caught by the flag which flew from that flagpole over Lastima. He shook his head to see that it was a bright red, white, and blue, and he noted that it had been there every day long enough to become faded and tattered.

"Lastima," he said to himself, "aie, Lastima, my poor home town. Until just a little while ago we were an old village in Mexico – and then the General signed the Gadsden Treaty with the gringos, and now we are a new village in the United States of America. I don't know, maybe it's a good thing. Maybe I'll get used to it.... if I live to be a hundred... .or two hundred."

The door of the saloon opened, and Flaco heard someone call out loudly, *"Hasta luego, Amigos."* He smiled to see Mayor Sapogrande step out into the plaza. He was only a few years older than Flaco, but he carried himself like a much older man, with a certain ponderous dignity usually reserved for patriarchs. He bore a substantial paunch, which he adorned with a gold watchchain and displayed by wearing a short-waisted coat of black brocade. His boots were tipped with silver, and bits of silver wire had been woven into the embroidery on his great black sombrero. Flaco strummed a loud fanfare on his guitar, and the mayor turned to him and laughed with appreciation. *"Hola, Flaco. Que tal?"* he asked.

"Bien, gracias," Flaco replied. "How about you, Emilio? Are you feeling as good as you look?"

"Well, I guess I am at that," said Sapogrande amiably. "I've had a very productive day. Christmas is a favorite time of year to me, almost as joyful and uplifting as an election."

"Ha!" laughed Flaco. "Then just for you, Señor Mayor, we should arrange to have an election every year."

"That's not as bad idea," the mayor agreed, "but we would need many more candidates. Why, we might even have to put you to work."

"Me?" Flaco exclaimed. "Oh, no, I'm sure we will never be that short of people who would like to be in charge of things."

Sapogrande sat down beside Flaco on the time-polished hand-hewn beam which made the step up onto the bandstand. "I will never understand you, Flaco my friend — an intelligent man who can read and write — you could have a good job working for me, or Romero the banker, and make something of yourself. Instead you scratch out a few pesos writing letters of condolence for the *viejitas*, and you live like a peon. Except you don't work like a peon, you lazy dog."

Flaco shrugged. "I am a man of very simple needs," he said.

"Flaco, think," said the mayor, sliding closer to him on the step. "What do you imagine would happen to our society if everyone did like you and just sat around drinking wine and thinking all the time?"

"Why, there would be nobody to do the work," Flaco conceded. "But of course, if everybody worked, there would be nobody to sit and think."

"Ah, I see. The world wouldn't be complete without some philosophers, eh? So how come you chose to be a philosopher instead of choosing to work like an honest man?'

"What?" asked Flaco, setting his guitar aside and looking with sympathy into the mayor's face. "Didn't you get to choose? So how come you chose to work hard all day when you could have been a philosopher?"

The mayor sat up straighter and smiled in smug triumph.

"Why? I'll tell you why. Because I believe a man ought to do something for his community. And if you're too lazy to serve, Flaco, the least you could do is get out and vote."

"I did vote, Emilio. . . .for you."

"Well, there you have it. One hour every few years you do something useful."

"It's not enough I vote for you?" Flaco asked. "I have to work for you too? I thought you ran for office because you wanted to work for me — that's what you said, *que no?*"

"Well, of course, Flaco, but how can the mayor serve the people without resources? If the people have no resources to contribute to the government, then the government can do nothing."

"Oh," said Flaco, "you mean, if I went to work for you, I'd have money to pay your taxes."

"Exactly," said Sapogrande eagerly. "Then the government would be able to do something for you."

"I see," said Flaco enthusiastically. "It's like you want to feed your dog a nice piece of meat, so you cut off his tail."

The mayor slapped his thigh in exasperation. "Flaco, think. Meet the rest of the world halfway - - if you only worked halftime, you could afford to take a vacation the rest of the time."

"That's good thinking all right, Sapo. And if I worked full time, I could afford to pay someone else to take my vacation for me."

" *Va!* So instead you take a vacation all the time."

"*Seguro!*" agreed Flaco heartily.

"But how can you go anywhere if you're broke all the time?" Sapogrande persisted.

"Where should I go? Where is a better place to be than here in Mexico... that is, here in New Mexico?"

The mayor laughed and shook his head. "How your thinking can be so right and your conclusions come out so wrong is beyond me, Flaco."

"*Bueños dias, Mayor Sapogrande,*" called an old woman walking by. "*Hola, Flaco.*"

"*Bueños dias, Abuelita,*" they replied. "*Feliz Navidad!*" The old woman was great-great-grandmother to almost everyone in the little town, or at least was so acknowledged. "When I was born," she was sometimes heard to say, "there was no United States of America." The two men nudged each other and suppressed their laughter as Abuelita stopped in front of the church, crossed herself, then turned and stepped sprightly toward the saloon, La Fuente. She had just reached the door when she was hailed from across the plaza.

"*Buenos dias, Abuelita. Que Dios bendiga.*" Recognizing the voice of the village priest, she nodded and waved, then ducked inside.

Flaco and Sapogrande laughed as they were joined by Padre Cabrito. Though he had once had a full head of curly hair, and had once been lean and drawn, he had become round-bellied, with a curly and gray natural tonsure and a broad beatific smile with toothbrush moustaches at the corners. Though he had never been to catechism, and had never been ordained, he had been accepted as the town's religious leader, and the church had been built for him. He was on his way from the bakery with a basket of fresh hot empanadas to take back to the church. "Good morning, good morning, the Lord bless you. What a lovely day, isn't it, Mayor Sapogrande. My, isn't the holiday season exciting? Just two more weeks, and we will have our holy Christmas procession of La Posada. This year, I'm sure everyone in the whole town of Lastima will come out to walk with us and sing. *Hola, Flaco. Que tal?*"

"*Bien, gracias, Padre,*" said Flaco. "Isn't this beautiful weather for the Holiday?"

"Beautiful weather to sit and loaf, he means," said Mayor Sapogrande. "I don't understand it, Padre, why this man chooses to do nothing with his life."

The Padre nodded. "Maybe you should let sleeping dogs lie, Sapo. If he is really as talented as you say, he might take away your job."

"Well, perhaps he would at that," the mayor conceded gruffly, "but it still troubles me to see him live by just getting along."

Flaco waved a hand in dismissal of the notion. "If I were a religious man, it might be said that I live by faith — trusting in the righteousness of my humble life, I let the Lord provide for my simple needs, and seek not after the vanities of wealth and position. But....since I am not a religious man, it is said of me that I am irresponsible and suffer from lack of ambition."

"Well," said the Padre with a chuckle, "perhaps you should spend more time in church, so people would speak more highly of you."

"Padre, please," said Flaco. "If I were not called to the faith, it would be a vanity to profess it for the sake of reputation. And unlike you, Padre Cabrito, I have never met the Lord — nor the Devil either — so all my testimony would be heresay at best."

"Well, don't be surprised if either of them shows up sometime," said the priest, patting his shoulder.

"I'm ready to believe it's possible," said Flaco, picking up his guitar again. "To think that the Lord likes to become involved in our day-to-day lives — that's a very lovely idea. Who knows — maybe something will happen to convince me. Until then... ." He shrugged and began to pick at the strings.

"My friends," said Emilio Sapogrande, "I would like to stay here and chat with you all day, but I must attend to the duties of my office."

"I must go also," said the priest. "I am meeting with your wife, Sapogrande, and her Women's Civic League to discuss plans for the grand procession Christmas Eve."

The mayor laughed, shaking his head in a grandfatherly patronizing way. "My wife and her League of Women. Ha! That a girls' gossip club should give themselves such airs."

"Yes," said Padre Cabrito, "but I'll bet if they could vote, you'd be in there now talking sweet as *piloncillo*."

"Women vote? *Valgame Dios*, God forbid!" exclaimed the mayor, looking genuinely shaken. "But perhaps you're right. Perhaps I should organize a town rally for our Christmas celebration this year, and you, Padre, could...."

"No, no, don't even get started, Emilio," interrupted Cabrito quickly. "I will play the town chaplain in your show any other time of the year, but Christmas belongs to the Church. This time you must come and play the faithful steward in my show."

"What?" asked Sapogrande, looking wounded. "You think I'm only trying to steal your thunder?"

"You would steal the Lord's thunder, Sapo, if you could find a way to get yourself elected to His job."

The mayor laughed heartily and pounded the little priest affectionately on the back. "You might be right about that, Padre. What an idea!"

"Come, Señor Mayor, I'll walk with you a way. *Hasta luego, Flaco*. The Lord bless you."

"*Y a ti tambien, Padrecito*," called Flaco as his friends turned and walked together toward the church. As soon as they were out of sight, a young girl peeked out from behind the church and ran across the plaza to sit next to Flaco. She was about ten years old, slender as an ocotillo, with long shiny black braids and wide dark eyes. Holding her knitted wool shawl tight around her shoulders, she snuggled up close to him with an air of conspiratorial excitement. He wrapped a fold of his big heavy *zerape* around her. "Hola, Chulita," he said. "You certainly look lovely today."

"Oh, Flaco, I'm so excited!" she bubbled.

"Because it's Christmas, of course," he said.

"Yes, but much more than that. Oh, I'm just going to pop, I need so much to tell somebody."

"Tell somebody what, Chulita?"

"Flaco, I had a dream," she said in a hushed voice, then added quickly when she saw him smile, "no, no, I mean a very special dream."

"Will you tell me?" he asked.

"Yes, I came to tell you first, even before Padre

Cabrito, because I know you believe in the magic of God's love, even if you don't like to go to church. Flaco, I think this is going to be the most wonderful and important Christmas of my life."

"You're going to get married," guessed Flaco.

"No, silly, I won't be old enough to marry for at least another year or two. This is serious. Listen, Flaco, I was sleeping in my bed, and I dreamed that I woke up and sat up, and the room was full of light. But I could see that I was still there sleeping."

"You mean you saw yourself sleeping?"

"Yes, and there was somebody standing by the foot of my bed."

"Who?" Flaco asked.

"It was the Blessed Virgin, Flaco, I just know it. She was wearing clothes like the Sisters at the cathedral in El Paso, except that her robe was the most beautiful blue you can imagine, like the most perfect sky. And she felt so warm and wonderful that it was just like sitting in the sunshine. And right then I decided what I was going to do."

"What?" asked Flaco breathlessly.

"In the big cathedral, there are the most beautiful statues of the Saints and the Apostles carved in wood. Our tiny church has no statues at all, and we even have to make the shepherds and the Holy Family out of straw and corn stalks for the *Natividad*." She sat up and turned to face him, and put her hands on his knee. "But I know the love of the Lord is here," she said earnestly, "so I prayed to the beautiful Blue Lady to help us get a new statue of the Virgin of Guadalupe to carry in the procession of La Posada this Christmas. I shall find the best woodcarver in the whole country and tell him about my dream, and he will make it for us."

"Well, that is a very beautiful prayer, Chulita," said Flaco, hoping she would not take his amused smile as mocking. "I hope it comes true — even if it is only a very short time until Christmas."

"Oh, I'm sure it will come true," she said. "Aren't you?

After all, how could the Lord refuse such a request, especially on Christmas?"

Flaco chuckled wryly. "Chulita, what He will grant or refuse is always a mystery to me, but I'll believe that anything is possible for one who has a heart as good as yours. There is one thing I can do to help you, though."

"Oh, please tell me!" she said eagerly.

"Well, did you know that one of the finest woodcarvers in all of Mexico lives right here in Lastima?" he asked her.

Her eyes grew wider, and she clasped her hands together. "Why, no, I didn't," she said. "You see, Flaco, the answer to my prayer is happening right here already. Who is he?"

"He is Caterino Medina."

"Caterino?" She stood and looked down at him, perplexed. "Why, he is just a lonely old man who drinks too much."

Flaco smiled and nodded. "That's the kindest thing anyone has said about him in years. But, yes, poor old Medina was once the finest woodcarver for miles and miles. The last piece of work he did was those great doors there on Padre Cabrito's church."

"Really?" she asked, surprised. "I thought they had been sent all the way from Santa Fe or Chihuahua. They're the most beautiful in the valley — in the whole world, maybe."

"Yes, maybe so," Flaco agreed. "He worked very hard on them, and was very proud of them. But the day he finished them, his wife died working in her garden. And since that day he has never entered those doors, nor ever carved a single stick. He lives alone and hangs around La Fuente begging for drinks. He could certainly carve your statue, but it would take a miracle to make him do it."

Her face lit up with a grateful smile and she nodded with certainty. "Well, then we shall have a miracle," she said simply.

"Ah, I see," he said. "Your faith is so beautiful,

Chulita. I hope you get everything you want. Maybe you should go to Padre Cabrito and see if he'll talk to Caterino for you."

"No, Flaco, I'm going to ask him myself," she said with determination. "Where do you suppose I can find him."

He laughed and shrugged. "Where else? La Fuente. He is sure to be there a little later today."

"Then I will find him," she said. "She was so beautiful, Flaco, the most beautiful blue you can imagine. I know she'll help me." She gave Flaco a quick peck on the cheek, then turned and skipped across the plaza.

Flaco looked after her and shook his head with patient affection, then began to pick at the strings of his guitar.

Chapter Two

Thanks to Lastima's new status as territory of the United States, Señor Arturo Melendrez, the owner of the saloon called La Cantina La Fuente, was able to obtain a loan from Señor Alonso Romero, the banker, to buy a fine new hardwood bar with a mirror. It was a handsome piece of furniture, fully six meters long, and its glass shelves were lined with fine hand-blown glassware from Chihuahua. The warmth and hospitality of La Fuente were well known among residents of the area and travelers alike. Some said they believed Melendrez never slept, because he was always on the job in the saloon, dressed in black brocaded vest and white apron, smiling genially from behind his enormous moustache.

Muchacha, his cocktail waitress that afternoon, carried a tray of drinks from the bar to one of the several tables along the wall. The girl was...well, very plump, but she was young and bright and full of laughter, and was liked by everyone. She set drinks before Mayor Sapogrande and Abuelita. The mayor paid for the drinks, and Abuelita shook her head and put an extra ten centavos on the little tray for Muchacha.

At the bar stood Pancho Huarache, gaunt and long-moustachioed, in the short jacket of a *vaquero,* his long black hair just starting to streak with gray. He was one of a respected family in the valley, a fact which many of his relatives would have preferred not so. When Pancho was nineteen, he had decided his family's middle-class values were an affront to humanity, and he became a revolutionary. He acquired an enormous pistol, and an ancient rifle with a bandolier of bullets which fit across his shoulder, and he set out to proclaim the truth and thereby arouse the passions of the masses — beginning with those at his favorite forum, La Fuente.

Over the years since the border moved south, he had lived in and out of his little home town, and though he had become much more likely seen at political rallies than acts of militant revolution, he had remained at heart a would-be champion of the proletariat.

At the far end of the bar, an old man slumped on his elbows, hands guarding his tequila glass. His clothes were

ragged and dirty, and they hung on his body sloppily. His gray
hair was matted and his face bore a scraggly growth of
beard. He did not acknowledge any of the others in the
room, but stared morosely into his drink.. .or somewhere far
beyond it.

There was a wide-hearthed but very cozy fireplace at the
end of the bar, and Flaco sat beside it on one of the tall
barstools, strumming gently on his guitar and humming an old
melody.

"Well, I for one could not care less," Abuelita was
saying. "Life will be the same."

Pancho Huarache looked at her in astonishment. "*Aie,
Vieja*, how can you say that? All your life you have been
Mejicana, and still you can sit there and say it is no
different? You make me ashamed."

"Ashamed? Ashamed of what, Huarache?" asked
Melendrez.

Huarache drew himself up to his full height, a lean
sixty-eight inches. "Where is our pride, our patriotism, if a
greedy general can sell us to the gringos and our old people
do not even care? Why is it only the young like myself who
still take pride in our country, Mexico? *Viva Mexico!*"

Abuelita waved a bored hand at him. "Will you get over
it? So now you have a new country to be proud of, Panchito.
You should relax and enjoy it, and perhaps you will survive to
become an old *viejo* yourself."

As though he were an old *viejo* himself, Sapogrande
chuckled and patted the substantial belly he was trying to
cultivate. "Perhaps Capitan Huarache -- or is it Coronel
Huarache? — is ashamed to grow old because he did not die
for something when he was young," he said.

"You make fun of me because I am prepared to die for
the people?" Huarache asked, disillusionment wringing
astonished anguish from his reedy voice. "You hypocrite! You
call yourself public servant, but you serve only your own fat
career. You are a parasite on the masses!"

Equally astonished, Sapogrande let his jaw fall open.
"What! You call me a parasite? You who have never produced
a thing in your life, and who still put your dirty feet under

your mother's table three times a day? You astound me, Pancho."

Again Abuelita waved a bored hand. "Oh, be still, Sapo. He is absolutely right, you know. Most of what passes for government is a waste of everybody's time."

Huarache turned on the mayor in triumph. "Aha! The old woman has got your number for sure!"

"And yours too," she declared, "a silly boy who thinks Jesus should have been a *pistolero*. You think you serve us by telling us what you don't like about our lives. But what can you do for your precious masses? How about buying us all a drink?"

Huarache wrinkled his nose in distain. "The revolution is a life of sacrifice. If you want money, turn to those who make laws which say we must pay them fat salaries to rule us. Let the mayor buy the drinks."

"I was waiting for that," said Sapogrande. "Your mouth is wiser than your brain, Pancho. By your own words you admit only the government can do anything for the people."

"Fah!" spat Abuelita. "The government provides nothing. For you to buy us all a drink, Señor Mayor, you would have to collect taxes from us, then buy with our own money. Then you would come around at voting time expecting us to be grateful."

"It sounds to me like you are against both sides, Abuelita," said Melendrez.

"No, I am agreeing with both sides," the old woman declared, "and as long as one side doesn't tax me to death, and the other side doesn't blow up the bank, I can buy my own drinks."

"Spoken like a true American!" laughed Flaco.

"I think it will be good for all of us to be part of America," said Muchacha as she brought an ashtray for the cigar Sapogrande took from his vest. "Soon we will have a railroad from El Paso all the way to California."

"That will certainly be good for business," agreed Melendrez.

"Yes, and we can begin to have some culture here," the girl went on, jiggling with enthusiasm. "The railroad will bring the great thespian reviews from New York, and Pa-ree.

"*Mande?*" asked Melendrez. "What's that?"

"Why, the theater, of course, you old *baboso*," she said with the warm familiarity one might reserve for a grandfather. "The Stage! And when the great masters come here to perform, I will run away with them and become a grand lady on the stage in San Francisco."

"Hmmph," Huarache said with a derisive sneer. "You think the gringos will let you do that? You flatter yourself, girl. No, we will never get anything from them but what we can take."

"Just what do you propose to take, Generalissimo?" asked Sapogrande.

Huarache surveyed Sapogrande over his long bony nose as though deciding whether or not to honor the mayor with a reply. Finally he nodded condescendingly. "All right, I will tell you. The revolution will drive out the fat generals and governors, and then the new leaders of Mexico will take back the land which was sold to the gringos."

"Now that sounds like a very good trick," said Flaco.

Huarache turned on the troubador like a roadrunner after a lizard. "And what about you? What good is an educated man who does nothing about the problems of the world except lie in the sun all day and sing to the moon all night like a dog?"

Flaco shrugged. "Better to be a dog in the sun than a coyote in a cage," he declared.

"But to do nothing in the face of the tyrant?" Huarache persisted. "That, Señor, makes you a coward."

"You could be right," Flaco agreed amiably. "As I see it, only a fool or a very brave man hopes to prove in court that the judge who tries him is unjust. So would you let a coward buy you a drink? Here, Muchacha, pour another drink for me and my friend and put it on my account."

"Why, certainly, Flaquito," the girl said, flashing big brown eyes at Flaco.

Huarache nodded his head slowly up and down, looking from one of them to the other. "You think you're very clever. But when comes the revolution, you will all be standing in line to thank me." He took the drink which Muchacha handed him.

"To the revolution," toasted Flaco, hoisting the glass she had brought for him.

"I'll drink to that," declared Sapogrande. "And when you have died for the cause, Pancho, I will become President and build a statue of you."

"*Andale, pues!*" declared Abuelita, raising her glass also.

"*Viva Mexico!*" cheered the little group. Huarache looked disgusted, but he did drink the wine.

There was a timid knock on the door, a sound which caught the attention of almost everyone by its unlikelihood. After a second, the door burst open, letting in a gust of cold desert air. With it came Chulita. She stood for a moment uncertain after she closed the door, then turned to Señor Melendrez.

"Excuse me please," she said, speaking up politely. "I am looking for Señor Caterino Medina."

"Are you running an errand for your mother, Chulita?" he asked her.

"No, sir," she replied. "I have come to do the work of the Lord."

"What, here?" he asked.

"Yes, sir, if Caterino is here."

Huarache began to chuckle. "The Lord sent her to see Medina? Next we'll find out that is holy water he has been drinking all these years."

"*Quitate, huevon,*" the old woman scolded. "Señor Medina is right over there, Chulita dear," she told the girl as she pointed to the old man slumped over his drink at the far end of the room.

"*Gracias,* Abuelita," Chulita said, and ignoring the stares of the others, she walked primly to the end of the bar to where Caterino Medina sagged on his barstool, clutching a half-empty glass of tequila. "Señor Medina?"

Medina twitched, readjusted his arms on the bar, and grumbled, but he did not look up from his stupor.

"Señor Medina?" she asked again.

From behind her, Huarache sniped snidely, "Compared to this, raising Lazarus was easy."

Chulita turned a quick angry glance at Huarache, and looked for support from the others. Flaco smiled at her gently and nodded. She turned to Caterino with shoulders back and head high. Her voice rang out with authority. "Caterino! Wake up!"

Caterino stirred and turned a bleary eye on her. The girl wore a simple dress which hung straight from her slender shoulders, around which she clutched a heavy woolen shawl. She stood before him with the light from the fireplace behind her, its warmth adding a bright halo around her dark flowing hair. He gazed what seemed a long time at her, and then squinted, and then suddenly opened his eyes wide. He jumped up straight as though he had seen a ghost, spilling his drink. He stared at her in bug-eyed horror for a moment, then cried out in a terrible tortured voice, "*Valgame Dios!* Why do you come to haunt me?"

The little girl's voice rang out like a summons in the warm comfort of the saloon, "Caterino, the Lord has sent me to find you. I have seen the beautiful Blue Lady, and I have asked the Lord to give us a new carved statue of the Virgin of Guadalupe to carry in La Posada this Christmas. I asked Him to find me the best *santero* in all of the country, and He has sent me to you." She paused a moment as the man teetered on the barstool as though he might at any second fall onto his face. "In the name of The Lord, will you take up your tools again and carve us a new Madonna?"

There was a moment's silence...then Huarache snickered audibly and derisively.

"No!" Caterino suddenly howled. "No, get away from me! Get away! Why do you torment me? Leave me alone. I have suffered enough! I have suffered enough!" The man stumbled from his stool and scrabbled frantically half-crawling. He fell against the bar and knocked a stool flying.

Huarache laughed and pushed him toward the door. "What's the matter, you never saw an angel before? Haw haw haw!"

"Shame on you, Medina, frightening a little girl like

that," said Sapogrande indignantly.

At the door, the man turned and pointed a trembling finger at Chulita, his eyes wild and red. "No! You have no right! You're not real!" he wailed.

"Huarache, will you get him out of here," said the mayor. "Get him to his bed while he can still stagger, so we don't have to carry him later."

"My pleasure," said Huarache. "I prefer his company to yours anyway." Pancho helped Caterino stagger from the saloon, leaving everyone shaking their heads and clucking. There was a pause, then everyone at once remembered Chulita.

The girl was still standing in stunned silence at the far end of the bar. "Chulita, darling..." someone began.

"No. No, don't say anything," she said, her voice tiny and thin. "I know what you all think. You think I'm just a silly little girl." Then her voice found its strength again, and she declared, "But I did see her, I did see the Blue Lady. And if the Lord doesn't answer my prayer, it is only because you don't deserve it!" All at once, she burst into tears and fled from the saloon, running past them to the door.

There was a moment's uncomfortable pause, and then Sapogrande snuffed out his cigar in the ashtray and stood.

"Well. I for one have had enough. I bid you all a good night." He put on his big sombrero and stood pensively a moment. "Hmm. It gives one much to think about. *Buenas noches*, my friends."

"These old bones are ready for a rest too," agreed Abuelita. "Buenas noches."

"What an imagination," said Muchacha as she began to clean up the tables. "I can hardly remember what it was like to feel so serious about Christmas. If she could still feel things like that when she gets to be my age, what an actress she would make! Come on, Flaco, are you going to stay here all night?"

"It wouldn't be the first time," he chuckled. "You know, Muchacha, if there is a God anywhere who loves little girls, he ought to do something nice for that one."

"Amen," said Melendrez.

As the moon came up that evening, Chulita sat huddled inside her shawl on the steps of the Lastima town bandstand, sobbing softly into her arms. Then, as though she had stepped from the gathering mists of evening, a beautiful young woman appeared behind her, and sat down beside her. She took the little girl's head in her arms, and sat silently holding her and rocking her gently. Without looking up, Chulita began to cry her heart out. "There, there. Yes. Yes. Now, hush. Sweet Chulita," she said, her voice soft and soothing.

After a little while, Chulita looked up to see who it was, and she jumped to her feet. "It's you!" she gasped as she saw the tender-eyed young woman in the sky blue habit of a medieval nun. "Oh, please, forgive me," she wept, sinking to her knees.

"Hush," said the Blue Lady. "Hush, now, and stay beside me."

"Are you really...I...I mean, are you...?" Chulita began.

She put a finger to Chulita's lips. "Tonight I am only your sister, Chulita."

"Oh, my," said Chulita, and she began to cry again. "Oh, Sister, I'm so ashamed. I tried to tell them about you, and they laughed at me."

"Dry your eyes, now," she said, handing the girl the corner of her long, deep sleeve. "You mustn't worry about that. People have been laughing at me for a very long time now. And when Our Lord told them what wonders He had seen, they laughed at Him. Remember, He was only twelve once, too."

"I guess I always think of Him as much older," said Chulita, snuggling against her.

The Blue Lady wrapped her arm around the girl's shoulders. "Yes, most people seem to think of Him as older, or bigger, or stronger than everybody else, as though he were too grand to feel things like ordinary people do. But it's not true."

"It's not?"

"No. When He was twelve years old, and God spoke to Him, and told Him to go to the temple and say things to the elders that His father Joseph would never have dared to say, how do you suppose He felt?"

"I can't imagine," she said, breathless.

"He felt just like you did when you walked into La Fuente tonight," the Blue Lady said.

"How do you know that?" Chulita asked.

"Because He told me."

"Oh," the little girl said. After a moment she asked, "Do you come here... into the world... often?"

The Blue Lady laughed gently. "From time to time. To see someone special...like you," she said.

"Me? But why me? I'm just a little girl."

"Because little girls like you...and me...are God's hobby," she said. "It makes Him happy when we love Him."

"Oh, Sister, I do! I do! And I love you, too," Chulita said, giving her a happy hug.

"I love you too, Chulita." She sat and held the little girl for a long moment, then said, "Now you sit here and close your eyes tight, and tell Him you love Him with all your heart."

"Oh, yes!" She squeezed her eyes shut and held her breath. The Blue Lady stood, put her hand gently on Chulita's head, then slipped silently back into the shadows and disappeared. After a few minutes, the little girl finished her prayer. "Amen," she said. Suddenly she remembered her request, and she jumped to her feet. "Oh! But what about...." Looking around, she knew the Blue Lady had gone. "Oh, my, I forgot to ask her about...oh, dear, I'm afraid I didn't do that very well at all. I was so rude to poor Señor Medina, and in front of everybody, too. Now he will never be a *santero* again, and it's all my fault." From a block away, Chulita heard her mother calling her to come home, and she called back to her, "Here, Mother, I'm coming." She started to run from the plaza, then paused and called softly into the shadows, "Goodnight, Sister."

Chapter Three

Somewhere not far from the plaza of Lastima, a rooster crowed. The eastern sky was growing bright with the cool, clear pastel colors of morning — pink, gold, and the palest blue. Just as the disc of the sun blazed over the ridge of mountains to the east, the heavy carved doors of the church were opened from within. Padre Cabrito came out into the plaza to greet the new day. He yawned, stretched, and waved in blessing to the awakening little town. *"Que Dios bendiga,"* he prayed. He rubbed his hands briskly and stamped his feet in the morning chill. "What a lovely morning — crisp as an apple and crystal clear. And what a sunrise!" He began to applaud the sunrise heartily, then began to cry out as though in a great theater, "Author! Bravo! Author!" He enjoyed a moment's reflection on the humor of it all, then addressed his soliloquy to a Divine audience, drawing the passing attention of a curious dog. "Ha ha ha, that's a pretty good joke, huh, Boss? Yes, when You invented sunrise... now, that was some first class creation. Sunrise and chile plants... you know, Lord, I think the delicious agony of eating a really choice *jalapeño* is the finest single expression of the joy and suffering of human life. It is the perfect complement to the bread and wine."

The first to greet him that morning was Chulita. She came skipping lightly into the plaza, crossed herself in front of the church, then stepped up beside him. "Good morning, Padre Cabrito," she said.

"My, you're certainly out early today," he declared, "and filled with Christmas spirit, no doubt."

Chulita gave him a hug and a kiss on the cheek. "Oh, Padre, the most wonderful thing has happened, but I've been so foolish, and I'm afraid I've made a mess of everything."

He nodded kindly. "Yes, I heard about your evening at La Fuente last night. That was a very brave thing you did, and the Lord will bless you for it, even if it didn't work out."

She stood in front of him silently for a moment, and he waited for her to speak. Finally she asked, "Padre Cabrito, do you believe in the Blue Lady?"

He didn't answer at once, then nodded solemnly. "The Blue Lady. Yes, I believe I do, though I certainly would not admit that to everyone."

"But you do know who she is?"

"Oh yes," said the little priest. "She was a Franciscan abbess who lived in Spain over two hundred years ago. Her name was Mother Maria, and she claimed to have traveled in the spirit to our valley here in Mexico...that is, in New Mexico...to bring the church to the Indians."

"She did! It's true, you know," Chulita told him earnestly.

Cabrito smiled. "Well, the church says she was just a nun with too much imagination, but I have heard too many legends from the Indians — my mother's people — to say it is not true. In fact, some people say she still appears sometimes."

She reached up to take hold of the sleeve of his simple roughspun robe. "Padre Cabrito, I saw her... and not just in a dream. I talked to her, and I touched her, and she kissed me."

He stared at her for a long moment, then said, rather wistfully, "I believe she did. How wonderful, Chulita. I would love to meet her someday." Then he shook his round belly briskly and smiled. "I did meet the Devil one time... but that is another story," he said.

They were interrupted as two little boys came rushing into the plaza galloping, whooping, and waving wooden swords. They ran to the bandstand, where they staged a swashbuckling duel, leaping and slashing. As they fought, Flaco came out of an alley and stood against the wall of the saloon, wrapped in his heavy zerape.

"Hold on, Rebel!" yelled little red-headed Rusty. "You'll never escape the Captain of the Guard! Ha! Yah!"

"Ho! Take that, Villain!" cried black-bristled Paco. "Taste the cold steel of *El Coyote!*"

They departed in the same cloud of dust which brought them, dashing and slashing. From around behind the church Abuelita came to greet them. *"Buenos dias, Padre Cabrito. Hola, Chulita, dame chito."* Chulita gave her a kiss on the cheek. "My, my, it sounds like Armageddon around here."

"It's good for boys to dream of being heroes," said the Padre, "grown men too. If you don't let them get puffed-up a little, you can't get a thing out of them. Like our humble friend Flaco over there...a man that free of vanity is no earthly good at all."

Other townfolk began to come out to begin another day. Among them were Muchacha and her chubby little five-year-old sister Chiquita, carrying baskets of fresh hot apricot empanadas —delicious breakfast turnover pies. They were followed closely by a very hungry Pancho Huarache. "I can't understand you, Muchacha," he pleaded. "You have such a free spiri. You of all people should be with us...with the revolution!"

"Oh, don't be silly, Pancho," she scolded. "Good morning, everybody. Fresh hot empanadas!"

"With nuts and raisins today! Yum!" amended little Chiquita.

"Oh, I'll take one, Muchacha," said Abuelita. "Are they still five centavos?"

"Every day. How about you, Chulita?" Muchacha asked. "Your mother can pay me later."

"*Gracias*, Muchacha," the girl said, happily plucking a particularly tasty looking one from Chiquita's basket. "Mmm, they smell wonderful."

Padre Cabrito patted his round belly and rubbed his fingertips together, tempting himself with the confection he had been informed his health would not permit him to eat. With a beatific smile, he reached for an empanada from the same basket, but the sagacious child drew it back and waved an admonishing finger at him. "Now Padre doesn't eat sweets," she said.

Huarache looked longingly at the diminishing pile of pies and made another attempt to recruit Muchacha. "Well, if you won't join the revolution, Muchacha, how about at least supporting it with breakfast?"

"I may have a free spirit, Pancho, but no free empanadas," she informed him.

"Here, Muchacha, I'll take one," said Flaco, "and one for the people's advocate there too. Feliz Navidad."

"Thank you," said Huarache gratefully. "You are a man who understands the fight for freedom, Flaco. I always wonder why you refuse to join us."

"I am already free. So what should I fight for?" Flaco asked as he bit into a fat empanada.

There was a commotion, then the two boys came back out from behind the church, still fighting mightily. "Ow! Hey, you hit me on purpose, Paco!" cried Rusty.

"I did not. You're just crying because you're losing, Rusty," taunted his friend.

"I'll show you who's losing. *Cabron!*" Rusty dropped his sword and swung a big wide looping fist at Paco.

"So you want to fight, huh? *Huevon!*" Standing about four feet apart, they both swung punch after punch furiously, without either of them hitting the other even once.

Padre Cabrito ran to break up the fight. "Here! Here! You boys stop this. It is too cold for a funeral today, so you must not be killing each other. Go rescue a prisoner somewhere."

The two boys cast dark glances at each other, stood up straight and said, "Yes, Padre," then scooped up their swords and ran away.

Flaco chuckled and pointed to the two departing boys. "There go your recruits, Huarache. You should be trying to convince them."

Huarache snorted derisively. "Little boys? The *revolucion* needs men!"

Flaco nodded sympathetically. "And in a hurry, I guess," he said.

They all turned as Señor Melendrez came out of one of the shops with Señora Luzelena Chavez, one of the members of Corona Sapogrande's Women's Civic League. "Well, I guess you have all heard about Mayor Sapogrande's town meeting this morning," said Melendrez eagerly, as they approached the group gathered in front of the church. "I am going to be very interested to hear what he has to say."

Everyone turned and stared blankly at him, uncertain

if he were joking or not.

"Are you, now?" Abuelita asked finally. "My, every time our Mayor opens his mouth, I am just sure the Millenium has begun."

Everyone turned and stared blankly at her.

"Empanada?" asked Chiquita.

"Don't mind if I do, thank you," said Melendrez. "Señora?"

"No, thank you," she said. "I have just attended breakfast with the Women's Civic League."

"And the other ladies are not attending the town meeting?" asked Abuelita.

With a smug little smile, Señora Chavez said, "I will report to the Chairwoman if her husband has anything important to say."

"Ah, I see," said Abuelita. "They sent you so the important women would not have to be bothered. Good thinking."

"Here comes His Excellency now," said Pancho Huarache.

Mayor Emilio Sapogrande strode onto the plaza and walked among them as though he were about to receive a prize, greeting all, hugging, and even bestowing a kiss on the cheek of Abuelita. "Good morning. Yes. *Buenos dias. Que magnifico*," he intoned, grasping a hand, patting a shoulder.

Little Chiquita presented her basket of empanadas. He took one and started to bite it. "That's *cinco centavos*, Señor Sapogrande," she said.

"Ah, ha-ha. Yes, of course," he laughed, fishing into a pocket for a coin. He raised his head and looked around to find someone. "Ah, Chulita. Dear, sweet Chulita. Come here, darling, and let me give you a kiss. There now, you come with me. Come right on up here." He led Chulita up to stand with him on the bandstand, and readied himself to make a speech, and everyone gathered around to listen to him.

"Some of you were there last night," he began. "I was there last night. But maybe you didn't recognize what you were seeing. Maybe you didn't recognize the true spirit of Christmas right here among us. Now I have been thinking for many days about our little celebration of La Posada. Sapo, I said to myself... Sapo, what can we do to make our little village of Lastima special, so people might take a second look at us? And when I heard this innocent little child last night in La Fuente crying out to us for an answer to her prayer, my heart went out to her. I knew right then that she was the answer to my question, and I decided right then, *Caballeros y Damas*, that her prayer will be answered." There was some polite applause.

"Thank you. Thank you," the Mayor continued. "Yes, if I have anything to do with it, she will see the answer right before her eyes. I do not expect a new Madonna to materialize out of thin air, but if you will all help me, Chulita will still have her miracle. If you will all make a little sacrifice... a generous donation, a real donation, we will buy our new Madonna from a professional *santero* in El Paso. And to make sure we get just the right one, I will personally go to El Paso, or all the way to Chihuahua just to answer little Chulita's prayer myself."

Everybody applauded and cheered, except Huarache, who stood aside looking quite disgusted.

Padre Cabrito stepped up onto the bandstand with Sapogrande and shook his hand. "A wonderful idea, Emilio. Surely we are blessed to have such a Mayor."

"There, Señora Chavez, take that message to the ladies of the club. They should make the biggest contribution of all," declared Abuelita.

Giving the older woman a long cool gaze, Señora Chavez replied, "And you, dear Abuelita, take the message to the other residents of the saloon. Surely they should make the biggest contribution."

Pancho Huarache leaned against the wall of the church, groaning louder with each mention of contributions. Finally he could take no more. "All that money could buy supplies and ammunition to defend ourselves from the gringos and the generals," he cried.

As though with a single voice, everyone turned to him and began to shout him down. "Boo! Hiss! *Afuera!*" they cried. "*Callate!* Hiss! Boo!" Huarache glared malevolently at them, and skulked off down an alley.

Padre Cabrito took up the lead. "All right now, everybody. Let's get out and knock on every door in Lastima, so we can send the Mayor to the city in style. There is hot coffee in the church, and we can make our center of command there."

Chulita gave Sapogrande a big hug. "Thank you, Uncle Emilio," she said.

"Did you hear that?" he crowed. "You bet I'm her Uncle Emilio, and it is Uncle Emilio who gets things done, isn't it?"

"Well, here is our empanada money," said Muchacha. "That makes us the first. Who is collecting it?"

"You have the basket. Why don't you collect it?" suggested Flaco.

Abuelita took Muchacha by the elbow. "That's a good idea, Muchacha, but why don't we let these strong men do the collecting, and we'll go get some of Padre's coffee."

"That sounds like a marvelous idea, ladies," agreed the mayor heartily. "I'll join you in the church." Still holding Chulita, he began toward the beautifully-carved doors.

"Would you put me down, please?" she asked him. "I want to go tell my parents."

"Why, of course, dear. Bless your heart." He set her down, and she skipped away toward her mother's home. Muchacha set her basket on the steps of the church, and entered with Cabrito, Sapogrande, and Abuelita. Everyone else departed to go ask their friends and relatives to contribute to Mayor Sapogrande's plan.

Rusty and Paco ran into the plaza, then looked around surprised to find nobody there. "Where is everybody?" asked Paco.

"Maybe it's a gold rush, and they all went to stake a claim?" guessed the young carrot-top.

"Oh, yeah, and maybe they all went to the moon, too," said Paco sarcastically. Then his eyes widened. "Hey, look, there's one of Muchacha's baskets." They ran over to it and peeked inside. "Hey, Rusty, there's two left!"

"Looks like we struck the gold, Paco. Gimme one!" They grabbed the empanadas and departed running.

There was a quiet little pause in the plaza, a pause enjoyed only by a few passing birds looking for warmer weather to the south, and by a neighborhood cat who wished the birds would stop and hang around for lunch. Then as though they had planned it to the second, they found themselves all gathering again in the plaza, bustling and buzzing excitedly. Muchacha and Chiquita hurried around to gather the coins everyone threw into their baskets.

"Why, it's just wonderful!" cheered Muchacha.

"Praise the Lord. What a blessing! Thank you," Cabrito gushed as he listened to the coins tinkle into the baskets.

Melendrez came out with a big double handful of coins and tossed them into a basket. "Here, Muchacha, we collected this in the saloon," he said happily.

"Now this is more like the old-fashioned Christmas spirit I knew when I was a girl," declared Abuelita.

Finally even Pancho Huarache came back, stood looking confrontational, and then a little grumpily tossed some coins into the basket.

"Why, Pancho, bless your heart!" said Padre Cabrito.

Huarache shrugged. "The revolution can wait until after Christmas, I guess," he said.

Then Señora Chavez stepped forward imperiously and put a heavy leather pouch into the basket.

"That does look like a very generous gift," Abuelita admitted. "Madame Chairman La Doña Corona must have been very impressed with her husband's suggestion."

"Very impressed," said the woman with her tight smug little smile. "And the Mayor will surely be delighted to find that he is the largest contributor."

"What a clever wife!" said Abuelita, genuinely impressed. "I wonder if Sapo knows how lucky he is? Keep up that way, and I might even join your Civic League myself."

"I am sure we could all profit from the wisdom of your years, *querida*," said Señora Chavez, dripping sweet.

After a few minutes, *El Mayor Don Emilio Sapogrande* strode in triumph to the bandstand. Muchacha and Chiquita followed him and presented the baskets to him. "This is magnificent! What a blessing! This is more than I had dared to hope for," he said, wiping tears from his eyes. "You are all so wonderful. We have collected so much money that I have come to a decision. Yes. I am going to declare this a yearly tradition. That's what I'm going to do, officially. After a few years, we will have the best collection of the most beautiful Santos in all of New Mexico. And when I am gone, I could think of no greater honor than to be remembered as the founder of the Sapogrande Memorial Collection. What a blessed thing that would be."

There was a round of applause and a few hallelujah's.

"All right now" he went on. "Thank you for coming out on this cold morning, and thank you for your wonderful generosity. Now let's all go to our homes and get ready for the greatest Christmas celebration we have ever known. And I will get ready for my journey to the city to fulfill little Chulita's dream."

The people applauded, and Sapogrande made a grand exit. The others left also, happily chatting and laughing. In a little while, Sapogrande passed again through the plaza, wearing a heavy greatcoat, and carrying saddlebags. He stood a moment looking around the plaza, then sighed happily. "*Andale pues*. Time to get going."

Then as he began to depart, a tiny figure wrapped in a big woolen shawl hurried out from beside the Church and confronted him, a little bit timidly. "*Señor Mayor?*" called out Chulita.

"Chulita, how nice to see you," he said. "I am off to El Paso to bring back your new Guadalupe. How do you feel about that?"

She smiled and shivered a little as though the cold were slipping beneath her shawl. "Very grateful, Sir. Thank you, and thank the Lord too. Only...I didn't have any money to give, and...oh, please, would you take this? Perhaps you could sell it in El Paso and use the money to help pay for the Madonna." From beneath her shawl she took a delicate white lace *mantilla*, a mantle so fine it looked as though woven of spider's web. She held it unfolded on her arms and extended it up to him. "It was my great-grandmother's," she said. "She brought it with her when she came here from Spain. I know it is very old, but it is the only thing I have that you might be able to sell."

The mayor gazed down at her fondly and put his hand on her head. "Why, bless you, dear. You have the sweetest heart in the world. I will take the very best care of this." He put the *mantilla* into the inner pocket of the greatcoat, hefted the saddlebags, and turned to leave. "They're all waiting for me at the stable. Give me a little kiss for luck?"

"*Seguro, Tio Sapo. Buena suerte,*" she said, giving him a warm smack on the cheek. "Good luck, Uncle Sapo. I'll pray for you every day you're gone." Then she stood and watched as he strode mightily down the street toward the stable.

Chapter Four

The days went by quickly after Mayor Sapogrande left to go to El Paso, but on the day of the celebration of La Posada, he had still not yet returned.

On the plaza, the townfolk of Lastima were busy decorating their community for the event. On the side of the bandstand which faced the church, they had built a nativity scene using a feed trough for a crib and some boards for a roof. The figures were made of cornstalks and straw, but were nicely dressed by the women of the town, and wore faces of painted papermache.

"What a beautiful morning!" declared Padre Cabrito. "A perfect day for our celebration of La Posada." In fact, it was a still, cold, gray day, and clouds hung heavy and dark over the town.

"Cabrito, you would call any day a perfect day, no matter what the weather," said Flaco with a fond chuckle. "Look at those clouds...why, it might even rain."

The little priest waved a hand at him and shook his head with solemn certainty. "Flaco, if you had been educated by Indians instead of the gringos, you would know something about the weather," he said. "It is too cold and clear to rain, and look at those clouds...see how they are round on the bottom like clusters of grapes? If we get anything from them tonight, it will be snow."

"Snow!" At the mention of the word, Rusty and Paco dropped the evergreen branches they were carrying and ran to the priest. "Did you say snow? Oh, boy!"

"Yay! Snowball fights!" cheered Paco.

"Yeah, but you better not put rocks in them this time, Paco," warned his friend.

Nearby, Señora Chavez, Chiquita, and some of the others were setting out long rows of little paper bags, and pouring a few inches of sand into each one.

"All right now, how are you coming with the *luminarias?*" Cabrito asked them.

"Just a few more, Padre," said Chiquita.

"Be careful to put enough sand in them so the wind doesn't blow them over," he said, peering into several of the little bags. Following behind the girls, Señora Chavez carefully placed into each one a little votive candle, and neatly nestled it down into the sand. "There, that's right," Cabrito said, "and make sure they're straight up, now, so the candles don't burn the paper.

"How nice it is the Women's League was able to get these little sacks from the mercantile supply in Santa Fe this year," Señora Chavez said. "Why, I remember when I was a child, we used to make our *luminarias* from sheets of butcher paper."

"Well, let me tell you something, Señora," said Abuelita. "I can remember when the *luminarias* were just little piles of sticks set on fire along the way of the procession of La Posada."

"*Va!* Not even you could be that ancient, Abuelita," the woman laughed.

"Oh, you would be surprised what I know!"

Flaco walked by them carrying an armload of tall yucca stalks. Each stalk was topped with a cluster of dried seedpods, each of which had been painted red and yellow in a flamelike design, so they looked like big candelabras. "Did you know they don't call them *luminarias* in Santa Fe?" he asked. "No, they call them *farolitos.*

"*Farolitos?* What a pretty name," said Abuelita. "I think I would like to visit Santa Fe someday...perhaps when I get old."

At the *Natividad*, the nativity scene, Padre Cabrito and the boys were setting up the figures. "Here, you boys. Let's get these in the right places," he advised. "That's right, the Shepherds over there. My, didn't the ladies do a fine job of dressing them this year?"

"Where do these dogs go?" asked Rusty.

"They're sheep," said the priest, "and they go over here by the Shepherds." Each of the beasts was made of a straight-legged wood frame covered by a curly goat pelt, and topped with a cone-shaped papermache head.

"Maybe they're sheep dogs," said Paco, looking at them doubtfully.

"Then what are these...dog herders?" Cabrito snapped good-naturedly. "Where is the burro?" he asked, looking around. "Ah, Flaco, you have him. Good. Oh, Chulita, darling, you have some straw for the manger. Good, good, just put it right in there. You can make a soft bed for *El Niño*." He bustled happily around the plaza, more and more delighted with each step in the progress of the decoration. Finally he was satisfied that everything had been done for the nativity scene. "There now. Everything set for the arrival of our new Lady of Guadalupe. Sapogrande should be home any minute now, and everything will be just right."

"That Emilio," clucked Abuelita. "He should have been home days ago. Somebody should have gone, with him to keep him from getting lost."

"Oh, be still, Abuelita," Padre Cabrito said. "He is probably just making sure he gets the best one he can find."

"He is always biting off more than he can chew," the old woman complained. "I can remember when he was just a little boy, and..."

"*Callate, vieja!*" admonished Señora Chavez. "He may puff himself up like a frog, but he has a good heart. Who else has ever tried to do such a thing for this village?"

"Ladies, come, come," said Padre Cabrito entreatingly. "Sapogrande will arrive just in time. You watch and see if he doesn't. Now let's go and get the *ristras* and the mistletoe, and we can finish decorating the rest of the plaza."

"Yeah, and the *piñata!*" sang out Paco, speaking of the hollow decorated papermache Star of Bethlehem which they would hang from a hook on a long rope.

"Full of *biscochitos* and *piloncillo!* Yum!" cried Chiquita, speaking of the shortening cookies and sugar candy with which the *piñata* would be stuffed. The children looked forward to the hour when each of them would be blindfolded, handed a long club, and given the chance to swing at the brightly-colored star until one of them broke it open to spill its treasure for all to gleefully scoop up.

"I think I'll go have a glass of wine and see what's going on in La Fuente," said Flaco, happily surveying the results of their work.

Inside the warm and friendly saloon, he found Señor Melendrez, Muchacha, and Pancho Huarache together at the long polished bar enjoying a cup of hot spiced wine.

"Ah, Flaco, we were just talking about you," said Melendrez.

"About me? Well, you'd better quit it. I can only take so much praise, you know. I'd like a cup of that delicious-smelling wine, please," he said.

"As a matter of fact," Pancho informed him, "we were discussing your resemblance to the Devil."

"*Va!* That's some puny devil, don't you think?" Flaco laughed.

"That's what I told them," said Muchacha. "You're too easygoing to be the Devil. Now Sapogrande would make a great Devil."

"The Devil's job is open?" Flaco asked, perplexed.

"No, silly," Muchacha laughed. "It's for Los Pastores, the shepherd's play. It is being presented in El Paso. Yes, Sapo would make a great Devil." She paused, frowned, then said with a wry chuckle, "In fact, if he doesn't get home with the new Madonna, he might as well be the Devil already."

Huarache snorted derisively. "He is lost, I tell you. I knew this would come to no good, because that fat rooster is only interested in making himself look important."

Flaco gazed at Pancho a moment, then shook his head in resignation. "Huarache, how you torture yourself. Always making yourself angry about something, always hating people for being so much less than what you would like them to be."

"What, am I supposed to praise people like him for being incompetent?" the revolutionary demanded.

Flaco shrugged. "You would probably feel much better if you found something to praise him for."

"Anyone who could feel good in a world as rotten as this one has got to be just plain crazy," Pancho declared positively.

"Gee, Pancho, I don't think it's really all that bad," said

Muchacha, gazing at him with concern.

"Huarache, my friend, I'll tell you something...just because it's Christmas and I'm feeling foolish and idealistic," said Flaco. "I have seen a bit of this world you are talking about. I have seen how things are in the powerful places. I have seen a few rich men get together and call themselves the law, and say everyone has to pay them taxes for the right to live on the land. I have read the history of the church, how many tribes and cultures have been damned and destroyed in the name of spreading the gospel of peace. It would be easy for me to justify being angry about all that. But, you see, Pancho, I don't like that feeling. I don't like being angry. I like being at peace. I can't change much of the world...my anger certainly would change nothing at all...so if I am to select and justify a feeling, why shouldn't I choose to feel good?"

"What could possibly make you feel good about the way people are in the world today?" Huarache demanded.

"Why, the best feeling in the world. Forgiveness," said Flaco simply.

"Forgiveness?" asked Muchacha.

"Sure," said Flaco. "If you truly forgive those who are too weak to resist the temptations of the world, then you do not have to feel the anguish of rage, or hate, or vengeance every time you think about them."

"That's very easy to say," scoffed Huarache.

"The power to forgive comes from knowing who you are," Flaco continued. "You have to separate yourself from material things, to know that no worldly loss is so great that you cannot forgive it. If someone steals your money, for example, you can say, 'I was happy before I had it, I enjoyed it a while, and now I can still be happy without it.'"

"What about somebody trying to kill you?" Huarache persisted. "How could you forgive that?"

Flaco sipped his hot wine and smiled. "Your body is just temporary property like the money. If you believe your spirit survives the loss of it, then you can forgive the person who takes it from you. Then you don't have to die in anger or fear. You can die in peace. That makes it possible for a person to happily sacrifice his life for a higher purpose. I know you understand that, Pancho, that such a sacrifice must certainly be the most joyful way to die. So to live with a peaceful heart, ready every day to die for your ideals, and forgiving the rest of us for being weak and foolish — that must certainly be the most joyful way to live."

"That is just beautiful, Flaco," sighed Muchacha.

"Well....maybe you're right," Huarache agreed reluctantly. "Maybe I ask too much of the world, expecting people to be more like myself."

"Give us a chance," Flaco laughed. "Maybe we are more like you than you think. Like Emilio, for instance.

"*El Gran Mayor?* He is puffed-up and proud like a fat frog!"

"Well, yes, he is," Flaco conceded, "but if you can forgive him for that, then he is not a villain any more...he's just a big-hearted boy, and a pretty funny one at that."

"It's getting awfully late, and he still hasn't come home," said Muchacha, a note of worry in her voice. "It would be a terrible shame if something happened to him and he doesn't get back in time for the procession this evening."

"Chulita would be heartbroken if something happened to him,"

Flaco agreed. "I'll go over to the church, and see if anyone has heard anything about him. See you all in the plaza tonight."

In the plaza, the townfolk were continuing to decorate, hanging long *ristras*, strings of bright red dried chile peppers, bunches of mistletoe from the cottonwood trees which grew along the Rio Grande river, and bright pyracanthis berries. Padre Cabrito was the center of attention as he hung up the gaily-colored *piñata* from a hook high in the very center of the roof of the bandstand.

"This *piñata* is filled with *biscochitos* and *piloncillo*, the sweetest cookies and candy the ladies could make, and Christmas morning we will give all you children a chance to break it open with a big stick," he told the little ones gathered around him.

"Those children had better be quick, Padre, or you will run in and get all the best pieces yourself," cackled Abuelita.

Flaco came out from behind the saloon, bringing a squat and scrubby-looking tree, and wearing a huge smile. "Here, Padre. I brought a piñon tree we can decorate. Shall we put it up here in front of the church?"

Padre Cabrito gazed at the gnarled little tree and nodded. "Marvelous. A beautiful tree. Where did those two boys go?"

"Here we are, Padre," called out Rusty from nearby.

"There is a basket by the bandstand with some things you can use to decorate the tree," he told them. Then he added, to Flaco, "There are also some lovely little *Ojos de Dios* in the church. The ladies have been making them for weeks."

The boys quickly found the basket and began to decorate the tree with red chile peppers, some strings of popcorn, and cookies from the basket. Abuelita, Señora Chavez, and Chulita brought out the *Ojos* and hung them in several places around the plaza. These were each a little sunburst pattern of bright yarn woven like a spiderweb around a frame of two or three crossed sticks.

Flaco dug into the pocket of his pants and produced a little bell, which he rang, and then hung on the tree.

"There now. Isn't that beautiful?" said Padre Cabrito. "Look at that Christmas tree. Why, there couldn't be a finer one in Mexico City."

"Or Santa Fe," added Flaco.

"And when it gets dark, our *luminarias* will be just beautiful, just heavenly," mused the Padre.

There was a long moment of uncomfortable silence, then Señora Chavez said, "Padre Cabrito. We ought to give it some thought. What if Mayor Sapogrande does not get back in time for the procession? We did not make another Madonna, you know."

Padre Cabrito nodded. "Yes, I know, Señora Chavez. But he will be back, you wait and see. All right now, let's all go home and rest, and get ready for the celebration tonight. *Feliz Navidad*."

"*Feliz Navidad!*" they replied, and they began to leave,

each in a different direction. The last to leave the plaza was the Padre. He stood before his church and sighed, then just before he turned to go inside, he saw Chulita, wrapped in her shawl, huddled among the figures of the *Natividad.*

"Why, Chulita, dear, you should go home also and get ready. Mayor Sapogrande will be home any minute now, you wait and see. And you don't want to catch a cold sitting here, do you?"

She looked up at him with great sorrowful but hopeful brown eyes. "I'm not cold, Padre. I'll wait for him here. I just know he'll get here in time."

Slipping in between Joseph and one of the shepherds, Cabrito sat down beside the girl. "I have been thinking, Chulita... and praying. I have been thinking that maybe the Lord is trying to show us something."

"Yes, Padre?" she asked, so trustingly.

"Well, sometimes even our best prayers don't get answered just the way we think we would like them," he said, hoping he did not sound foolish. "God is not a magician we can just hire to do tricks for us, and when we ask Him to do things for us, well, sometimes He would prefer that we did it ourselves, so that we can grow by the experience."

"Do you think I prayed for too much, Padre Cabrito?" she asked in a tiny voice.

"Why, no, of course not," he quickly assured her. "That was a lovely thing to pray for."

She sat silent for a moment, then asked him hesitatingly, "Do you think...that the Lord would not answer my prayer if I did something bad?"

"Why, what do you mean, dear," he asked her.

She began to cry softly, and her words were choked and hardly spoken at all. "When I went into La Fuente to ask old Caterino to help, and everybody laughed at me, I told them the Lord would not answer the prayer because they didn't deserve it. I cursed them...and now it is coming true!" She turned to him and fell against his shoulder, weeping piteously.

"There, there, now," said the priest, patting her back

and head. "No, dear, the Lord wouldn't do a thing like that. He is very merciful, and He loves you very much. Maybe He just had a different plan for us this Christmas. Maybe something even better than getting our new Lady of Guadalupe this year."

"What do you mean?" she asked, sitting up and looking at him fearfully. "You don't believe the Mayor will be back?"

"Well, I pray he will," said Cabrito. "but even if he is a few days late, we will still have a beautiful Guadalupe to carry in the procession. And that is what I have been praying about."

"How can that be?" the girl asked, perplexed. "I don't understand."

The priest turned to her and took her hands in his, and looked into her face. "Chulita, you will be our Virgin of Guadalupe this year, because it was you who prayed. We will dress you in a beautiful blue robe, and four men will carry you the streets. You will be the most beautiful Guadalupe ever, and everyone will praise the Lord when they see you. Now, what do you think of that?"

She put her head onto her knees and sat huddled a moment. "I had really hoped..." She paused a moment, sighed softly, then went on. "...but, of course, if that is how the Lord answers my prayers, I will be grateful. I will do it, Padre."

"Why, bless you, child," said Cabrito, much relieved. "I'll go get the robe ready, and you go home and get warm and eat something."

"Oh, it isn't too late yet," she pleaded. "Mayor Sapogrande could still get here."

Suddenly from a block away they heard a voice cry out, "Look! Look, he has come back! It is the Mayor!" People began to pop out of their homes and to gather quickly in the plaza, looking around and chattering excitedly.

"Oh, I knew it!" cried Chulita. "I knew the Blue Lady would get him home."

"Well, praise the Lord," marveled Cabrito, "and not a minute too soon."

Even Pancho Huarache was excited. *"Viva Sapogrande!"* he cried out.

"Come on, everybody! The mayor is coming!" shouted Rusty.

Then suddenly everyone fell silent. Mayor Emilio Sapogrande came out of a sidestreet into the plaza and stood before them. He was on foot, covered with mud, beaten, downcast, and clearly empty handed. Slowly he stepped up before the *Natividad*, took off his great — and now battered — sombrero, and dropped it at his feet. "I'm sorry," he said. "I... I am today the most miserable of men. I have failed you. When I got to El Paso, I rode all around looking for the very best, bragging about how my village and my people had collected such a great sum of money. When I left one of the shops, two robbers followed me. I am ashamed to tell you that they robbed me of my horse, and all the money, and they left me beaten in the mud."

A groan of disappointment rose from the crowd. Pancho Huarache took off his sombrero and hurled it at his feet in disgust.

"I found out that in El Paso it did not matter very much that I am the mayor of Lastima," Sapogrande continued. "After today, I am afraid it won't matter very much here either."

Then Chulita stepped up onto the platform beside Sapogrande, and took his hand. She wiped her eyes and stood up bravely. "We mustn't let a little misfortune keep us from our celebration, *Tio Sapo*," she said. "It is still the night of La Posada, and the Lord still loves us. In fact, only a few minutes ago, Padre Cabrito told me that..."

Suddenly she was interrupted by a loud voice from behind the crowd. "Wait! Wait a minute. Let me through." They all gasped in surprise as Caterino Medina appeared among them. He had shaved and cleaned himself up, and though it was clear he was still a sick and tired old man, there was a new flash in his eyes, and his voice was clear. He was pulling a large wagon containing something covered with a canvas tarp. "Thank the Lord I have made it in time," he said. "I was afraid I couldn't finish it in time."

The crowd began to buzz, but he waved a hand to stop

them, and stepped up onto the platform with Chulita. "Please. Please, let me tell you. When I lost my beloved wife, I cursed the Lord for cheating me, and I cried out for death. And God help me, I have lived like a dead man since. But because of you, Chulita, He has given me a new life instead. When I saw you standing before me in La Fuente that night, you looked so much like my dear Celeste that I could not keep from crying out, and I had to run away to hide. But I could not hide, not this time. I went to my room, and I fell into my bed, and tried to make it all go away. And then...and then, I saw her! I saw a light, and there she was, standing at the foot of my bed. She was dressed in Blue, and there was light all around her. And then she spoke to me. You know what she said? She said, 'Caterino, your grief is a sin!' Aie, I fell to my knees when she said that. 'Yes,' she told me, 'In your self-pity, you deny yourself to the living, who need you.' Then she reached out her hand, and she touched me. And she blessed me. I cried like a baby to see how hardened my heart had become. And then...then I picked up my mallet and my chisels, and I soon found out how soft my hands had become."

He opened his hands and displayed the palms which were a mass of bleeding blisters. He sagged a little and began to laugh and cry, tears streaming down his face. "But I finished it! I finished it!" He pointed toward the wagon. The people turned to it, and then Flaco took hold of the canvas and pulled it back to reveal a beautiful life-sized statue of the Virgin of Guadalupe, wearing a gown of sky-blue folds. "You see," the man said, his voice cracking with emotion, and tears springing to his eyes again. "You see? She has the face of my Celeste."

Everyone saw, and everyone noticed, and nobody mentioned that she also looked very much like little Chulita. They all began to cheer and laugh and shout praises, hug one another, jump up and down.

Sapogrande had stood through it all in awe, his great sombrero still at his feet.

"Hola, Sapo!" called Padre Cabrito. "The Lord has brought us our Guadalupe, and has restored our *santero* to life. What do you think of that?"

Sapogrande stood a moment looking from one of them to the other. He picked up his hat and walked around the statue, looking at it as though sniffing for foul odor. He placed his sombrero squarely on his head, then said, "It is not quite right."

There was a moment of shocked silence, then everyone began to clamor at once. "What? I don't believe it!"

"Emilio, how could you say such a thing?" pleaded Padre Cabrito.

Sapogrande held up a hand to silence the crowd. He reached into the inner pocket of his heavy greatcoat and brought out the beautiful antique lace *mantilla* which Chulita had given him to sell. "This is the only thing the robbers didn't get."

The townfolk sighed a breathless and amazed, "Oooohh," as Sapogrande reverently placed the long delicate mantle of lace over the head and shoulders of the statue of the Virgin of Guadalupe.

Then their mayor turned to face them. "Today, we have seen miracles," he said. "A foolish mayor has seen that the Lord does not demand greatness of those He chooses to do His work. With love and faith, even the simplest child among us can work miracles. A little girl's prayer has been answered, and the Virgin now wears as a mantle the symbol of our Chulita's generosity. And what's more, our brother Caterino is restored to us a whole man."

"I am a new man!" declared Caterino Medina. "I will make you all a promise. Every year for the rest of my life, I will make one more Santo for the church. Every year. And when the Lord figures there are enough saints in there, He will call me home to rest. So, Sapo, you may have your collection yet."

"Then may the Lord grant you long life. But please, we'll call it the Caterino Medina Memorial," said the Mayor.

"Please, yourself," admonished the old *santero*. "We don't have to call it anything. If we just remember whose birth and life we celebrate, that will be the best memorial of all."

Everyone applauded and laughed, and they began to talk happily among themselves, admiring the decorations and the beautiful new icon, and feeling the joy of the moment.

"So, Caterino, you old burro, the Lord has restored your hands, eh?" Abuelita said, "So what about your feet?"

"*Mande?*"

"Is there still a dance left in you?"

His eyes widened, then a great smile spread itself across his face like a sunrise. "*Aie, que Abuelita chiquitita!* I am going to dance every step I take for the rest of my life," he said. He offered her his arm and they danced around the plaza, to the cheers of all.

"Oh, this is lots of fun," said Muchacha, "but I hope next year we can put on a performance of Los Pastores. It has some wonderful character parts for a woman with a little talent."

"I think you're absolutely right, Muchacha," agreed Pancho Huarache. "You'd be really great. I am going to recommend that just as soon as I get elected."

"Elected?" asked Melendrez, overhearing him. "Elected to what?"

"I've been thinking. I had it all wrong," declared the revolutionary. "Someday they will make this whole territory a state, and I have decided I am going to be the Governor."

"Why, Pancho, how wonderful!" said Muchacha.

"God bless our country, the United States of America," said Pancho fervently. "I think I'll start by running for Mayor in the next election."

Melendrez laughed. "You are starting to think like a gringo already, Huarache. Only Santa Claus could bring you that election."

Mayor Emilio Sapogrande gave Chulita a big hug. "So, my sweet Chulita, look what you started."

"Thank you, Uncle Emilio, for trying so hard to help the Lord," she said, squeezing him around the neck.

"You're welcome, dear, but I think from now on I'll try to let Him help me instead," he told her. "As long as any of us are left alive, we will never forget that it was you, Chulita, who asked the Lord for this blessing. But come now, it is getting late. Why is our Padre standing around with his fingers hanging down? Let's begin our celebration!"

"How you can fall on your face as hard as you do and still come out looking like a hero is a miracle in itself, Sapo, my old friend," said the Padre with a laugh.

"Well, I guess I must be the Lord's hobby," chuckled the mayor.

"Where did you hear that?" asked Chulita.

Sapogrande shrugged. "I don't know. I heard it in a dream, I guess."

Señora Chavez stepped up to Cabrito and whispered into his ear. "Oh, yes, thank you," said the priest, and turned to the townfolk. "Señora Chavez has just reminded me to remind you all to be especially thankful for your wife, Mayor Sapogrande, and the ladies of the Women's Civic League, who have spent all day preparing a great feast, which we will all enjoy, when we find the right house. *Entonces, vamos a La Posada!*"

Enthusiastically, everyone ran off to prepare for his part in the procession. Some hurried to the church to reappear with a cross on a pole, some torches, and handbells. Several people ran quickly along the rows of *luminarias* carrying little candles with which they lit the decorative lights to form warm flickering lines of welcoming glow. Flaco brought his guitar from the saloon, sat down on the bandstand, and strummed a lively chord. Rusty banged a small drum and took up the lead of the parade, followed by Mayor Emilio Sapogrande with Chulita sitting high upon his broad strong shoulder. Muchacha and Chiquita brought more baskets of *biscochitos*. Melendrez and Huarache lifted the statue and began the procession around the plaza. The townfolk followed happily, singing a Mexican Christmas carol.

For a few moments after the parade started down the first of the village streets, Flaco stood alone in the plaza. He jumped up from where he was sitting, and danced around in a circle, happily singing to himself. "What a night! *Que noche buena!* I don't know if the Lord had anything to do with it all. Maybe it was all in the hearts of these good people. Either way, I can only say Amen! Happy birthday, dear Lord, and many happy returns." He spun around again in joy, dancing a little step in the spirit by himself. As he did, someone stepped silently out of the shadows and stood watching him. He saw her there and greeted her as though he had seen her there every day of his life. *"Buenas noches, Hermana,"* he said to the beautiful young woman in the sky blue habit of a fifteenth-century nun.

"Buenas noches, Flaco," she replied.

With his arms sweeping wide to include the entire world and all the heavens, he called out to her and to everyone, "Look at our little town! Surely this must be the holiest place in the whole world tonight."

Suddenly he was struck by the reality of what he had just seen. *"Eres Tu!"* he cried out, and turned around quickly... but she had disappeared. He stared dumfounded into the night for a moment, then began to laugh and dance around again as the procession returned to the plaza, and the townfolk continued to sing. They put the statue into its place in the *Natividad*, and put *El Niño Santo*, the baby Jesus, into her arms. They piled gifts at her feet, paper flowers, baskets of cakes and candles as they sang, and everyone agreed that their own Guadalupe with the flowing mantilla of purest Spanish lace was the most beautiful in the world.

THE END

THE HEALING WATERS OF CACIQUE SPRING

Chapter One

"The Anasazi have gone from here," Buck Tyler whispered, "gone so long their graves have Navajo names." He looked out upon the pre-dawn horizon, and in the perfect focus of still, clean air, he could see landmarks to the south and to the north, which he knew were ninety miles away. Though the sky above him was already a swirling palette in cool pastels, and high cirrus clouds were touched with pinkening gold to the east, the desert two miles below him was still dark, its features obscured. Then the gleaming blade edge of the disc of the sun broke over the horizon, the color of live blood on polished gold, and bright as pain.

In a quiet bedroom in Santa Fe, dark but for just enough pre-dawn light one might see its simple furnishings and viga ceiling, Sharon Hightower lay sleeping fitfully. As though caught in a dream she struggled to awaken from, she squirmed and moaned softly. Her hands moved across her body, one on her breast, and the other down her belly, as though her dream might be erotic, but not pleasant.
In her dream she lay sleeping fitfully in her bed, and beneath the sheet there was a movement, and the movement was a huge snake sliding sensuously against her, and wrapping itself around her. It was not a natural snake, not an errant boa or python, but a surreal and glowing incarnation of the sacred Water Snake, with zig-zags of bright turquoise along its russet pipestone scales. The snake wrapped itself around her, rose over her, and she cried out in her bed as though in fear and in desire, as though she could not tell if she were being seduced or devoured. She tried to turn away from the eyes of the Snake, but she was held transfixed as it swayed and slithered toward her, glistening, phallic, leering hungrily

at her helplessness. Then from the leering jaws came a sound, the voice of a hundred bull-roarer paddles, a grumbling of thunder, but sharp and cutting. To her horror she felt herself gush wet as the Snake took her, opening its fat pouting moist lips to slurp her up. The hot caressing lips slipped up over her hips and over her breasts and neck, sucking her whole body sensuously. She drew her sleeping body into a ball as she surrendered herself to orgasm and the Snake swallowed her. Down the long slippery tunnel she flowed, and then fell, turned and twirled, and then flew toward the light where the rippling sides of the tunnel flashed past her like hypnotically expanding circles. Then suddenly she burst out into the light.

As though startled awake, Sharon jumped to sit up in her bed, clutching her sheet around herself, eyes wide with astonishment, sweat matting her long black hair to her neck. She is about thirty, quite pretty by the standards of the Native American tribes of northern New Mexico, to one of which she was born. To her astonishment, her bed was no longer in her room in Santa Fe, but on the top of a high sandstone tower in the cliff country of her childhood. The canyon below her still rang with the roaring of the Water Snake's voice. She looked up to see that it was not the Water Snake making the sound, but a hawk, a bright red hawk circling above her. Then she gasped and clutched her homespun robe around her shoulders and stood where the bed had been as she recognized it was not a hawk, but an airplane.

High above her, Buck Tyler felt a pat on his helmet from the rear cockpit of the big 450 Bull Stearman. "Now I gain one sunrise, and borrow a day from the ghosts of the Anasazi," he resolved, and he turned around and nodded vigorously. Then he unbuckled his lap belt and shoulder harness and stood up in the open cockpit of the biplane. "See you later, Sakata," he shouted with a grin into the roaring propwash, hardly expecting the pilot to hear him. He reached up to grasp a handle on the top surface of the upper wing, stepped up onto the fuselage, and pulled himself to stand upright behind a thin chromed ladder fastened to the top of the wing with taut guywires. Like Perseus dancing upon the feathered withers of the flying horse, he thrust forward his chest and felt the smooth undisturbed morning air press against him and slide past him like a rushing flow of mercury, with awesome power, immediate, and demanding. The exhilaration charged his body with the muscle-rush of adrenaline, and his forearms felt like the same chrome steel as the ladder they gripped. He placed his feet apart carefully and tested the grip of his custom desert boots on the pebbled walkway surface of the wing, then he lowered his center of gravity and pressed out with his thighs and pulled in with his feet to assume the inverted U of the rooted Kibadachi stance of his martial arts training.

The disc of the sun was almost all the way above the horizon as the pilot nosed the red-and-gold showplane down about twenty degrees and accelerated directly into the sunrise. Buck hung on fiercely, willing himself to be part of the airplane as the pressure of the mercury slipstream tried to squeeze him from the top of the wing like a melon seed. The glare of the sun dazed him, and the flat tabled horizons of northwestern New Mexico seemed too starkly cut, too stylized to be real. "Sand-painting horizons," he marveled, laughing in delight at the effect.

Then quite suddenly he felt a tremendous weight come over him. Pressing harder with his legs against the G-forces he shouted, "Kiyaaaahh!" as the nose of the airplane rose quickly up through the horizon and higher. The bull-throated roar of the big Pratt & Whitney radial engine on the barrel-chested fuselage of the Stearman deepened a harmonic into the bass as the broad blades of the prop loaded up to drive the machine into a dizzying vertical climb. Just as the nose reached vertical, the pilot pushed the joystick forward, and the resulting negative-G effect neatly parted Tyler from the top of the wing. His momentum hurled him straight up another hundred feet, and then for just an instant, he hung motionless in the sky twelve thousand feet above the desert and faced the rising sun. "Ki!" he cried, in salute, and in challenge.

With his arms outstretched and his feet together, he dropped his head back and fell in a long, impossibly slow back layout. He plunged backward and inverted through the still-gray horizon of the departing night, rolled through to level, and let his arms and legs spread out to the comfortable flying-frog position in which he could control his fall and look around. Far below him, the floor of the Kim-me-ni-oli Wash was still in shadow, but he could see from the yellow just touching the tallest of the mesa tops and peaks to the east that the shadow was very shallow. He steeled himself and fell toward that thin wedge of night below, keeping his eyes on the rising sun. As he fell toward the earth, he saw the disc begin to descend once again beneath the horizon. Dazzled, fixed like a rabbit in the beam of a locomotive headlamp, he plunged toward the sandy floor of the remote uninhabited valley.

"Can I cheat time?" he asked himself as the slipstream whipped at his jumpsuit. "If I miss, I have made my own last sunset." The chisel-cut sandstone horizons loomed up to engulf him, but he held his arms outstretched until the disc winked out beneath a mesa. Then in two very fast, very precise moves, Buck snapped his arms in to his chest, grabbed his D-ring, and snapped the arms out again smoothly. The cable slid out with four finger-tip-perceptible tiny clicks as the pins popped free. Event by event, microsecond at a time, he felt the pack spring open, and the drogue fly out into the slipstream, and the neat bundles of shroud lines stutter free of their elastic holders, then a shock, a jolt. Good chute!

Only then did he look down, and he heaved a great sigh of relief. The ground was still two hundred feet below him. He pulled on the control cables of his parachute and swung in a circle to take a look around. East of him on the edge of the wash ragged sandstone cliffs rose with sloping buttresses of talus. On the west the wide wash extended flat and dry for miles. And high up on the slope of the wash, up close to the ragged cliffs lay his objective, a little tattered rubble of ancient Anasazi walls. The ground swung up to meet him, and he struck solidly in soft sand. He rolled, stood quickly, and dumped the last air from his collapsing chute.

Above him the bright little biplane circled, and he waved. The pilot rocked the wings, jazzed the engine, once, twice, then turned and departed to the southeast. Buck Tyler stood on the ruins of the ancient home, and watched as the first bright edge of the sundisc blazed above the horizon. "Today belongs to the Anasazi," he said.

He spent the morning walking among the ruins of a building which had once housed several hundred people at a time. Its long north wall stood for more than three hundred feet, and in some places it was still three stories tall. He shook his head and marveled as he wandered along the stumps of walls two feet thick. From the highest point to which he could climb, he saw the ground plan of the great pueblo laid bare to reveal an E-shaped structure of scores of rooms. At a glance, he could count at least six kivas. Intended for clan ceremonies — and no doubt also the equivalent of neighborhood pubs — the circular chambers had been built partly above ground. Though the walls stood two or three feet high in some places, the kivas were for the most part filled with the dusts of centuries.

It was the day before the summer solstice, and the sun soon sent hot shimmering columns of rising air up from the baked ochre soil of the arid wash. The silence was eerie, not cold, foggy, hollow eerie like a Boris Karloff cemetery, but hot and bright, silence with pressure, like the instant before a scream. Buck peeled off his shirt and put it with his jumpsuit and parachute, and stood in shorts and boots in the 120-degree glare. He inhaled deeply with pleasure and winced as the hot rushing air burned along the edges of his nostrils as though he were in a dry sauna. The sweat soon began to trickle down his temples from beneath his sandy curls, and his lean and well-muscled body began to collect a patina of oil, dust, and salt as his perspiration evaporated. He took pleasure in the heat, and found the glassy-eyed giddiness it provoked a little frightening, and deliciously so.

The season had been wetter than usual, and Buck saw the yucca, creosote, and mesquite were green, and in the protected hollows in the rubble he saw clumps of Rocky Mountain bee plant. He smiled to recognize the Anasazi potters' source of black for decoration of their work. In the low spots, the little arroyos which led through the midden hills to the wash, he could see the dark olive-green vines and white trumpet flowers of the datura, source of a terribly toxic — often lethal — hallucinogen. "I can pass on that one," he said to himself, "but I wouldn't mind finding some *lophophora* up here somewhere." In the middens, the trash dumps of the ancient community, he found the ground littered with potshards and lithics. Had he wanted to, he could have filled a backpack with them in minutes, but he was content to pick up a piece, recognize it as corrugated Cibola Gray ware, or smooth Chuska White, and then to throw it back down.

Mid-afternoon, the winds came up, listless shifting winds which generated the thousand-foot-high swirling pillars of dust devils, the desert twisters, and swept them back and forth across the wash. To escape the largest of the sand-blasting wind demons, Buck took refuge in the stone circle of one of the kivas. It was deeper than most, almost five feet from the top of the wall to the floor of blown sand, and about twenty feet across. After the twister had blown through, he noticed there was already a wedge of shade along the west side of the kiva, so he crawled across the sand toward it. He rested there for a few minutes with his eyes closed, letting the glaring purple and green of his retina burn-in fade. Then he opened his eyes, and looked around close beside him.

He was sitting on the old stone bench which ringed the lodge, near where a few feet of the wall had caved in. Growing on the rubble were a few sparse grasses, a few wildflowers nursing fat seedpods, and a little clump of cacti about half the size of a dinner plate. Around a dark-green muffin-sized central button of the cactus grew several waxy, multi-lobed young daughter buttons, each crowned with a ring of little white tufts. "Peyote!" exclaimed Buck Tyler in delight.

Though he had included plenty of food in his jump kit, he had not felt hungry in the heat all day. All he had consumed was two quarts of his water. That was not as good as having fasted for two days, he knew, for the cactus that gives visions is best taken on an empty gut, but he laughed softly and reached up to pat the stone wall beside him. "I've come to look for the Anasazi," he said aloud. "I guess I might as well go for it like I meant it. And I guess if this wasn't meant for me, it wouldn't be here."

He reached to the scabbard built into the outside calf of his right boot and drew out a long thin double-edged knife, a perfectly-balanced weapon and tool wrought from a single piece of fine old 19th-century Wilkinson steel. Taking his time, he carefully cut off the top inch of four of the daughter buttons, and neatly trimmed the crown of tiny toxic bristles from each one. He poured a little water from his canteen onto the polished surface of a near-by metate, a corn-grinding stone, to rinse away the dust. Then he sliced the buttons into thin pieces and laid them out on the rock in front of him. He picked up the biggest slice and put it on his tongue. He gagged. His throat constricted with revulsion at the loathsome taste, but he controlled the urge to retch and chewed and swallowed. Then he picked up another slice, and another. In about half an hour, he washed down the last of it with water and sat back against the wall of the kiva to wait.

It seemed he had dozed for a while. He found himself returning to the kiva, surprised that he had been drifting, and was again surprised to see that the wedge of shadow extended clear across the circle. He noticed that the red color of the light filled up the space above the shadow, and that it lay tangible on the rock surfaces across from him. It quite suddenly occurred to him that he was feeling the texture of that interface of light and rock, not as an abstraction in his mind, but feeling it where it stood. He felt a staggering, a disorientation in the shape of space, and his body jerked suddenly, as though locating itself. With the jolt of self-awareness came the realization that he was horribly sick to his stomach. He flashed with tingling cold sweat when he stood, then broke out hot across the forehead and neck when the ground began to slosh like mud. He took hold of himself, walked across the sloping sandfill in the kiva, stepped out of the circle and began to vomit violently.

After a few minutes the paroxysm passed, and his ears began to ring. He heard, or felt, a great sizzling, as though of sand rushing down the side of a huge gourd, and he turned around. The sizzling hissed to a stop as though the sands had flowed swiftly to their appointed places and all stopped at the same focused instant. He was caught outside himself with awe as he beheld the grand panorama of the blazing desert sunset spread before him cleanly drawn in the crisp perfect stillness of sand. The sky and the land were both wrought in sands of the same sun-gold, blood-red, stone-ochre colors. He could see each grain of sand in the vast painting, from the coarse rubble of ground shards of the stonework in the foreground to the fine grains of purest gold glowing just red hot in the fat-sided orb of the setting sun. Grain by grain, the colors changed, and the long straight rays cast from behind the perfectly-domed cumulus tilted up and up, as though the sun god were drawing up the ladder-poles to his castle for the night.

As the last of the precious gold disappeared from the sandscape, Buck Tyler became acutely aware that the night was come upon him, and he was alone in an alien world. He stepped into the kiva again, and they all turned to look at him. He couldn't see them yet, but he knew they were there, as a little boy at a birthday party knows the others are watching when he is brought in blindfolded and turned round and round. His heart began to beat harder, and in the kiva they began to mock him by picking up the anxious beat with their drums. He felt himself stagger across the floor and drop again onto his place on the stone bench.

"They can see me," he thought. "They will see my fear, and know that I am false." His thoughts scurried, looked for hiding. "They will know I am not worthy of being here." Someone laughed at him, as though from behind a mask.

As the sky darkened, the sand in the kiva darkened with it, and faded to leave his vision unobstructed. The bench on which he sat extended all the way around the chamber. Near the center a stone altar bore objects he did not recognize. Four awesome pillars supported the roof, rising up to disappear into the darkness. Above him, the domed ceiling was black with smoke, and on it was painted a map of the stars, each a little cross, except the few which wandered with the running legs of the swastika. Fire glowed from two pits, and there, that hole in the floor, the hole from which flowed strange-smelling smoke, that surely was Sipapu, the gateway from the underworld below.

"Are you a wolf? Are you a bird?" they demanded of him. "Why should you be admitted to the Fourth World, as though you knew right from wrong?"

"I am not a bird," he replied.

"Are you a goat? A lizard? What are you?"

"I am a man."

They laughed at him, and he flushed with embarrassment, not certain he had answered truthfully. "You are a do-do," they said mockingly. "You are a little boy with dirty pants. You have no magic, and you have no penis."

"I do so!"

"Then get it up, or we'll cut it off." He was made small by an unexpected wave of shame at his awareness of the pitiful vulnerability of the tiny bit of flesh in which he took such pride, and when they laughed at him again, he was suddenly afraid that they could take it away and leave him impotent in... in that other dream. It occurred to him that he had just failed in his first test, and he couldn't quite remember what it was about.

"If you fail here, you don't go back to the other world," they told him. "If you fail, the Kachina Tunwe-up will destroy you. You will die of a natural cause, and your body will be given a burial name, and you will never be spoken of again."

The drums began to beat more fiercely, pounding, pounding, demanding more and more of his racing heart. Then he knew what they meant. They would drive his heart to a spasmed standstill with their drums, and it would be blamed on the toxins in the cactus he ate. "You thought to steal our power when you took the sacred peyotl, and instead it has given us power over you," they informed him seriously.

Knowing they spoke the truth, he began to weep. "I've gone too far!" he realized in horror. "Oh, my God, this is real!"

"Yes," said the fearsome Tunwe-up. "The blindfold shall be taken from your eyes, and you will see the reality and face the fate your arrogance and your theft have earned you. Tell us, while you try to hide your precious little pee-pee: what is it you fear most to lose? What is it you fear most will happen to you now?"

The walls of the chamber began to move, to pulsate and ripple, to flow toward him reaching out to feel him, to taste him. To his horror he saw the sands of the floor rise up and take the form of the Kachina, a man-bear-wolf monster with huge jaws, and eyes that fixed him with the intensity of their focus, the eyes of the mantis. The room began to echo round and round with a muttering roar, like the strident chanting of many voices in a cave. "You have come to the kiva of Fire Clan," said the Kachina with a deep ringing voice, "but you are not worthy." Crack! The whip in his hand lashed out and bit a burning welt across Tyler's shoulder. "I am taking you down through Sipapu into the Lower World where you belong, and I will use you for what I want. Your fate is to become one of the lower forms!"

He felt his body convulse through shapes. His toes grew and spread like frogs' webs, then his shoulders shrugged helpless squab wings. He crouched on the bench of stone, felt his clumsy legs bound together, and felt the rope around his neck, and he heard himself utter a bleat of terror. He knew it was the kid goat who stole the grain and first got fat who went into the roasting pit while his less-presumptuous brothers grew old rutting in the safety of the fold. Tonight it would be him who died struggling wild-eyed in the hands of the hungry laughing chef, not the Chosen Initiate, but instead the fatted sacrifice.

He jumped to his feet and ran from the kiva, fleeing from the unknown horror of the life and death of the dumb anonymous beasts. He ran headlong into the Kim-me-ni-oli Wash, and was astonished to see the sky above was just like the star-chart on the ceiling of the kiva, and that the mesas on the sides of the wash looked just like the benches in the kiva, and that the pueblo stood in exactly the place of the altar stone below, and that he had suddenly become the size of a tiny bug on the floor of the kiva. To the west a hot night thunderstorm flashed and rumbled, and in the light of the bolts, he could see it was the huge Kachina, with his lightning flashing down like whipstrokes to the earth below. Sobbing in shame and fear, he fled running into the night.

He ran a long time. The sands of the wash flowed beneath his feet, and his body began to burn with exhaustion. The agony began in his chest and lungs, and in his legs, and spread to his belly, his kidneys, and the back of his neck. "I will eat this fire and grow strong on it," he muttered thickly, driving the burning pain into the crevices of his body. "I will burn this body pure, or destroy it."

"Are you a wolf?" the Kachina laughed, voice rumbling on the horizon. "Are you a deer?" His legs became short, and thick, and he hopped and shuffled along like a fat little toad. Behind him he heard the huffing and panting of the great bear, and he ran in slow-motion panic without looking back, up to his knees in the syrup-thick sands of the mandala he had violated.

There was a bit of moon, and he saw that he was running alongside the huge Water Snake, a snake as long as the part of the wash he could see. "If I get to the head of the snake, he will eat me," he thought, "but if I stop running, the Kachina will eat me." He ran like a lizard, like a mouse alongside the snake until the fire in his body went out, and then he became terribly thirsty. Knowing the snake knew where water lay, he cried out in anguish to the meandering god to reveal himself. The snake flowed silently down the wash into the night, and Buck staggered along beside it, his mind growing numb with fear, thirst, and fatigue.

High upon the sandstone above, Sharon Hightower stood beside her grandmother, herself a child of twelve, and in awe. The old woman sat on the red sand beside her loom, weaving a rug with a pattern that changed and flowed, a moving record of the great cities in the caves, and the cities in the sky atop the great red towering mesas. The tapestry flowed from her loom and became the land around her, and she looked at the dreamer and smiled, and her face grew young, the wide flat planes of her cheeks growing round and smooth. Her long gray hair flowed down and became shiny black, then flowed up and became dark clouds on the horizon. The wind made her hair and clothing flow and tatter in timeless slow motion as she reached out her hand holding a large red pipestone pipe. From its stem like smoke flowed the great Water Snake. Dressed in her finest ceremonial robe and wearing a wreath of squash-blossoms made of living blue stone, she raised her arm silently and pointed along the dry desert wash.

At first Sharon saw only a little hawk, a pale hawk with gold and red plumage along its back and tail. It appeared to be hurt, or bound to something and unable to fly. Then she saw it was a man, and he was bound by a vine to the red pipestone altar at the center of the valley, and was struggling against it blindly, without direction. She saw he was a very pretty man, young and strong, and she sucked in her breath as her heart went out to him. Then her grandmother called out to him, in a name she could not understand, but a name she knew was his ancient spirit name.

Sheltered by a bend in the wash, BuckTyler fell to his knees sobbing. He was aware that the dawn colors had still not come, but he could just see the rocks above him. He saw also that he was dressed only in boots and shorts — to protect his shameful weaknesses, the thought occurred to him wryly -- and he had no water. In frustration and thirst, he cried out a name he had learned from a book, had told to others, but had never called before. "Gogyeng Sowuhti!" he cried.

Near him, a voice, a strong old woman's voice, called back to him. "Come here, pale little hawk. You have run long enough." He turned, and to his astonishment he saw an old woman standing in a cleft in the rock high above him. "Come up here and rest. I am Gogyeng Sowuhti. I am Old Spider Grandmother, and I have your water." She led him into a little space behind two leaning rocks, high up on the side of a cliff where she had built a little shrine, a little web of masonry. She showed him a little barrel cactus, about a foot tall. "This cactus will relieve you of that other cactus," she told him.

"Thank you, Grandmother," he said gratefully. Falling to his knees before the cactus and taking his knife from his boot, he cut off the little nipples from which the clusters of sharp, stiff needles grew, exposing the top of the fleshy green trunk. Then he cut out and lifted off the top like the lid of a jack-o-lantern and began to carve out the juicy interior pulp. He carved, cut up, squeezed, and sucked the plant, and drank almost a quart of water, not sweet like melon, but alive, and good. It took a long time, and it was hard work, but he soon lay back refreshed.

As though he had dozed for a moment, he was suddenly surprised to see that it was already quite light, almost dawn. He lay in the little cleft in the rock, and marveled at the perfection of each photon of sand in the desert mosaic. Then the sun broke over the horizon and he felt the warmth of life flow over him like healing water, and he wept in gratitude. When the tears sprang to his eyes, he saw the Water Snake come out from the brush and climb up onto the flat rock surface. Round and round the Snake coiled, and then it turned upon itself, swallowed itself, and emerged with a head on each end. Then suddenly the little grotto was filled with light. Between the two leaning rocks, Gogyeng Sowuhti stood with her arm extended, and her arm was a dazzling shaft of light like the sun flashing on polished gold, and she reached out her finger and touched one head of the Water Snake, the head which held a fat ripe gourd in its mouth. And the Snake turned around, and began to crawl in the other direction.

As the shaft of light began to fade, he saw that the ancient grandmother had grown young, and was beautiful and flush with life and promise, her dark skin like copper-red mahogany polished with oil and lighted from within. He also saw her eyes were wide with astonishment, as though she were as surprised to see him as he was to see her. For a moment he thought she was wearing not a blanket-woven robe, but a silk chemise nightgown.

He looked, and she was not there. The snake was not a Snake, but a reversing double spiral, carved into the surface of the rock before him. The arm which had reached out to touch the symbol was a beam of sunlight cast by the rising sun through a crack between the leaning rocks. "Today is the solstice," he remembered. "Today is the longest day, the day when the sun cycle reaches its peak and starts back the other way, and the snake she touched has a gourd in his mouth because it is summer." He looked at the other head of the snake, and saw that its forked tongue was in the symbol of a young stalk of corn, for the winter solstice, when the sun, and the lifegiving corn, begin their long slow cycle of return. "This is the shaman's calendar!" he cried aloud, and pressed both palms against the ancient stone, astounded by the secret it had just revealed to him.

"I've got to remember where I am," he said to himself, "and I've got to get back to Kin Bineola." He stepped out of the cleft and his breath caught in his throat at what he saw. He was high up on the sandstone mesa above the wash, and before him the desert moved and flowed in waves like the sea, a sea of straight lines and strata flowing up and down through one another. Nearby yucca stalks pulsed bristle-topped, and swayed not with the wind but as though dancing.

It was incredibly beautiful, and totally unfamiliar to him, but he knew that the pueblo was somewhere northeast of him, up the wash. He put the sun on his right, carefully climbed down from the rock, and began to walk back up the wide arroyo, amazed as it flowed and rippled in peacock colors beneath his feet.

It was mid-afternoon when he arrived back at the ancient townsite where he had left his belongings. Though he was still giddy and light-headed, completely exhausted from the long walk in the sun, and burned in spite of his good summer tan, he had for the most part recovered his awareness of the empirical world to which he had returned. He stumbled into the old ruin and hurried to his pack to get a canteen of water, and as soon as he had drunk some, he became hungry and wolfed two concentrate bars. He ate all of his chocolate, licking the sticky melted paste from the paper greedily, and only then remembered what he had seen in the cleft.

He shook water onto the back of his neck, dampened a loose shirt and put it on, and sat down on the edge of the kiva. He picked up a rock, tapped on it with his knuckles, and threw it down again. Somewhere, a four-hour walk from Kin Bineola, he had seen a shrine built up on the rock, and in it were petroglyphs intended to mark the motions of the sun during the cycles of the seasons. But had he? Had he not also seen a Water Snake two miles long, and had he not been chased by a Kachina made of sand? No, the calendar was real, and he could find it again. He could get a grant, make a computer study of the terrain, utilize students... it would be the find of the century.

As he sat on the edge of the kiva wall, he suddenly remembered what the ceremonial chamber had looked like when he saw it through the eyes of the Peyotl god. Over there, under about six feet of sand, would be the smoking hole Sipapu, and there, by the lowest point in the sand filling the chamber, would be the stone altar. If it were still standing, the top of it would only be about a foot beneath the surface. He chuckled, unwilling to believe that he had learned its true location by the vision. He had seen many kivas, and that was a likely place for the traditional altar. He scoffed, kicking the sides of the wall with his heels and looking away. Then the hair rose on the back of his neck as he felt again the peculiar sense of audience he had experienced in the night.

"Primal fear, the root of superstition," he muttered, and he jumped down into the kiva. "Sure that's where the altar will be. That's where they all are." He took a small shovel from his jump pack and began to scrape at the red sand in the kiva. About a foot down, he found the surface of the altar, and on it a handsome blood-red pipestone pipe, a perfect artifact inlaid with turquoise in the waving symbol of the Water Snake. "Tyler, you've done it again!" he exclaimed in satisfaction. "Call it a hunch, call it luck, call it an educated guess, but this thing is real." He turned it back and forth in his hand and whistled softly. "We just might not need a grant."

Late afternoon, he sat with his equipment all packed — and with his specimen bag loaded with some lithics, points and scrapers, a nice grooved axehead, some potshards, and the exceptional pipe he had taken from the kiva. About six o'clock, he heard a droning, and as it grew louder, he recognized the deep-throated rumble of the Bull Stearman's big P&W, and he stood to spot it in the sky. In a moment, the red-and-gold showplane was circling overhead. He took a canister from his pack and ran toward the wash, pulled the pin, and hurled the smoke grenade to make a plume of purple smoke to show the pilot the wind. The beautiful flying machine floated to a soft touchdown on the smooth arroyo sand, and taxied to a stop near the ruin. The pilot pulled off her helmet, shook out her long black hair. "Well, Professor, did you find the Anasazi?" she asked playfully, smiling in delight to see him.

"Hi, Sakata," he said with a grin. "I sure did." He stepped up onto a footrest and reached into the cockpit to embrace her and to pull her to his lips. When he kissed her she giggled happily. "Barbra, you won't believe what I found," he said eagerly. "Come on, get me out of this place. I need to be in my Jacuzzi, with you."

"Sounds good to me," said the slender little pilot, "but I've got to make a pitstop. You get your gear loaded, and I'll see if I can find a friendly bush."

A few minutes later, they looked down on the little patch of crumbling ancient walls casting long shadows across the desert. Buck Tyler shook his head. "Ghosts," he muttered. Then he leaned back in the seat and let the cooling wind blow past him.

Chapter Two

With the setting sun on her right wingtip, Barbra Sakata set the high-powered biplane down on the strip at Coronado Airport in north Albuquerque. Buck leaned back in his seat and laughed with weary delight as she taxied to the hangar where her father kept his showplane. On the door, and also on the side of the Stearman was painted his logo, Japanese-style letters reading, Alton "Kamikaze" Sakata. His big gimmick on the wing-walking-and-sky-diving circuit was dive-racing. He had a standing offer to pay $10,000 to anyone who could beat him to the ground from ten thousand feet. Buck had tried it once, and when he chickened out and pulled the ripcord, Al was still head-down below him, arms at his sides at 150 mph.

They took her new Nissan and drove up Tramway Blvd to the Sandia Peak Tramway, where they caught the cable car for the ride to Sandia crest, four thousand feet above the mile-high valley floor. Though he made the trip several times a month, and though she had spent several nights in his apartment downtown, it was the first time they had ridden to the crest together. The ride on the world's longest tramway span was exhilarating, and they rode much of the way in silence, holding each other and looking at the lights of The Duke City sprawling below them.

At the top, they passed quickly through the lobby of the resort lodge, hardly drawing a second glance among serious students trying to look liberal in long hair and boutique jeans, blow-combed Hispanics trying to look professional in double-knit suits, and G-rated gringo couples trying to look acculturated in guayabera shirts, square-dance skirts, and turquoise jewelry. Barbra had her long wavy black hair tied up in a loose bun on the back of her head, and her lithe hundred-pound figure was completely lost in Buck's voluminous sky-diver's jumpsuit. Wearing his backpack, shorts, boots, three days beard, and a uniform coat of dirt, he looked like a man who had just come in from a desert backpacking trip — or a really burned-out hippie.

He led her to the parking lot of the lodge, where he threw his gear into the back of his chromed and polished 1970 Eldorado. She settled comfortably onto the tooled-leather seat and began to shuffle through his music. "Sorry there's not much there," he apologized. "I should carry more CD's in the car, but it's only a couple of minutes drive to the cabin."

"Leo Kottke, Johann Pachelbel, jazz by Willie Nelson... these all sound pretty good to me," she said, putting a disc into the player.

Only a couple of miles down the road from the Sandia Peak ski resort toward Tijeras Canyon, Buck turned into the driveway of a small, rather plain-looking cabin tucked among the trees in a piñon grove. Automatically he noticed that the window shutters were still securely in place, concealing the wrought-iron bars behind them from the casual observer. He turned the heavy dead bolt, pushed open the solid hardwood door, and led Barbra inside.

Buck Tyler's resort hideaway was plush and exotic. Though at first glance it looked like a photo spread from a slick men's magazine, a closer look revealed a rustic simplicity in the built-in shelves, polished hardwood floor and bench furniture, and the stonework around the fireplace. The lavish effect of the room was almost entirely the result of Tyler's collection of art and artifacts. The shelves were lined with pots, huacas, and stone tools; carved wooden Uchu and Vodu figures, and strangely-similar Kachinas; with necklaces of shells and seeds, of stone and amber beads, turquoise, and crystal amethyst; with masks, and phalli, and long smoking pipes made of bone. On the amber-warm oak floors lay rugs of fur and wool, fluffy alpaca, yarn-shags in bright colors of Aztlanic sacrifices, and tight-woven subdued Navahos. On the walls hung framed Cuna Molas, reverse-appliquéd cloth panels in shimmering electric color combinations depicting a bizarre vision of tropic island life. The benches were covered by thick pillows, upholstered in crushed velvet and leather.

Barbra had been around a bit for an undergraduate in anthropology, but she still gasped quite involuntarily when he first turned on the light. "Why, Buck, the place is like a museum!"

He chuckled indulgently and set his pack down against one wall. "There are a few really fine pieces here, but most of this stuff is just inventory. Some people like to have real cultural artifacts in their homes instead of other kinds of art. So I keep a few things around. I don't make a pile of money doing it, but it does enable me to have this place." He opened a pair of cabinet doors to reveal the controls of a fine modern sound system.

"I can hardly wait to see the rest of the house," she purred.

"Put whatever you want on the disc player and make yourself comfortable. I'm going to get a bath."

She zipped open the flight suit, dropped it from her shoulders, and turned to him, a Buddha-lipped and olive-nippled pixie. "Put on something that soothes you, and I'll join you in that bath. I'm going to make you comfortable."

"You better watch out," he said with a grin. "I've been eating peyote and running with the Anasazi, and I haven't seen a woman since about 1130... A.D. How about getting that bathtub warmed up? I've got to make a phone call."

She dropped her shorts, wagged her round-muscled, black-bushed mini-buns at him, and disappeared naked into the bedroom. He put on a Chopin disc, picked up his phone, ran through its memory to locate a number, then placed a call. He nodded, not surprised when he got a taped answer. He waited until the machine beeped, then spoke softly. "Gordon, this is Indiana Jones. I just found a really unusual piece, maybe the best one I've ever found, a ceremonial pipe. I don't know what kind of numbers we're looking at yet, but you'd better bring both checkbooks, if you know what I mean. Thought you'd want to be the first to know. Bye, now." He hung up the phone, raised his arms to stretch his shoulder muscles, then sighed and turned happily toward the sound of gushing hot water in the other room.

At nine o'clock the next morning, Barbra sat in her second-row seat in a classroom in the Henry H. Frost Memorial Wing for Anthropology on the campus of the University of New Mexico. At the podium, Dr. Buck Tyler sipped coffee from a large mug and addressed his class.

He began by acknowledging the invaluable student assistance he had received from Ms. Sakata on his research expedition, which got her glares of envy from a few of the others, and which got him a glare of contempt from one rusty-sideburned serious student. He was a wild-eyed Texan out to prove that it was only the Lone Star Republic that had saved the Indians from extinction, by driving the Spanish slave-traders of Mexico south of the Rio Grande.

Tyler described the anthropologically significant events of his long weekend, up to the point of his discovery of the Water Snake calendar in the stone of the canyon. "My mind was so dysfunctioned by the powerful psychoactive drug in the Anasazi ceremonial cactus that I was unable to objectively record much important data, in particular the exact location of the petroglyphic solar calendar." Tyler paused and indulged his class of sixteen students as they passed a knowing chuckle around the room. "I believe I detect an implication that some of you may also have done a little anthropological exploration into the natural pharmacopoeia." The Texan guffawed insolently. He was the one person Tyler knew who admitted to having eaten the deadly datura plant, the white trumpet vine of Castaneda fame, and his description confirmed Tyler's decision to let that particular experience go past him. The young professor nodded, sipped his coffee, and slipped Barbra a little wink. "Just remember, as long as you do it for class, you're an anthropologist. If you do it on your own time, you're a degenerate dope fiend." He let them laugh, then waited a moment before continuing.

"But whether you want to call me a scientific researcher or a drug-crazed lunatic, I believed I was led to that site by a vision of the great Water Snake from Indian mythology... maybe I should say Indian theology. If I had not eaten the peyote, I am sure I would never have run half the night across the desert, and I would not have discovered the calendar site. Because I had eaten the peyote, I could not locate the site precisely on my topographic chart of the area. So what took place? An act of serendipity, luck? Bizarre coincidence, and nothing else? An act of God? Which god, Gogyeng Sowuhti? Maybe I was acting upon hidden knowledge from a past lifetime I spent living in Kin Bineola. Was it my destiny? What are we dealing with here, objective science or manifestation of some mysterious unseen influence? It is along the knife-edge of this paradox that we must tread: if we deny the vision which perceives meaning where the eye sees only substance, if we deny the intuitive vision that can know directly what no eye can see, then our lives are reduced to materialistic goals. If, on the other hand, we deny the empirical, if we deny the fact that facts are facts, and the laws of nature are unbreakable, then our feet soon become tangled in the hard-rock reality, and we stumble, and our vision thus becomes useless.

"Somewhere between these mutually-exclusive views of the world must lie an optimum middle ground, somewhere between the illusory and the absolute, between fantasy and firmament, between prophecy and physics. I believe it is within the proper function of an anthropologist to contribute to mankind's understanding of that middle ground, though some might say it is more properly a job for the psychologists, or the priests, or the philosophers. As I have said before, at least once every class period, and in every TV interview I've ever had...(he got an appreciative chuckle from the class)...it is my personal and professional position that long-surviving primitive cultures often demonstrate a certain deep, very pragmatic understanding of some of the things which are basic to human life. Though these cultures failed over the millennia for one reason or another, some of those basic down-to-earth human-life things they knew may be very valuable in an empirical, practical way to us today. While we grow ulcers and break out in hives under the pressures of such artificial fields of survival competition as commodities exchange and pro football, we may be overlooking a solution to our anxiety that might have been more accurately isolated by people who were working against real survival stress conditions.

"The Anasazi were not into documentation, nor for the most part, were they into making big changes in their environment. The one exception to that is the network of big stone buildings, the pueblos, which cover the Southwest. Our study of these places reveals a high knowledge of long-distance trade involving many tribes and even the development of certain kinds of currency. The discovery of the solar calendar carved into the side of a rock indicates a very sophisticated understanding of celestial motion and its relevance to seasonal cycles. I suspect the deeper we are able to look into their most fundamental beliefs and activities, their mythology, psychology, and religion, the more likely we are to make some discovery which we have been prevented from making by factors within our own cultural belief structure. I mean that one of the factors which make us so much more 'advanced' could be keeping us from knowing something they understood very well. By studying their culture, we can use their vision to peer into areas in which we are blind." He paused to let the note-takers catch up. Barbra Sakata grinned conspiratorially, having heard him make the same speech to her over brie and coffee one recent dawn.

"That sounds to me kind of like a blind man using a seeing-eye ghost to help him find his glasses," said a gray-bristled older student from his seat in the back row.

Buck laughed with the class. "Well, Mr. Simmons, I guess I'd have to allow that it does. However, the fact that I am able to convincingly present that argument to the Department here at UNM enables me to be here, and that enables you to be here for this summer special course. I have read all of your topic outlines — and your completed paper, Mr. Abdulaziz, which is remarkably well-written — and I'm looking forward to reading all of your papers. All of your subjects are approved as submitted, but I've made some notes to some of you." He handed the stack of papers to the student nearest him, and paused to enjoy his coffee. He smiled to see that the tall handsome blonde rancher sitting across the room from Barbra was doing her best to catch his eye without raising her hand or taking off her clothes. "I'll be very interested to see what you write about the dwelling site you believe you have located on your family's ranch, Mary," he said to her, making a mental note to be sure to write a "See me after class" message on her next paper.

"While you all are sweating about how hard it is to write a decent research paper," he continued, "let me tell you about my own little assignment — which some of you might want to get in on. First I've got to make a computer study of the best topological data I can get on that section of the Kim-me-ni-oli Wash. There are only so many places where the canyon wall is at the right angle to the rising sun to facilitate a solar calendar. Using that analysis, I will write a proposal which will obtain the funding to spend a week or two checking out the sites selected by the computer as the most likely. Sometime next spring, I will make the trip into the wash, and I will locate the calendar. I will, I promise! (Another chuckle from his appreciative audience.) Then the real work begins. I write a tentative script for an hour-long documentary film about the Anasazi and the discovery of the calendar, and I sweet-talk somebody like the National Geographic Society into filming it. On the solstice next summer, we go in with the film crew and duplicate what happened to me last weekend... without the peyote. A producer makes a buck on his film, and I get my picture on TV again, which is good insurance against staff cuts in the Department, and which makes it easier to sell my next project for a bigger piece of the action. The Department gets credit for the work in academic circles, which doesn't hurt my feelings too bad, and science goes merrily along.

"I tell you these things so you can understand that our profession is not totally devoted to going on interesting digs and spending nights by the campfire talking to the old people with a recorder in your lap. It takes a certain amount of attention to such superficial matters as position, security, and acknowledged success — that is, the almighty buck — to give you the stability and the mobility necessary to accomplish anything more worthwhile than writing research papers on the published works of others. But it's a place to start, so I hope you take to it with enthusiasm. When you get enthusiastic enough about a research project that you start going after information that nobody else has written down yet, then you're on your way. Then is when you enter the adventurous, back-breaking, mind-bending, and heart-wringing world which is the operating arena of the professional."

He actually got a round of applause from some of the students on that, and with twenty minutes of class time yet to go, he dismissed the class. Casting an amused smirk over her shoulder toward the ambitious cowgirl, Sakata waved to him and departed quickly without speaking. He smiled and put her out of his mind, knowing it was her habit to disappear for a few days after she had spent time with him. The cowgirl stayed for a few minutes, but she saw she would be unable to quickly gain Tyler's exclusive attention, and soon departed. The red-headed Texan immediately engaged the professor in a discussion about the inability of the Spaniards to assimilate the nomadic Chichimec Indians of northern Mexico though the urban-dwelling Aztlanics of the south had been easy victims for their predatory cultural expansion forces. Tyler found the matter of passing interest and made a few comments intended to conclude the conversation on a positive note. He turned to leave, and saw that another person had remained after class to talk to him.

It was John Simmons, a man of about fifty who wore his hair in a gray-bristled flattop, always dressed in wrinkled khaki workman's clothes, and somehow managed to maintain what seemed to Tyler a constant three-day growth of beard. Tyler recalled that Simmons' work had impressed him. He wrote well enough to have developed a style — a folksy semi-historical patter — but seemed to give greater credence to the stuff of rumor and legend than to matters of historical record. His class essay papers were poor science, but good reading. He sat patiently reading a magazine, then looked up and smiled when it became apparent he did not have to compete for Tyler's attention.

"Well, Mr. Simmons, what can I do for you?" Tyler asked.

Simmons stood and stuck out his hand. Tyler shook it automatically. "Dr. Tyler, I know you're very busy, what with teaching and trying to get funded by Smithsonian, or somebody like that, but I just kept thinking about what you were saying today in class, about how a scientist has got to make a buck if he's going to be able to do any kind of significant work."

"It's a useful commodity," Tyler agreed.

"I've got a proposition for you, a project. Travel expenses for about a week, a couple thousand up front, and guaranteed publication of the paper you write when we get back. Interested?"

Tyler took a second look at Simmons, curious. "Sure, I guess so. What do you mean, publication? By whom?"

Simmons handed Tyler the magazine he had been reading, Vol.I, No.2, of "Western Gold Lore", three years out of date. "It's one I published," said Simmons. "I run a little printing operation out of my garage — a couple of magazines like this one, and a line of short paperback books. I'm into lost mines, Spanish treasure caves, missing Confederate shipments, that sort of thing, OK?"

Buck eyed him coolly. "A treasure hunter," he accused, with an undertone of amusement.

"Don't burn me at the stake yet, please. Last time I got that look I was talking about astrology at the planetarium. But look, regardless of our motives, it seems to me that grave robbers, treasure hunters and archaeologists have something in common. That is a desire to discover the intimate secrets of people who have long passed from the Earth, and to use those secrets to improve our own situations in some way or another. I make a living with a mail-order publishing company. Whether we find any treasure or not, we will end up with a publishable report on a very special investigation. You write the report, I publish it and market it on my mail-order lines, and you get a royalty."

"Why me?" asked Tyler.

"I enrolled in this class just to check you out," said Simmons matter-of-factly. He picked up a folder from his desk and handed it to Tyler. Buck was surprised to find it contained newspaper and magazine clippings about himself, including the story from the national personality magazine "Who" about the making of his PBS documentary film on the Penitentes of northern New Mexico. It also contained a copy of an article Tyler had written for an obscure journal called "The Pendulum", published by an organization identified on the cover as ISPI. Titled "Dowsing To Find His Roots", the article described an Indian Tyler knew who used the techniques and devices of dowsing, that is, water-witching, to find artifacts of his ancestors.

Simmons reached across and tapped the little journal. "I want you to get me through to these people," he said.

"They don't participate in treasure hunts," said Tyler flatly.

"I know that. The Inter-world Society of Parasentient Investigators takes itself quite seriously, as seriously as academicians, which is why I need you. I want to pay you to take me to the ISPI Convention next month, as the sponsor of my project."

Tyler shook his head. "Look, they aren't going to lend themselves to a treasure hunt just because I show up with it."

Simmons pulled his face into a taut and self-satisfied smile. "It isn't a treasure hunt," he said, "and I'm not paying you on the basis of their reaction. I just want you to get me there and get me the opportunity to make my case. Can I buy you a drink? Something to eat?"

Buck Tyler shrugged. "Sure, why not, John? I could use a drink, and frankly I don't need much reason to spend a week in Jerome, so how about we go find a quiet booth at Jodido's and you can tell me about this project of yours."

"Now you're talking, Doc." Simmons enthusiastically scooped up his papers and magazines. A few minutes later, they found a booth in the quiet and comfortable basement dining room at Jodido's Mexican restaurant and bar. They agreed to order a pitcher of beer and a double plate of nachos, and Simmons outlined his plan.

"I've got a theory," he told Buck. "I'm not trying to convince anybody to believe it, but it motivates me. I think the ancient Indians, the Anasazi, and their ancestors used to believe that gold had great healing power. Sometimes I think maybe it does, and that's why God supposedly gave it such significance in his instructions to Moses to build the temple. At any rate, I believe if it were possible to locate the places where the people of that culture performed their healing ceremonies, you'd find gold artifacts there. What do you think about that?"

Buck sucked the head off his beer pensively. "I suppose it is as good a totally-unsupported notion as the next," he said.

"Good," said Simmons. "Because it doesn't matter whether or not it's true, or whether or not you believe it. I just tell you because I want you to understand my motivation clearly. I want the members of that society to use the same techniques and parasentient powers they use to solve crimes and locate lost things to conduct a collective search for a particular thing that I'm seeking. That's all."

"You mean Indian healing sites?" asked Tyler.

"Precisely. You are a professor of Anthropology, an acknowledged investigator into the mystical, ceremonial, mythical side of ancient cultures. You have been to their meetings before, and you are published in their journal. If you tell them we are trying to locate places used as healing sites, for scientific purposes, and that you will make professional site inspections of any place they get a lot of agreement on, there's a good chance they will actually make the psychic search." Simmons popped a large jalapeño nacho into his mouth and sucked air anxiously as the hot chile grabbed him by the tongue.

"What if they refuse?"

Simmons shrugged and took a long pull on his beer. "You pocket the two thousand bucks and come home. If they agree to do the search, you can write up the proposal made to them, compile the results of their searches, and then do whatever we want with the data. Maybe we just write it up and forget it. Maybe we go check out some of the sites. If we can find anything at one of the sites, then the article starts looking more saleable, maybe as a small book. If I'm right, and we find gold, I'll cut you in for a nice piece of the action."

Tyler nodded and smiled. "You know, it actually sounds pretty good. We can leave the Friday after the summer school session ends and have a week to spend in the Verde Valley. I'll really enjoy seeing the ISPI crowd again. They are very interesting people. I missed the convention last year, but I was there the year before, when I gave that paper they put in The Pendulum."

"They seem to hold you in pretty high regard."

"Maybe so," Tyler chuckled. "I think some of them figure that anybody from the academic community is most likely too pig-headed to consider them seriously, so it pleases them to have a token scholar on their membership rolls. We'll have a good time. And by the way, I'd like to take a look at some of the other stuff you've published, particularly the books. If we can find something at one of their target sites, we can sell a ton of books through ISPI's mail-order channels. They'll pay plenty for a record of their own success."

Simmons pulled his face into his taut, self-satisfied smile. "I like the practical way you look at things," he said, clinking his beer glass against Tyler's.

Chapter Three

Buck Tyler and John Simmons were delayed getting out of Albuquerque until after sunset on the day before the ISPI meeting, and they drove through the night along Route 66 toward Flagstaff. Buck was disappointed that he could not see the terrain as they drove west through Grants, Gallup, and the sandstone wonderland south of the Navajo, Zuni, and Hopi Indian Reservations. He could not see the pueblos built on the tops of the sandstone mesas, but he knew each of them well, and he smiled when they passed the highway turnoff which led north to the ancient cities in the sky called Oraibi, Moenkopi, and Wupatki. The pueblos were like condominiums built of stone and mud along the flat tops and ledges of high red sandstone bluffs, and though they now housed only a few hundred people, he knew some of them had been occupied for hundreds of years.

Buck enjoyed the drive. Simmons said they would need a 4-wheel-drive vehicle, and he had insisted Buck rent a new Blazer. The truck was comfortable and had a good sound system, and Buck would have preferred to listen to the music and keep his thoughts to himself. To his discomfort, however, Simmons insisted on helping him by keeping him awake with conversation.

"It's a passenger's duty," he informed Buck earnestly. "That and keeping a second set of eyes on the road. I learned that when I was a waist-gunner in a PBY in the south Pacific back in the war. I was just a kid, but it stuck. Every person in an airplane is a member of the crew, an observer. If people did that in cars, there wouldn't be half the accidents."

"Yankee teamwork, right?" said Buck Tyler.

"No joke, it won the war," Simmons agreed. "If we'd have stuck by the lessons we learned then, things would be a lot better today, let me tell you. I had just been discharged from the Navy when Korea broke out, and I came back to

New Mexico to get away from it all for a while. I took my coffee pot and my goldpan and my trusty old Winchester 30-30 and lit out for the hills, and spent the next two, three years up in the Gila wilderness prospecting. I've been hunting for gold veins, lost mines, and missing treasures ever since. I still love to sit on a rock in a cold mountain stream and pan for gold — got to be one of the most relaxing things in the world — and every little once in a while you see a flash of color in there, and you just got to smile. There's no feeling in the world the same as finding gold, even just a little bit of the stuff."

Tyler laughed. "I can sure relate to that, but I get double the kick out of it if I can find something somebody made out of gold a long time ago."

"That is wonderful, isn't it," said Simmons, with his tight, smug smile.

They turned south on Arizona Highway 17, then took the cutoff to Sedona. As they came into Oak Creek Canyon, the sight caught Tyler's breath. There had been a little low cloud cover, light fog and scud, during the night. The sun just coming up behind the travelers was quickly burning off the rising mists, and it cast a pale but perfect rainbow above the towering red cliffs and domes of the spectacular sandstone formations of the canyon.

"God, that's beautiful," Buck breathed.

"A dawn rainbow — a good omen," said Simmons.

Buck pointed to a high slope overlooking the picturesque little town of Sedona. "According to the local folks, there is a psychic vortex up on the side of that slope. It's supposed to be a place where you can most easily make contact with people in other dimensions — kind of a doorway."

"Weirdoes everywhere," Simmons chuckled. "There's a familiar looking place," he said, indicating a prominent outcropping of the towering red rocks. "Seems like I've seen it somewhere before."

"Only in half of the western movies made since Randolph Scott got his first pair of boots," Buck said. "Come on, we'll catch some breakfast at the Gold Dust Cafe." He drove into the center of the quiet little resort town and parked the Blazer on the almost deserted main street. The morning was already warm, and the sun shone with rich-toned intensity on the high red cliffs, and cast cool wet shadows on the waxy deep green vegetation growing in the narrow gorge of the canyon.

They stretched, looked into the windows of shops carrying a variety of Indian-looking paintings, clothing, and craftwork, then went in and sat down in a booth in the cozy little cafe. A waitress brought them big mugs of coffee, which they sipped gratefully until she brought plates of scrambled eggs, sausage, and huge, fluffy homemade biscuits with country gravy. Half an hour later they were on the road again, heading south through the rugged red hills to the Verde Valley, and to the ghost city, Jerome.

When Buck first pointed it out to Simmons, the little town looked like a few buildings and mine tailings high up on the slope of the rocky hillside, but as they drew closer, it could be seen to be a good-sized community of steep-roofed houses and old hotels and apartment buildings several stories tall. It was perched high on the impossibly steep side of the mountain, and many of the smaller buildings could be seen to have struts propping them up on the slope, like the houses in a L'il Abner cartoon strip.

"Good grief," said Simmons as they started up the long switchbacks leading from the valley floor, "what ever made anyone build a town on the side of a hill like that?"

Tyler chuckled. "About half of that mountain is hollow," he said. "Until they closed the mine in 1938, this little place was a major world producer of copper. In fact, Jerome had a lot to do with Winston Churchill's ending up the Prime Minister of England. You may remember his mother was an American named Jennie Jerome. She was one of the family who owned this mine."

"Well, I'll be dipped," Simmons marveled. "I didn't know that."

"I thought you knew about mines, John," said Buck.

"I know a lot about mines," said Simmons gruffly, "but

I've always been more interested in little mines, the kind where some old geezer with a burro strikes it rich. This kind of mine has always looked to me more like industry than adventure."

"This town used to have about fifteen thousand people," Buck informed him as they drove through the narrow winding streets. "These days the population is about six hundred, mostly artists, tourist shop owners, and some old folks who just keep the history alive." He pointed to a large multi-story yellow-brick building on a promontory overlooking the valley. "That's the old high school, where the society holds its conventions. We're a little early, but some of the people will probably be there already."

When they pulled into the parking lot of the old school building, they saw that one of the main doors was open, and when they went inside, they found several people setting up chairs in one of the larger classrooms. They gave Buck and John friendly but noncommittal glances, then one of them broke into a wide-eyed and delighted smile of recognition. "Buck, how nice to see you! I'm so glad you made it this year," she said, and hurried to give him a warm hug.

"Hi, Ivy, it's good to be here again this year," he replied, bending down to return her embrace. She was tiny and delicate, with ivory-white skin, long black hair framing a pixie face, and large flashing dark eyes. "I'd like you to meet a friend of mine," he said. "This is John Simmons. He runs a little printing business in Albuquerque, and he'll be documenting my project this year."

"Nice to meet you, John," she said pertly.

"This is Ivy Jongers, the president of Inter-world Society of Parasentient Investigators," Buck told him. "Her father founded the organization, and she has been running it since he died three years ago."

"I just answer the mail," she said. "The members are who keep ISPI going. We have a wonderful program this year. Alex St. Luc is going to talk about the Sedona vortex, Stan Lidey will do a presentation on Huna and the works of Max Freedom Long, and Sharon Hightower is going to talk about psychometry. I'm hoping we'll get a visit from Beth, too."

"Beth?" Buck queried. "Oh, yes, I remember. Beth is Ivy's spirit contact," he told John. "I remember Alex and Stan, too, but who is Sharon Hightower?"

"You'll love her," said Ivy with a knowing wink and a grin. "She is Indian, from one of the tribes of northern New Mexico, and the best psychometrist I know of. I've seen a lot of para-normal things, and I have some talent myself, but I still get goosebumps watching her work. The detail she gets is just astonishing."

"Just to be sure I know what you're talking about, what is psychometry?" asked John Simmons.

"Psychic touch reading," Ivy replied. "She can touch a ring, or some other personal item, and she gets all kinds of data about the people who have owned it in the past. Last year Alex St. Luc — he's a dowser and psychic who lives here in the valley — spent a couple of months trying to verify some of the things she got in her readings at the convention, and he got real confirmation on almost every detail. She is also very well known for her forensic work, and she has solved several crimes, including the kidnapping of the daughter of a Senator from Illinois back a couple of years ago. Maybe you remember that case?"

"As a matter of fact, I do," replied John, impressed. "Wasn't that where they found the child buried in the garden of one of his political opponents, but couldn't get conviction because the information had come from a psychic?"

Ivy snorted with disgust. "That was the one. The court said it was an invasion of his privacy because she didn't have his name on a warrant when she made the psychic search, and the warrant they issued to investigate the garden after her search was declared illegal because the court wouldn't acknowledge that her information constituted sufficient cause to issue it. They even tried to indict her for withholding information about how she knew where the body was buried. The defense attorney said the only way she could have known was to have been involved in the crime herself."

"You know how it is," Buck concluded wryly. "Lawyers don't give a hoot for the truth if it gets in the way of legal process."

"You should talk," she teased him. "Scientists don't care much for the truth either, if they can't work it out on their computers."

"Well, I for one am delighted to hear you have a touch reader," said John enthusiastically. "I have brought some things related to our project which I sure hope she might give us a reading on."

"Yes, your project sounds really exciting," said Ivy. "I told Buck on the phone it was too late to put you on the official schedule, but I'm sure we'll have time to let you present your idea. In the meanwhile, can I talk you two big strong men into helping us set up the room?"

Buck and John pitched in to help, and they had the chairs, slide projector, and tables ready for the meeting before time for lunch. Simmons brought in a box from the Blazer and took from it several pieces of what looked like a little boy's junk treasures — a few pieces of rock, pottery, and wood, and a weathered old glass bottle turned purple by years in the sun. He put them on one of the tables.

"Just what kind of things do you publish, Mr. Simmons?" Ivy asked him, looking at the pile of things.

Simmons laughed self-indulgently. "Oh, a little of this and a little of that," he said. "I have tried all kinds of things that have caught my interest over the years. Mostly western history, I guess, and stuff for the mail-order market. I did a series on the tax revolt a few years ago — Fifth Amendment tax return, good faith challenge return, that sort of thing. I gave that up when it became apparent nobody cared that the IRS and the Fed have long since junked the Constitution. My favorite was a magazine on the legends of the Southwest, lost explorers, missing Confederate cannons, that sort of thing. I also put out three issues of a magazine on UFO's and the unexplained — you see what I mean."

She laughed, a merry tinkling. "You and Alex will get along fine, I'm sure. He's a UFO nut, too. He has some marvelous tapes he made of conversations he had with Beth, my oversoul contact, about UFO's."

"Oh? How does that work?" Simmons asked.

"It works good," she said. "Actually, I trance-channel Beth, and she talks through me. I don't get to hear it until I play the tapes back later."

"So what did she say the UFO's are? Spaceships, right?"

"Not really. She said they are visible psychic projections used by people from a parallel dimension to visit our world. When astral travelers here on earth go out, they sometimes psychically create an astral body to travel in. Apparently in that dimension they prefer to create astral vehicles. Same principle, different shape. How about some lunch? If you and Buck don't have other plans, maybe you'd like to join me for a sandwich."

The main street of Jerome was a winding switchback which worked itself up the side of the mountain, and the buildings looked as though they had been built on a staircase, with each row higher than the last. As they drove into the center of the little town and parked the truck, they could see along the top most level a row of beautiful old homes with high peaked roofs and gingerbread-trimmed bay windows. Most were in a state of crumbling decay, with gaping windows, broken glass, peeling paint, and sagging porches. The few which were clearly occupied had the appearance of Aquarian-age restoration — macrame plant-holders, hanging tapestries, astrology symbols painted on the walls, and the like. The lowest floors of the old business buildings had been converted to gift shops, antique shops, art shops, and tiny restaurants, their windows filled with the remnants of mining and refining paraphernalia, and the household goods of seventy years ago.

"That's the Spirit Room," Ivy told John and Buck, pointing to a corner saloon where several chopped and chromed motorcycles were parked. "It's the night spot in town, and the top floor is still kept up as a hotel. If you don't have other plans, I recommend you get a room there. It will take you back a generation, and the beds are comfortable."

She led them into a cafe, a long room with a high ceiling and big slow-turning fans. The walls were covered with framed photographs of the town in its heyday, streets lined with square black cars and groups of rough-looking miners wearing floppy fedora hats and huge moustaches. A long-haired young waiter swished across the room to greet Ivy with a sisterly kiss on the cheek, and led them to a table.

"Oh, there's Sharon Hightower now," said Ivy, waving to a young woman sitting with some other people at another table. Buck looked at her with friendly curiosity, and was surprised when she glanced up at him, gasped as though startled, then blushed and dropped her eyes. He too was shaken with a deep and unreal sense of recognition, as though both knew they were not strangers in some other world. He could see she was small like Ivy with long black hair, but round-figured and dark. Her face was wide, with high strong cheekbones, soft dark doelike eyes, a small sharp-planed nose, and a generous mouth. Her dark skin glowed with the rich copper-red overtones of the American Indian. She wore a long purple skirt in pueblo style, but of a lighter material than the heavy velvet favored by the women of the reservations. Her hair flowed smoothly down her back, held from her face by two small braids which met at the back of her head. Her blouse was bright blue and loose-fitting, and the way she moved under it seemed just, just right. For a moment, the ISPI convention was forgotten as he indulged himself in speculation of amorous adventure, perhaps as though to reassure himself that were to be the subject of their immanent destiny, and not something more portentous.

She and her party were just finishing their lunches, and they stopped briefly on their way out to let Ivy make introductions. Sharon shook his hand and smiled with gracious professionalism that told Buck she was used to a lot of public exposure. "I know who you are," she said to him. "I live and work in Santa Fe. I'm a Social Services liaison to the

Indian tribes. You have quite a reputation, Dr. Tyler... for scientific work, that is."

He laughed. "Maybe it would be better if I left it at that... and it's Buck, please," he said. "I have heard something of your reputation also. Ivy tells me you are a visionary."

"My people acknowledge the spiritual vision, and I was raised with it," she said with a little moue. "I didn't know it was something unusual until I started going to school with white people."

"Ha! Sounds like you've been listening to my lectures," he said.

"I have," she confessed. "I've considered contacting you, but my work hasn't left me the time. Are you going to present a paper at the convention? I didn't see your name on the schedule."

"If there is time," he said, giving a nod to Ivy. "I hope you might be interested in working on a project Mr. Simmons and I are organizing."

"Maybe," she said, flashing her dark, soft eyes at him. "Please don't let me keep you from your lunch. It was very nice to meet you, and I'm looking forward to hearing about your project."

He shook her hand again, with both of his, then sat a moment and watched her as she saucily tossed her raven-sheen hair and left, unable to take his eyes from the smooth round curves of her wide hips.

Ivy kicked his leg under the table, and he turned guiltily to see her grinning at him. "I told you you'd love her," she said. "But watch out. She's hard to lie to." When he tried to cover his embarrassment with a wide-eyed, innocent, and hurt expression, she chuckled. "I've heard something of your reputation too," she told him.

Chapter Four

The convention drew a good crowd, about forty people, a few of whom had come from as far away as St. Louis and New Bern. Most were either residents of the Verde Valley or Sedona, or had come from the affluent psychic community in Phoenix.

Ivy Jongers welcomed the group to the convention and introduced the first speaker, Stan Lidey. He was young and slender, with wide bright eyes, a boyishly sincere smile, and an air of relaxed but aggressive eagerness. He had flown to the convention in a silver-and-black Rotorway personal helicopter, which he had deftly landed in the parking lot of the school.

"I'm the first speaker because I'm going to talk about Huna, which gives us a good frame of reference for understanding what is actually going on here with this business of parasentient investigation," he began, speaking from a comfortable desk chair he had placed on the raised dais at the front of the classroom. "Huna is the ancient psychic science of the people of Hawaii, the Polynesians. Some people call it the Hawaiian religion — including Max Freedom Long, who made the definitive academic study of Huna only about sixty years ago — since it makes use of ritual magic and acknowledges higher spiritual levels than human consciousness. I prefer to call it a psychic science because that is what they actually used it for, doing those things we would call psychic phenomena.

"Parasentient investigation as it is presently being practiced relies heavily on three psychic techniques: dowsing, channeling, and psychometry. These are very different forms of gaining information, but the fundamental principles of Huna are a good way of explaining how all three work... and the fact is that they all three work the same way!

"The best known form of dowsing is what we call water-witching. You know, finding water in the ground with a forked stick. But there are a lot of other forms of the technique. Some people say that Moses was water dowsing when it was recorded that he struck water from the rock with his staff. By dowsing I mean any use of a mechanical device operated by the dowser to obtain information which is not accessible to the normal physical senses. In addition to forked sticks, which some people call Y-rods, other people like to use L-shaped angle-rods made from bent clothes hangers, spring-loaded wands, Hieronymous boxes and such psionic devices, and lots of people like to use the pendulum in one form or another. Psychometry means touch-reading, obtaining information about past situations by touching or otherwise contacting something which was present in those past events. Channeling is the word being used these days for what we used to call being a medium."

Lidey looked enthusiastically around the room, assuring himself that everyone understood what he was talking about. He moved his chair another foot closer to the front of the dais, and continued. "The Kahunas, that is, the Huna practitioners, regarded man as a trinity, a three-level entity, having a Low Self, what we would call the autonomous and subconscious minds, a Middle Self, what we would call the conscious mind, and a High Self, what we might call a superconscious, or spiritual mind. The Hawaiian word for that high self is aumakua, which basically means spirit father. The aumakua, the oversoul, the spirit entity, is not limited by the physical senses like the conscious mind, and it knows things about the world and can do things in the world that the conscious can not. But because of the conscious mind's concern with ego, emotion, and sensation, the aumakua usually can't communicate with the conscious directly. However, the communication between the aumakua and the low self, in Hawaiian called the unihipili, is much easier, particularly if the conscious willingly permits it." He paused to sip a glass of ginger ale, then continued.

"Huna is no longer widely practiced in Hawaii. When the Christian missionaries made enough money selling sugar to take political control of the islands, they made Huna illegal.

Most Huna techniques were used for healing, and for causing effects upon human relationships, and also for the cursing or destruction of opponents. It is probable they had techniques for gaining information about what we would call navigation and meteorology also, since they lived so close to their environment as sea-faring people. The techniques all involve ways of accumulating the psychic energy — mana — necessary to send messages to the aumakua requesting certain action or information. Then through the Kahuna's willing submission of control of his body to the subconscious, the low self is placed in a state where the answer can be manifest. All three of the parasentient investigation techniques I have mentioned can be easily explained using this frame of reference.

"The dowsing method is the most complicated, in a way, because it relies on the use of a mechanical device. The dowser agrees to let certain motions of his dowsing device mean certain things, then he asks a particular question, takes the device into his hands, and prepares himself to receive the answer. Then he takes the motions of the device to be the requested information, in the code agreed upon. The supposition is made that the superconscious mind understands the question and can tell where the water is — that is, the aumakua is clairvoyant — and is willing to reveal its location to the dowser. It is able to control the body at the subconscious level to make the device move in the correct pattern at the right time. In a more sophisticated form, a pendulum is held in the hand, and its motions are used to choose letters from a board like a Ouija-board. When it starts spelling out in plain language things you don't know until you read them, you're on the right track, and you have entered into the realm of channeling.

"The thing which sets channeling apart is that the agent supplying the information takes on the characteristics of a distinct personality, and often passes information in the form of personal conversation. Here the mechanism is the same. The aumakua, your own superconscious parasentient high self, or some other aumakua-level being, is permitted to take control of the body through the subconscious low self, and to speak or write things directly. As I'm sure all of you know, that is how Ivy is able to channel Beth, who is certainly one of the most delightful, wise, and spiritually profound persons I have ever had the pleasure to meet. For those of you who have never met Beth, or who have never seen any of the videotapes of the channeling sessions, I can tell you that she is quite a different person from Ivy, even if she does use the same body. Her gestures, facial expressions, voice, sense of humor, use of language — all are very different. And she knows things about all sorts of things that Ivy could not possibly have learned through her normal senses."

Ivy laughed and put in, "I'll say. Sometimes I have to go do a lot of reading and research just to understand what she was talking about. And so far, she has always been right."

"In the third form, psychometry, the aumakua is able to send information to the conscious mind not just from another place, but from another time," Lidey continued. "The information is presented to the consciousness directly, bypassing the normal sensory system, and coming across as a complete full-sensory moving picture — at least, that's what Sharon Hightower has told me. Most psychometrists I know of indicate they just get impressions of one kind or another. What is implied is that there is a kind of superconscious memory, and that memory is somehow associated with every tangible thing in the present-time objective world. The concept matches what some other mystics and mediums have called the Akashic Record.

"The Kahunas said there is a spiritual substance, a sticky stuff called aka, which forms threads to every thing a person knows of or touches psychically. Living beings have an aka body — like an ectoplasmic aura — around us, and the Kahunas practiced psychometry by following the aka threads, or by extending their own aka out to contact things. I see a certain parallel to the electron paths in the memory banks of a huge computer. And this collective aumakua memory, connected by aka to every thing, contains a record of every event that has ever occurred, or has ever been experienced, or has ever been known in the world. And further, the aumakua is able to gain access to that memory, and to present it to the conscious mind in the form of mental pictures very much like normal physical sensations.

"What is taking place in all three cases is the same. The middle self — the human psychic person — uses some method of requesting the superconscious high self to locate specific information not available to the senses, and to transmit that information to the conscious mind through the subconscious low self by some kind of action or sensation of the body."

Stan led the group through some basic mana-raising exercises involving deep breathing and visualization, and everybody began to relax and enjoy themselves.

"I see a trip to the south Pacific in my future," Buck said aside to Simmons. "That supports my hypothesis that spiritual understanding is most likely to be found in cultures with lower technological development."

"You mean, you think engineers and mystics don't mix?" Simmons asked him.

"They don't much like each other, do they?" Buck chuckled.

Alex St. Luc, the speaker who followed Lidey, was a local dowser and writer who claimed he was in contact with a person in the parallel dimension of Atlantis whenever he was sitting in the exact center of the Sedona vortex, the location of which he had discovered by dowsing using an angle-rod ball-bearing-mounted in a pistolgrip. He was a tall gaunt man like an El Greco saint, with the comic sad-eyed face of a borzoi hound. He had a certain angular awkwardness about him, as though he had been assembled of body parts that did not all match in size.

"The world of the Atlanteans and our world spiral about each other like the strands of a DNA molecule," he said, with a high reedy voice. "They never actually touch, but are constantly in a pattern of relationship. It is really pretty simple if you can think in more than four dimensions. In the way in which the stack of pages of a typed manuscript occupy the same two-dimensional space, but are stacked in a third dimension, the moments of our lives are three-dimensional pages, stacked in the same three-dimensional space, but extended into a fourth dimension. By looking at them in sequence — that is, by moving along that fourth-dimensional axis — we obtain the experience we call time. Now take that axis of sequentiality and bend it into a spiral. Viewed from inside, it still feels like time is going in a straight line, but viewed from outside, that is, from one dimension higher, it is seen to go in cycles.

"Atlantis occupies the same three-dimensional space as we do, but its axis of sequentiality is one-hundred-eighty degrees out of phase with ours. Seen from outside, we spiral around each other. Now take the axis of that double spiral and bend it into a circle, and fasten the ends together. The two worlds meet and join like a five-dimensional Mobius loop. From inside, we each see the other as appearing to be in the extreme past or the extreme future. By looking across the spiral, that is, by looking ninety degrees from our own axis of sequentiality, ninety degrees from our time axis, we can see into Atlantis as it is today.

"When I am sitting on that hillside in Sedona in the center of the psychic vortex I can do that, and I have learned to communicate with somebody over there. He comes to sit in the vortex also, on his side of course, and we can chat. The languages are different, but the meaning gets across — like the vortex was a kind of psychic modem that lets one computer talk to any other kind of computer. His name is Beeackque, and he is an avuncular sort, always ready to fill me in on the latest news. Unfortunately, what I get from him is not exactly enlightened stuff. It is the kind of celebrity fortune-telling gossip that passes for psychic revelations in the supermarket tabloids, goofy stuff about the love lives of local politicians — I mean local in his dimension, Atlantis. They are more aware of parasentient phenomena over there, and tend to take it for granted. I think he considers me like the kind of contact people have over amateur radio. You know, 'What's your call sign, how's the weather over there, and did Aunt Winnie ever have that baby?' Right. I have never tried to get in touch with his superconscious, but his conscious doesn't know the first thing about where the loot is, or whodunit over here. Uncle Beeackque is exactly worthless as a parasentient investigator, believe me."

He got a good round of laughter. "So we can forget about him," he continued. "However, before he died a few years ago, and wrote the final chapter in the most recent of his long string of lifetimes, Ivy Jongers' father Bill taught me everything he knew — well, everything I know, anyway — about location dowsing with a map and a pendulum. I like to use a six-and-seven-eighths-inch chain, same as my hat size, and a small brass pendulum bob. I'm pleased to say it works pretty good for me, and since I live here, I can sit down with Ivy and run a complete map survey on every case which is sent to ISPI for a psychic search. It's a lazy man's way to do the job, and believe me, I don't have much use for anything that takes me away from my little spread over by Red Rock Crossing, or that starts looking too much like organized labor. It's good to be a psychic, right? I can live in Sedona and work anywhere in the world."

St. Luc spent a few minutes demonstrating the basic techniques of map dowsing, using his pendulum directly over the map. He also showed a method preferred by some other map dowsers, involving the use of the pendulum over a target card marked to indicate directions and distances, and a separate pointer on the map. Though some pendulums were passed around, and everyone enjoyed going through the motions of conducting a basic map-dowsing search, the segment was concluded several minutes before the time allotted.

Ivy suggested it would be a good time for Doctor Tyler to make his presentation. She introduced him as a professor of anthropology, an adventurer, archaeologist, and a published expert on mystic and psychic powers in different cultures all around the world.

"Don't let all those fancy titles throw you," Buck told the group. "Titles are what they give to academicians and bureaucrats instead of money, the way they give medals to soldiers and athletes. Actually, I think most of my conservative colleagues would prefer to call me a professional dilettante, a pothunter, and a superstitious publicity-hound." He nodded wryly at the group's understanding laughter.

"The reason I do the things I do is that I believe we can learn a great deal about the true nature of human life by studying cultures which were — or are — very spiritual minded, like the Huna culture Stan spoke of. Another group which seem to have been very spiritual minded are the Anasazi, the people who lived in this part of the world before the Navajo and the Hopi, and who built these huge pueblo and kiva complexes which we find in ruins all over the southwest. There is much evidence to suggest that these places were kind of like religious convention halls. That is, they were not places in which people lived full time, but were like hotels where the Anasazi gathered to participate in mass spiritual activities of one kind or other in the kivas. Every one of these great buildings has at least one of these big round underground ceremonial rooms, and some of them have as many as eight or nine.

"I believe the Anasazi very likely took advantage of certain places, like the Sedona vortex for example, where psychic forces are more effective than at other places for healing. If I could find some of these places, and document some kind of objective evidence that they conducted ceremonial activities there, it would support the notion that they used psychic or spiritual healing techniques."

He got a good murmur of positive comment from the crowd, and every eye was on him. "There is a problem, however. The problem is that psychic vortices and psychic healing sites don't show up in the physical world. There is no ball of blue light, no sword in the stone to show us where these places exist. The only way they could be located is by psychic means." He stepped down closer to the edge of the lecturers' dais and looked around the room dramatically. "The reason I have come here today is because I believe if anybody in the world is capable of locating those Anasazi healing sites, it is this group of people assembled here in this room right now. You, the members of the Inter-world Society of Parasentient Investigators."

The group of psychics applauded. "I have come with Mr. John M. Simmons, who is a publisher from Albuquerque," Tyler informed them. "That's him there sitting in the back of the room." Looking more like a janitor in his rumpled khakis than a journalist, Simmons raised his hand and passed around a grizzle-bearded grin. "What we would like to do is to conduct a psychic search for Anasazi healing sites," Tyler continued. "That is, we would like you to conduct a parasentient investigation, which we will document. Whatever parasentient technique you happen to use, we will direct toward locating psychic healing sites here in Arizona, in Utah, Colorado, or New Mexico. We will record what you find on a map, or on tape, or by drawing, or whatever is called for. Where agreement shows up in the search, I will actually go to the site sometime in the next few weeks, and I will record what I find there, in the manner proscribed by the science of archaeology. If something significant shows up, Mr. Simmons is prepared to publish a book I will write on the project. So what do you say?"

The group applauded enthusiastically, and Ivy suggested they all take a break for a few minutes, and then return to decide how and when Buck Tyler's search should be conducted. During the break several people came up enthusiastically to congratulate Tyler on his work, and to offer their support. He was delighted when one of those was Sharon Hightower.

"To be honest," she said, "I have suspected you of being a dilettante and a pothunter myself, but I admit I find this interesting."

"Well, that's good to hear," he said.

"The Anasazi are my ancestors," she told him. "We

have always been more conscious of spiritual matters than the Europeans, both the Anglo and the Hispanic groups. The Anglos are too intellectual to believe in the subtle visions, and the Hispanics are kept blind by their superstitions. I would really like to see you find what you are looking for, just to let the so-called civilized world see who we are."

"I am more and more impressed every minute," said Tyler, drawing her off to one side, "and I am delighted you're interested in the project. I'm really looking forward to the chance to work with you."

"Oh, really? Doing what, Mister Tyler?" she asked innocently.

"Well, uh, doing this search, to begin with," he replied, "and please... it's Buck, ok?"

"If you insist."

"It's Buckminster, actually. My Daddy was a rocket scientist at White Sands. He named me after Dr. Fuller."

"I see. I'm sorry, I thought it was just a little too cute," she confessed. "So OK, Buck, but I'm not sure what use I can be. My vision only works in the other direction. I can touch a thing and get impressions, but I've never been able to start with an impression, and find a thing that matches it." She paused to let him register his disappointment, then added, "but I'm sure we'll be able to find something. Aren't you?"

"I am sure," he said, and permitted himself to be interrupted by Alex St. Luc.

"Buck, that sounds like a great idea," Alex said eagerly. "How about I coordinate the map-dowsing part of the search as my demonstration? We've already got the equipment passed out."

The program schedule called for two hours before supper break to be devoted to parasentient readings on cases sent to ISPI for investigation. The group eagerly agreed to devote that time to Buck Tyler's project. Alex provided the group with a stack of maps, and drawing paper and pencils, and let them do their thing. Several used pendulums, and others worked with pointers and wands.

Another used a Y-rod to obtain lines of direction and distance, which he plotted on his map. Several of the parasentient investigators did not use maps, but drew impressions of one kind or another on paper. One drew a portrait of an old Indian with a strong wise face and deep wide eyes focused upon infinity. On the horizon behind him rose a butte, not a vertical column like the sandstone towers of Sedona or Canyon de Chelly, but a steep-sided flat-topped mound. "Red", the psychic wrote, drawing an arrow to the butte.

One of the older women used a pendulum over a letter board, a system she called her "talking pendulum." While she held it over the board, it swung back and forth, changing the angle of its swing to indicate one letter after another. When she had finished her reading, she brought it to Tyler written letter for letter on a piece of paper. "I'm sorry," she said, "I usually get so much more. Sometimes I get the most beautiful quatrains. But all of this is just gibberish, except that the word 'pity' appears five times — and it's the only legible word there."

John Simmons was sitting nearby, and he turned with interest when he heard her. He looked at the paper, then smiled, shrugged, and put it with the others. Buck got the distinct impression that it meant more to him than he wished to reveal. He made a mental note of it, and went on to other things.

Ivy Jongers, Sharon Hightower, and a few of the others went into a small adjoining room which had once been a teacher's office, so they would have privacy and quiet while Ivy tried to make contact with Beth. After a few minutes, Ivy began to nod dreamily like an opium eater, then all at once she sat up and began to speak in a voice quite unlike her own. Beth recognized Sharon immediately, and began to converse animatedly with her. She was willing to speak about all sorts of interesting things, but would not offer any comment at all about Buck Tyler's interest in the Anasazi. She stayed only a few minutes, then departed leaving Ivy sagging asleep in her chair.

Alex collected the maps, drawings, and notes, and Buck thanked the group profusely and promised to keep them informed about the results of the project. Ivy called for a supper break, and most of the conventioneers went together to a restaurant in Jerome. The place had been decorated using timbers, lighting fixtures, ore cars, drills, and other equipment taken from the mine, and it was a fascinating museum of mining engineering. It was clear that Ivy and Alex were well known and liked there, and the staff went out of their way to show they considered the ISPI convention to be an important event in their little town. The marinated venison prime rib, roast turkey, and country-baked ham were excellent, and the group got quite mellow drinking the fine Sonoma County wines which the owner, Perry "Tinker" Bell, selected himself on his frequent trips to California.

At eight, they returned to the classroom. Ivy hoped to be able to give more of the members the opportunity to meet and talk with Beth. There were two others whose parasentient ability also was manifest as a separate personality, and they also hoped to enjoy good channeling sessions. Sharon Hightower had promised psychometric readings, and several people had brought items for her to hold. John Simmons returned immediately to his hotel room above the saloon, to begin compiling the results of the afternoon's parasentient investigation. Buck Tyler took a seat among the group with Sharon, and settled down happily to watch the show.

Chapter Five

"When I was a child I took my vision as something quite natural," Sharon Hightower told them. "I was taught by my grandmother and by the Medicine Chief of my clan to use it — or more accurately, to let it happen."

Buck Tyler leaned back in his chair to watch her, hardly listening to what she was saying. He had generally found himself less attracted to Indian women than to others, but he was drawn to her more strongly than he felt comfortable with. He expected to enjoy the demonstration, but in spite of his participation and status in the group, he put little credence in the tall-dark-stranger impressionizing of psychometrists and scryers. Yet there was something about her that drew him, as though she were someone he had known a long time, and didn't quite recognize. He tried to dismiss the notion as the usual grist of a convention romance, and assured himself he would permit himself to indulge the fantasy just as much as was needed to attract her.

"When I was twelve, I was sent away to a mission school," the young woman told them, speaking from a chair on the edge of the dais. "In school I was told that my vision was a childish fantasy, that it was not possible to do what I said I was doing. If I insisted what I knew was true, I was punished for lying. In church I was taught that my vision was real, but evil. The pastor and the other people of the church used to gather around me, and put their hands on me, and pray that I would be delivered from the demon spirits which brought me the delusions, sometimes all night long. I learned pretty quick to keep my mouth shut, and I learned to keep myself busy with the tasks at hand, and not go looking after visions. After a while I almost forgot. I started to believe that it really was just a fantasy of my childhood."

She caught Buck's eye and smiled warmly, and he was suddenly aware that he had been staring slack-jawed at her, the room and the other people quite forgotten. He smiled too, feeling a little foolish.

"I became accustomed to keeping to myself," she continued. "I had been taught in my tribal family life to be obedient, and so I did what I was told to do, and I said what I was told to say. After that, they always treated me very well, and I could devote myself to education, which I loved. After six years at the mission school, I was able to enter college. I studied psychology, education, and social work at the University in Albuquerque, and when I got my degree, I went to work for the State as a social work administrator."

She paused to sip iced tea.

"So there I was, a grown woman, an acculturated Native American, educated, and employed. Then two things happened which challenged everything I had learned. First, my grandmother died, and a few days after she was buried, she came to visit me. I saw her in the vision, of course, and she brought her whole world with her, her hogan, the rocks and clouds, her sheep. It was as though I had gone to visit her. She told me that all I had learned did not change who I am. She told me that people could declare whatever truth they wished, but that would not change what I had seen, or what I could see. It was a very disturbing experience for a Christian psychologist, even one with my background."

Buck laughed, appreciating the irony of her position, and becoming more impressed with her. He began to get the strange feeling that he had heard her tell this before, and that he already knew what she was about to tell him.

"That experience freed me of both of those forms in which I had been trained, though I continue to practice both," she said. "Then something else happened. A friend of mine disappeared, a woman with whom I worked. She had been gone a few weeks. It was in all the newspapers, and nobody had the least idea where she was. I went into her office to get a reference book, and I sat down in her chair to read it... and I knew what had happened to her. The details are not important, but it was not pleasant, and it was not over.

"I was confronted with the knowledge that I was going to have to call up the magic of my childhood, and to learn to live with it. I was going to have to use it to find my friend, and then I was going to have to go to the authorities and convince them that I knew where she was, and what was going on, so they would go to rescue her. The alternative was to call it superstition, to tell myself it was coincidence, and to continue to mind my own business."

Buck knew she could only make the right choice, the choice with courage and love. She smiled at him again, and he felt the space between them grow tangible. He noticed the solidity and strength in the full curves of her compact body, and the fluidity and economy of motion with which she used it, and he was surprisingly aroused.

"I went to her house, of course," she said. "I touched her things, and I tried to remember the little Indian girl who knew how to see them. When I was sure of what I knew, I went to the wife of the State Governor, whom I knew from her involvement in social work. We went to the police, and my friend was saved. Of course, I did have to go before a Grand Jury. They had to be convinced that I was not concealing material evidence. That wasn't the last time I was put on the grill for knowing things only a witness could have known. It has been five years now, and my background has been documented well enough that the law enforcement agencies just take what I give them, and they cross their fingers, and nod and wink, and say, Thank you, Ms. Hightower, we'll check it out. Then when they go check it out, they say, 'I'll be darned. It's a good thing we check out all these crackpot leads, or we never would have solved this crime'."

The group laughed, and some began to applaud, but she went on quickly. "So far the National Enquirer hasn't slandered my love life, or called me an extra-terrestrial, and my vision has become a beautiful and very wonderful part of my life. Maybe best of all, it has enabled me to meet wonderful, gifted, and loving people like you."

The group laughed again, and applauded enthusiastically.

Most eager of them all was Buck Tyler. "I've got to find out where she is staying tonight," he thought, and when she turned to face him and laughed also, he flushed hot, sure that she had heard him.

"There it is, my whole life story," she said. "Now let's see what we have here this evening." She stepped to the long table placed on the lecture dais to hold the speakers' materials. There were some of Ivy's tapes of sessions with Beth, several small books her father had written and locally published, some assorted pieces of antique jewelry and household goods, and the box of rocks and bits of glass and rusted metal which John Simmons had left. She ran her hands over some of the things casually, picked up an interesting-looking old brooch, then set it down and took from Simmons' box an old sun-purpled glass patent-medicine bottle. "This is practically shouting to be picked up," she declared.

She brought the bottle back to her chair and sat down in front of the group of people, holding it lightly in both hands. She took a few slow, deep breaths, unfocussed her eyes, and stared off into space for a moment.

As Buck watched her, the hair suddenly stood up on the back of his neck, and he felt perspiration break out on his forehead as he became aware they were watching him. It was the same peculiar sense of presence he had felt in the kiva at Kin Bineola. "Good lord, I'm having mescaline flashbacks from that peyote," he thought, as he watched a glow begin to form behind her, as though her body were brightly back-lighted. The colors of her skin, hair, and clothes became richer, as though wet, and he was struck again by her radiant beauty, the doll-like perfection of her features, high-cheeked, full-lipped, and flashing-eyed.

He felt a moment's trepidation, a sort of stage fright, as though he feared the judgment of the unseen watchers he could sense mocking him just out of sight. As he had learned to do when using the hallucinogens, he released his fear and submitted himself to the experience. He let himself appreciate her, let himself flow out to her unshielded, and sat in awe of the wisdom and the beauty of spirit which shone from her.

He watched her become more like the women of the reservations, with her hair braided up in the style of the Hopi, and wearing the heavy dark-colored skirts and velvet blouse of the Navaho. Behind her, in the glow of her aura, he could see the massive granite spires of a rugged mountain ridge baked tan as crust in desert sun, and the rust-red of the little outcropping of sandstone on which she sat. He could smell the spicy aromatic smoke of a mesquite fire, and the pungent oily musk of creosote bush. Over him flooded a warm sensation of affinity, and of appreciation for her, and for her people, and for the vibrant goodness of God manifest as an Indian woman. Tears sprang to his eyes. He could see that she was speaking to someone, but he heard only his heart beating in time with the throbbing of a tom-tom.

Then as he watched her, she changed again, and he was astonished to see it was not Sharon squatting beside the mesquite fire in the little red sandstone grotto, but an old man, an old Indian. His long hair was still black, but streaked through with gray, and his dark, deep-set eyes gazed with patience from his wrinkled and tanned face as he tapped his hypnotic rhythm with a long slender bone on a little drum.

He blinked, and it was again Sharon, sitting on her chair in the middle of the grotto, holding the bottle in her hands. She looked at him, their eyes met, and both were surprised to recognize they shared the vision in common. The schoolroom in Jerome and all of the other people had dissolved, leaving the two of them staring at each other in astonishment in the midst of the peculiar fluid world of the vision. He felt visceral disorientation, and the light of the vision suddenly waned. He saw the schoolroom again on all sides of himself, but as though viewing it from a distance.

"There is more," she said to him, holding her eyes locked with his. Recklessly, he abandoned his disbelief, and allowed himself to be drawn into the raven-bright obsidian-clear windows of her mind.

They saw a street, wide and dusty, between the low adobe buildings of an old Mexican town. The sky above was overcast, with clouds the same grainy sepia as the dust and the mud brick walls. The clouds swirled eerily behind the stark unmoving skeleton of a leafless tree etched in jagged darker planes in the monochrome tan. They saw chickens scurry, and dogs slink into ochre shadows as a dark enclosed wagon moved with funeral slowness along the street, pulled by two dark horses which galloped fiercely and silently. The steam from their bodies swept back in tendrils from their withers and swirled to mix with the dust churned up by their hooves, and whipped past the saturnine face of the driver of the wagon to flow into the eddies of the stormy sky.

He was tall, angular, and heavy, drawn in severe straight lines, none parallel. He wore black, for the most part, black as an undertaker's top hat and a physician's frock coat can be with a patina of sepia dust. His shirt was ruffled like a gambler's, and he wore a bone-handled Colt revolver in the front of his belt through an opened button of his vest. He wore his face shaved clean, but for long spidery sideburns in salt-and-pepper gray. The lines of his face were many and deep, but without expression, fixed in a dour countenance. His eyes were hidden behind smoked glasses, flattened-hexagon lenses in wire frames. He raised his hand, turned to face Buck and Sharon, and held up before them the patent-medicine bottle. The horses' hooves began to thunder, and the sound was the booming of the Indian ceremonial drum.

"I have a name," said Sharon to the group sitting raptly before her in the schoolroom. "His name is... a Hebrew name... no, no, that's not right. It is Hiebert... Heebs. Reverend Heebs. Yes, I'm sure that's it."

Buck was surprised to find himself instantly back in the schoolroom, and to find that he remembered having been there all along, listening to Sharon describe to the group the impressions she had received from the bottle. He was also surprised to find that he had held up his hand for her attention. "What about the old Indian?" he asked her. "Who was he?"

She smiled, and her eyes twinkled. "That's very interesting, Buck," she said. "I didn't mention him." The others turned to look at him, and they laughed delightedly at the dumbfounded expression on his face. "I may have your answer, though," she continued. "I see here on the bottle that the name of the product or company is molded into the glass. See, it says, 'El Cacique'."

"Ah," he said, as though that explained everything. "El Kasiki... and what do you make of that?"

"It is the name which sometimes has been given to the senior Medicine Chief of the Indian tribes in a region," she said. "It is actually a misnomer, since a cacique is technically an Indian who is given political power by an occupying colonial government, whereas the Medicine Chief has no political power, but is given authority by the people because of his spiritual wisdom."

"Of course," said Buck, "a good name for a patent medicine."

"Yes, isn't it? Let's have a look at some other things."

He watched her read from another item, but he kept himself apart from her and listened to her describe what it was that she saw. Then when she took a break, he got up and went into another room to listen to Beth speak. Half an hour later, the sessions began to break up, and except for a few of what were clearly going to be all-night raps, everyone left to retire for the night.

Sharon smiled and waved at Buck as she left the classroom, and for a moment he stood abashed and sweating like a schoolboy, reluctant to step up and confront the woman with whom he had just shared an astonishing intimacy. Then he hurried after her. "That was a very interesting reading," he said.

"Wasn't it?" she agreed.

"I've never seen anyone do anything like that before," he said. "Does...does that sort of thing happen to you often?"

"What sort of thing?" she queried, walking briskly down the long hall.

"Well, I mean when...when other people...do other people

ever tell you that..."

"That they can see it too?" She looked at him sharply, but with amusement. He nodded. "No," she confessed simply. "That was a first time for me, too."

"I see," he said. "Wow." They walked in silence the rest of the way to her car. He opened her door, then held it open after she sat down. "Are you staying here in Jerome?" he asked her.

She waited a moment before answering, then said, "Yes. I come here several times a year, and I stay in an apartment which belongs to friends. Why do you ask?"

"Well," he said, "I thought maybe we could spend some time together...this evening."

"Oh. It seems to me there isn't much left of the evening but the rest of the night," she said.

"So how does that sound?" he asked.

She turned to look at him, and asked, "Are you sure you really want to?" For a moment his knees weakened, and he felt a rush of vulnerability remembering how she had shared with him a part of his being he had never been in before, and knowing she was a person of power there. "No, Doctor Tyler, I don't think so," she said conclusively, before he had time to register and react to his feelings. She reached out and closed the car door. "See you in the morning, Buck." Then she smiled delightedly and leaned out of the window to grasp his hand. "Wasn't that an amazing experience, though?"

"I'll say it was," he gushed. "I've...I've never..." He grinned lamely, and squeezed her hand. "Good night, Sharon," he said.

He found John Simmons waiting for him in their room above the saloon. "Well, how did it go?" asked Simmons. "Learn any thing?"

"I'll say I did," said Buck with a weary laugh. "I met my first bonafide psychometrist tonight. Say, tell me something. For what purpose did you bring that box of rocks and junk?"

Simmons chuckled. "Just to see if anybody would get

into it, and to have some things if anybody asked for
something. Why, did somebody get into it?"

Buck told him what Sharon said she had seen when she
picked up the bottle, omitting his own experience. When he
told him about El Cacique crouching beside a fire in a rocky
grotto, John put down the paper he had been reading and sat
up seriously. Then when he described the dark saturnine
driver of the wagon, Simmons began to pace around the room
in agitation. "She said his name was Reverend Heebs," he
concluded, "and I assume he was the man who sold whatever
was in the bottle."

Simmons sat back down and ran his hands over his stubby
gray flattop. He shook his head and slammed one fist into
the other palm, one, two, three. "Kiss my mother dawg," he
declared. "Come here. Come look here at this master map."
He led Buck to a table and showed him where he had plotted
the results of the individual parasentient searches. The
ISPI members had made twenty-eight searches, and John
had transferred them all to the master. Most of the sites
indicated were solitary marks, scattered across the
northern deserts of Arizona and New Mexico. One site near
where Buck had jumped into the Kim-me-ni-oli Wash had
three marks. One site had eleven marks, all grouped very
close together. Simmons put his finger on it. "Here," he
said.

Buck frowned. "That is south of Truth or Consequences,
John. There isn't much archaeological data to indicate the
Anasazi got down that far."

"I know. I know," said Simmons, "but listen to this. That
bottle was used to sell El Cacique Indian Medicine Tonic in
the early 1870's. It was very popular for about three years,
then the company suddenly went out of business. They
operated out of a little town called Lastima, New Mexico."

"OK," said Buck. "That fits with what Sharon saw. But
what is our connection?"

Simmons pulled a Geodetic Survey topographic map from
a pile near the master map. "This is the sector where those
eleven positive readings fall. See, right here where the Rio

Grande bends on the big map. Now, look here on the topo. There is the river bend just north of the ruins of old Fort Selmore. See that little town there, so small it doesn't even have a paved road into it? Read it."

Buck bent down and looked closely at the detailed small-scale map. "Lastima," he said, feeling his neck begin to prickle again.

"Lastima!" said Simmons triumphantly. "It is astounding, Buck, just astounding. I couldn't have asked for better. Hell, I would have been ready to jump on half this much corroboration. Here's the clincher." He tossed Buck the paper on which the woman with the talking pendulum had written the scrambled letters her swinging crystal had selected. "Lastima is the Spanish word for pity!" he said.

Buck noticed that John had brought a six-pack of beer to the room, and he opened one for himself. "I guess we tell the group tomorrow morning, right?" he asked.

Simmons shook his head. "No. No, what we do instead is pack up and leave. You tell Ivy that you have to get back to the University, and ask her to tell the group you'll send the results as soon as you finish compiling the data, and then we are pulling out."

"Back to Albuquerque?" Buck asked, frowning in confusion.

"Buck, I'm going to up the ante," said Simmons. "There is another two G's in it for you if you will stick this out for another week. We're going to Lastima."

"You mean to try to find that site?"

"Exactly," Simmons confirmed. "Which brings us to the catch."

"Catch?"

"Yeah," said Simmons, eyes squeezed almost shut by his tight, smug grin. "You have to persuade Sharon Hightower to come with us."

Chapter Six

Sharon rose early and went for breakfast to the Go-4-Broke Cafe, where Buck had first seen her. She smiled and greeted a few other ISPI visitors, but chose a seat in a secluded corner. She ordered without looking at the menu, spooned honey into her coffee, and had just begun to dig into a plate of *huevos rancheros de chile verde* when a man stepped up to her table.

"*Ya-at e-heh,* Hightower," he said, using the Navajo greeting common among several of the southwest tribes.

She looked up surprised to recognize the tall barrel-chested and long-haired young Indian, a man about thirty, who stood gazing down at her with a certain distain. "Asher Quaptewa! What are you doing here in Jerome?"

"Missionary work," he said dryly. "May I sit down?"

She gazed at him with cool appraisal a long moment, then sighed and nodded. "Politics," she said. "Sure, sit down, Asher. Have you eaten breakfast?"

"I will have some coffee," he said, taking off his tall feather-banded hat. He signaled the waitress, sat silently for a moment, then asked, "How is your...what do you call it, a seminar? How is it going?"

"Fine," she answered, continuing to enjoy the hearty platter of eggs, corn tortillas, beans, and green chile sauce.

"What do they have you doing? Looking for robbers? Parlor tricks with old jewelry?"

"Something like that," she replied noncommittally.

"You should use your gift for our people, Hightower," he said abruptly. "This is sacrilege."

"Look, Asher, you have been trying to tell me what I should and shouldn't do as long as I can remember," she said, setting down her fork. "If you have come here all the way from the reservation just to give me a bad time about using my vision for whatever I want to, you can save your breath and go home."

"No." He shook his head, accepted his coffee from the waitress without acknowledging her presence, and drank it hot and black. "It is more than that. I am not here on personal business... though I do have a very personal interest. This is about the preservation of an endangered people. Our people, Hightower. Our resources are being taken away from us, and in return we are given the white man's machines to destroy the land, the white man's materialist addictions to destroy our people, and the white man's churches to destroy our spiritual understanding. You are one of the resources which has been taken from us. You could be very important to us now, more than ever. You could do something about what is happening...if..."

"If what?" she demanded. "Asher, I am doing something about it. I work where the changes are actually being made, and I would like to think I am having a real effect on the future. The real future is not a narrow-minded tribal future, but the future of the United States of America, including those of us whose ancestors came from the caves of New Mexico." She shook her. "Unlike you, I am not just drumming up the emotions of old men at the tribal waterholes by yelling for radical and completely impossible goals."

"Yes, I am a radical," he conceded. "I know it no longer considered possible to seal off the reservations, and to drive out all of the influence of the white man, but I will always continue to speak out for doing exactly that. Most Indians do not agree that should be done, so I guess that is why you call me a radical when I say we should be who we are."

"No, Asher," she said curtly. "I am saying we should be who we are. You are saying we should be who we were."

He nodded solemnly. "I follow your work, Sharon. I listen to your speeches, and I read your reports. You are a radical also, a radical in a position of influence, and what you are doing makes me want to throw dirt in the air and howl like a chained wolf. I am trying to find some way to make all of the tribes see that anything we let the government do for us, and anything we buy from the machine-state will eventually destroy us. We will all become like them, and then there will be no more of us. There are many of us in all the tribes who believe we should find ways to reduce government influence over the tribes, and to minimize our contact with the white man and his ways. And then I read that you are proposing the abolition of all the reservations! That is not just radical — that is madness! It is genocide!"

She nodded, and thanked the waitress who had brought her fresh coffee. "Most reservation Indians do not like that idea either," she said archly, "but it happens to be the one course of action which is in accordance with the reality."

"What reality?" he asked hotly. "The white man's reality, the destruction of all of us!"

"Wake up, Quaptewa," she said patiently. "We are not destroyed just because we no longer live like stone-age man. We are still here, and we have every right to take advantage of our opportunity to become anything we want, bankers, senators, or astronauts."

"What if we want to be Indians?" he demanded.

"This is not 1880, Asher, and it is certainly not 1580. There is no longer a separate nation, if there ever was one, of Indians apart from Americans. We are all just Americans now, and we all came from somewhere, even Indians. Our ancestors may have been here a thousand years, but you and I are really like first-generation immigrants. We're the newest Americans. If we preserve our cultural heritage, it will be because it is meaningful to us, and we will do it ourselves, no matter what our position in American society. We do not need laws to force our own cultural limitations upon us. We certainly do not need a separate set of laws which impose on us an obligation to remain undeveloped. That would reduce the Indian culture to some kind of a museum exhibit, a living diorama."

"I agree with you about that," he conceded, growling. "What we are being made to do with your programs is to preserve our culture by staging our tribal rituals and ceremonies for the benefit of tourists and television cameras. It is a mockery, Sharon, a set of commercial formulas like Christmas. What are you going to give us next, robot kachinas and Kiva Kids dolls?"

"What do you want me to do, Asher?" she asked. "Do you expect me to go back to work next week and start saying we should close down all the reservation schools and hospitals, and tear the plumbing out of our homes? You know I am not going to do that."

"No, Hightower, I do not expect you to do that," said the strong, broad-faced young man. "But I have come to make a request."

"A request. Well, all right then, what is it?"

"I remember you when we were children together," he said, shaking back long black hair plaited down the sides. "Even then I saw you were close to nature, and you had the wisdom of nature. But you have been taken from nature, and made to see things another way. You have been taught in school to think in certain other ways, and perhaps you have forgotten what it is to live the life of an Indian. Sharon Hightower, I ask you on behalf of our tribe, and on behalf of our race. Before you become a powerful person in the white man's government, come back to our pueblo for a time, not as a visitor from the outside, but to live, and to see if you can remember who you are. Then you could go into government as our champion."

"And not as the white man's lackey? Is that what you are implying? Listen, Indian, who is this white man you keep talking about? General Custer and who else? What about the black ones, and the brown ones, and the yellow ones?" She paused, and lowered her voice. "Every kind of people make up America," she said, "and the fact that we have an identifiable cultural heritage does not make us different from all of those others. It makes us the same as all of them."

He stood and picked up his tall black flat-brim hat from the chair beside Sharon. "I won't keep you," he said. "You have studied the ways of the white... of mainstream Americans, and you think you are ready to make changes which will affect the lives of all Indians. But you do not know the ways of the Indian. You do not know what there is to preserve, and that is probably why you do not give it much value. When you were sent to that mission school over in east Texas, you were only a child. Now you are a woman, and you have proved that you are intelligent and unafraid. I believe you will see what we are asking is very sensible. Come back to the reservation, and live there for a few years, and learn the ways of your own people also. Then when you have seen both sides of the river, then make your own decision as to where...or if...we should build bridges." He stopped, nodded, and put on his hat. "Goodbye, Hightower," he said, and turned to leave.

"I will think about it, seriously," she said to his departing back. He nodded curtly without turning, and left the cafe.

A few minutes later she saw Buck Tyler enter the now-bustling cafe, looking around anxiously trying to appear quite casual. He spotted her, grinned winningly, and headed for her table like a puppy. He stopped behind the chair Quaptewa had just vacated. "Hi," he said. "You, uh, you really get up early."

"It's the early bird that gets," she said.

"It's the early worm she gets, don't forget that," he said. "May I join you?"

"Please do. Sleep well?"

"Could have been worse," he said. "Simmons kept me up half the night with the results of that search. Look, Sharon, I want to begin by apologizing for last night."

"You don't have to," she said, spooning more honey into her coffee, "but go ahead. I'd like to hear it."

The waitress brought him coffee and a menu. He glanced at Sharon as she cleaned the last of the egg yolk and chile sauce from her plate. "I'll have whatever she had," he told the woman.

He put his hands in his lap, then on the table. "Sharon, I guess that must have looked like a typical convention-hall pickup, pretty crass. But it wasn't, it really wasn't. It was some thing very different, and I just didn't stop to think how it would appear. Sharon, what happened in that classroom had me pretty shook up. I'm still pretty shook up about it. There is something about you that draws me to you, and I can't deny that I find it a bit frightening. The... the intellect is stimulated, as a scientist, an anthropologist, and, and... the psychic implications are just astonishing, and I can't deny either that I find you very disturbingly attractive... sensually. So I guess I just manufactured myself a romantic fantasy, and acted on impulse."

"That's very nice of you, Buck, and I'm sorry it didn't work out the way you dreamed it," she said, "but I'm afraid I'm just not that impulsive. I know too much about where impulses come from...and where they lead. What happened to us in the room is something I can no more explain than you can — but we both know it is a real thing, whatever it is. If it really means we have some special kind of relationship, we will find out, won't we?"

He stared at her solemnly. "I guess so," he said finally. "We'll just have to trust...our fate, I guess. In the meantime, I have another proposition for you."

"Now that is penitent," she exclaimed, laughing.

"No, no, this is a professional proposition," he assured her.

"You couldn't afford it, believe me," she bantered.

"If you're getting what it's worth, you're probably right," he countered. "But seriously, I have a professional offer to make you, Sharon Hightower, professional psychometrist, Buck Tyler, anthropologist, writer, lecturer, and blah, blah. Want to hear about it?"

She studied him with amusement. "All right. I'll listen."

"Thanks. First, let me say that I don't want to make any premature announcements to the ISPI convention today. We haven't compiled proper reports on the data, and we haven't followed up on any of the results yet, so we are not going to make a statement. However, we did get enough positive readings on one spot that we are going to make a special trip to go there, leaving today, if we can. We want you to come with us."

"It is the site with the bottle, isn't it?" she said positively. "It is El Cacique's medicine cave."

He nodded. "El Cacique was a tonic, bottled in a little town called Lastima, New Mexico, which turned up in several of the parasentient searches. We want to go there and do some investigation. Simmons has the historical material on it, I will do a scientific archaeological assessment, and we need you to make a psychometric investigation on the site. You said you would like to find a way to work together, and the truth is I'm not sure we can do this one successfully without you. It would be a few days, that's all, maybe three or four."

"I see," she said, packing butter into a fluffy sourdough roll. "I seem to remember it was you who said he wanted to find a way to work together, but we won't worry about the little details. Just what am I offered for my professional services, other than your lily-white body, I mean?"

"Ouch!" he winced. "You bite pretty deep, for a nice girl. The truth is, we can't offer you very much, I'm afraid," he said lamely. "Your expenses would be covered, of course, and we could probably arrange for a small honorarium, maybe a few hundred dollars."

She shook her head. "Actually, I was planning to take a short vacation and spend some extra money just fooling around. What else you got, Professor?"

"How about documented acclaim?" Tyler suggested. "About half of my act is getting my name in print, so I know how to do it. You could count on full recognition in all the reports, books, or whatever we do on the project. I'll get you in the National Enquirer, I promise."

She laughed. "Now that actually sounds pretty good. However, I would not be able to leave until tomorrow in any case, since I've agreed to stay through the convention. But your trip sounds interesting, and I can't deny I find you interesting, too, Buck, so I will think about it." She stood and picked up her slim leather purse, and Tyler noticed for the first time she was wearing a light and very stylish summer dress. "Ask me again later," she said condescendingly.

"I'll do that," he said, standing also and preparing to leave with her.

"Here comes your breakfast," she said, pointing to the waitress approaching. "You had better hurry, or you'll be late for the first session." She left quickly, leaving him staring with jaw agape at the huge plate of *huevos rancheros.*

"She ate all this?" he asked himself in disbelief.

As Buck Tyler addressed himself to the plate, another person got up from the table closest to him, one separated from view by a row of plants in long macrame hangers. He was very thin, very white, with a long black moustache and short hair, and he was dressed in the jeans and leathers of a Harley-cult fanatic. He paid his bill and left the cafe in a leisurely fashion, then strolled up the hill from the Go-4-Broke Cafe to the Spirit Room, where he found Asher Quaptewa waiting for him.

A few hours later, the young tribal traditionalist met Sharon in the parking lot of the school building. "I must talk to you," he insisted, getting into her car with her.

"What is it, Asher?" she asked impatiently. "Something you forgot to tell me...on behalf of the tribe, of course?"

"Girl, don't you know who that man is?" he demanded.

"What man?" she asked innocently.

"Don't treat me like a stupid redskin, Hightower. He is a grave robber, a treasure hunter! Don't you know he just wants to use you and your vision, the vision of *Gogyeng Sowuhti,* a gift to our people, to desecrate our sacred places? Don't you see that?"

She looked at him sharply, her dark eyes flashing. "I see that you have become psychic yourself," she said coldly, "or else you have ears in very strange places."

"I told you I have made it my business to know what you do."

"For the tribe."

"Yes, for the tribe! Yes. You are a very special member of the tribe, Hightower, and you are in a position to do a lot of good, or a lot of harm. I do care about the tribe...and I care about you, too."

"About me?" she said, surprised. "What is this I'm hearing? What do you care about me? You are a thorn in my side, a troublemaker who gets in the way of everything I have tried to do for our tribe, and for the Navajo, and the Hopi, the Zuni, the Tiwa, for all of us." She stopped, then turned on him accusingly. "You don't mean you are going through all this just because you don't like seeing me with white-eyes?"

He sat silently for a moment, clenching his jaw and breathing deeply. "When I was a boy," he said, his voice gruff with emotion, "I watched you beginning to become a woman, and I said, 'This is what I want from life — the high desert, a horse and some sheep, and this beautiful Indian woman to be my wife.' When they took you away, I promised myself I would not let them take you forever. I would go after you, and bring you back."

"Well, I certainly never suspected that, Asher," she said softly. "I'm very flattered. On the other hand, I'm sure you must recognize that I am not very likely to let your adolescent fantasy run my life, neither my professional life nor my personal life."

He nodded solemnly. "I know. I have no right to tell you anything, and no reason to expect that you will listen to me. But I tell you this, and I hope for the sake of our people that you will listen to me. You are dealing with things that you do not understand. You must not associate with that man. You must not go anywhere with him, and you must not prostitute your vision to his desire to rob us of our past as well as our future!"

"I see. Well, I must do what I must, mustn't I? If you are finished now, would you please get out of my car? I have only an hour for lunch." She turned her head away from him and waited silently while he got out of the car and closed the door behind him, then she drove away without looking back.

She ate at the Go-4-Broke cafe again, and sat with three

of the other conventioneers, enjoying a lively conversation about parasentience, and its future in society. Then she spent the afternoon casually placing herself in Buck Tyler's view, and making a show of politely keeping him at a distance. During the break just before the final hour-long session of the convention, she approached Buck at the water-fountain in the hall. "Enjoying the presentations?" she asked him.

"Yes, actually, I am," he said. "I'm glad we stayed."

"I've been thinking about what you said," she began, "and I have almost come to a decision."

"Almost?" he asked, bravely trying to muster a friendly but completely-respectable smile. "What's left to decide?"

"I have almost decided to go," she said, "but it all depends on one thing."

"What's that?" he asked.

"It depends on what happens tonight."

"Tonight?"

"I don't think I want to spend my vacation cooped up in a motel somewhere with a man who doesn't do something for me," she said, looking boldly into his eyes. "So why don't you come up to my apartment tonight about eight, and if we're still talking when the sun comes up, we can get an early start."

When the evening's activities at the ISPI convention hall were wrapped up, Buck met Sharon leaving the building.

"Hi, that was really interesting, but I couldn't think of anything but you. So... your place?"

"I've changed my mind," she said.

"What? I mean... why?"

"I just don't think I can handle it, that's all. But I have decided to go with you."

"You have? Well, OK, that's great."

"But I want to leave now, tonight."

He looked at her, perplexed, disappointed, but ready to take advantage of her mood. "Now? Well, all right, I'll go fire up John."

"You do that," she said. "I'll get packed."

Chapter Seven

They hit the Camp Verde entrance to Highway 17 at 9:00, turned south toward Phoenix, and put some music on the cassette player.

Buck drove, with Sharon beside him. Simmons sprawled comfortably in the back seat, smoking a sweet aromatic pipe mixture and enjoying a Dave Brubeck tape he had brought along. "I'm just tickled as can be," he said enthusiastically. "I've never seen anything like it. I consider it an honor just to be the publisher on your project, Doc, and Miss Hightower, you can't imagine what a thrill it is to see a psychic of your caliber working with him. Even down to getting the name right — it's just astonishing."

"What's that about the name, John?" she asked.

"Heebs," he said. "I made a couple of phone calls to, ah, some historical sources I use, and I found out that 'El Cacique' was a tonic bottled in the 1870's by a company called Morton & Heebs, in Lastima. I'm hoping we can find the site of the old bottling plant itself. That's why we're going there, in fact."

"What do you expect to find there?" Sharon asked him.

"I'm hoping you can pick up a lead of some kind which will give us the link between the tonic and the Indian healing site we are looking for," he informed her. "If we make use of whatever channels you can pick up with your psychometry to find the site identified by the parasentient searches, then we have the basis of our book to support Buck's theories." He spread his hands and beamed expectantly at her.

"It would really be a shot in the arm for ISPI, too," Buck put in.

Simmons kept a running line of chatter going. "So whaddya think? You want to hear about my mail-order multi-level free traders club, or do you want to tell me about your experiences as a psycho spook for the cops?"

"Oh, is that what I am?" she asked. "Well, I have always

wanted to meet a genuine chain-letter scam artist, so why don't you tell me about that?"

"OK, but let me warn you," he said, "I'm not going to try to get you to buy into this. You're going to have to beg me to let you in. OK, here's how it works..."

They had a late lunch in Tucson, then finally dropped down from the lava flows of the west mesa into the Mesilla Valley of central New Mexico about 6:00.

It was a hot afternoon, and the sun was still two hours high in the sky. Above the Organ mountains on the east side of the valley rose a huge anvil-topped thunderstorm, a rumbling free-standing column of boiling clouds driven up into the clear summer sky by the jagged sun-baked ridge of rock which rimmed the valley like a crust. They decided to check into a motel in Las Cruces, and then to drive up the valley north to see if they could locate Lastima.

The little town was not marked at all. They found it by following the topographic features on the map Simmons had used. "We must be pretty close," Buck told John. "We're north of the old fort, and south of that hill there marked Tenuco." He looked around and saw only a few adobe buildings and old cottonwood trees. The entire area was sparsely built up with scattered new residences, many of them converted mobile homes, but there was no centralization to identify a town. One building caught his eye. It was an old adobe church, a squat single-story hall with thick, sloping walls and a tall bell tower. "Let's ask at the cathedral here," he said.

The church had a small courtyard surrounded by a low adobe wall, and as they entered through an old wooden swinging gate, Buck was struck with a strange sense of disjointedness of time. He glanced at Sharon, who just smiled. The sun was settling low in the west, casting a warm subdued light over the valley, a light the same mud-brick sepia as the adobe walls of the church. There was a small garden in one corner of the courtyard, and though it appeared to be well tended, it was sparse, and dry.

"Gosh, look at these doors!" exclaimed John Simmons,

reaching out a reverent hand to touch the beautifully carved heavy wooden doors of the little church. "These look like they ought to be in some kind of a museum, not drying out here on the front of this nowhere place."

Sharon reached out and touched the doors also, then drew back her hand. "There is something terribly sorrowful about them," she said. "Someone put his heart into these doors, and it was broken."

The doors had been fitted with a modern lock, but it was open, so they went inside. It was an elegantly simple church, a place which had not changed in a century, with sturdy handmade pews, unpadded but highly polished, and with niches in the walls containing beautiful carved wooden santos, icons of the saints. The sanctuary was dominated by the most beautiful carving of all, a petite but lifesize statue of the Virgin of Guadalupe, dressed in sky blue. Framing her compassionate face was a real lace mantilla, an ancient hand-knotted spiderweb of Spanish linen thread, turned a warm sepia by the long years.

"May I help you?" asked a deep voice. All three of them were surprised when they saw the priest step through a door into the sanctuary. He did not look like a twentieth-century cleric. Absent were the lightweight black suit, the stylish business haircut, the wristwatch and the briefcase. He was a large man, slender but strong looking, apparently in his late 40's. He wore the floor-length cassock and tonsured pate of the Franciscan friars who had first brought the Church of Rome to the valley in the 1520's.

"We are looking for the old townsite of Lastima," said Buck.

"How interesting," said the priest. "We get a few visitors here, mostly collectors of out-of-the-way churches who see us from the road, but you are the first I can recall who have come looking for Lastima. You are in Lastima. Your truck is parked in what was the town plaza, and for one hundred and thirty-two years, this building has served as the Temple of Almighty God, and a shrine to the Blessed Virgin of Guadalupe. I am Father Justiano."

"How do you do, Father," said Buck, stepping into the sanctuary to shake the padre's hand. "I am Buck Tyler, of the Department of Anthropology at UNM. These are my associates, Mr. John M. Simmons, an Albuquerque historian and publisher, and Ms. Sharon Hightower, a noted Native American psychic."

"I see," said Father Justiano. "Then do I take it you are not of the Catholic faith?"

"Uh, why no, I'm not," said Buck, taken a little off balance. "I've had a pretty broad background in religion, which I guess keeps me from settling on any one of them."

"Lutheran by birth, heathen by choice," said John Simmons, with a friendly grin.

"I was saved through the Body of Christ Non-denominational Mission," said Sharon.

The priest put his hands into his sleeves and smiled very tightly and very politely. "Perhaps then I might inquire as to your interest in Lastima?"

Buck explained briefly that their project was part of the research for a publishing venture, and he told how the members of ISPI had located an Indian healing site near Lastima, and had concluded it was somehow associated with a patent medicine company called Morton & Heebs. "We hope to find the actual place where the healing site was located, and to obtain some kind of archaeological evidence."

Justiano stared at him a long moment before speaking. "You used witchcraft?" he asked.

"Oh, no," Buck assured him. "Not witchcraft, extra sensory perception, ESP. It is a natural phenomenon."

"And it has led you here? Most interesting," he mused.

"We were hoping maybe you could help us find the site of the old Morton & Heebs bottling plant," said Simmons.

"Perhaps you would like to come into my office where we can sit down," said the priest. He led them into a small but comfortable room in the back of the building. It was set up as an efficiency apartment with a small refrigerator and stove, and a large desk. On a narrow bench built into one wall, a bed was made up, covered by a heavy brown blanket pulled tight like a soldier's bunk. Along one wall a set of shelves bore a number of books and other objects. He motioned them to chairs which sat before the desk. "You know, the story of Orville Heebs and his Indian Medicine Tonic is very much a part of the history of this town, and of this church," he told them. "Do you know about it?"

"No, we don't," said Sharon. "We are just now discovering it. If it doesn't take too much time from your work, could you tell us about it?"

Father Justiano hesitated a moment, then nodded. "Well, all right," he agreed. "The whole incident began because of a lapse of faith on the part of Padre Cabrito, the priest who founded this church in 1850," he began, speaking in the manner of a tour guide. "He was a fascinating character, unorthodox almost to the point of heresy, and not actually ordained by Holy Church until several years after he had firmly established his ministry here. It was probably a mistake, I mean to have accepted him into the Diocese. He was half-Indian, an Apache, and apparently he retained a certain degree of pagan superstition, no offense intended, Miss Hightower. The fact that he had not been trained in the discipline of faith by an established seminary was probably the root of his weakness. He suggested as much in his final confession, which he wrote down and committed to the archive of the church."

"Is that document available for historical research?" asked John Simmons.

The priest looked at him with patient astonishment, nostrils flared in distaste. "I should say not," he declared. "It is not an historical document, it is a record of the sacrament of confession. For me to permit it to be used for secular purposes would constitute a betrayal of God's confidence."

"Ah, yes, of course," agreed Simmons.

"In fact, it was just such a lapse of confidence which allowed the influence of evil to predominate in Lastima," Father Justiano continued. "You see, Cabrito was tempted to believe in witchcraft, and he abandoned faith in the healing sacraments of Holy Church."

"Excuse me, Father," Sharon interrupted, "might you have some item of Padre Cabrito's personal effects, something he used or wore, which I might examine?"

Justiano frowned at her intently, and for a moment the three explorers thought he was going to simply ask them to leave. Then he nodded with a tight little smile, as though agreeing to a bet, or a duel. "All right," he said. "Yes, I have some of his personal effects." He stepped to his shelves, and brought back an old and worn rosary, its thong dried and stiff. The crucifix was rough carved from a piece of mesquite root, and it was dark and smooth with the rubbed-in oil of years of handling. He presented the beaded mnemonic to her by holding the crucifix at its base and dramatically thrusting it at arms length before her, like the vampire hunter of a horror film.

For an instant Buck expected to see her fall writhing to her knees with red light and smoke gushing from her eyes. Then she took the string of old wooden beads from Justiano's hand gently and smiled at him. "Thank you, Father," she said warmly. "My, what a beautiful thing this is. You can practically feel the man's character just flowing from it. But what did he have to do with the tonic seller?"

"Well," he said, sitting down again. "Yes. That was Heebs, the Reverend Doctor Heebs, he called himself, though there is no evidence to suggest he was either. He had come out of the south somewhere after the Civil War, and was making his way here as the local dentist, bone setter, undertaker, and seller of one kind of tonic or other. He also was known to preach, and the accounts which remain of his activities suggest he was an orator of considerable talent, a man capable of creating an atmosphere of hysteria by railing against sin and calling upon the holy name of Jesus Christ. Apparently, Padre Cabrito found Heebs' blasphemous use of that most sacred name to sell his wares to be very amusing, and it is reported that he often attended Heebs' so-called revivals."

Buck cast a sidelong glance at Sharon, who sat primly on

her straight-backed chair, holding the rosary in her hands, and gazing with rapt attention at the priest. Quite suddenly, the hair rose on the back of his neck, and he felt a sound around him, a sound like sand sizzling across a flat expanse of rock. He took a deep breath and exhaled it slowly, hoping the shuddering he felt would not show. He crossed his legs and tried to assume a nonchalant air as he watched her, waiting with some inner apprehension for something to happen.

As he listened to the familiar high bleating voice of the little Padre, he felt reassured, soothed by the knowledge that he could so clearly see the face of the gringo medicine man. He had been a handsome man once, but the war had made his face hard and cut with lines of pain, and then booze had made it soft and shot with tiny veins. His eyebrows bristled over piercing hawk-like eyes, and his skin looked like old parchment that had been crumpled and stained by years of careless handling.

"He told us he had been a surgeon's aide with the Army of the Confederacy," said the voice of Padre Cabrito. "He was left behind after the defeat of the Confederate forces at Glorietta Pass, and he wandered south through the mining towns, Winston, Chloride, and Mogollon, before settling in Lastima."

At a small gathering like a town fair, Buck saw Orville Heebs standing on the lowered back gate of his wagon, his tall heavy-boned figure dressed in black even in the summer sun. "Now that you have heard the Good Word, Brothers and Sisters, you are probably expecting me to take up a collection," he cried out in his great ringing baritone. "Well, I want you to know that I do not take up collections! No, sir. Would you have me think you believe the Lord is broke? That He or His people must go about begging for handouts? No. I will tell you the truth, Brethren, the Lord is rich. He doesn't need your charity, and neither do I. Yes, sir, He gives you something real in return for your contribution, and so do I. For a contribution of just two bits, the Lord God has empowered me to give you one whole large size bottle of this healing tonic, made with the same wonderful ingredients used by the good people of the time of Jesus and His disciples. Jesus and His disciples, Brothers, just think of that! Hallelujah! Just step right up here — thank you, Brother — just step right up. Yes, sir, just two bits. Bless you, Brother, bless you."

As Heebs hawked his tonics and preached his version of the gospel, a group of cavalrymen from the nearby garrison at Fort Selden arrived, bringing with them a sick boy. "He was called Chato," explained the Padre, "and he was the son of a cavalry trooper and a young Indian woman from one of the Tiwa villages in the valley. The doctor from the fort was gone on a journey to another fort, so they brought the boy to the medicine peddler's revival. It was very clear to me that Heebs knew he could do nothing for the boy, so I went to him. I spoke to him, and then I took him to a place I knew in the mountains of Doña Ana — the camp of the medicine chief, the man who was called El Cacique. In a few days, Chato returned from the mountains, and he was soon working and playing again. Then Brother Heebs came to see me here at the church."

Buck Tyler sat wide-eyed in his chair in the simple monk's chamber behind the sanctuary of the church at Lastima. Beside him Sharon sat calmly, smiling and listening attentively to the stocky little cleric who sat across the heavy carved table in the middle of the room. He had a round and friendly face, and a mass of curly black hair like that of a little goat.

"The boy you took from the soldiers' town, Padre," said Orville Heebs, standing beside the table between Buck and Sharon. "I see he is healed. Praise the Lord you were able to help him."

"Amen," said Padre Cabrito. "The Lord is very good to us."

Heebs took off his black top hat and set it on the table. Though he wore his gray-streaked black hair and sideburns quite long, and his face was sunburned and dark, the top of his head was almost bald and very pale. "I am, of course, always interested in His ways and methods," he said smoothly. "Perhaps you might share with me some small teaching I could put to His service. What did you give the boy?"

The little Padre looked at him coolly for a moment before answering. From a large pocket on the skirt of his cassock he took a pouch and a red pipestone ceremonial pipe. He packed the pipe from the pouch of sweet-smelling dried herbs, put it to his lips, and blew a cloud of swirling smoke. "I did nothing," he said. "Chato's mother is Tiwa, you know. I just took him to his own people."

"You mean to a medicine man?" asked Heebs skeptically.

Cabrito waved a deprecatory hand. "We Indians are very superstitious, and we believe many strange things," he said. "It is sometimes good medicine just to believe things. Who knows what really happened. The Lord will do what He will do."

"You see," said Cabrito to Buck and Sharon, "he was already convinced that I was concealing from him a source of great power. I did not tell him what he wanted to hear, so he went to see the boy."

In the subdued light of a cloudy afternoon, they sat at Cabrito's table beside a crumbling old adobe wall, the remains of a building not far from the church. "A great miracle has happened to you," said Orville Heebs, offering a chunk of horehound candy from a little bag to the ten-year-old boy who crouched beside the wall. "I want to be sure that the good people who have helped you get all the recognition and thanks they deserve. So tell me, what was it Padre Cabrito said to you when he took you away?"

The boy peered out from beneath an unruly shock of long black hair with his strange pale blue eyes. "He asked me in the words of my mother's family if I was the son of a Tiwa, or the son of a soldier," he said, taking a second piece of horehound. "I didn't know what to choose, so I said the Great Spirit is the Father of us all. And then he took me to El Cacique."

"Tell me, son," said Heebs, giving him the rest of the bag,

"just what did El Cacique give you? Some tea, perhaps?"

The boy nodded and took the candy. "Yep," he said, "but it was just *Canutillo*, like your tonic. My mother always gives me that. And then he gave me some more when we went to the sacred spring."

Buck Tyler felt the hair again rise on the back of his neck, and a strange excitement gripped him deep in his gut.

"The trouble began when Heebs brought in a partner, a young man from Santa Fe named Randolph Morton. They rented a building in town and began to market 'El Cacique Indian Medicine Tonic' which they claimed was made with water from the Indians' ancient healing spring," said Father Justiano. "There was quite a fight for several months over the rights to the water, then very suddenly, Heebs disappeared, Morton returned to Santa Fe, and the Tiwa moved their villages. The town, and also the spring, just dried up." The tall hawk-faced priest smiled politely and spread his hands. "That is about all there is to tell," he said.

"What about the location of the spring?" asked John Simmons.

"The spring has been dry for over one hundred years," Justiano explained patiently. "Now the Rio Grande is dammed and managed, and there are cities which have changed the water table. It could be any one of dozens of little arroyos or hollows in the rocks. If anyone left alive still knows where it was, there is probably only one, a member of my parish, but she has never told anyone, not even me, and I am her confessor...and friend." He stood behind his desk as though about to escort them back into the church, then hesitated. "Are you planning to go looking for it?" he asked.

"That is what we have come here to do," said Buck with a friendly smile, as he and the others stood also. "We're staying down in Las Cruces, but we'll be back up here in the morning. We hope to spend a couple of days just peeking around in some of the little canyons between here and a place on the map called Tenuco."

"The red mountain," said Father Justiano, with a nod of

recognition. "That's up by Rincon." He gazed at them pensively. "You certainly seem to have the general area located," he mused. "And with divining rods, and visions... remarkable. Look, I'll tell you what. Let me offer you my facilities here as kind of a headquarters for your search. As a man of faith, of course I have some reluctance to acknowledge the validity of... of your practices, but I would be very interested in knowing how the results turn out. I should hope you will keep me informed of your progress, and I will be glad to help in any way I can."

"Of course we will," Sharon assured him. "Thank you, Father Justiano, for sharing this wonderful evening with us."

"It's almost dark," said Buck. "We had better get back to Las Cruces before they close all the restaurants — I've had my tongue set all day for a big plate of *tostados compuestos*." As they returned through the church to the truck, he felt light-headed, dazzled, uncertain of his reality, as though he had taken some strange drug. In the courtyard, John Simmons kicked up his heels in a little jig as he swung open the old wooden gate.

They returned to Las Cruces, ate dinner, and then John dropped Buck and Sharon off at the motel, then drove off.

"Dinner was great, thanks," she told him.

"Welcome. Glad you didn't want to go out for drinks with John."

"I hate bars," she said. "I'd really rather get some sleep."

"Not really my thing either," Buck agreed. "Maybe you'd rather watch a late movie or something?"

"Or something?"

"Look, I'm not trying to start anything."

"I know. It's all right, and I'm sorry about the other night. I shouldn't have led you on."

He shrugged.

"It's not that I'm not attracted. It's... more that I am attracted. It's just not as simple as I would like."

"You mean the vision?"

"Mm-hmm. My dreams are... well, sometimes very erotic. I think that might have a lot to do with why we both see things together."

"And that frightens you?"

"Buck, when I was taken from the reservation, and put in a Christian home, they used to... to punish me when I spoke of what I saw."

"They told you it was evil?"

"Yes. You see... I've never talked about this before. I don't know why I'm telling you, but, after my parents were killed in an accident, I lived with my grandmother, and she taught me things. I found that the visions were stronger if I... well, if I touched myself. I didn't know it was wrong, it was just... natural, that's all. Then in the church, when they found out, they made me... they made me..."

Buck took her hands, and he could see young Sharon crouching in the middle of a Spartan room, surrounded by a group severe looking dark clad white people. Holding court, the preacher directed the women of the church. "Take off her clothes," he commanded, and the women leaped to obey. "The Devil is on you, girl. You have a lot of nerve, bringing that wicked, lustful spirit into this home, do you hear me? Spawn of Satan, you heathen savage, did you think you could get away with that in this house of The Lord? Show us, show us the evil you have dared to practice in this home. Do it!"

Naked, trembling, and sobbing with fear and shame, the girl put her hand between her legs, then fell weeping to her knees.

"That's right, on your knees before your Lord God. Now repent, and call upon the Lord to free you of this evil."

"Please forgive me," the girl wept.

"Hallelujah, Amen! Lord Jesus, drive the spirit of lust from this girl. Shundala! Shundala cundaie!"

The people crowded forward, pressing themselves upon her to put their hands on her head and shoulders, fervently babbling in tongues. "Shundala babbala, gaggalashalaga achala babbala."

The preacher leads the girl to her bed, lets her put on

her nightshirt and lie down, and then motions to the others to leave the room. He shuts the door behind them, then sits down on the bed beside her.

"There, there, now. Amen, amen. Yes, the Devil is very strong and very frightening, and he makes us to desire that which we should not. But the Lord is good, yes, and He does provide for all the needs of our nature. Yes, yes, every good and obedient Christian woman deserves the reward and comfort of the covering of a man of God. There now, there, don't be frightened."

As he speaks, the preacher strokes her head, and then draws up her nightshirt to again expose her naked body. Pressing her legs apart, he rises over her. "There, there now. You are provided for, yes, yes."

"Then you were abused?" Buck asked her.

"Yes, and expected to be grateful," she said. "Some of the girls used to compete for the prophet's favor. I learned to turn my head, to not look."

"And the visions?"

"I learned to turn my head from that also. Eventually I learned to forget."

"Until the girl at the job disappeared?"

"Yes."

"Wow, I'm sorry. Then you've had no lovers since?"

"No, I've had many lovers, many, but always... at a distance."

He nodded. "You mean, guys like... well, like me?"

"Yes. Guys like you, Buck, but, I'm sorry, I just... well, you're different, and I just... can't."

"Wow. I guess I should be flattered, but..."

She turned to embrace him, and she let him kiss her, and then turned quickly to enter her room, closing the door to leave him standing alone.

Chapter Eight

"What about Barbra Sakata?" he asked himself, lying alone in his room. He was surprised for a moment when his world in Albuquerque came rushing back to him, surprised because he saw how completely he had ignored the consequences in that other world of his feelings for Sharon. "What about Mary, long, blonde, and luscious, and that weekend coming up in the ruin on her father's ranch? What about the bird nest on Sandia crest? And what about the weeks spent on interesting projects with interesting women on trips like this one? Come on, Tyler, this is what romantic adventures are all about, isn't it? Relax and play the part, and two weeks from now, you'll be back in the classroom."

He looked around the motel room, trying to get himself firmly attached again to the reality. He wished he were back in his downtown apartment, so he could get up and fix coffee, and he wished she were an adventurous co-ed he could send back to her dormitory. "Well, isn't she?" he asked himself. "Who says this is more than a good safari with some romantic potential with a two-week run? Just what is there about this fat little Indian girl that is so very captivating?" The first answer was obvious, and undeniably frightening: he was in awe of the psychic awakening he had shared with her. So was not his feeling then just a case of a crush on the teacher? And what about that psychic awakening? Would he soon be able to do it by himself, or would he have to give it up if he chose not to stay with her romantically?

It was clear to him if they were to stay together, the potential for their growing close was profound. He feared to think the word 'soulmates'. The notion that two people should be born to share a relationship which would persist across the boundaries of time and human personness... it was a loss of options, a mandated future, as implacably horrifying as knowing the hour of your death. And at the same time,

what a future, what a destiny it offered! To travel the
world together as a famous team with remarkable powers,
seeking out great relics and great stories with their
knowledge and skills. "If I believe it," he thought, "there is
a good chance it will turn out to be true. It is disturbingly
tempting."

They met John Simmons for breakfast in the motel's
cafe. "Better get a hurry on," he said, glancing at his watch,
"if we want to get on the road by nine o'clock." When he
stood, Buck noticed he had shaved and put on a fresh suit of
starched khakis, the shirt with short sleeves and epaulets,
and a silver belt buckle bearing a natural gold nugget of
respectable size. He spread his hands genially and invited
them to sit down, wearing a jaunty smile. "Today is the day,"
he said.

"When we get to the area specified on the map," he
began after they had ordered breakfast, "you should get a
good look around, Buck, to try to identify any likely terrain
features or evidence of human development. I'm going to
try out the pair of ball-bearing angle-rods I bought in
Jerome."

In the truck on the way out to the site, Buck and Sharon
sat in the front seat, enjoying each other's company, and
enjoying the drive along the river. The Rio Grande was
running full. Though its banks were carefully controlled by
dams, levees, and rockworks, it flowed smoothly and swiftly,
a broad band the color of cafe-con-leche winding its way
through the cotton fields and pecan orchards of the valley.

They drove past the turnoff to Lastima without stopping
at Father Justiano's church, and continued up Highway 85
looking for the complex of arroyos and canyons at the foot
of a steep-shouldered round bluff which was described by
the topographic figures on Simmons' map.

"Little Lady, I hope you can get some sense of the honor
and excitement I feel just being able to work on this
project with Buck," said John eagerly. "I don't mean to
belittle your technical specialty, of course. It is a wonderful
break for him that you were able to come on this project.

With one of you looking in the present, and the other looking in the past, I just can't wait to see what you two discover."

"I'm glad I was able to come," she assured him.

"It just amazes me that we have come so far and our data has been so accurate," he marveled. "I have a really strong deja vu, as though I already knew all of this, and I'm just being reminded of things I have forgotten. I guess that's kind of how it is for you, when you see the visions — kind of like deja vu, but really clear, right, Sharon?"

"Something like that, yes, John," she replied, laughing.

"You don't have to give me all the credit, John," Buck protested. "After all, this was your idea in the first place."

"Well, sure," John said with exaggerated self deprecation, "but only as a publishing venture, remember."

"Of course I remember," Buck quickly assured him, "and it is looking like a better one every day. We might just get one hell of a book out of this."

Sharon cast a quizzical glance at Buck and John. They both seemed to be relaxed and enjoying the conversation, but she felt something like a skip, as though she had missed a part of what was going on. When she was a child, her grandmother had taught her to use a certain polite restraint in peeking into other people's lives and intentions. She had both by habit and by her own intention come to respectfully look the other way, and to give people the benefit of the doubt. Even so, she could not deny that she felt a certain uneasiness about John's intentions... and Buck Tyler's.

They passed through a narrow place in the valley, a place where salt-cedar clumps grew along the river, and the steep hills of crumbling sandstone and eroding adobe were covered sparsely by creosote and mesquite. As they rounded a bend, all three of them exclaimed at once, "There! There it is." Standing by itself among the khaki-tan ridges and hills stood a massive steep-shouldered bluff of rust-red earth. As they approached the mountain called Tenuco, they could see an area just to the south of it where the iron-rich red strata met the softer soils of the sandy ridges in a dendritic pattern of steep and twisting canyons.

"That is the area indicated by the psychic search at ISPI," said John. "There is a bridge a few miles ahead, and a power-line road we can follow back to get in there."

A few minutes later, Buck made his way across a washed-out arroyo and up an erosion-rutted rocky hill, and then down onto the sandy bed of the complex of canyons. He was glad Simmons had the foresight to have insisted on bringing the Blazer instead of a highway car.

"Wait. Wait a minute," said John. "Stop here. I want to try something." He jumped out of the truck and took his new angle-rods out of their box. They were each made from a 24-inch piece of 3/16 chromed rod, bent ninety degrees at the 6-inch point. The short ends were mounted into tube handles on ball-bearings. "I want to see if I can get some kind of a reading with these," he told them. They relaxed and listened to music on the truck's sound system while John made his search. Carrying his map, a compass, and the two angle-rods, he tramped eagerly out to the middle of the flat sandy wash and began to lay out a wide circle on the ground, marking the cardinal points of the compass with head-sized rocks. As Buck and Sharon watched, he stood at the easternmost point of the circle facing north, holding the rods like pistols before him. With his head up and eyes fixed on the horizon, he began to goose-step slowly around the circle like a comic sleepwalker.

He walked about halfway around with the rods pointing forward. Then quite suddenly they spread apart and pointed straight out to the sides. He marked the spot with his boot, dipped the rods forward to reposition them, and continued around. Then he turned around and began to walk back the other way. Two more times the rods swung apart, and each time he made a mark on the ground. Then he squatted in the center of the circle with his compass and made several notations on his map. It was a good half hour before he returned to the Blazer, looking quite satisfied. "Well, according to my gizmos here, what we are looking for is up that first big canyon on the left," he declared, "the one that goes right up into the red strata."

"That's good enough for me," said Buck lightly. "Let's go check it out."

Buck snapped off the tape player as John got into the truck. He reached for the key, but Sharon touched his hand. "Wait," she said. "I thought I heard something." She cocked her head and listened a moment, forehead pulled into a frown, then she opened her door and stood up to put her head out of the vehicle.

"What is it?" asked Buck. "What did you think you heard?"

She sat back down again. "It sounded like thunder, or cattle running... some kind of a rumbling."

"I wouldn't worry about it," said Simmons. "It was probably some jet fighter plane or a rocket. There is a lot of that kind of thing going on in this part of the state. The next valley over is where they blew up the first atom bomb, July 16, 1945. Who knows what you might hear out here."

The bottom of the narrow canyon was fairly flat, and made up of sand and rocks washed back and forth by the arroyo's occasional cloudburst runoff floods into a network of criss-crossing erosion ridges, filled by the wind with soft patches of blow sand. The new Blazer negotiated the terrain easily, and they made their way up the twisting little gorge. Each of the arroyo's switchbacks produced a hollow undercut place, a little secluded grotto with a sandy bed and an overhanging, enclosing shell of rock. On the north side of the arroyo, the red cliffs rose quickly, jaggedly, cut by fast erosion and fracturing into the already-steep side of Tenuco.

"Our site could be any one of these hollows," said John Simmons. "All we have to go on is what you might be able to discern examining the area, Buck, and whatever Sharon might be able to pick up by going in and touching things."

"That and the fact the place used to have a good-sized spring," agreed Buck. "Let's stop here at this one and get out and just walk around for a while. We can't get much idea of the feel of the place as long as we stay inside this truck."

They stopped, got out of the vehicle, and began a

leisurely walk up the canyon. Buck was surprised that the moist summer air carried such a wealth of smells in the desert. In the sandy floor grew stands of tall desert willows, a few of them still flourishing lavender blooms that looked like snapdragons. On the slope above towered the tall candelabra of agave century plants, and the bristle-headed shaggy trunks of the yucca. In the sunny places along the edge of the arroyo grew clumps of the dark-green vines of datura, and near them gray-stalked thistles with white blooms, which he knew produced a bright yellow dye in the sap. The sky above them was the soft blue of Taos turquoise, but intense and keenly clear, a blue that was bright like a screaming note just above the upper limits of hearing.

"This is a very beautiful place," Sharon said to Buck as they walked around the first bend, leaving John to walk back and forth beside the truck with his angle-rods. "But for some reason, I just don't feel comfortable about this."

"Is it something that happened back then, back in Heebs' time?" Buck asked her.

"I don't know," she said. "I just feel unsafe —as though someone were watching us with great malevolence. And I know it must be eighty degrees already, but I keep feeling a chill every time I step into a shadow."

They stopped, and stood together for a moment, listening to the sounds of the arroyo. It was strangely quiet, except that the wind twisting back and forth through the canyon and around the rocks and through the willows made a deep, almost silent sound, a sound like the rumbling of water, the muted booming of a flood-crest's headlong rush, a surging wall of water driving before it a herd of thunder-lunged cattle in a crazed stampede.

Suddenly there was a sharper sound, a crumbling which cut through like riflefire, and a shuddering of earth beneath their feet. They heard John Simmons scream like a wounded animal, and saw a plume of dust rise up from the tumbling shower of rock and red dirt which crashed down the steep side of the canyon to fall only a few feet from him and the Blazer. Buck and Sharon both ran to see if he needed help.

"Let's get out of here," said Buck, as Simmons struggled to his feet. "There may be more of it loose up there. It must have been a tremor of some kind that broke it loose."

"Tremor my eye!" declared John. "There was somebody up there, and they tried to kill me. Get moving!"

Buck turned the truck away from the rock face and began to drive back out of the canyon. "What do you mean, there was somebody up there? Did you see anybody?" he asked.

"I saw something, yeah," Simmons said, gasping back his breath. "I saw something, just out of the corner of my eye, up on the slope above us. I looked up and saw something move, just for an instant, like a deer or a man moving behind a rock or something. Then I heard the rock start to roll, and it came crashing through the brush. If I hadn't been watching, it would have got me for sure."

"Aw, come on, John, you probably just saw a yucca being knocked down by the slide, that's all," Buck assured him. "Why in the world would anyone be out here in the middle of nowhere rolling rocks down on top of you?"

"Maybe they know something we don't," said Simmons. "Maybe that was just a warning that we should confine our search to some other canyon."

"But why?" asked Sharon. "Why should anyone care about a Tiwa medicine spring used by a bottling company to make quack tonic?"

"That is what I would like to know," Simmons declared. "What say we go back to Lastima. I would like to have another go at that Justiano fellow. I intend to find out why someone would start a rockslide to keep us out of that canyon."

"It was just an accidental fall," Buck assured him. "Let's go ahead and drive up the canyon and see if we can spot anything obvious. Then we can stop and ask Justiano about it on the way back to Las Cruces."

"That would be fine as long as you are right," said John.

"But if I'm right, going back in there could get us killed. I have an idea that priest knows a lot more than he told us last night. Just to set my mind at ease, all right? Let's go back now."

They found the cassocked cleric carrying water in a wooden bucket from a faucet beside the church to his little garden in the courtyard. With Buck and Sharon a few steps behind him, Simmons strolled to the garden, nodded to the priest, and squatted down in the sun beside the adobe wall. He watched Justiano empty his bucket onto a chile plant and walk without hurry back to the faucet to refill it. When he brought it back filled to the little vegetable patch, Simmons asked him, "Why don't you use a hose?"

Father Justiano looked at him seriously a moment, then smiled a little tight smirk of private amusement. "It would be out of period," he said. He and Simmons shared a chuckle.

"Listen, Father, I sure don't want to seem to press you for things you might not want to volunteer, but something happened this morning in a certain canyon up by Tenuco mountain, and I'm hoping you might be able to shed some light on it," Simmons told him.

"I would certainly like to hear about it," said Justiano.

"Somebody tried to kill me," Simmons announced coolly, "or at least to scare me pretty bad — to keep us from going into that canyon. I would like you to tell me anything you know about anyone who might for any reason be likely to do something drastic like that to keep people out of there."

Justiano frowned. "No, I don't know of anyone at all," he said, continuing to water his plants.

Simmons stood up and walked alongside him. "As I told you last night, I publish stories about the history of the Southwest, stories about lost mines, and ghosts, and famous gunfights. People send me all kinds of stuff, and so I've heard a lot of tales, and read a lot of history. I was impressed last night," Simmons told him. "I was impressed by your grasp of the history of your office here, and I am impressed that it is the church which is the repository of the truth here, and not the newspapers and state records."

Justiano nodded solemnly. "In the rise of this land from heathen savagery, it has always been the church which identifies a place. The homes and the businesses come and go, but while the church remains, a community still exists. As long as those old carved doors are still opened to invite those who are faithful and penitent to the Lord's table, there will still be a place called Lastima. If the church goes, there will be nothing left, regardless of the number of homes on wheels and the shops which serve them."

The sun was quite high in the sky, and Buck and Sharon found a narrow wedge of shade on the north side of the church from which relatively cool vantage they could watch Simmons and Justiano and follow their conversation.

"You know, Father," Simmons said, "One thing which keeps cropping up in those stories is the fact that certain places get a reputation for collecting dead bodies. Like the Lost Dutchman Mine in the Superstition Mountains over in Arizona — people go in there looking for something, and they don't come out. Now I am sure if there is really something here of historical importance, even if it is just legend, you know about it. Are you sure you never heard any local stories about any kind of a lost mine, or Conquistadors — something somebody believes in so strongly they might arrange an accident for anybody else looking for it?"

"No," said Justiano positively. "No, it was never anything more than a promotion scheme to sell patent medicine, and the last person who disappeared up there was Orville Heebs. The spring dried up, and nobody has been up there since that time."

"Over one hundred years ago?"

"That is correct, sir. The story of El Cacique Medicine Tonic is a big part of the history of this little place, but of no great consequence to anyone else." Justiano poured his bucket of water onto another chile plant. "However," he said, "I would like to see on the map just where you were when this happened. Would you step inside?"

"Why certainly," Simmons agreed. He and the others

followed Justiano into the church, and into the surprisingly-cool chamber of Justiano's apartment office. The priest poured them iced tea.

Simmons placed his folded topographic map on the desk, and stood there with his hand on it. "Strangest thing," he mused. "I was just thinking about what you told us last night, and it suddenly struck me why it was so familiar. I remember years ago somebody sent me a story for my magazine, about a spring, and about how they almost had an Indian war over it. It wasn't a very good story, and it wasn't very well documented — I didn't publish it — but it keeps coming back to me. The person who wrote it said his grandfather had told him about it before he died. His grandfather had been there, and he said he saw some thing, an artifact..."

Buck saw the priest tense, as though to ready himself for a fight without giving himself away.

"...an artifact, like a black stone knife, he said, a black stone knife with some kind of a very decorative handle, like a Mayan or Aztec ceremonial blade. Does that ring any bells with you, Father?"

"Who told you that? Who was he?" asked Justiano.

Simmons leaned forward and looked Justiano pointedly in the eye. "You know we are getting close," he said, "and you know what is out there. You know why someone tried to stop us this morning, and you probably know who did it. I am not surprised that you claim you know nothing, but I would like to ask you something. Are you going to be one of those who gets credit for helping us find it, or are you going to be one of those who goes into the history for trying to stop us?"

"Mr. Simmons, Dr. Tyler, Ms. Hightower," said Justiano seriously, sitting down behind his heavy wooden desk, "to the best of my knowledge, there is no Mayan treasure or lost mine out there, or anything like that, and I don't have the least idea who might have been out in that canyon this morning, or why anyone might have wished to harm or frighten you. That is the simple truth of the matter."

"We are not expecting to find treasure," said Sharon.

"We are only interested in locating the place used by the Indians as a healing site. Once we find it, and have a chance to make an inspection of the site, we'll show you exactly where it is, and if anyone wants to search there for treasure, they are welcome to it. It is your history, Father Justiano, so we will be happy to discover whatever we can, and to leave it in your hands."

"Thank you," he said, "but I don't know what else I could do to help you."

"Last night you said there might be one person alive who may know exactly where that spring was located," she said. "Would you take us to her? Perhaps the only reason she has never told anyone else is because no one ever asked."

"If we find the place, this story could make a great PBS-TV special," put in Buck. "You could put the church of Lastima back on the map, Padre."

Father Justiano sat for a long moment staring from one to the other of them. "It amazes me that you have come so far," he said. "I do not know from what source the information has come which has led you here, and yet you have come, like divers following echoes in the sea to seek out a sunken ship." He sighed. "Well, perhaps you have come to solve the mystery, and to release the ghost of Orville Heebs from whatever fate he met in that canyon. I will take you to meet Concepcion Gutierrez. She has always claimed she actually knew Orville Heebs."

"But didn't he disappear in the 1870's?" asked Tyler.

Justiano nodded. "She is very old," he said.

Chapter Nine

Father Justiano took them walking a short distance from the church along the dirt road which led to Highway 85 from the windblown patch of bare adobe and sand which had once been the busy plaza of Lastima. They passed a part of an ancient adobe wall, a weathered remnant almost two feet thick, about five feet high at its highest point, two at the lowest, and about forty feet long.

"Wow," said Buck, "talk about deja vu! I feel like I've been right here sometime before this."

Sharon laughed. "I know just what you mean. I can almost see Orville Heebs standing right there now talking to little Chato."

Buck Tyler's body flushed fire and ice, cold in the heart and hot at the skin like lust and fear of the same lover, like frozen chile when you're burning with thirst. He remembered where he had seen the wall before, and how she knew he had seen it. It was personal objective evidence, something he knew he would never be able to prove to anyone else, nor to deny to himself. "You're right," he laughed, trying to remain casual and relaxed, "I'll bet he and Padre Cabrito used to stand right there talking, too."

"That's a sure bet," chuckled Justiano. "That is the last remaining wall of the old Morton and Heebs building. After the business folded, the place was a livery stable used by travelers between El Paso and Santa Fe."

"You know, that's one of the things I like best about publishing a local history magazine," said John Simmons enthusiastically, "going around and finding places like this and trying to imagine what they were like when they were filled with life."

Justiano led them to a little hollow place beneath several huge mistletoe-festooned cottonwood trees near the river, to a low settling ancient adobe house. The yard was well tended, free of weeds and of grass as well. In stone-walled little planters, and in gaudily-painted Mexican flowerpots grew irises, daisies, and columbine, as well as aloes and delicate, spindly Christmas cactus. The priest knocked at the heavy carved door, and after a minute or so, it swung inward slowly.

The woman who greeted them had the eyes of a child, open, unshielded and accepting, very aware, dark eyes which flashed from one of them to the other. Her eyebrows and her hair were powder white, and her skin was like parchment, thin, and tenuous in substance, as though the eyes were bright garnet gems in a setting carved translucent-thin in meerschaum and rubbed brown with handling. "What is it, Justiano?" she asked, in a soft but still-melodious voice.

"I have brought some people who would like to meet you," he told her.

"Is there some reason why you think I should want to meet them?" she asked.

"Well, I don't know," said the priest apologetically, "but I hoped perhaps you would not mind seeing them. They have come all the way from Albuquerque to find out about the history of Lastima."

She glared at them reluctantly, then nodded, and led them into her home. "For a little while then," she said. The interior of the house was much larger than it had seemed from outside, and might as well have been a museum of life in an earlier time. It was filled with beautiful old cabinets, sofas, trunks, and tables, and one entire wall was lined with deep shelves. Hardly any space at all was free of the collected properties of the woman's lifetime. The furniture was heavy Spanish hardwood and glass, with dark brocade upholstery, and pictures on the walls were framed in ponderous gilded curliques. Along the wall opposite the book-filled shelves, a tiled bench hearth and a heavy mantle carved from a single beam framed a large fireplace. She invited them to sit on sofas, then sat opposite them on a slender straight-backed chair.

Justiano introduced them as an anthropologist, an

historian, and a psychic investigator, and briefly outlined to her their purpose. "This delightful lady is Señora Concepcion Gutierrez," he told them. "She is quite certainly the only person still alive who actually knew Padre Cabrito and Orville Heebs."

"Why, good heavens," exclaimed Sharon, "that was over one hundred years ago!"

"I was only one month old when Abraham Lincoln was shot," the old woman said with a smug little smile. "I was sixteen when they sent that man Garrett out to shoot Billy Bonney, and I first became a grandmother in 1908 when Oliver Lee and Albert Fall and their thugs from the Tularosa valley murdered Garrett and took over the territory."

"You are sure of that?" asked Simmons.

"Of course I am sure," she snapped at him. "Everyone back then knew exactly what happened, but Fall and the Santa Fe ring controlled the courts, and they controlled the press. They even created a new county just so they could try each other in their own court. They got away with it, too, and lived to write the history books themselves. Orville Heebs was one of them, one of those Santa Fe boys, in the beginning. That's how he got title to that land where old Cacique's spring was located."

"When did that happen?" Simmons asked.

"Oh, I was just a child," the old woman replied. "Heebs had a partner, a slick young fellow from Santa Fe named Randolph Morton. He was the one who pulled the strings for Heebs. He became a Senator in later years."

"Then you must have known where the spring was located," Simmons pressed.

"I went there once or twice when I was very young," she said with a deprecatory gesture, "but I wouldn't know where to begin these days. It is probably a gas station or a supermarket now."

"Señora Gutierrez, we are hoping to find that location as part of our study of places which were used by the Indians as healing sites," said Buck.

She chuckled softly to herself. "Young man, you sound

just like Orville Heebs," she told him. "You can't imagine the lengths he went to looking for that spring."

"Would you tell us about that?" Buck asked.

"We would really appreciate the chance to set the history books straight," added Simmons.

She hesitated a moment, then nodded and stood. "Father Justiano knows I do not care to talk to curious strangers," she said, giving the priest a sidelong glance, "but since he seems to feel this is an exception..." She walked across the room with short but brisk and sure steps, and took a framed newspaper clipping down from its place on the wall of her living room. The paper was brown with age, but still quite legible.

Buck read it aloud to the others. It was a testimonial, a report given by a traveler from Atlanta who had passed through Lastima on his way to California. In stilted language which could only have come from a bombastic orator, the traveler was reported to have described how his young son had fallen sick on the trail, and how he had been taken by one Reverend Doctor Orville Heebs to a spring used by El Cacique, the medicine chief of the local Indians, and how immersion in the healing waters had miraculously cured the lad.

"What a slick old devil was that Heebs," declared Señora Gutierrez, sitting up perkily and speaking with the sureness and vigor of a woman half her age. "He waited months for his chance, ever since he got the idea somewhere there was a profit to be made in that spring. He just had to find out where it was. The only one who knew was El Cacique himself, and just about the only one of us who could talk to him at all was Padre Cabrito. He was half Apache, you know." For a moment her bright eyes misted over, and she shook her head softly. "Dear Cabrito, he was so sweet. Of all the people I have ever known, if I could see only one of them again, it would be him."

"Then did Padre Cabrito tell Heebs where the spring was?" asked Simmons.

"Oh, no, Padrecito didn't know where it was," Señora

Gutierrez assured him, "but he did know how to find El
Cacique, and Heebs knew that. When the traveler came to
town with his sick boy, he went to Heebs, and Heebs brought
him here to my father's house, where we had room for him.
He stayed in the back bedroom, right down that hall. The
boy was about my age, about seven or eight. I remember I
liked him because he had long golden hair in curls. I have
always liked pretty men." She laughed a little and winked at
Buck Tyler, and for a moment it was clear the tiny wisp of
ancient flesh and gossamer hair had once been a very
beautiful woman.

"Heebs came here, and he told the traveler about the
spring," she continued. "'I have seen this fever before,' he
told him, 'and there is only one sure cure. But the secret is
kept by the priest, and he will not tell anyone.' Then he took
the traveler and his boy to the church, to beg Cabrito to
take the boy to the spring."

"Did you go with them?" Simmons asked.

"Oh, no," she replied, "I stayed at home and helped my
mother, and I helped to take care of the traveler's dog. It
was a hunting dog, hardly more than a puppy, which they had
brought from the Confederacy when they left there after
the war, the Civil War, you know. But Padrecito told me
about it many times. He was an old man when he passed away
at the turn of the century, and we had spent many evenings
together talking about the old times.

"When Heebs came to him, Cabrito was surprised that he
wanted to take the boy to Cacique's sacred spring. 'Why do
you want to do that?' he asked him. 'The boy is not Indian.'
And Heebs told him, 'It is in the water, Padre. The water
can heal the boy, just like it healed Chato.' Cabrito tried to
tell him it was not in the water. It was in El Cacique, and in
the faith of his people. It was in the magic of the old
Indian's love, which is the greatest healer of all, *gracias a
Dios*. 'I can not take you there,' Cabrito told him. 'It is a
sacred place to them, and I would betray their trust if I
took you there.' He told him that.

"The traveler begged Cabrito on his knees with tears in

his eyes. 'Is their shrine so sacred that you would deny my Christian son the chance to live?' he asked Cabrito. 'If it is in the water, like Doctor Heebs says, then it will still work for the Indians after we have gone. If it is something only El Cacique possesses, then no harm will be done by placing the boy in the spring. How can you refuse?'

"'I can not take you there,' Padrecito told him. 'That is not mine to give you, but I will take the boy to El Cacique.' So just before sundown that day, Padre Cabrito came to this house alone, and he put the boy into the back of his buckboard, and he rode away into the Robledo mountains near here. When they left, we had to tie the dog to a tree with a piece of rope. Aie, how that poor dog cried when they left. When the morning came, the dog was gone. The rope was loose, and the dog was gone. In a few days, the Indians brought the boy back to a place on the river near town, and he was much better. In a week, the traveler left to go to California, but not before Heebs got him to sign a letter saying he had been healed by the water from the spring, in the care of Reverend Doctor Orville Heebs. The dog never came back.

"Then Heebs took the letter, and he rode away to Santa Fe. He was gone about a month, as I remember, and when he came back he brought with him a new partner, that Morton boy, a pretty dandy as slick and greedy as Orville Heebs himself. The two of them set up their business in the back of Heebs' barn, and they began to sell El Cacique Indian Medicine Tonic. They said it was made from the water of the Indians' sacred spring, and they had a piece of paper from someone in Santa Fe, which said they owned the land where the spring was. Oh, they made a lot of money, a great deal of money." Señora Gutierrez sighed and shook her head.

"Then it was El Cacique's medicine spring?" asked Buck.

She nodded. "Heebs must have followed Padre Cabrito. But very soon the Indians began to make trouble, and they sent word to the Padre to tell the white men to stop the desecration of their spring. Morton and Heebs took their paper from Santa Fe to the commanding officer of Fort Selmore, you know the fort a few miles from here, and they told him that he ought to take the cavalry and go out into the mountains to defend their property from the Indians, to drive El Cacique away from the spring. Everyone was afraid there would be fighting."

"Then there really was a chance that the spring would be the cause of an Indian war in the valley?" asked Simmons. "I heard a story about that, but I wasn't sure this was the place."

"Oh, yes," affirmed Señora Gutierrez, "El Cacique's people were very angry, the Apache, the Tiwa, the Tewa, all of the tribes respected the medicine chief. Their farming lands had been taken, the animals they hunted had been killed and replaced with cattle and sheep which grazed the open range to destruction, their people had been murdered, and their villages had been burned ever since the white Spaniards first came three hundred years before, and the Anglos two hundred years after them. But the medicine spring was too much, too much. There was much talk of war."

"It didn't happen, did it?" asked Sharon. "I don't think I have ever read about an uprising of the tribes then."

"No," the Señora said, "it didn't happen. The commanding officer, Major Cooley, did not want to fight them, but the politicians, and the bankers, and the businessmen all thought the money from the tonic was a good thing for Lastima, and for all of New Mexico."

"What did happen?" asked Buck.

"Nobody knows for sure," said the old woman with a shrug. "Padre Cabrito blamed himself for starting it all by taking the boy to El Cacique, so he went to find a way to make peace. He left one day to go to the camp of El Cacique, and when he came back, it was all over."

"What do you mean?" Buck persisted.

"There was a terrible storm that day," she told him, looking down at the floor between her feet, and speaking almost in a whisper. "I watched Cabrito ride off into the rain and I ran and spent the whole night hiding under my mother's bed, the big bed, there in the front bedroom, where I sleep now. It was a terrible storm, and when Cabrito came back the next morning, he was very upset. He was never the same. For days he would speak to no one, and he was never the same. He was only about forty years old, I think, but that night he became an old man. Heebs was never seen again. People searched for him everywhere, but they never found him. Morton, the dandy boy, took all of his money out of the bank, and went back to Santa Fe, and was never seen in Lastima again. A few people knew where the spring was because they had helped Heebs to bring the water in barrels on his wagons, and they went out there. They found El Cacique dead, like *carne seco*, jerky meat, like he had been cooked dry by lightning. But no sign at all of Orville Heebs. The spring was stopped up by mud, red as blood, and it has never flowed a drop since. And not a trace of Heebs."

As Buck listened to her, he noticed a painting hanging on the wall of an adjoining room, and again he felt the hot chill of excitement in the face of the unknown. It was a portrait of an Indian, an old man, with deep lines in his face. His hair was braided on the sides, and he wore a simple headband. Though the style was naive, a sort of globby pointillism in the rust-earth colors of the river valley, the strength of the man's character was clearly evident in the set of the jaw, and the warmth of the dark compassionate eyes fixed on infinity. Behind him, drawn in the almost-black red of drying blood, rose the square-shouldered bluff of Tenuco mountain. Unlike the soft lineless texture of the pointillist portrait, the bluff had been drawn in carefully with a knife or small brushes, and its skyline was sharply defined against the pale ochre sky.

Buck stared fascinated at the painting, almost dreading to point out to Simmons and Sharon that it was very similar to one of the parasentient impressionists' drawings. Noting his slack-jawed stare, Señora Gutierrez said, "That is El Cacique. The picture was painted by one of my friends."

She smiled and shook her head a little as she remembered him. "His name was Manuel Elizondo Lopez, but everyone just called him Flaco. I always thought I would marry him when I grew up. He was older than I, and I was quite taken by him."

"Tell me, Señora, was Flaco also a friend of El Cacique?" Buck asked her.

"Well, I don't know," she laughed. "I think Flaco was everyone's friend."

When John Simmons saw the picture, he also was astonished by its similarity to the drawing he had been given in Jerome, and he gave Sharon a meaningful sidelong glance. "Mrs. Gutierrez, you said Morton and the Padre came home that morning looking like they had seen something terrible," he said. "Did Cabrito ever say anything to you about what it was he saw that night?"

The woman seemed to withdraw within herself. "No, no, it was just a terrible storm," she said.

Glancing pointedly at Sharon again, Simmons pressed on. "Do you recall if the Padre might have brought back some kind of unusual item, an artifact, perhaps?"

Seeing Simmons' line of questioning was causing some anxiety, Sharon tried to relax and let herself feel out into the room as though to locate the focus of the woman's discomfort. The old woman looked up at her quickly, and Sharon was surprised to recognize that she was aware of her power, and was frightened, trying hard to conceal something from her parasentient vision.

"No, no, there was nothing," she insisted, and turned to the priest. "Justiano, I am tired now," she said, the imploring note in her voice not quite covered by her imperious tone.

"Yes, of course, you must be," Sharon quickly interjected. "You have been so kind to give us so much of your time." She stood and stepped forward to shake the Señora's hand gently.

"I must be going also," said Justiano, standing with her.

"Perhaps, Miss Hightower... if you could just be permitted

to touch some things..." Simmons began.

"Buck, will you take me back to town now, please?" asked Sharon firmly, interrupting him.

"Yes, of course," Tyler immediately agreed. "Thank you, Señora, for your help," he told the old woman. "You have been very helpful."

After the four visitors left her home, Concepcion Gutierrez stood for a time staring after them. Then she stepped wearily to the heavy mantle over her fireplace and took down an old wooden box, like a silverware case. Standing in the warm slanting beam of afternoon sunshine coming in through her living room window, she opened the box. The ruddy beam gleamed brightly from the gold handle of what appeared to be a wide, short-bladed knife, or a cleaver of some kind. It was made from a single piece of black obsidian, beautifully shaped by precise flaking of the volcanic glass stone with the highest level of lithic craftsmanship. The gold handle was more crude, as though the stone had been partly immersed in molten gold, cooled, and then carefully peened to create a uniform surface. She gazed at the black knife for a long moment, then sighed, closed the box without touching the ancient artifact, and replaced it on her mantle.

They walked back to the church in silence, except for the polite amenities of thanking Justiano for taking them to see the old woman, and commenting on how interesting her story had been. The priest shook their hands perfunctorily and wished them a good day, without inviting them to return. Once they were back in the truck, John Simmons was beside himself. "Dammit, girl," he spluttered, "what did you do that for? It didn't take a psychic to see she is hiding something! She knows about the artifact, I'm sure of it, and all you had to do was..."

"Of course I could see she was hiding something," Sharon replied coldly. "That is why I refused to invade her privacy. And I don't have to be psychic to see I have made a big mistake about you two. It is clear to me that you are hiding something also, and I did not come here to look for treasure.

Hidden gold is a curse," she said. "It makes men go crazy."

They rode in silence half an hour back to the motel in Las Cruces, where Sharon immediately began to pack her things. "Hidden gold makes men go crazy," she repeated to Tyler as soon as they were alone in their room, "and I guess hidden passion makes women go crazy. It has certainly made a fool of me."

"Sharon, please," he pleaded, "I don't know anything about a treasure, I swear. I'm only here, like you, because of what showed up on the search at the ISPI meeting."

"I'm afraid I just don't believe you any more, Doctor Professional Anthropologist," she told him. "Will you drive me to the nearest airport, or do I have to call a taxi?"

He sighed and reached for his own suitcase. "I'll do better than that. I'll go with you."

"What?"

"I said, I'll go with you. I'll drop the project and come with you."

"With me? To where, and why?" she asked, surprised. "And what about John Simmons?"

"I don't care where, and I don't care about John Simmons. I care about you."

She stopped packing and gazed at him doubtfully. "I wish I could be sure of that," she said, "and I wish I could think of one good reason why I should care."

"I know where the spring is now," he declared. "I know how to find it, and I could go right there tomorrow morning. But I will still leave with you right now if you won't stay with me another day. If you do stay, and I'm wrong about the spring, I'll leave with you tomorrow. I promise."

She frowned, started to speak, then pursed her lips and sat on the bed. "If you are lying to tempt my curiosity to make me stay, you are wasting your time. Something I learned a long time ago about seeing things: I don't have to know everything, and some things I would prefer not to know. This feels more and more like one of those things. But if this is a treasure hunt, and you really have found what you're looking for, then this would be the right time to let the naive little girl run away in a snit, none the wiser."

"That would be the thing to do, you're right," he said.

"Tell me what you know," she demanded.

"The picture," he told her, "the picture of El Cacique. The only details in the background were very recognizable features on Tenuco Mountain, the red one just north of Lastima. Unless I am very wrong, that picture was painted at the site of the spring. All we have to do is go to the spot where those features can be seen, and take a good look around."

She stared at him a long moment. "I believe you're probably right," she said finally. "All right, Buck, I'll stay one more day. I admit I'm curious to see what we will find... but if that man Simmons says one word about a treasure, I will leave, right then and there."

They heard the shower running in Simmon's room next door, then after a few minutes he knocked lightly on their door. "If you two don't mind," he said, "I would like to take the Blazer and go find myself a decent little bar. I could use a couple of drinks, and I guess you'd probably like a little time to yourselves."

"Sure," Tyler told him, "we'll get some dinner at the restaurant here and call it an early night. See you in the morning."

Late that night, in the silent living room of the old adobe house under the cottonwood trees, someone moved stealthily, following the slender beam of light from a tiny pocket flash light. He shined the little spot around from bookshelf to bookshelf, and from table to table. Then it fell on the carved wooden box on the mantle. He opened it, and the light glinted coldly from the black blade. Suddenly he heard a noise behind him and turned to see Concepcion Gutierrez advancing on him, holding a fireplace poker in her hand. "What are you doing here?" she demanded. "Get out!"

Without an instant's hesitation, the intruder struck the tiny old woman backhanded, knocking her to the floor. Then he rushed past her, taking the box with the gilded obsidian blade.

Chapter Ten

John Simmons came into the motel's restaurant for
breakfast about half an hour later than Buck and Sharon,
looking rumpled, bleary-eyed, and unshaven. He scratched
his gray-bristled scalp and chin, mumbled an apology, and
ordered only coffee and a roll.

"Late night?" asked Buck, with a rather unsympathetic
chuckle.

Simmons nodded. "Yep. I ran into a couple of other old
geezers and got to talking about the early days around here.
Next thing I knew it was two o'clock. Happens to me all the
time."

"Did they tell you anything useful?" Buck asked.

The old treasure hunter shook his head. "I was hoping
they could tell me something that might give us a lead on
who it was that rolled that rockpile down on top of me."

"But no leads?"

"Nope. I'm afraid the best shot we've got is just to go
back up to the canyon and take another look around."

"Well, I have something," Buck said. He took his pen
from the pocket of his shirt and began to sketch on a napkin.
"Do you recall the picture of El Cacique we saw in Señora
Gutierrez's house?" He carefully drew the skyline of the
red mountain Tenuco as he had memorized it while sitting in
the old woman's home. "Here on the north side, the artist
put two round objects, like boulders, which line up with the
lighter-colored rock in the foreground, and over here on the
south side, a tall piece of rock which looked like it had
cracked away from the hard formation on the top of the
bluff, but didn't fall down the slope. I noticed it because it
looked a little like a figure kneeling in front of an altar. I've
got a hunch those features are not just some fantasy of her
friend Flaco the artist. I don't remember seeing that rock
up there, but if that cleft between it and the bluff is quite
narrow, then it will only be visible from one angle. I'm

betting if we go to the spot from which it can be seen, we'll find our site."

Simmons' eyes widened, and he sat up excitedly in his chair. "Tyler, you're a genius!" he declared. "You're worth every penny of what you're getting...for the book, of course."

Sharon had been paying close attention to her pancakes and sausage. She stopped for a moment, glanced suspiciously at Buck, then shook her head and continued eating.

"Well, I hope I'm right," said Buck, "because Sharon says she wants to leave after today's search. She has her own life to get back to, you know."

"What, when we're so close?" said Simmons plaintively. Then he nodded in acquiescence. "I guess we'd better get started then. I would sure hate to have come all this way, then leave with nothing to show for it."

An hour later, about mid-morning, they drove past Lastima, crossed the Rio Grande, and drove up the sandy wash behind Tenuco. They left the truck near the spot where the rocks had tumbled from the slope the previous day, and continued on foot. The sun was already high in the sky, and the shadows it cast were narrow, but very dark, and the temperature was quickly climbing past one hundred degrees. Buck shook beads of sweat from his sandy curls and wished he had remembered to bring a hat. Carrying the napkin on which Buck had sketched the mountain, Simmons led the trio, peering up onto the slopes above with a large pair of binoculars. Sharon trudged along resolutely, paying little attention to the surroundings, and laconically fielding her companions' attempts to engage her in conversation. Buck walked behind her, eyeing the skyline and trying not to be too distracted by the swaying of her round rear end, dressed in tight denim jeans.

As they approached a bend in the narrow canyon about a quarter of a mile beyond the rockfall, Simmons yelped excitedly. "Look! There it is!" He pointed up toward the side of the massive red bluff. Separated by only a few yards from the crumbling cliffs at the top of the mountain stood a single slab of rock which had cracked away from the hard formation which capped the butte, but which had not fallen onto the talus slope below. It was clear the narrow gap would no longer be visible if they were to walk another fifty yards. The place where they stood was a sharp bend in the canyon, a place where the mountain had been eroded away by the meandering arroyo to form a hollow grotto with dark overhanging walls. The water running down the sides of Tenuco had cut several clefts into the surrounding rock, and had left small wind-swept dunes of iron-rich red sand. "We must be right on top of it," Simmons declared eagerly. "Are you getting anything?" he asked Sharon.

"Hush," said the dark-eyed young psychometrist suddenly. "Listen." She frowned and looked around the little grotto. Buck and John stopped and stood for a moment holding their breath. There was no wind at all, and the hot silence pressed upon them like molten glass.

"What is it?" whispered Simmons.

"Like thunder," she replied, whispering also.

Buck stepped close to her and took her hand. From a long way away, so far he could feel it more than hear it, came a rumbling, a sound like the wind mumbling in the mouth of a cave. Eyes wide, he looked at her, and she nodded slightly. Warily, he looked up, as though expecting any instant to see rock tumbling down upon them. The sky seemed to grow more intensely blue, and darker, like turquoise growing wet from the inside out. The rumbling swept around the curves in the narrow canyon as though a wall of water were only seconds away, a wall of water which pounded and throbbed like the hooves of a thousand horses. The sky grew darker, and Tyler's vision began to glass over, creating a landscape drawn in planes of glistening purple and green, like the retina burn-in from staring into the sun. The hooves pounded in driving rhythm, the insistent throbbing of hide-covered drums.

The glaring darkness closed in on him. It was night, and the sky glared blue-black, obsidian glowing with the unreal purple of pressure on the eyeballs, and the throbbing of a tom-tom drove his heart to pound against his ribs and to echo from the rock walls of the grotto. Light flickered, electric like the blue-white of an arc, flashing against the rock from the little fire where the old Indian sat drumming. His chanting was a rumbling, a grumbling, a droning of a thousand voices in the vault of a cavern.

Beside the fire lay the settler's boy, shaking and moaning, with sweat pouring from him and flowing past their feet. His voice rose and fell like howling wind as he struggled to follow the chant. Beside him the medicine chief's clay pot bubbled on the fire, and the water tumbled and mumbled like the sound of muffled hooves thundering on the sand.

Then from somewhere not far off came a baying, a howling like a hound on the trail, like wind in reeds, like a tormented soul. The old Indian stood, his eyes flashing green like phosphorescent seafoam as he peered into the night. Again the hound bayed, closer, and again. Then, with the sharpness of a rifle shot, the dog yelped, a scream of mortal pain, and was silent. El Cacique stared into the night. Then he raised the bubbling crock high above his head, poured the water onto the fire, and disappeared with the night in a cloud of rushing steam.

"That's it!" declared Buck Tyler. "That was how Heebs found the spring. He used the boy's dog to track him down."

"This is it, isn't it?" Simmons demanded excitedly. "You can see what happened here, can't you?" He rushed around the little grotto, looking into the clefts in the rock eagerly.

Suddenly they heard another sound, sharp and piercing like the yelp of the settler's hound. "Eee-haw!! Eee-haw!!" All three of them jumped as though burned and stared in astonishment as a mule stepped out from behind a jutting outcropping of rock.

"I've got a very bad feeling about this," said Buck.

"Hey, look here," called Simmons, pointing to the ground before one of the clefts in the rock. "Someone has been here, and recently. There are footprints leading into this cleft." Buck and Sharon hurried to join him, and saw the footprints, clear and unmistakable, the footprints of a large man. In the back of the cleft the red sands had been washed away by erosion, leaving a narrow tunnel less than two feet high, a tunnel which disappeared into the heart of the mountain. "There are two big battery-powered lights in the truck," Simmons told them. "I'll wait here while you go back and get them, Buck. It looks like whoever was here has crawled back into this hole."

"You're going in after him?" asked Sharon.

"Damn right I am," said Simmons, with his tight, humorless smile. "I haven't come this far to be ripped off."

Buck left at a trot and quickly returned with the two battery lamps from the truck, and he followed Simmons into the tight little hole, crawling on his belly. "Coming?" he asked Sharon.

"I guess so," she replied grimly. "I don't think I want to be left out here alone."

The tunnel was too small for them to crawl on their knees, and too narrow to permit them to turn around inside it. Carrying one of the lights, Simmons crawled on his belly like a snake, followed by Buck, and Sharon struggled along after them with the other light. It was cool inside the rock, and they could hear each other's heavy breathing as they dragged themselves with their elbows along the sandy bottom of the cramped little passageway. "Look at the top of the tunnel," Buck commented to his companions. "It's all blackened with soot like there has been a fire in here."

Quite suddenly the tunnel opened into a larger space, and John Simmons cried out in astonishment. They were in a vault, a steep-walled cavern with a floor of sand and a ceiling which disappeared up into black shadows thirty feet above their heads. The walls were decorated with petroglyphs and pictographs, some chipped, some stained, and some smoked onto the stone surfaces. The artistry was varied, some sophisticated and eloquent, some crude and indecipherable, as though many people had passed through and left a mark. In the highest places Buck could see the patterns of constellations marked in small crosses, and among them were interspersed the running swastikas of the moving planets, exactly like those he had seen on the ceiling of the kiva at

Kin Bineola in his peyote vision. Niches chopped into the rock still bore the charred stumps of torches, and two of them still smoldered as though they had just been extinguished, filling the cave with the bittersweet tang of mesquite smoke. Against the back wall, an altar had been cut from a single massive block of blood-red pipestone, a stone Buck knew immediately must have been brought from the beds of northern Arizona, hundreds of miles away. His jaw fell open, and Sharon gasped as the light of their battery lamps glinted from thousands of nuggets of raw gold which were scattered on the sand like grain on a threshing floor, and which were heaped on the glossy polished altar. Sitting on top of that block, with handfuls of the precious bits of metal falling through his fingers, was Father Justiano. His mocking laughter echoed in the ancient hidden shrine.

"Thirty years I have prayed to claim this prize in the name of Almighty God, in fulfillment of His command," he cried out in exultation, "and today I have snatched it from the hands of the agents of Satan, and brought it home to Mother Church!"

"You no-good son of a bitch!" spluttered John Simmons. "How the hell did you..."

"Did you think you could cheat God, you fools?" asked the big priest, jumping down from the altar. He took from the pocket of his cassock a cigarette lighter, stepped to the smoldering torches, and relighted them. "Do you think God was guilty of your own materialistic greed when he ordered Moses to build His ark and His temple in the wilderness with gold, according to the Holy Scripture beginning in the 25th Chapter of the book of Exodus? Do you think Holy Church sent forth her consecrated priests into this desolate land in the 16th century of Our Lord seeking pagan gold for no better reason than the lust for power which drives the basest of pirates and the corrupt kings of the earth? Hah!" In the flickering light of the torches, the gold twinkled and gleamed at the priest's feet. He scooped up a handful of the glittering nuggets and held them up above his head. "The gold of Exodus has spiritual power because it is sacred unto God! Holy, and incorruptible! It is His, then and now, and forever!"

"You are a lunatic!" Simmons declared.

"I am the last of the faithful," Justiano retorted. "The Church of Rome has grown weak, full with politicians, social workers, and Sunday saints like the Protestants. But I alone have kept the faith, and today, today I am fulfilled!"

"Aw, fer Christ sake," muttered Buck Tyler, turning aside and sitting down on a mound of the dry red sand which the shifting waters of time had heaped against the wall of the cave. He chuckled with irony. "What the hell, John, it's still going to make one hell of a book," he said. "So how did you find this place, Padre?" he asked the exultant priest.

Justiano's face darkened, and he nodded seriously. "Late last night I was called to the side of Señora Concepcion Gutierrez to hear her last confession," he said. "Perhaps one of you may know why." He looked pointedly from one of them to the other, and seeing their blank expressions, continued. "She was visited by a demon incarnate, a diabolical villain, and struck down in her own home. Before she died, she revealed to me a secret she had kept an hundred years, revealed to me so Our Father's precious gold could be brought unto Him before the altar of the humble church her friend Father Cabrito built."

From the shadows where she had stood near the entrance to the cave, Sharon glared at John Simmons. "A few drinks with the old timers," she scoffed accusingly. She moved away from the others, toward a recessed place in the back of the ancient Indian sanctuary.

"You think I killed the old woman?" Simmons called after her. "You think I went there to force her to talk, is that what you think? Well, you're wrong. And what makes you so sure this gold-damned fanatic didn't do it himself? You don't think he has been sitting in that nowhere old church all these years for nothing, do you? Holy gold, my eye!"

"Blasphemy!" snarled Father Justiano. "Witches! Spiritists and liars! Murderers! I'll see you imprisoned for life for this, by Almighty God, I swear it."

Simmons began to chuckle with a sinister tone. "You think that's how I found this place, don't you, by witchcraft and murder? No, my sanctimonious and superstitious friend, I found this cave because you led me to it. You provided me with what I needed to know, and you did it because you secretly feared Ms. Hightower's psychic vision would lead me to it before you got the secret out of the old woman. I suckered you in, you greedy bastard."

"What are you talking about, John?" asked Buck. "What about the ISPI people, and their parasentient search?"

"Hah. What a joke," scoffed Simmons, clearly enjoying himself. "I suckered you in too, and you suckered her. You two wanted to believe that twitchy-witchy stuff so bad you actually swallowed that story about half of those starry-eyed bead-waggers all coming up with the same results. I put those marks on that map where I wanted them to show up."

"Then you knew about this place all along?" Buck asked accusingly.

"Well, of course I did, to a point, just like Saint Francis here. I only needed some help with the little details."

"Very clever," said Father Justiano, "but as you can see, your duplicity was futile. I was here first, and the gold belongs to me, and to God."

Simmons began to chuckle again, and then to laugh out loud. "That's what you think," he said, strutting back and forth before the lean, broad-shouldered priest.

Suddenly they heard Sharon cry out from the recess at the back of the cavern. "Oh, my! Oh, look over here!"

The three men turned toward her, then quickly moved to join her, carrying the battery lamps. On a raised ledge about shoulder high they found the desiccated skeleton of a man who had last been dressed in a heavy black greatcoat. "Orville Heebs," gasped Buck Tyler.

Chapter Eleven

Buck moved close to Sharon and put his arm around her shoulders in the cool dry cavern. She shuddered a little, then reached out her hand to touch the crumbling remnant of the dead man's coat. From somewhere far above them in the dark shadows came the rumbling of distant thunder. As though the rock had become transparent, they could see the little grotto outside the cave. Above them, a storm began to gather quickly. Dark clouds swirled like huge tattered tendrils to form a vault, a great cathedral which dwarfed the canyons and ridges of the desert mountains. Around them, rain began to fall in dark slanting columns enclosing the space where Tenuco Mountain rose like a blood-stained altar. The winds began to rise, and to howl like a demon chorus in counterpoint to the booming of the thunder, a basso-profundo litany chanted in strident rhythm by a horde of sepulchral monks.

At the mouth of the cleft, Orville Heebs struggled to load a wooden cask of the healing waters of El Cacique's spring onto his great iron-wheeled buckboard, the wind whipping his black greatcoat up around his head like the frenzied flapping of the wings of some huge buzzard. He struggled, staggered, and tripped as the sand beneath his feet turned to slick red mud which sucked at his boots, and the heavy cask fell to the ground and shattered, further soaking him. He raised his fists to the storm and howled his curse unto the God who drove the rain into his face. The two black geldings which pulled his wagon began to stamp and scream, their eyes in horror bulging white in the sky-splitting flashes of the lightning which crashed around them. They reared and bucked, and kicked madly at the singletree and harness of the wagon, and at each other. Tangled in the traces, one of the great beasts fell beneath the other and screamed and screamed as the iron-shod hooves chopped again and again into its flesh.

On the steep slope of the canyon wall another horse appeared, a huge pale horse of shadow-gray and powder blue, whose mane and tail swirled and flowed like the tattered clouds above, like steam gushing forth from boiling water dashed upon rock heated to blue-white. The great spirit horse reared and tore the air with its flashing hooves, and when it stamped and reared again, the red rock shattered and sent knife-edged shards tumbling down the slope toward the dark figure below. Astride its back rode El Cacique, his skin glistening the color of wet pipe stone, the contours of his muscles standing out as though chisel-cut in planes like the rock from which his mighty steed split flying shards. On his chest he had strapped a macabre war-shield, a plate made of human ribs bound up with sinew, and upon his head he wore the bone-white rack of the antlers of the mountain buck, a rack which stabbed the sky like lightning flashing upward. His long hair, black and silver-gray, stood out from his head as though static-charged, and blue-white sparks crackled in the warrior's mane around his shoulders. Across his face was painted a band of black and slashes of glittering powdered gold. Over his head the medicine chief raised his spear, a stone-tipped shaft of awesome size, which stood starkly against the darkening sky like the dead trunk of a lightning-scarred high mountain pine. In his other hand he held his drum, and when he beat the spear shaft against the tanned hide drumhead, the thunder boomed, and the rock trembled. His eyes shone from the band of black like banked coals in a the heart of a smoldering tree, like living gems of fire, and his voice rang out like the tolling of a bell, shaking the earth at the feet of Orville Heebs.

Heebs staggered and fell against the hoof-shattered side of the buckboard, his face a mask of terror, stark and white. Then from within him rose a rage, and he thrust his fists up toward the fearsome vision of the medicine chief and roared out his curse in a torrent like a hell-struck preacher with the tongues of Pentecost.

As Buck and Sharon watched in gaping awe, they saw another man coming up the canyon struggling against the whipping wind, and not far from him, a fourth. His heavy homespun cassock soaked and dragging, Padre Cabrito fought the raging violence of the storm, crying out to God in anguish to forgive him for the horror that his weakness and his pride had wrought upon the peaceful valley. His feet churned the mud to drive his stocky body forward, but he was blocked and hurled back again and again by the force of the downpour. He fell to his knees, his cassock torn, and the rocks beneath him rent the skin of his arms and legs to release his blood to flow as one with the ruddy earth. Prostrate, he dragged himself forward, his prayer whipped from his lips and lost in the howling of the storm.

Behind him, cringing in a hollow in the rock stood Randolph Morton, his fancy suit reduced by the power of the elements around him to the tattered rags of a clown. Like a child trapped before the hungry jaws of a raging bear, he screamed and wept in helpless horror as he saw El Cacique raise up his spear and gather to its long obsidian tip a ball of shimmering green fire. Like a thing alive, the emerald fire wrapped itself around the shaft of the war lance, crackling like burning flesh, sizzling like blazing fat from the blue-white sides of the great spirit horse, and from the red-hot skin of the wrathful shaman upon its back. Then the old Apache swept the point of his weapon down toward his enemy below, and cast the fire like a cannonball toward him.

When the fireball struck the ground at Heebs' feet, the mud splashed up like a fountain, and the floor of the canyon shook. Heebs' black horses in their frenzy tore free from their harness and the one still standing fled madly up the canyon, leaving the other struggling and kicking on the ground, its last breath forcing a final scream of terror from its bloody foam-flecked mouth. Like a tornado's roaring funnel, the green fire swirled down from the churning cloud above, and El Cacique swept it up and hurled it again toward Heebs. The medicine peddler drew his bone-handled pistol and fired shot after shot toward the horseman above him, each barking report of his firearm producing a ball of angry yellow flame, and a fiery streak across the narrow canyon.

El Cacique swung his drum, and the streaks boomed against it like cannonfire, and ricocheted to burst against the tortured rock.

"I never miss! God damn you, I never miss!" the black-cloaked madman screamed. When his pistol clattered empty in his hands, he hurled it in frustration at his tormentor and ran to seek shelter in the cleft of the spring. Again the green fire encircled El Cacique, and the wind howled like the damned at judgment as he hurled the seething power of his weapon into the cleft. With a rumbling like the pounding hooves of buffalo hordes, the spring suddenly gushed forth a torrent of mud, red as blood, and surging like a ruptured artery.

Then, like a flash of lightning, but deep yellow, a light glinted in the cleft. From the widening passageway which the flow had cut into the rock flashed forth a burst of brightness. Eyes suddenly wide with awe, and his adversary instantly forgotten, Heebs pounced upon the glowing artifact, a foot-long blade of crystal ice, nightmare-black, with a handle of the brightest gold, which pulsed and gleamed in cold temptation. Like a madman possessed, like a zealot who has looked into the eyes of his god, Heebs held the black blade over his head and bayed out fiendish laughter. Teeth bared in the face of the storm, he rushed out of the cleft and again confronted the shaman's power. El Cacique swung his spear shaft again, and hurled his green fire. With a roar of savage triumph, Heebs swung the blade backhand like a sword, splattering the ball of sizzling green to tatters, which were swept away by the relentless bitter wind.

From his hiding place in the hollow of the rock, Morton watched him, his eyes bulging from his head in his horror of the supernatural, and in the fascination of his greed. Lying prostrate in the mud a few yards away, Padre Cabrito also saw the raging huckster raise the blade, and he saw the blue-white flash of lightning, and the seafoam green of El Cacique's fire gleam from the heavy golden handle. "Oh, no," he prayed, "oh, Dear God, no. What evil have I unleashed?"

The great spirit horse reared up, its massive body surging upward like a cloud of hot blue smoke, and its mane swirled with the vortex of green as the shaman gathered his fire. Then the flashing hoofs struck the rock again, the thunder drummed down upon the canyon in crushing hammer blows, and the fireball of green spat forward like a blazing comet. Heebs swung his blade and sent it back in a flaming arc to burst around the horseman and his mount. Lightning stabbed down again and again, filling the canyon with the reeking acrid smoke of ozone and scorched rock. The drumhead burst, the spearhead shattered casting white-hot shards, and the old Indian fell rigid from his horse, and tumbled down the slope to lie motionless in the blood-red mud which oozed from the cleft in Tenuco Mountain's side.

As though the earth itself were stunned in awe, a sudden silence fell upon the canyon. Heebs stood a moment gasping for breath. Then he turned quickly and looked toward the cleft of the spring. The mudflow had stopped, and had eroded from the rock a passageway large enough to crawl into. Throwing the obsidian blade to the ground at his feet, he ran to the broken remains of his buckboard and dug through the jumbled things beneath the seat. He pulled forth a tightly-sealed metal tin, twisted off the top, and cried out, "Hah!" in satisfaction as he saw his matches were still dry. Stuffing the tin into the pocket of his rain-soaked greatcoat, he hurried to the cleft, and began to work his way back into the tunnel.

Morton watched him, not yet daring to move from his place. After a moment, he heard his partner's triumphant laughter ring out from the cave. He started to move forward to join Heebs in his victory, then his breath caught in his throat. Without a sound, without a tremor, the earth above the cleft began to sag. His jaw fell open, and worked in horror up and down. He reached out his hand in futile gesture as the mud slipped, and flowed like clotting blood to fill the cleft completely, cutting off the avaricious cackle of the Reverend Doctor Orville Heebs. "I told him," he gasped. "I told him!" he cried, finding his voice a tortured squeak in his knotted throat. "I told him not to fool with that old witch doctor. It's a curse! This place is cursed!" He leaped from the hollow in the rock and ran madly down the canyon, without ever once looking back.

Cabrito lay on his face sobbing into the mud. Above him the sky rumbled softly, and the clouds began to disperse. The little priest rose to his knees and crawled forward to where the black blade lay before him on the sand. Raising his face to the last gentle showers of the desert cloudburst, he wept.

John Simmons began to hoot and prance with delight. "It is! It is Orville Heebs!" he crowed. "This proves it, don't you see? This proves this is the very same cave which Heebs and his partner Randolph Morton found...and claimed!" He turned to Father Justiano and rudely poked him in the chest with his finger, his face a leering mask of triumph. "It also means that you are trespassing on my property, Bozo." From the pocket of his khaki shirt, Simmons pulled a folded paper, one he had obviously carried for a long time. He unfolded it and waved it under the priest's nose. "This is a photocopy of the earliest recorded deed of title to this godforsaken chunk of worthless desert, a title to the land, to the water, and to all mineral and natural deposits found hereon. It is dated in 1871, and issued to one Reverend Doctor Orville Heebs, and to one Randolph John Morton, who happens to have been the grandfather of one John Morton Simmons, who happens to be me!"

Justiano snatched the paper from Simmons' hand and held it under the light of one of the battery lamps. "Hah!" he snorted. "This piece of paper is worthless. It was issued by a private law firm in Santa Fe forty years before New Mexico became a state. The territorial capital was south of here in Mesilla then, and your claim is no more valid than that huckster's." He pointed to the remains of the 19th century entrepreneur lying before them.

"You think so, do you?" said Simmons with a sneer. "Grandfather Morton lived to become a Senator in this state, and believe me, he took the necessary steps to cover himself...and me...with legal paperwork. Because he was a superstitious man, he never came back here, but he lived to be well over ninety, and before he died, he told me about this place, and he told me what he saw the night Heebs disappeared. I'm sure you know exactly what I'm talking about."

"You mean the Indian sacrificial knife you stole from Concepcion Gutierrez last night," the priest accused.

"If you know about that artifact at all, it is only because you stole it from the old woman yourself," the treasure hunter retorted. "Either that, or it will show up with old Cabrito's stuff, back at your little cathedral. I knew when I mentioned it I had you cold. I thought you were going to pop a gut, right there."

"What was the artifact?" asked Buck Tyler.

"A stone knife with a gold handle," Simmons told him. "My grandfather saw it that night. I was pretty young when he told me about it, but I never forgot what he said, and now after the better part of half a century, this is mine, all mine. You'll get your share too, Tyler, just like I promised, and you too, Miss Hightower. You both have been very helpful." He spread his hands and waved at the piles of nuggets. "How about all you can carry out of here today? At three hundred dollars an ounce, you could carry fifty grand in your pockets."

Sharon's lip curled with distaste. She cast Buck a dark look and turned her back on the three men.

"How about you, Justiano?" Simmons continued. "I'll make you the same deal, all you can carry out of here, if you'll take it now and get out. Of course, if you give me a rough time about it, you can go back to Lastima and wait for my lawyers to tell you that you don't get zip."

Tyler shook his head as the two men bickered, and stepped away to stand again beside Sharon, who was staring dejectedly at the body of Orville Heebs. "I didn't believe him when he told me about the gold," he began lamely. "I thought he was just saying that so I would help him with his book project."

"He paid you to come, didn't he?" she asked.

"Well, yes, he did, but it was just expense money, that's all. Come on, I take lots of projects like this — it's what I do for a living."

"What about me, Buck? Did he pay you for that too?" She turned and looked into his eyes.

His shoulders fell, and he looked down at the ground between his feet. "He offered to, yes, but Sharon, please, you've got to believe me. I didn't do that for the money, and I never knew about a treasure. The things I said to you, and the way I feel about you...those things are true."

"It's the things you didn't say that hurt, Buck," she said softly.

"I know this must sound awfully stupid now, but I really wish I had been straighter with you from the start. Sharon, I have always been inclined to take the easy way out of things. But I want you to know, whatever you decide to do, that I...I've fallen in love with you, and for the rest of my life, I will regret the way I have treated you, and I hope someday you can forgive me."

"I just hope someday I can forget you," she said, starting toward the entrance tunnel. "I'm getting out of here. The air in this place is starting to stink."

Buck turned to follow her, and Simmons grabbed his arm. "Hey, Buck, come on, we've got a book to write, remember?" he said. "Don't be a fool," he said as Tyler shook off his hand and moved after Sharon. "Let her go. There's a fortune here."

"It doesn't matter, sucker," said the priest. "It isn't going to be yours."

Then all four of them stopped and looked toward the narrow tunnel as they heard a scuffling sound. "Someone else is coming in here," said Buck in a hushed voice. They stood in astonishment as the head and shoulders of a man appeared, a man with long black hair and a powerful barrel chest. In a moment he stood before them.

"Asher!" said Sharon Hightower in surprise. "Asher Quaptewa!"

"Yes," said the big Indian, swatting the sand from his jeans and leather vest with his thick, muscular arms. "The secret of this place has been kept faithfully for a thousand years. Your Apache priest kept El Cacique's secret all of his life, and the old woman kept it all of her life." He reached beneath his vest and drew out the gold-handled black blade, and he held it up before their eyes to gleam darkly in the cold light of their battery lamps and the flickering golden glow of the torches. "Now you are going to keep the secret also."

Chapter Twelve

"Yes," said Asher Quaptewa, "You will keep this secret also...all of you."

"Now just a minute," began Father Justiano. "What makes you think you can..."

"Stop right there," the Indian commanded, pointing the black blade at the priest. "I have something to show you." He reached behind his back and brought forth something he had tucked into his belt. It was a foot-long cylinder of dull aluminum about two inches in diameter, with a red knob on one end. Archer gave the knob a deft twist with his thick powerful fingers, then with the thumb of the hand which held the device, pressed down a button in the middle of the twist knob. "It is a dead-man switch," he told them. "If I release this button, it will activate the timer, and that will detonate the contents, one quarter-pound of C-4 plastic explosive." He grinned humorlessly. "White man's magic," he said.

For a moment, the four of them stood speechless, then John Simmons grunted and clasped his hands behind his back. "All right, you have our attention. What do you want?" he asked.

"Why should I want anything?" Archer replied mockingly. "I have everything already."

"Look, uh, whatever your name is, this isn't going to get you the gold. I have a legal claim," Simmons declared.

Archer snorted derisively. "I have come to defend a much older claim than yours, grave-robber," he declared.

"Aw, come on, whatever you have in mind, put that thing away. Any idiot can tell that's a bluff," said Buck Tyler. "You haven't come all this way just to blow yourself up."

"Haven't I?"

"You had better listen to him," said Sharon softly.

"You know this guy?" Buck asked.

"She knows me," Quaptewa affirmed, "and now she knows

you, too, 'professor'." With the bomb in one hand, and the stone blade in the other, he waved them back farther into the cave, back beside the heavy red altar, and he stood between them and the entrance tunnel. "The arrogance of white-eye grave-robbers with college degrees is always amazing to me. You would go back to your schoolroom and write in your ignorant books about the history of my people that you discovered this place today, as though it did not exist until a white man stumbled upon it, as though no man knew about anything until a white man knows about it, and gives himself credit for discovering it in his books." He spat derisively into the sand. "And you, a mangy, greedy old dog, a garbage scratcher," he said to Simmons, "you think all of this belongs to no one until a white man has written a paper that says he owns it. Fah!" He glared at them malevolently.

"I am going to tell you something, and this might be a surprise to you also, Hightower. This cave was never lost. It has been known and kept by certain people, people, do you hear me, for a thousand years. The Anasazi made this place, and made it sacred to the true and living spirit of God who brings timeless life to the people, the Great Spirit who brought the people up out of the lower worlds into the Fourth World, and who made us men and women."

"Blaspheming heathen savage," growled Justiano.

"Your tongue rots in your head," said Quaptewa. "You are the worst of the lot. Four hundred years my people have suffered at the hands of your cult of guilt and greed. Four hundred years they have swallowed the lie that your blood-thirsty cruel white god holds their spirits in pawn, and will take them to eternal torture in the lower world if they do not become the slaves of gold-hungry priests. It was not the soldiers of the Anglo whites who have reduced my people to a remnant, but you, the priests of holy ignorance, the pimps of the Mother of Lies, who have robbed us of our spiritual maturity, and who have tried to keep us children in the ways of the Great Spirit to make us slaves of the Whore of Rome, and to sell us into servitude in the homes of the corrupt aristocracy of Catholic Mexico."

Father Justiano recoiled in astonishment before the bitter assault. "May God deliver your wicked flesh unto Satan," he hissed, "and forgive your poor, damned soul." The priest raised his hand and dramatically made the sign of the cross in the air before the Indian.

"'Mandrake gestures hypnotically,'" Asher scoffed. "Don't bother trying to frighten me with your simple-minded sorcery. I too am a priest. You see, there is a remnant which has not been spoiled by the spiritual blackmail of your cult of fear and death. Among the tribes of the children of the Anasazi there is a lodge, a secret lodge, which has kept the truth alive all of these centuries. One of the mysteries and secrets which our elders have preserved is knowledge of this kiva, and of others like it. I have been sent here today by the medicine chief of that great and ancient lodge to perform the sacred duty of protecting its secret from you." He looked from one of them to another, and he held the little bomb up before them. "And if I have to blow myself up with you to perform that duty, then it is a small sacrifice."

"Have you come here to kill us, Asher?" asked Sharon.

The Anasazi priest glared at her grimly. "You are of my tribe, Hightower," he said, "and you are of the Purple Bean Clan, which is given in marriage to my clan, according to the old ways. When you told me in Jerome that you were coming to Lastima because of what you had seen in your vision, I knew what you had found. I tried to stop you then, but this lying white snake had already succeeded in deceiving you. I followed you here, and I tried to stop you before you found the entrance to the cave."

"You rolled those rocks down on me," Simmons accused.

Quaptewa nodded. "It was a mistake. I was trying to move a larger rock, but I slipped. This time I will make no mistake." He turned again to Sharon. "Now that you know what kind of people these white devils are, come back with me, Sharon," he said imploringly. "You have the ancient vision, the gift of Gogyeng Sowuhti to all of the Dineh, our people. You can free yourself of the lies they have told you, and be now what you were born to be. Come back with me, back to the tribe, and to the old ways."

Sharon's eyes widened, and she stared at him in horror. "You mean, you expect me to let you kill these people, then go back to the reservation and be... your... your..."

"My wife, yes, and a priestess in the inner lodge. You have earned the right, and you have seen the truth."

She shook her head in disbelief. "Asher, please, you can't be serious! This is insane! This is murder. Asher, this is America. You just can't do that to people, not for... for gold, or a bunch of artifacts, or even for tradition!"

His face grew darker and his mouth turned down in a scowl. "So. After all that you have seen, you still turn your back on my love, and on the spirit of our people. Would you desecrate our most ancient temple to save the lives of three greedy, lying white-eye gold-hunters? Then I have no choice. You will die here with them!" He raised his head and threw back his broad, powerful shoulders. "You are right, grave-robber," he said to Tyler. "I do not intend to blow myself up to do this. What I do today is the sacred privilege of a warrior and a priest, and I am not afraid to do it eye to eye." He hefted the black blade like a meat cleaver and glared at Justiano. "Say your prayers," he growled, and moved purposefully toward the priest.

Justiano gurgled out a strangled cry and began to stumble backwards. Moving quickly, John Simmons stuck his thumb behind his wide silver belt buckle and brought out a tiny brass pistol, a Derringer about three inches long. Without hesitation, he shot Asher in the side, just over his kidney. With a look of shock and astonishment, the big Indian stopped, gasped, and turned toward the bristled-bristled old treasure-hunter. When Simmons fired his second shot into Asher's chest, the man dropped abruptly to his knees. The black obsidian blade fell from his hand, and the sinister aluminum cylinder fell beside it. The bomb made a single sharp cracking sound, and began to issue a thin stream of smoke.

Sharon screamed, her hands clutching at her face. "No!"

cried John Simmons. "No, you can't stop me! Not now!" He turned and dashed madly toward the entrance tunnel. "Get out! Get out!" he yelled at the others as he dived head-first toward the little passageway and began to scrabble at the sand to crawl into it.

His face a mask of agony and determination, Asher grabbed up the smoking grenade and lurched after him on his knees. Simmons squealed in fear and kicked frantically at the hands and face of the red-skinned giant who clutched his khaki trousers and struggled to follow him into the narrow wormhole. With blood spurting from the wound in his back, Asher held Simmons' leg against his chest and roared out his final defiance.

"Get back," shouted Buck to Sharon and Justiano. He grabbed Sharon's arm and pulled her toward the recessed area in the back of the cave where lay the grisly skeleton of Orville Heebs. He pulled her to the ground and threw his body across hers. Justiano dived to the sandy floor of the cave beside them, and held his hands over his head in terror, babbling an unintelligible prayer. Then Simmons' horrified squealings were cut off by the muffled roar of the explosion which slammed the three against the ground and filled the cave with choking dust and smoke.

The terrible shock of the explosion was a visceral experience, a pressure far beyond what could be described as sound, an impact like a fighter's kick on every point at once, an instant of white-hot blackness felt by every cell. Several minutes passed before anyone moved. Buck first became aware of a ringing in his head, and a burning sensation in his chest. He struggled to his knees and began to cough, and he felt Sharon move beside him. The torches had been extinguished by the blast, but one of the two battery lamps still cast its pale light into the dusty space in the ancient temple. Even at first glance from the back of the cave, it was apparent that the rock wall above the tunnel had collapsed, completely sealing off the passageway which led to the world outside.

While Buck sat holding Sharon sobbing in his arms,

Justiano climbed unsteadily to his feet and staggered across the nugget-strewn floor of the cave to the pile of rubble. He scrabbled at the rock a few minutes, but it was obvious no escape route was offered. All that remained of the two men was a single boot with a foot still in it.

Father Justiano sagged to his knees and began to pray in a mumbling, sing-song voice. He beat his fists against the ground, and he picked up handfuls of sand and threw them into the air to fall upon his head and back. He tugged at the heavy material of his cassock as though to rend it, with tears making streaks down his dusty cheeks. Clutching his rosary, he began to babble the formulae of its prayers, his words running together in a meaningless stream which rose and fell as he bowed his head and began to rock himself like a mother with an infant. Then suddenly he screamed in frustration like a child throwing a tantrum, and he hurled the string of beads across the cave. "Oh God, oh God, I've failed you, I've failed you! I waited so long, and I...I blew it! I blew it! Aaawww!"

Buck and Sharon had sat leaning against the side of the cave watching him in silence, then Buck stood and walked past him to relight the torches with his pocket lighter. "For Christ sake, Justiano, will you shut up," he said.

The tall sinewy priest turned on him like a snake, like a wounded dog snapping viciously at whoever was first to get near enough. "You! If it hadn't been for you, this never would have happened. You two and your Goddamned witchcraft! Oh, God! Oh, Lord, forgive me. Forgive me for my lack of faith, for I have fallen into the same unholy pit which claimed Father Cabrito. If I had not been tempted to believe in the power of your Satanic trickery, I would have run you out of Lastima the day you arrived. Concepcion Gutierrez would have told me. She loved the church! She would have told me, and all of this would have served the glory of God. But instead I welcomed you. I harbored you like vipers in the very bosom of the church. Witches! Sorcerers! You tempted me, and I failed. And now I am going to die here with you, imprisoned like rats." Staring madly from one of them to the other, he rose shakily to his feet. Then he began to shake his head. "No. No," he said, eyes suddenly gleaming with fanatical purpose. He took two quick steps and bent to scoop up the heavy blade of obsidian and gold. "With my last breath I shall resist you. In the name of Almighty God, I shall send you both to the Hell you deserve!" With abrupt and awesome power, he leaped forward and attacked Buck Tyler with the gleaming weapon of stone.

The black blade swung down in a sinister arc toward the smaller man's head, and Sharon screamed in horror. Buck moved so quickly it seemed to her he had already blocked the swing before it was begun. "Kiya!" he shouted as his left leg snapped back and planted his heel solidly at the same instant as the outside edge of his left fist caught Justiano's wrist, knocking the blade from his hand. "Ueess!" he cried as the leg snapped forward like a whip and the top of his foot slammed Justiano's lowest rib two inches into the soft tissue of his liver. Reaching across his face with his right hand to block the priest's left, Buck stepped in sideways, swinging his left arm down hard to strike a hammer fist into Justiano's groin. Without ceasing his motion, Buck snapped up his elbow to catch the point of his assailant's outstretched chin just as he bent forward double. The priest sank to the ground retching and gasping for breath, then collapsed sobbing in despair.

"A little Tae Kwon Do goes a long way," Buck said aside to Sharon. He picked up the gold-handled blade and stepped back to where she crouched against the stone wall of the cave. He sat beside her, picked up a handful of the heavy little raisins of the raw precious metal, and let them trickle between his fingers. After a while, he shook his head and laughed ruefully. "I'm sorry, Sharon," he said. "If I weren't such a coward, I would have admitted to myself long ago that I was in love with you, and that I knew my life was not going to be the way it was, and we could have avoided all this. But it all looked so easy, I just had to keep taking one more step."

Chapter Thirteen

Sharon reached over and put her hand on his, and leaned her head on his chest. "A fine mess you've got us into, Dr. Buckminster Butthead," she said. After a while, she took the black blade from his hands and sat turning it over in the light of the torches. It began to pulse and shimmer under her touch. Buck was immediately aware of what she was doing, and the thought of what they might see together was suddenly very frightening to him. For the first time since the explosion, he felt his terror sweep over him, his mind and body cringing from the horrifying recognition of the finality of their situation. He clutched her hand, and the obsidian blade, and he struggled to control his shuddering body and submit himself to the experience.

The walls of the cave became transparent, and from where they crouched, they could see a little distance away an ancient camp of Indian nomads, a circle of conic tipis, leaking pools of firelight into the night. From each tent came the sound of soft drumbeats. In the shadows, they saw a young man slip into the camp, enter the largest of the tents, the ceremonial tent, which is empty. Across the central firepit from the entrance was an altar of polished wood. Sitting upon the altar was a drum, and upon the drumhead was the black obsidian blade. The young shaman candidate snatched it up, and fled the tent.

In another of the tents, older shaman elders in ceremonial garb sat waiting and listening, drumming softly. One of them was El Cacique. As though hearing the thief run past, he smiled softly and nodded his approval, at which signal the drumming picked up harder and faster.

The candidate ran to the mouth of the cave, passed the little spring seeping up through the sand to form a small pool, and crawled up into the tunnel. Behind him, the shaman elders rose, and took up their drums and armloads of firewood. They packed the firewood deep into the tunnel, and packed more in behind it, and more. Then El Cacique brought a blazing torch, and set the wood on fire. Inside, Buck and Sharon watched as the candidate sat down on the sand beside them.

"That is why the walls of that tunnel were blackened with smoke," Buck said. "It was a test, and they were sealed in here by fire."

"Which means there is a way out," said Sharon.

"Hell, let's hope so. It might have been one of those fasting things, and he just had to stay in here until the tunnel cooled off."

"That's very reassuring, Buck," she said.

The vision faded like smoke rising up a chimney. Buck and Sharon stood in awe before the red pipestone altar, then turned to look into each other's eyes. "There is a way out of here," she said.

"I know," he replied, "and I know where it will be. That lesson is intended for me. All my life I have taken the easy way out. The way out of here will be the most difficult place in the whole cave to get to."

She nodded seriously, then suddenly broke into a delighted smile. "Buck, remember there is no hole Sipapu, no entrance up from the Lower Worlds in this kiva," she said excitedly. "I think that is because we are not at the top of Sipapu, we are at the bottom."

"Aaahh!" Father Justiano suddenly groaned. He struggled to rise from the fetal position in which he had lay on the sand trying to recover from the pain and shock of Buck Tyler's precisely-focused blows. He looked up at them from his knees with fearful hope contorting his face. "I have had a vision from God!" he cried out. "He has shown me a vision of the ladder of Jacob leading up to heaven. He has shown me there is a way to climb out of here!"

All three of them raised their eyes and looked up into the dark shadows above the altar. Buck snatched up the battery lamp, and pointed the beam upward. The ceiling of the cave was rounded near the front, but at the back it rose steeply in what appeared to be a fracture in the rock.

There seemed to be nothing at all to grasp onto, and the near-vertical cleft was too wide at the bottom for chimney-technique climbing until almost halfway to the top. No matter which way Buck pointed the beam of light, there was one small place which still was left in shadow. "There," Buck declared. "That is the one place in this monkey-trap we cannot see without going up there to look. That is where our way out will be."

"We could never get up there," said Justiano. "There is nothing in the cave we could use to make a ladder." Then he rose to his feet, eyes wide. "Wait, I have an idea. We can make a ladder of ourselves. It would mean only one of us could get out, but he could go get help."

"That won't work," said Buck positively. "If we sent Sharon to get help, only one of us would still be alive when they got back to dig us out."

"And she is the least likely to make it out," Justiano added, earning him a disgusted look from Sharon.

"We all know how far we could trust you to go for help," Buck continued. "You would just happen to discover this place along about Christmas, next Christmas. And as for leaving you here with Sharon while I went for help..."

"Only one of us would still be alive when you got back," Sharon concluded, fixing Justiano with a cold gaze.

Buck stepped up onto the altar, and began to run his hands over the rock wall behind it. "Set that light down here on the altar, close to the wall, as though it were a little fire," he said to Sharon. The light of the lamp cast a shadow from each bump and groove in the near-vertical wall. Sharon gasped aloud. Shown clearly in the heightened relief of the shadows was a set of staggered little handholds chipped into the rock. "There's your ladder," he said to Justiano.

The priest began to laugh and jump up and down, capering like a schoolboy. Then suddenly, he remembered the gold. "Hah!" he cried out, looking around again at the piles of nuggets. He began to rapidly unbutton his cassock. He pulled it from his body and spread it out on the sand, and, wearing an undershirt and a pair of black pajama-like underslacks, he began to throw handfuls of the nuggets onto the broad skirt of the ceremonial garment.

"Come on, let's get out of here," Buck said to Sharon, shaking his head solemnly at the scrabbling priest. "These batteries aren't going to last forever. I'll go first, and Sharon, you come up after me, with that obsidian blade. I don't know what it is yet, but I have a feeling we're going to need it."

"Wait," she said, pointing at Justiano. "If we go out now, what will happen? Is he going to get everything after all? What about the Anasazi? I don't want to sound like a crazy woman, but perhaps it would be better for everyone if we also keep their secret."

"You mean, stay here and die?" asked Buck. "I for one would be happy to walk away from this place and forget I ever heard of it. But I'm not ready to die here if I don't have to, Anasazi or no."

"I'm afraid I agree with you," she said, "but what about him?"

They watched as Justiano piled thirty or forty pounds of the gold on the cassock, rolled it into a tube, and bound it around his waist with the sleeves and waistcords. "God will have this gold yet," he declared.

"I won't die for the secret, but I won't kill for it either," said Buck. "Let him have the gold — the church will just put it in their treasure caves, or give it to the banks to put in their treasure caves. To hell with the gold. Let's get out of here."

Using the fingerholds of the Anasazi, Buck began to climb the wall behind the altar. He had some experience in rock climbing, enough to recognize the wall would not have offered a great obstacle to an expert boulderer, but he had only ascended a few meters before his forearms and calves began to shake. "It's not fatigue, it's only fear," he tried to convince himself, pressing his cheek against the cold stone. He did not look down until he reached the point where the cleft was narrow enough for him to reach his leg across. He wedged himself into the chimney and breathed heavily, taking advantage of the easier position to rest.

Below him, Sharon started up the rock face also, then jumped back down. "What is it?" he called down to her. "Can't you make it?"

"It's an easy climb," she assured him. Spreading her legs apart like a Sumo wrestler, she raised one foot and then stamped it back down to squat deeply. With an audible rip, the crotch seam in her tight blue jeans parted. "That's better," she said, moving back and forth to test her increased flexibility. She hopped back up onto the altar stone, grasped the shallow finger and toe holds, and began to climb the rock more quickly and steadily than Buck had. "You better get a move on," she said as she approached his position.

The opening in the shadow at the top of the chimney was very narrow, and Buck was able to pull himself up through it easily. "How does it look?" Sharon called up after him.

He pointed the light upward, and groaned. The chimney widened too far for him to reach both sides at once, and the beam of light disappeared into the shadows forty feet above him. Extending upward along one side was a crack a few inches wide. "It looks pretty scary," he replied, "but we'll make it." Without further hesitation, he wedged his fist into the crack above his head, wedged his boot into it below, and began to climb.

"Wait a minute," called Justiano from the chamber below. "You can't leave me down here without the light. I can't see the handholds by what's left of the torch."

"You think I can climb this crack in the dark?" Buck demanded.

"Just wait there for me to catch up with you, then I can shine it up ahead of you," the priest suggested. Reluctantly, Buck passed the fading flashlight down to Sharon, who dropped it to Justiano below. He took a piece of the rope sash he wore with his cassock and bound the light to his forearm, then began to climb. He struggled with the weight of his booty, the clumsy roll of cloth and gold he had strapped around his waist, but he soon scaled the first wall and shined the light up into the long shaft so Buck could continue. "The Lord shall have the victory today, I promise you," he called up to the others with a hysterical cackle. "You're dealing with The Big Guy Himself now, I hope you know that."

"Right," growled Buck as he began the long climb up the narrow crack.

The three climbers labored without speaking for a long time, their gasping and panting echoing dully in the narrow chamber. A fold opened up in Justiano's makeshift pack, and a few of the nuggets began to dribble out, making a forlorn clattering sound as they disappeared into the shadows below. "Damn," he muttered. "Damn, damn, damn."

Just when Buck thought he could endure the pain and stress of wedging his fists and arms into the vertical crack no longer, his hand felt a horizontal ledge above him. With his heart pounding in his chest, he uttered a sigh of relief and pulled himself up to where he could put his arm up onto the ledge. Then suddenly a wave of horror and nausea swept over him. He heard a scream reverberate from the stone walls above, and the thudding and scraping of a body falling toward them. Hugging the rock in terror, he screamed also, and very nearly fell backward from the ledge as he saw a naked young man plunge from the darkness above to strike the rock before him. "Buck, no!" Sharon cried out below him. "It's not real. Get ahold of yourself!"

With tears springing from his tightly squeezed eyes, he sobbed and struggled to regain control of his racing heart and trembling body. He opened his eyes and clenched his jaw to control his revulsion at the sight of the gaping eye sockets of the shattered skull on the ledge a foot from his face where his groping hand had touched it.

"Go on up, Buck," she called to him urgently. "We can't stay like this forever."

"Right," he said, getting a grip on himself. With an angry gesture, he swept the skull and a few other ancient crumbling bones from the ledge. They fell a long time, then clattered crustily against the rock far below. In a few seconds, he stood on the narrow ledge breathing heavily, and he was soon joined by Sharon. There was room for only the two of them, but Justiano was able to put both of his arms up onto the secure little platform and rest there also.

"Are you all right?" Sharon asked Buck, touching his face gently.

He nodded, took several deep breaths, then shined his lamp upward again to see where their path led. "Oh-oh," he groaned. "I have a feeling we've made a big mistake. I think we have climbed the wrong side of this hole." Above them the shaft made a sharp bend and disappeared horizontally away from them. From the wall on which they were climbing extended a flat overhang of about twelve feet. "We'll have to go back down until we can find a way to get around to the other side," he said, resignation heavy in his voice.

"We had better find it quickly," said Justiano, indicating his lamp, which was beginning to glow a murky orange. He started to move down the long crack.

"No, wait a minute," said Sharon, pointing up the shaft. "There on the opposite side, right at the top of the bend. There is some kind of a pole up there, fastened into the rock." By moving as far as he could to the side on the ledge, Buck was able to point the lamp to clearly reveal a lodgepole about four inches thick and three feet long, wedged into a crack with several small stones. "That was put there deliberately," she pointed out. "I think we are expected to jump."

Buck felt the cold visceral shudder of vertigo renewed as he visualized himself at the top of the chasm falling out away from the rock to leap. "I'm afraid you're right," he whispered hoarsely. "There must be another ledge on this side just before the top."

"Just as well," said Sharon. "If we had to go back, he would end up above us on the other side, and I wasn't looking forward to that."

"We might have to anyway," said Buck, a chilling realization coming over him. "That pole up there could be six hundred years old. Those bones down below were like chalk.

The chance of that wood still being strong enough to hold our weight is pretty small."

"Can we change places?" Sharon asked him. "I'm the lightest. I'll jump first."

He saw the seriousness in her eyes, and he relaxed and laughed. Calmness came over him he had not felt since the explosion had sealed them into the cave. "I guess if we've had it, we've had it, right?" he asked. She smiled and nodded, with a philosophical shrug.

"Watch this," he said, and began to climb quickly up the last few meters. In minutes, he stood on the top ledge, a tiny platform of rock a few inches wide, slightly above the pole sticking out from the opposite side of the yawning black gulf beneath him. With his back and his palms pressed against the cold wall behind him, he took a deep breath, afraid if he were to hesitate even an instant he would freeze in terror and fall. "And now," he cried out loudly, "zee Great Buckelli will perform zee triple flip!" He pressed hard with his hands, fell outward from the perch, then hurled himself forward in a swimmer's racing dive toward the outthrust stake. "Yaaaahhh!" he yelled. He grasped the pole, clung to it tenaciously, and slammed against the rock. The pole held. He clung to it for several seconds, fighting the shuddering of his body and the ringing pain in his face and chest. Then he scraped his toes across the rock to find footholds, and pulled himself up. The wall sloped away gently, and he found himself standing on the floor of a small round chamber.

"That looked like fun," she called to him bravely from the diving perch across the shaft, "but I sure wish I was a foot taller." She drew a deep breath, and fixed the pole with a gaze like a hawk about to pounce on a rabbit. "GeeRonimo!" she shouted, and dived for the pole. She grabbed it near the end with both hands, and planted her feet against the wall. The pole creaked loudly, and gave a few inches. One of the rocks wedged in beside it moved, sending chips flying. She quickly found handholds on the rock and took her weight from the pole. In seconds, she clambered up the rock and stood beside Buck.

"Lady, you are one hell of an athlete!" he declared, hugging her happily.

"You've got to be tough to be a fat little Indian in a Jane Fonda world," she laughed breathlessly. "I pump iron twice a week."

Father Justiano stood on the narrow ledge panting and sweating. Clinging precariously to the rock face with one hand, he struggled to tighten the knot he had made in the gold-laden cassock he had strapped around his middle.

"Get rid of the gold, you idiot," Buck called to him. "That stake is only going to take so much weight."

"It is God's gold," he replied. "Do you think I have no faith? He has promised me that I will bring it unto His temple." He closed his eyes, crossed himself, then leaped across the chasm. He grabbed the pole. The ancient wood cracked, then held, but suddenly the stones wedging it into the rock slipped. "Oh, God!" the priest cried in horror as the end of the pole dropped to point downward. "God?" he gasped as his hands slid along the smooth dry wood. His fingers clutched at the pole, and failed to hold it. "Oh, God!" His scream echoing horribly in the narrow shaft, he fell into the darkness, gold nuggets clattering against the stone around him, and the light of the flashlight winking out below when he finally struck the bottom.

"Amen," said Sharon.

Chapter Fourteen

For a moment they sat in the dark silence, and then Buck struck a match.

"Where did you get that?" she asked him. "You don't smoke."

"I always carry waterproof matches in a little pocket on my boot," he told her.

"Oh, Buck, look," she said. He turned around to see they were on the edge of a good sized chamber with a rounded top, several visible passages and holes leading out, and in the center, a ring of rocks forming seats around a fire pit. He touched his match to the pile of ashes and charcoal in the pit, and a flame immediately came up, soon producing a pile of glowing coals to light the room.

Then again Sharon cried out in surprise. She pointed to a row of niches in the wall of the cave, in which were piled several skulls and other bones.

"Yeah," said Buck. "Are these the ones who failed the test, or the ones who passed? Heck we don't even know what the questions are."

"You're the anthropologist, aren't you, the great expert on Indian mysticism? Isn't that what you taught, Primitive Anthropology?"

"Hey, you're the Indian, aren't you? Isn't Indian wisdom supposed to be some kind of cultural or intuitive thing?"

"Is that what we're looking for, Indian Wisdom?" she asked sarcastically.

"Well, if this is some kind of initiation cave, then whatever they taught here might be clues to getting out," he said reasonably.

"Right, clues hidden in how many generations of myth and metaphor?"

"Well, we are not going to die here metaphorically," he pointed out. "I don't know what's going on here, but at least part of it seems to be real, the rock part."

"And the rest of it?" she asked.

Heard at first like muttering deep in the tunnels to the sides, a sound began to rise, the sound of people breathing and shuffling, of drums beating softly. From the shadows they could almost see ghostly figures.

"Oh, no, I've been here before," said Buck.

They laughed at him, and he felt himself blush, as he remembered his nakedness before them. Just out of vision, they gathered and muttered among themselves. As before, at Kin Bineola, he struggled to control his racing mind in spite of the maddening sensation that he was not alone in that inner chamber of his thoughts and feelings. Though he did not turn to look at her, he knew she stood naked before them also with him in the kiva, and he was surprised to become aware that she also was frightened. On the ceiling of the cave they saw the running swastikas of the wandering planets moving through the fixed-cross stars of the constellations, growing close to some appointed time, as though the kiva had been waiting centuries for their arrival.

"What are you?" they demanded. "Are you wolf? Are you deer?"

In the flickering torchlight they heard the beating of drums, a tom-tom throb which drove their hearts and sent their flesh pulsing in waves, as though it were that rhythm which gave substance and form to their being, as though without it they would collapse into the formless void from which flowed the visions they perceived to come and go.

"This is the kiva of Blackwater Stone Clan," chanted the voices which drove the mighty drums, in a tongue which was strange, but without misunderstanding. "If you are not worthy of entrance to the Fourth World, where men and women dwell, then you shall not leave this place alive. Your flesh shall be destroyed by the Kachina Tunwe-up, and you will be taken back to the Lower Worlds."

For a moment Buck felt his water grow cold and loose. If the kiva was sealed, their fate was sealed, and they had already therefore failed their test. As if in response to his fear, the floor of the kiva began to move, to pulse and creep, to reach out to feel him, to taste him. The bits of gold which were strewn around began to move together, to coalesce into a glowing form which rose up over them and stood upon the altar, shimmering, throbbing in irrefutable power. To his horror, and to Sharon's also, the gold took the form of Tunwe-up, the whipping Kachina, a man-bear-wolf monster with huge jaws, and eyes that fixed them with the intensity of their focus, the eyes of the mantis. The room began to echo round and round with a muttering roar, like the strident chanting of many voices.

A new fear took them, a fear beyond the mortal horror of their flesh. They felt their bodies change like the slipping of sand, and they stood as little children, as they had been in the ancient stone cities of the tribes. When they were disobedient and guilty, the Kachina had come to the caves and hogans of their parents, to demand that they be taken back down through the hole Sipapu to be destroyed. They remembered how their parents had cried out to the Kachina that they were only children, and begged the fearsome whipping god to let them pay him off with offerings of corn, meat, turquoise, and silver. They remembered how they had cringed behind their mothers' skirts at the sound of the fluttering bull-roarer the Kachina twirled over his head, and at the vicious crack of his lightning whip. They remembered, and their terror was fresh upon them.

"Where are your mothers now?" the thundering voice of the Kachina rumbled. "Where is the corn to pay for your childish transgressions against the people? Where is your turquoise and silver? Have you nothing except your own pitiful scraps of drying meat?"

Buck's thoughts scurried, looking for hiding, and beside him Sharon moaned at her awareness of her shame.

"You have taken something from the people which is not yours," the Kachina thundered, mighty golden jaws snapping, clashing, and huge golden eyes probing relentlessly into the corners of their minds, eyes cold and sure and implacable, like the eyes of a hungry puma closing upon its cornered prey. "You have stolen life and vision from the people, so there is no room for you in the Fourth World."

Guilt and despair flooded over them, for they knew the Kachina had spoken the truth. As clearly as if it lay on the altar before him, Buck saw the red pipestone pipe inlaid with the symbol of the great Water Snake in bits of turquoise, the pipe which he had taken from the kiva of Fire Clan at Kin Bineola. "It is by the power of the Water Snake pipe that the elders of the people are able to call forth the Water Snake," the Kachina told them. "If they cannot call him, there is no corn, and the people cannot live on the land. If men and women cannot live on the land, then only the creatures of the Lower Worlds exist, and that is what you must be, a scorpion, a turtle, a rat. If you have stolen the medicine pipe which calls the Water Snake, you have stolen the life of the people, and there is no room for you in the Fourth World. You are mine, and doomed."

Buck dropped his head in shame, and he knew the horror of his certain death.

"Gogyeng Sowuhti, the wise Old Spider Woman who is grandmother of all creatures, gave you, proud and faithless daughter, a bead when you were born. It was a bead of the Blackwater Stone, one of her tears as hard as ice, and black as night. She placed it between your eyes and pressed it into your head with her finger, and in it you can see what she shows you, like a reflection in a pool of still dark water. Where there is no vision, the people perish, for they stumble in the darkness, they forget who they are, and they strike out at each other like beasts without wisdom. They turn their backs upon each other and they are scattered by the winds, and swallowed up by the wilderness. The great kivas of the Anasazi are filled with dust, and the mouths of the great chiefs are filled with dust, and only the lower forms live in the house where wind whirls, because the vision has been taken from the people. You have kept from them the gift of Gogyeng Sowuhti, and for lack of it, they perish, and so there is no room for you in the Fourth World. You are mine, and doomed."

"This is real," said Buck Tyler to himself, and the realization weighed heavy and bleak upon him. "All the things I have ever hoped about my destiny, and about the nature of my existence, have been only prideful illusion, and have all come to this reality. I came into the world to be tested for the right to my humanity, and I have failed. I am going to die here, and whatever it means to descend into the Lower Worlds, I will suffer that."

He turned to look at Sharon, and his heart went out to her in sympathy, for he saw she was small with shame and fear, a fat little polyp of soon-corrupt flesh, with the haunted eyes of a rabbit in a snare.

"Now," said the fearsome Tunwe-up. "Now I take you." The monster rose above them, and around him blazed up fire. The roar of chant thundered in the cave, and the beast of gold reached out to claim his prizes. In the cold and final horror of certain death, Buck cried out with all his heart, and gave himself up to the Great Spirit, to God the Father of all living souls. It was a solitary act, his own, and for a moment Sharon was forgotten, as though left behind.

Then the roar was hushed, and a calm golden light came upon the dark little cave. He realized in an instant that she had left him also, to whatever fate his own heart decreed, and she had abandoned herself to the mercy of the God she also knew in spirit as surely as he. The Kachina Tunwe-up stood before them in radiant glory, and he reached up and took from his head the golden mask with the fearsome jaws and cold accusing eyes. Behind the devil's mask of terror they had been taught in their childhood to fear was revealed the face of El Cacique. "It is our father's brother," they gasped in astonishment.

"The fear of God is the beginning of wisdom," said the medicine chief, "but you must never forget that the forgiveness of the One who is Grandfather to us all is absolute. With such faith in God's perfect love, you may enter into the Fourth World not as ignorant children kept within the law by fear, but as understanding adults, prepared to take responsibility for preserving the rituals by which the people are preserved. If the Fourth World is to exist where men and women may live, it is only because you create it, and protect it." The gold began to fall from him in a glittering shower, making piles of nuggets and flakes on and before the altar on which he stood, and in a moment he stood before them naked also.

"So come and sit beside the fire with me," the old man said, finding a comfortable rock and holding his hands to the warm coals. "The young in spirit sometimes seek to find wealth in gold, so as to gain power to create change for good in the world, because it seems the easiest way to greatness. But there is no greatness in the greed which gives gold its power, nor in the pridefulness which comes of taking power over others in the hope of serving them more generously than they could serve themselves. The wise men of ancient times brought this gold here, because they knew to keep useless wealth hidden away in the heart of a mountain, not to protect it from the people, but to protect the people from its cruel power. To abandon pride and wealth in the hope of good is a narrow and difficult path, but it is the way out of the bondage of our inheritance from the Lower Worlds. When your path seems blocked by the obstacles of the world, have no fear, for you are loved by the Father of all spirit, and by the Grandmother of all creatures, and you possess their gift, the key to Sipapu, and the Fourth World."

Buck sat down across from him, staring at him in awe. "So it's you after all, and we have stumbled into your favorite haunt."

"Who do you think I am?" the old Cacique asked. "Would I be here if you were not?"

"So what are you, our Spirit Guide, or something?" Buck asked.

"Spirit Guide," the Indian chuckled. "In the Indian culture, Spirit Guides are usually animals, so I take that as a compliment." He took up his pipe, and lighted it with a long stick from the fire.

"Then is this some kind of test, and if we fail it, we

die here?" Buck asked him.

"Oh, you will die if you fail it, all right. You also might die even if you pass."

"Then this is not about escaping?" Sharon asked. "Like the Tibetan and Egyptian books of the dead, it's about dying?"

"Why do you look so surprised?" the ancient one asked. "Why shouldn't dying be a rite of passage? And if you are ready to think I am the ghost of an Anasazi medicine man, why should the idea of dying bother you?"

"I'm not afraid to die," Buck declared. "I jump out of airplanes just to dare it. But if there is a way out of this hole alive, I plan to find it."

"Good, good," Cacique said with a nod. "So tell me, when did your journey to this place begin?"

"That's a good question," said Buck.

"You entered into this place through the kiva of Fire Clan at Kin Bineola, when you ate the cactus and stole the Water Snake pipe. The pipe is a tool of civilization. It is not about the smoke. In the dark, the glow of the pipe is enough to see, and in the pipe, fire can be carried safely from one place to another. Building a fire is like nurturing a live thing. It must be fed at the right rate, and overfeeding it can kill it as quickly as starving. If you throw your kindling at a big log trying to set it on fire, soon you have only the log, and no kindling to start it with."

"Tending a fire is like tending a bean plant," he said to Sharon. They are two sides of the same skin, one creating life out of earth and air, and the other returning life to earth and air. Likewise a clan is not something which can be created all at once. It must become like a bank of coals, which is kept burning by the glowing remains of the great logs of the past. If fire rages through the house of the clan, or through the forest, it destroys everything. Only the Water Snake can bring the rains to control the fires. In the Kiva we learn the wisdom of keeping small fires in our pipes and stone pits, and of quenching the fires which might threaten the safely of the clan."

"Is that why Asher was sent," Sharon asked, "to quench us?"

"No. He was rash, like you. Too much fire."

"Then he failed the test we are now facing?" Buck asked.

"Failed? Are his lessons over because he is dead? His sacrifice was very pure, even if unwise."

"And the priest?"

"Is not the god of the Anasazi the same god sought by Abraham? Is God a racist? When the believer sees through the eyes of the Buddha, does he not find that the Buddha has always seen through his eyes? When the Kachina takes off the mask, what is beneath? Another mask? Are we Indians, Christians, Democrats?"

El Cacique picked up a gourd rattle lying beside him. "The pipe makes smoke which rises to the clouds to call the Water Snake, which brings the rains to make the Purple Beans grow. By tending the fire, and tending the beans, the clans can survive. As the roots of the bean and the gourd go deep into the earth to find the Water Snake, the sound of the water in the rattle can lead the shaman to water."

"You mean the rattle is used for dowsing?" Buck asked.

"Exactly," said Sharon. "My God, Buck, I know what is inside this rattle."

"What are you talking about?"

"Beans," she said. "He said the bean plant follows the water. Those are been seeds in there, the purple bean of the Anasazi, which haven't been seen for hundreds of years."

"Do you think they might sprout?"

"If they do, they might be worth a lot more than that gold."

"In a few hours, we're going to wish we could trade it all for enough water to cook them in."

"Why would there be a dowsing device here?" she asked.

"Where there is no water? Where better? Do you think you can do it?"

Sharon picked up the rattle, and she began to shake it and swirl it gently. She began to dance with it, and to listen to the different sounds it made. In one direction it sounded like pebbles in a gourd. In the other direction it sounded like splashing, gurgling water. Following the gurgling sound, she danced, and he picked up a glowing stick and followed her. Her dowsing search took her down one of the smaller passages to the end of the cave, a rounded area sealed in the back by what appeared to be a large chunk of fallen stone lying at an angle. At the far end, against the wedge of stone, lay a shallow crusted pool of water, about five feet across and a few inches deep. Above it on the stone is a large pictograph of the Water Snake, not a double spiral like the one at the solstice calendar, but with a forked head. Beside the pool squatted El Cacique.

"Well, I'll be damned, there is water in here," said Buck.

"But not the way out. How long do you think we'll last down here, now that we have water? Waiting for what? Rescue? By whom, and when?"

"Too bad you can't just turn that vision of yours on and off," Buck complained.

"My vision? Aren't you doing it too?"

"All right, yeah, but not alone. So why can't we just start touching everything here, and see somebody getting out, and follow him?"

"I don't know," she wailed.

"I can show you the way to see the vision," said El Cacique, "and then we all can get out of here."

"That would be wonderful," said Buck. "These guessing games are driving me nuts. So what is the big secret?"

"Sex," said El Cacique.

"Sex? Are you out of your mind?"

"No. I am all in your mind. It is all of us or none."

"Stop it, I understand," said Sharon. "I understand, Buck. When I have had visions, my dreams are often very... erotic. It uses the sexual energy, don't you see? In the family, the church, they... they punished me, they made me close my eyes to what I saw, and to look the other way to what they did. Since then I've never... I've never..."

"Never what?"

"I have never taken a lover. Never."

"Then you're a... well, you're not, but then why did you...?"

"Invite you to my room? Because after what happened in the meeting I... I knew I was attracted to you, in a way I didn't understand. Then I couldn't do it, because I was frightened, of that attraction."

"You are saying if we want to use your vision... our vision, to find the way out of here, we've got to... you mean, here?" he asked her, incredulous.

"Yes, and that's not all. Buck, he said we all make it out of here, all of us, or none of us."

El Cacique nodded. "That's right. You, Hightower, you let your field lie fallow, and plant nothing for the future. And you, Tyler, you plow every field you meet, and harvest nothing. You both have forgotten what sex is for."

Suddenly Bucks eyes widened, and he sucked in air in a gasp. "Ooooooh. A baby."

Sharon gazed into his eyes in helpless submission.

"We are trapped in a cave, hallucinating our heads off in shock, ready to believe the way out is to make a baby for the ghost of a dead Indian." Buck shook his head.

"What would it take to make you believe?" she asked.

Buck turned to El Cacique. "Would you mind excusing us for a little while?" he asked. And then to Sharon, he said, "I guess this means we're sorta like getting married."

She extended her arms to him, and he embraced her. Without a word, they took off their clothes, and with a piece of charcoal, they made designs upon their bodies, and then they knelt together facing each other, hands clasped.

"Sharon Hightower, here in the presence of... well, of whoever is watching, will you be my wife, until... until death do us part?"

"Buck Tyler, I will, and I don't care who is watching. I love you."

They kissed tenderly, and their passion quickly came up. As they lay down together, their vision began, of the Water Snake coming down from the pictograph on the wall, into the cave with them. As it thrust itself smoothly toward them, green plants sprouted up and burst into bloom along its path, forming a Garden of Eden scene in the cave. While they clung together in passion, the Snake entwined itself with their limbs, and wrapped itself around them sensuously. As their passion peaked, the snake rose up before them, and they saw that it was forked, and had two heads. Then suddenly they were alone in the dark cave, clinging naked to each other in the pale warm light of a glowing torch.

"The Water Snake," she said. "It is always in my dreams, about passion and death and rebirth. It isn't about whether we die here, it's just about how."

"I don't think so," said Buck, looking at the wedge of rock and the little spring. "I think the two-headed Water Snake means a spring with two heads. I think the pictograph means this spring has two openings, this one, and one on the other side of that rock. See how it goes down like a fallen piece there."

"You mean the way out would be through the water?" she asked in horror.

"It rings all the right bells, baptism, firewalking, the birth canal, the ultimate test."

"If that's the test, I fail it," she said miserably. "I can't swim. I could never put myself under a rock to drown in the dark. I... I'd rather use your knife to cut my wrists."

"Always thinking about yourself," he rebuked her. "What about the baby? You don't have to swim. Just close your eyes, hold your breath, and think beautiful Indian thoughts." He picked up the black obsidian blade, and tucked it into his waistband.

"Why do you keep bringing that?" she asked.

"If the ceremony starts with stealing it and running in here, my is it ain't over until it gets returned. And I don't want to have to come back for it. Come on."

"Wait," she said. She picked up the gourd rattle and

twisted the binding so the gourd slipped from the stick handle. She shook out two dried dark purple beans, and put them into a buttoned pocket. Then she removed her own turquoise stud earrings and dropped them into the gourd. "Let the next guy figure that out. Now what?"

Buck took her hand, and led her out to stand in the little pool. "But Buck, it's only a few inches," she said, then shrieked as the thin limestone crust beneath them gave way, and they plunged suddenly into deep dark water. In darkness, they could hear the sounds of gurgling water, of boots scraping stone, of grunting and whining, and heartbeats pounding. He felt down with his feet, and when as he expected, they located the bottom of the rock, he pulled himself and her down. He pushed her in first, then quickly followed. With heart pounding and fear rushing upon him, he swam up, struck a surface, and then burst forth into open air. He could hear her gasping and crying in horror and relief beside him.

"Here, get a hold on this. There's a ledge here," he told her in the dark. "That's it. Now let's see if these matches are really waterproof." His match flared up brightly, revealing them to be in a little chamber with a ladder leading up.

"We made it," she said as she clambered up onto the ledge of rock. They climbed up the ladder through a hole in a viga floor, and found themselves in another kiva. It was very small, simple in layout, with a small altar at one end, and across from it, the hole Sipapu, from which they had just emerged. The room was dominated by an amazing structure. From the floor about halfway up to the viga and earth ceiling rose a stone platform with a carved curving hardwood top. Standing on end upon it was a slab of stone, fastened at the top to a notched-log ladder which stuck out into the room like the leg of an A. At the apex of the A, the stone held in place a trapdoor.

"I get it," said Buck. "If you put your weight on the ladder, it swings the rock up, and the trapdoor down. When you get out, the rock swings back and closes it after you."

He stepped up to the ladder and put his weight upon it. It moved about half an inch, and then snubbed up tight.

"Look here," said Sharon. "Look at the grooves cut into the top of this. I think there is something inside keeping the stone from moving."

"You mean, a lock? Come on, there is no evidence the Anasazi ever had that kind of technology," he scoffed.

"What, you find the evidence, and still don't believe your own eyes, Doctor Buttminster? Maybe Asher was right, you'll never think we are anything but stone-age savages."

"All right, I'm sorry," he said contritely. "So if it's a lock, how do we pick it?"

"We don't have to. You have the key." She pointed to the black blade tucked into his belt. He drew it out, and blew the dust from the notches in the ancient table. They looked at each other a moment, not asking the obvious question, "Which slot?" Placing the blade in her hand, and holding it with his own, they slid it directly into one of the slots.

He took a deep breath, stepped up onto the ladder, and threw his weight against it. Dumping dirt and spilling light into the room, the trapdoor swung open.

"We're free," she said. "So what now, Buck? Find of the century? Wealth, influence, books, a feature film... Keanu Reeves or somebody?"

"Keanu Reeves? You think so?"

"Well, some cutie. Your future as professor of Indian Wisdom is guaranteed."

"I don't know if I can still do that," he confessed. "What about you? Are you still going to be Indian Scout for the State government?"

"I don't know if I can do that either," she admitted. "But what about the three dead men in there? Can we really just walk away?"

"Or do what? Tell all, stand trial, let the lawyers fight over it? Simmons lived alone, ran a mailorder thing out of his garage. He won't be missed at all until his mortgage gets backed up. I'll write something for ISPI, about how nothing panned out. The truck and the rooms are all in my name, one of his little quirks, so I figure nobody is likely to put us together."

"Unless they have a parasentient working for them," she reminded him.

"People are going to wonder what happened to Justiano for the next two hundred years, but the legends here are already full of priests and snake-oil peddlers who disappeared. As for, what was his name, the mighty warrior..."

"Asher Quaptewa. I will take care of that."

"OK, then," he said, "I guess that takes care of everything but us."

"Yes, what about us?" She looked at him in the dusty light of the kiva.

"Are we still going to be married? I mean, really married?" he asked.

"I don't know, Buck, are we? What about the little girl with the airplane, and the big blonde one who rides horses in your dreams? Don't tell me you won't want to see them again."

Buck pulled from his pocket a fat gold nugget. "I cheated a little," he said. "I brought one of these out in my pocket. If I had it made into a wedding ring, would you wear it?"

"I'll tell you what," she said. "You go back to your job, and I'll go back to mine, and in a little while, you can call me to see if our beans have sprouted. Then we'll talk about your Indian gold."

"What about this?" he asked pointing to the black obsidian blade. "If we leave it in the rock, we can get back in here by pushing down on the trapdoor." She shook her head. "Not a good idea, right."

Buck pulled the black blade from the stone, let Sharon climb up the log ladder ahead of him, then climbed up after her. When he took his weight off, the door swung up and closed tightly behind him. He took a switch of leaves from a nearby creosote bush and swept the dirt to cover the hidden door.

Sharon ran down the hillside toward the parked truck below. It was late afternoon, and in the sky behind them rose the anvil top of a huge thunderstorm. As he ran down to follow her, the first drops of the coming downpour spattered the ground around them. As they ran past the spring cleft, they saw the tunnel was filled with dirt from the explosion, and the rain already was beginning to smooth it out.

Standing astride the red Tenuco Mountain like a drummer five miles tall in the storm, almost concealed by its boiling cumulus, the great Kachina cracked his whip, and the thunder rumbled like huge drums.

"All right, all right, we're going," called Buck over his shoulder. As they ran laughing to the truck, the healing waters of the summer storm began to patter around them harder, erasing from the sand the footprints of their passage.

Epilogue

On the day of the summer solstice, a few moments
before dawn, there was an air of great excitement among
the crowd of Indians of various descriptions arriving in
Jeeps, on horseback, or on foot. They were modern
ranchers, deputies, potters, traditionalists, and all had come
to look with wonder.

As the disc of the sun broke over the horizon, the
shrine of Gogyeng Sowuhti, Old Spider Grandmother, could
be seen bathed in light. The ancient matriarch reached out
her arm of sunlight and touched the Water Snake on the
wall upon its head, and it turned around and began to move
the other way, to the cheers of the Indians.

In simple but elegant ceremonial garb, Buck Tyler and
Sharon Hightower stood before a group of elder shaman
from the tribes, each wearing special robes and feathers.
Their clasped hands displayed matched gold wedding bands.
Buck stepped forward and laid the black obsidian blade onto
a blanket before the Medicine Chief. Sharon stepped
forward and laid a pot before him holding the sprouted and
fruiting Anasazi bean plants. Lying on a sheepskin on the
blanket was a beautiful baby boy, about two months old.
Laughing happily, the baby clutched to his breast the
turquoise-inlaid red pipestone Water Snake pipe.

The Medicine Chief wrapped a woven belt around their
clasped left hands, and Buck and Sharon shared a kiss in the
bright light of their new dawn.

THE END

Other books by James Nathan Post:

SACRIFICES -- A Novel Of The Vietnam War
LOST ILLUSIONS -- A Novel Of The Seductive 1970's
MERLIN'S PAWN -- A Doubled-Down Runner In Vegas
KALISNACHT -- A Cult of Serial Killers, Out To Save The World
KING'S KNIGHT -- A Science Fiction Anthology
HIGH ARENA -- Post-Apocalyptic Action Adventure
THE ANTI-CYCLOPS PAPERS -- Challenging Commentary
FUNDAMENTAL BLASPHEMY -- Debunking Bible Idolatry

With Shelly Waxman, JD:
THE SAM COHEN CASE ADVENTURES
  #1 The Black Messiah Murders
  #2 Piranhas On The Loose
  #3 The Josephus Enigma

With Bajram Angelo Koljenovic:
  Blood Of Montenegro -- An Epic Family History
  Forgotten Soldiers -- The Tragedy of Bosnia

With George Mendoza, Jr.:
  A Vision Of Courage
  SPIRIT MAN

www.postpubco.com

About the author:

James Nathan Post was a rocket base kid at White Sands NM in the 1950's, son of an engineer and an artist. Educated in Physics, a jet pilot and combat helicopter gunship pilot in the 1960's, he has since been an editor for an occult publisher, self-publisher, disciple to a fundamentalist prophet, psychedelicist, smuggler, actor, troubadour, Las Vegas sports-book high-roller, parent of two delightful people, founder of The Scribes Of Osiris, other curious callings. First published at twelve, he has always been a writer, in his words, "a blowhard would-be-pro opinion monger, and weaver of fantasies and spells."

CPSIA information can be obtained at www.ICGtesting.com
Printed in the USA
BVOW08s0324231015

423821BV00001B/3/P